CHAPTER 1

Three figures were observing from a distance—a older man, a middle aged woman and a young boy. They weren't using regular binoculars but hiking telescopes due to the distance they had to cover, almost a kilometer from their focus point. The terrain offered no closer hiding spots. The landscape around them was a mix of dry grass, rocks, and sandy soil, burnt into shades of tan by the relentless sun. The only shelter they found was in a dry gulch formed millions of years ago during a different climate when water had still flowed through the region to form the giant inland sea that was in the middle of Australia.

The man and the woman lay flat on the hot ground, peering through their telescopes while the boy moved around, making notes in his book, keeping an eye out for any dangerous wildlife, and fetching water. Snakes are common here as is the odd scorpion. They had arrived before dawn in a dusty ute, taking a longer, less direct route across the desolate land from the west. The ute was covered with a dirty black tarpaulin weighed down with rocks for camouflage. Now they were settled at the rim of the depression, watching the scene unfold through their lenses as the morning sun began to rise behind a cream-colored house, just under a kilometer away. It was their fifth morning observing the same place, and conversation had become sparse.

"What time is it?" the man asked, his voice muffled as he squinted with one eye closed.

The boy glanced at his watch. "Six-fifty," he responded.

"Any minute now," the man holding the telescope said, not looking away from his scope.

The boy opened his notebook, ready to jot down the same notes he had been recording for the past four days.

"Kitchen light's on," the first man said.

The boy wrote it down: *6:50 AM, kitchen light on*. The kitchen faced west, away from the rising sun, which left it in shadow even after daylight.

"She by herself again?" the boy asked.

"Same as always," the woman said, narrowing her eyes.

Maid's in the kitchen. Target still in bed, the boy wrote. The sun continued to rise, its light creeping up slowly, shortening the shadows. The cream-colored house had a tall chimney, casting a sundial-like shadow that shifted as the sun climbed higher. By seven in the morning, the temperature was already climbing; by nine, it would be scorching, and they were there to stay until nightfall when they could leave unnoticed.

"Bedroom curtains are opening," the woman noted. "She's up now." The boy scribbled down the time: *7:04 AM, bedroom curtains open*.

"Wait," the man said, listening.

In the distance, they faintly heard the sound of a well pump starting up.

"She's in the shower," the man confirmed.

The boy added another note: *7:06 AM, target starts showering*.

The man and the woman lowered their telescopes, taking a moment to rest their eyes, knowing nothing would happen while she was in the bathroom. After six minutes, the well pump shut off, and the boy recorded: *7:12 AM, target out of the shower*. They raised their scopes again.

“She must be getting dressed now,” the man guessed, prompting the boy to giggle.

“You think you can see her?” the woman, positioned twenty metres to the south with a better view of the back of the house, asked dryly.

“You’re gross.”The boy chuckled as he wrote: *7:15 AM, likely dressing*. A few minutes later, he added: *7:20 AM, likely downstairs, probably eating breakfast.*

“She’ll go back up to brush her teeth,” the man predicted.

“Absolutely,” the woman agreed. “She’s meticulous like that.”

“She’s closing the curtains again,” the man noted.

This was a standard practice during Queensland summers, particularly for bedrooms facing north, like hers, to prevent them from turning into ovens by nighttime.

“Get ready,” the man said. “She’ll head to the barn now, just like always.”

It was an easy bet. Four days in a row, she had followed the same routine.

“Kitchen door’s opening,” the man reported.

The boy quickly jotted down the time: *7:27 AM, kitchen door opens*.

“She’s coming out.”

She stepped outside, dressed in a knee-length blue gingham dress that left her shoulders bare, her hair still damp and pulled back.

“What’s that kind of dress called?” the boy asked.

“A halter dress,” the woman replied.

The boy jotted down: *7:28 AM, exits house in blue halter dress, heading to the barn.*

She moved across the yard cautiously, her steps small and uneven as she navigated the ruts in the baked ground—probably around seventy meters in total. She pulled open the barn door and disappeared into the shadowy interior.

7:29 AM, target enters barn, the boy noted.

"How hot is it now?" the woman asked.

"Probably close to 30 degrees," the boy responded.

"There'll be a storm soon. Weather like this, there has to be," the man predicted.

"Here comes her ride," the woman added.

Far to the south, a dust cloud was rising from a slow-moving vehicle on the road.

"She's coming back," the man said.

The boy wrote: *7:32 AM, target exits barn.*

"Maid's at the door," the man said.

The target stopped at the kitchen door, where the maid handed her a lunch box—bright green with a cartoon character on the side. She paused for a moment, her skin flushed and damp from the heat, bent down to adjust her socks, and then hurried toward the gate. She passed through the gate and stood at the roadside. The school bus approached, slowing to a stop, and the door opened with a soft hiss that the observers could hear clearly despite the distance. The chrome handrails on the bus glinted in the sun as the target lifted her lunch box onto the first step, grasped the rails, and climbed aboard. The bus door shut, and the men watched as her head, topped with licorice-colored hair, bobbed along the base of the windows.

The boy finished the note: *7:36 AM, target boards bus for school.*

The bus headed north, following a dead-straight road, and the boy tracked it until the heat waves on the horizon blurred it into a shimmering mirage. He then closed his notebook and secured it with a rubber band. Back at the cream-colored house, the maid had already stepped inside and shut the kitchen door. The watchers, nearly a kilometer away, lowered their telescopes and turned up their collars against the blazing sun.

It was 7:37 on a Friday morning. Time crept on.

At precisely 7:39 AM, more than three hundred kilometers to the northeast, a man named Mick Hunter climbed out of the window of his motel room. Just a minute earlier, he had been brushing his teeth in the bathroom. A minute before that, he had cracked the door open to check the morning heat, leaving it ajar. The mirrored glass of the closet doors near the entrance, coupled with the cantilevered mirror in the bathroom, gave him a rare glimpse—through a double reflection—of four men stepping out of a car and heading toward the motel office. Pure luck had allowed him to spot them, but Mick Hunter was the kind of man luck favored.

The vehicle was a police car, easily identifiable by the shield on the door. The sunlight reflecting off the mirrors allowed Hunter to read the insignia clearly: *City Police.* Beneath a decorative emblem, the name *Cloncurry, Queensland* was inscribed. All four men wore police uniforms, equipped with guns, radios, batons, and handcuffs strapped to their belts. Three of them were strangers to Hunter, but the fourth one was someone he recognized.

The fourth man was a large, heavyset individual with a blond buzz cut, his ruddy complexion accentuated by the bright morning sun. Today, however, part of his face was obscured by a shiny aluminum splint taped over what was clearly a broken nose. His right hand was similarly bound up in a splint and bandages, protecting what appeared to be a fractured finger.

The man hadn't been injured the night before, and Hunter had no idea at the time that the guy was a cop. He had seemed like any other bar patron. Hunter had only gone to the bar because he had heard the music was decent. It turned out it wasn't, so he had ended up sitting on a barstool, watching muted sports highlights on a TV mounted on the wall. The bar was crowded, loud, and cramped, and Hunter had found himself wedged between a woman on one side and the heavyset guy on the other. He had grown bored of the television and turned to observe the room, which was when he noticed the man eating.

The man was wearing an old white t-shirt and devouring a wings special. Marinade dripped from his chin and fingers, staining both his face and shirt. A dark, greasy stain spread across his chest, but barroom etiquette kept Hunter from staring for too long. Unfortunately, the guy noticed.

"Who you lookin' at?" the man muttered aggressively, though Hunter ignored him.

"Who you lookin' at?" the man repeated, this time with more menace.

Hunter had learned from experience that if someone says something like that once, you might be in the clear. But if they say it twice, trouble is on the horizon. The problem was, bullies like this one took silence as a sign of weakness, a signal that they were winning, and yet they never let you answer the way they wanted.

"You lookin' at me?" the guy asked again.

"Nah," Hunter finally replied.

"Don't look at me, boy," the man snarled.

The way he said "boy" gave Hunter the impression that

he was probably some kind of foreman—maybe at a mine or slaughterhouse—doing the kind of tough, physical work common in Cloncurry. At no point did Hunter think the man was a cop, especially since Hunter had only recently arrived in Queensland.

"Don't you look at me," the guy growled again.

Hunter turned and gave him a deliberate look, not to provoke him, but simply to assess the situation. Life, he knew, could be full of surprises, and one day, he expected to come face-to-face with someone who could genuinely challenge him. But today wasn't that day. Hunter smiled slightly and looked away.

That's when the man jabbed him with a grubby finger.

"I told you not to look at me," he said, jabbing him again.

Hunter glanced down. A smudge of marinade now marked his shirt.

"Don't do that," Hunter said, his voice calm.

The man jabbed him again. "Or what?" he sneered. "You gonna do somethin'?"

Hunter looked down again. There were now two greasy marks on his shirt. The man jabbed a third time, and Hunter clenched his teeth. He told himself it was just three greasy smears on a shirt, and he began a slow count to ten. But the man jabbed again before Hunter could even reach eight.

"You deaf mate?" Hunter asked. "I told you not to do that."

The man smirked. "You gonna make somethin' of it?"

"No," Hunter said evenly. "I just want you to stop."

The guy smiled wider. "You're a coward," he said.

"Righto," Hunter replied. "Just keep your hands off me."

"Or what? What're you gonna do?"

Hunter restarted his mental count. Eight, nine...

"You wanna take this outside?" the guy taunted.

Ten.

Hunter glanced at him and said quietly, "Touch me again, and you'll find out. I've already warned you four times, alright?"

The man hesitated for a second, but, predictably, he jabbed Hunter one more time. Hunter grabbed the man's finger mid-jab and bent it sharply, snapping it at the knuckle. Then, because he was annoyed, Hunter leaned in and delivered a swift headbutt to the man's face. It was a clean move, but not delivered with full force—Hunter wasn't trying to put the guy in the hospital over a few greasy marks on a shirt. He simply stepped back, giving the man room to fall, bumping into the woman on his right as he did.

"Sorry, ma'am," he muttered.

The woman, still focused on her drink, seemed unaware of what had just happened. Meanwhile, the heavyset man crumpled to the floor, and Hunter used the toe of his shoe to roll him onto his side, nudging his chin back to keep his airway open—a standard recovery position to prevent choking. Then, he paid for his drinks and left, not giving the man another thought until he saw him the next morning, walking toward the motel office in a police uniform.

Seeing the man in uniform made Hunter pause and think fast. The first thing he considered was the reflection—if he could see them through the double mirrors, it meant they could see him, too, if they happened to look in the right direction. In the second moment, he cursed himself for not picking up on the signs sooner. There had been clues—after all, who else would provoke a man his size unless they had some kind of protection or immunity? Only someone who thought they were untouchable, like a copper.

Now, what to do? The man was a local cop, and Hunter was a noticeable figure. Aside from his towering build, he still had the chicken stains on his shirt and a fresh bruise on his forehead, which probably lined up perfectly with the man's broken nose. That could easily land him in hot water, especially if the police decided to make a show of it—a loud arrest, maybe even some shots fired, followed by some rough treatment in an empty holding cell. After all, a man without a home address, with nothing but a wallet and a Swiss Army knife in his pocket, would look suspicious anywhere, let alone in Queensland. They could easily charge him with assaulting an officer, a serious offense that would have plenty of witnesses backing the policeman's version of events. The thought of serving time in prison wasn't appealing at all.

So, discretion had to be the better part of valor. He grabbed his wallet, crossed the room, and slipped out through the window. He unclipped the screen and gently dropped it onto the ground. Climbing out, he carefully placed the screen back in its frame before walking across a vacant lot to the nearest street. He turned right and kept moving until he was concealed by a low building. Now, he needed a way to leave quickly—preferably by car.

There were no buses, no taxis. He stuck out his thumb, calculating that he had about ten minutes to catch a ride before the cops wrapped up their business at the motel and started searching the area. Fifteen minutes at the very most. But deep down, he figured it wouldn't work. Who in their right mind would stop for a man in this heat, let alone a large, unkempt guy like him?

Yet, to his surprise, he was wrong. His first surprise had been the copper showing up in uniform, but now he got a second one—a ride pulled up in under five minutes. His shirt was still dry, and he hadn't even started sweating. The third surprise? The driver who stopped for him was a woman.

The biggest surprise came next—where their conversation

would lead.

Hunter had been hitchhiking for over twenty-five years, in more countries than he could easily count, and five minutes was about the shortest time it had ever taken for a ride to stop. Hitchhiking wasn't as common as it once was—commercial truckers had insurance issues, and private drivers were too cautious, worried about who might be standing on the roadside, serial killers etc. People no longer wanted to pick up strangers, let alone someone like Hunter. He wasn't a harmless-looking guy, after all. Standing not far under two metres and weighing in at about 105 kilos, he was often disheveled and usually unshaven, his hair of/ten a mess. His size alone made people wary, and now, with a fresh bruise on his forehead, it was even less likely that someone would pick him up.

Yet, here was a woman pulling over, offering him a ride.

Typically, there was a hierarchy when it came to hitchhiking —a young woman could get a ride from an older man without much difficulty, while a big, scruffy guy like Hunter getting picked up by a neat, slender woman driving an expensive car was near the bottom of the list. But it happened. In just five minutes.

He was walking quickly away from the motel, his thumb stuck out in the heat, when a large, white car pulled over with a soft hiss of tires on the hot pavement. The sun bounced off the hood, momentarily blinding him, but he heard the driver's window slide down on the far side.

"Where to?" the woman called out, as if she were a taxi driver.

"Anywhere," Hunter replied, immediately regretting it. That was the kind of response that made drivers suspicious—vague, aimless, like someone drifting with no clear destination, making them worried they might never get rid of you.

But the woman simply nodded. "Okay," she said. "I'm headed up past Mount Kalka."

Hunter hesitated for a second, surprised. Her face was half hidden in the shadows of the car, but she was looking up at him expectantly.

"Great," he said.

He stepped off the curb, opened the passenger door, and slid into the freezing cold interior of the car. The air conditioning was on full blast, and the leather seat felt like ice against his skin. The woman buzzed the window back up as he shut the door.

"Thanks," Hunter said, trying to warm up. "I really appreciate this."

She didn't reply, just made a vague gesture, almost dismissive, as she checked the traffic in her rearview mirror. People had their reasons for picking up hitchhikers, but they were all different. Some drivers did it because they remembered hitching rides in their younger days and now, having settled down, they felt a need to repay the favor. Others were charitable by nature, or maybe just lonely and in need of some conversation.

However, if this woman wanted to talk, she didn't show it. She waited for a couple of trucks to pass by before pulling out without a word. Hunter glanced around the interior. It was a BMW, a two-door coupe, but long and luxurious—probably a few years old, but impeccably clean. The seats were upholstered in a red-colored leather, and the tinted windows gave everything a soft, dark hue. A small purse and a weathered leather bag were casually thrown on the backseat, the bag unzipped and stuffed with folded papers that looked like legal documents.

"If you want more room, you can move the seat back," she said, still focused on the road.

"Thanks," he replied, fiddling with the seat controls until he had enough space. He leaned the seat back slightly and lowered it so he wouldn't be so noticeable from outside.

"That better?" she asked. "More comfortable?"

Her own seat was pulled up close to the wheel, clearly adjusted for her small frame. Hunter glanced over at her. She was slim—maybe fifty kilos, with long, wavy black hair and a finely boned face. She appeared to be in her early thirties, with smooth, dark skin that suggested a Pacific Islander background. She wore a sleeveless cotton dress that seemed both simple and expensive, her arms and legs polished to a perfect shine. Everything about her radiated confidence and ease.

"So, where are you headed?" she asked, then paused and smiled slightly. "Oh wait, I already asked you that. You didn't seem very sure about where you're going."

Her accent was distinctly Australian, though more urban than rural. She steered with both hands, and Hunter noticed rings on her fingers—a slim wedding band and another ring with a large diamond.

"Anywhere," he repeated. "Wherever I end up is fine."

She smiled again, a bit wider this time. "Are you running away from something? Have I just picked up a fugitive?"

Her smile made it clear she was joking, but it still struck a chord with Hunter. She was taking a risk, picking up a stranger, and the fact that she was comfortable enough to make light of it surprised him.

"I'm just exploring," Hunter said.

"Exploring Queensland? Someone's already done that, you know," she teased.

"Like a tourist," he replied.

"You don't look like a tourist," she said, casting a quick glance at him. "The tourists we get are usually sunburned and arrive in buses."

She smiled as she said it, and Hunter couldn't help but notice how self-assured she seemed, comfortable in her skin, and entirely at ease behind the wheel of an expensive car.

Hunter felt suddenly aware of his disheveled appearance—his messy hair, the stain on his shirt, the bruise on his forehead—and how out of place he seemed next to her.

"Do you live around here?" he asked, trying to keep the conversation going.

"I live north of Mount Kalka," she replied. "About two hundred kilometers from here. Like I mentioned, that's where I'm headed."

"Never been there," Hunter said.

She didn't respond immediately, focused on waiting at a traffic light. As they pulled through the wide intersection, she stayed in the inside lane, her legs shifting slightly as she worked the pedals. He watched her in silence, noticing the tension return to her face. Her eyes narrowed, her bottom lip caught between her teeth, but she maintained control.

"So, did you explore Cloncurry?" she asked after a moment, trying to keep the conversation light.

"I went to the museum," Hunter said, keeping his reply vague.

She glanced briefly at the radio, as if considering turning it on. "You into museums?" she asked.

"Not really," Hunter admitted. "A little too tame for me."

She nodded, agreeing. "I prefer the big dam there. You saw that in Cloncurry, right?"

"I saw a poster of it in a shop," Hunter replied.

"How long were you there?" she asked.

"Just a day," he said.

"And now you're moving on?"

"That's the plan," Hunter said.

"To wherever," she repeated with a knowing smile.

"That's the plan," he echoed.

They passed a small metal sign marking the city limits, and Hunter smiled to himself, remembering the emblem on the police cruiser—City Police. As they drove further, Cloncurry faded into the distance behind them, leaving potential danger shrinking on the horizon.

***

Meanwhile, two men sat in the front seats of their Ford Falcon, with the tall, fair-haired man driving while the smaller, darker-skinned man rested. In the backseat, their female partner remained silent. The car cruised out of the motel lot, picking up speed as they headed north on Bruce Highway, leaving Brisbane in the rearview mirror. None of them spoke, their thoughts weighed down by the vast interior of Queensland ahead of them. The woman had studied a guidebook in preparation for their trip, which boasted about Queensland's sheer size—comprising seven percent of Australia's total landmass and larger than most European countries. But what had really caught her attention was the comparison of distance: top-to-bottom, Queensland was longer than the span between Paris and Moscow. That piece of information gave her a new sense of perspective—and a reminder of the long journey ahead.

Still, the car was quiet, cool, and comfortable, making it a decent place to relax before the mission truly began. They had some time to kill, after all.

***

Hunter, sitting beside the woman in the BMW, glanced over at her. "Is Mount Kalka worth visiting?" he asked, breaking the silence.

"It's mostly Islanders," she said with a shrug. "So, I feel at home there."

Her hand gripped the steering wheel a little tighter, the tendons shifting under her skin as she gave him a sidelong glance. "Do you like Pacific Islanders?"

Hunter shrugged back. "I like them as much as I like anyone, I suppose."

"You don't like people?" she asked with a hint of curiosity.

"It depends," he said.

"You like mango?" she asked, a sudden change in topic catching him off guard.

"Sure, as much as I like any fruit," he replied, smiling slightly at the unexpected question.

"Well, Mount Kalka grows the sweetest mango in all of Queensland," she said proudly, "which, according to the locals, means it's the best in the world. There's also a rodeo in August, but you've missed that for this year. And north of Mount Kalka, there's Katter Shire. Ever heard of it?"

Hunter shook his head. "Never been here before."

"It's the least-populated shire in Australia," she explained, "well, except for some places in the Northern Territory. But it's also the wealthiest, per capita. About 110 people live there, but there are over 500 active mining leases."

"Sounds like an interesting place," Hunter said. "Maybe I'll get out at Mount Kalka and have a look around."

"The area used to be wild," she said, her tone softening. "A long time ago, anyway. The railroad used to stop there, so you had pub shootouts and all kinds of lawlessness. People used to say, 'Mount Kalka someone'—which meant to shoot them and toss them into the Mount Kalka River."

"They still do that?" Hunter asked with a grin.

She smiled mischievously, easing the tension from her face. "Not so much anymore."

"Your family from Mount Kalka?" Hunter asked, continuing the conversation.

"No, I'm originally from New South Wales," she said. "I moved to Queensland when I got married."

Hunter figured keeping her talking might be wise, given the situation. "You've been married long?" he asked.

"Almost six years now," she replied.

"Your family been in New South Wales a long time?" he asked, trying to keep the dialogue flowing.

She smiled again, this time more relaxed. "Longer than any New South Welshman for sure."

They continued driving through flat, empty country, and she eased the car's speed higher on the dead-straight road. The hot sky, tinted green by the windshield, made the world outside seem even more desolate. The digital thermometer on the dashboard displayed the temperatures—42 degrees outside, but a cool 21 inside.

"You a lawyer?" Hunter asked, nodding toward the stack of papers in the backseat.

For a moment, she looked puzzled, but then she caught the connection and glanced in the rearview mirror at the bag on the seat.

"No," she said with a small laugh. "I'm a lawyer's client."

The conversation stalled again, leaving her tense and Hunter feeling slightly awkward. He decided to change tactics.

"And what else are you?" he asked casually.

She paused briefly before answering. "A wife, a mother. A daughter and a sister, I guess. I keep a few horses, too. That's all. What about you?"

"Nothing in particular," Hunter said.

"There's no such thing as nothing in particular," she insisted. "You have to be something."

"Well, I used to be things," Hunter replied. "I was somebody's son, somebody's brother, somebody's boyfriend."

"Was?" she asked, picking up on his choice of words.

"My parents passed away. My brother's gone. My girlfriend left me."

Hunter knew it wasn't the smoothest line he could have used, but he shrugged it off.

"I don't have any horses either," he added.

"I'm sorry," she said, genuinely. "Not about the horses, of course."

"Water under the bridge," Hunter replied. "It's not as bad as it sounds."

"You're not lonely?" she asked, clearly intrigued.

He shrugged again. "I prefer being alone."

There was another pause. "Why did your girlfriend leave?" she asked, probing deeper.

"She went to work in Europe."

"And you didn't go with her?" she asked.

"She didn't really want me to come," Hunter said after a moment.

"I see," the woman said. "Did you want to go with her?"

Hunter was silent for a beat. "Not really. I'm not one for settling down."

"And you don't want to settle down?" she asked, her curiosity growing.

He shook his head. "Two nights in the same motel is enough to make me uncomfortable."

"Hence, just one day in Cloncurry," she observed.

"And one day in Mount Kalka," he added.

"And after that?" she asked.

Hunter smiled, a bit of mystery lingering. "After that, I've got no idea. That's how I like it."

She drove on, the silence filling the space between them.

"So, you are running from something," she concluded. "Maybe from a settled life."

Hunter shook his head. "No, it's the opposite. I spent most of my life in the military—always moving, always unsettled. I grew to like it."

"I see," she said thoughtfully. "You got used to the chaos, then."

"I guess so," he said.

She hesitated, then asked, "How is someone in the army their whole life?"

"My father was military," Hunter explained. "I grew up on bases around the world. Then I stayed in after I came of age."

"But now you're out," she noted.

He nodded. "All trained up and nowhere to go."
The woman fell silent, considering his answer. Her knuckles tightened slightly on the steering wheel, and her foot pressed down a bit harder on the gas pedal. Without saying a word, she seemed more focused, as though something about Hunter's response had sparked her interest. The car's speed increased gradually, reflecting her heightened attention.

Meanwhile, the tall, fair-haired man driving the Ford Falcon pulled off the highway. They were somewhere in the vast open country between Brisbane and Townsville. He steered the car through a dusty turnout, likely about ten kilometers away from the nearest settlement, and parked. The small, dark-haired man in the passenger seat got out, popped the trunk, and pulled out a heavy valise.

The woman in the backseat unzipped the bag and handed a pair of license plates to the fair-haired man. He retrieved a screwdriver and quickly swapped the Queensland plates with ones from Victoria. The small man removed the plastic covers from the car's wheels, leaving the cheap black steel rims exposed. He stacked the covers neatly and tossed them into the trunk. The woman took out several antennas, which they'd bought from a shop in Sydney. She attached a few to the rear window with self-adhesive pads and then placed two more on the trunk lid, magnetized and easy to affix. None of the antennas were functional—they were purely for show.

With the transformation complete, the once-unremarkable Falcon now looked like a government vehicle, maybe one from the Australian Federal Police or some other official department. The fair-haired man slid back into the driver's seat and turned the car around, heading back to the highway. Now they were cruising in a car that would arouse no suspicion—a Ford Falcon with steel rims and a forest of antennas, sporting plates from Victoria. Anyone who saw them would likely assume they were federal agents on a mission.

Back in the BMW, the woman glanced at Hunter, her voice casual as she asked, "What did you do in the army?"

"I was SAS," Hunter replied.

"What's an SAS?" she asked, her curiosity piqued.

"Special forces, I was a sniper in the army during Kosovo before they drafted me into the SAS and I was in charge of counter terrorism," he explained.

She seemed to think about this for a moment, her expression pensive. "I didn't know we had a special forces," she said.

Another quiet stretch followed, and then she looked over at

him. “Would you mind if I asked you a few more questions?”

Hunter shrugged. “You’re giving me a ride. Go ahead.”

She nodded but added, “I don’t want to offend you.”

“That would be hard to do, given the circumstances. It’s a forty two degrees out there, and twenty five in here,” he said, gesturing at the cool air-conditioned interior.

“There’ll be a storm soon,” she predicted. “This kind of heat always brings one.”

Hunter looked ahead at the sky. The windshield’s green tint made the clear sky seem ominous, but he didn’t see any signs of a storm. “Doesn’t look like it to me,” he said.

She smiled, then asked, “Where do you live?”

“I don’t live anywhere,” Hunter answered. “I move around.”

“No home at all?” she asked, surprised.

He shook his head. “What you see is what I’ve got.”

“You travel light,” she observed.

“Light as I can,” he replied.

They drove for a while in silence, the road stretching out endlessly in front of them.

“Are you out of work?” she asked suddenly.

“Most of the time, yeah,” Hunter said, nodding.

“Were you good at being a cop? In the army?” she asked.

“Good enough. They made me a major and gave me some medals,” he replied, nonchalant.

The woman was quiet for a moment before asking, “So why did you leave?”

Hunter’s response came easily. “They downsized me. After Afghanistan and Iraq it wasn’t politically good to have a large army. So they did a big clean out and cut back our squadrons, which meant I had the longest tenure and I had also upset the most colonels."

She nodded as if this made sense. "That's like how it works in a town. If the population shrinks, so does the police force. Something about appropriations and taxes, right?"

Hunter didn't respond.

"I live in a very small place," she continued. "It's called Four Ways, south of Mount Kalka. It's a lonely place, and that's why they named it after the crossroad of the Burke and Wills roads after the explorers who died trekking up here. Or lonely like an Islander stuck in the red desert.."

Her voice had taken on a slightly hesitant tone, and Hunter picked up on it.

"Is that a problem?" he asked.

"It's mostly a white shire," she said quietly. "Not like Mount Kalka at all."

"So?" Hunter asked, curious.

"So you get the feeling that, if things went wrong, there might be trouble," she replied, choosing her words carefully.

"Has anything gone wrong so far?" Hunter asked.

She smiled awkwardly. "I can tell you were in the army. You ask a lot of questions."

"I thought you were the one who wanted to ask questions," Hunter countered with a slight smile.

She didn't answer for a while, and they drove in silence. Hunter noticed the subtle lines of tension returning to her face. Her hands, gripping the wheel lightly, belied the growing pressure she seemed to be feeling. He leaned back slightly, adjusting the seat again, watching her out of the corner of his eye. She was clearly troubled, but she hadn't revealed exactly why.

"What was life like in the army?" she asked after a long pause.

"Different," Hunter said simply. "It was its own world. Different rules, different situations. It was rough sometimes. Uncivilized."

"Like the Wild West," she said thoughtfully.

"I guess," he replied. "A hundred of thousands people, all trained to do whatever was necessary. The rules came second."

"Like the Wild West," she repeated. "It sounds like you enjoyed it."

Hunter nodded slightly. "Some of it."

She hesitated before asking, "Can I ask you a personal question?"

"Go ahead," Hunter replied, intrigued by her sudden shift in tone.

"What's your name?" she asked.

"Hunter," he said.

"Is that your first or last name?" she asked, looking over at him.

"People just call me Hunter," he said.

She paused again, clearly thinking over her next question. "Can I ask you something else personal?"

Hunter nodded.

"Have you ever killed anyone?" she asked quietly. "In the army?"

Hunter nodded again. "Some."

"That's what the army is, in the end, isn't it?" she said softly. "That's what it's about."

"Yeah," Hunter agreed. "That's what it's about."

The woman fell silent, her mind seemingly preoccupied with something important. After a while, she spoke again.

“There’s a museum in Mount Kalka,” she began. “It’s a Wild West museum, partly in an old saloon, partly in an old hotel. Out back is where they buried Benjamin Blackman. Ever heard of him?”

Hunter shook his head.

“They called him the Gentleman Gunfighter,” she explained. “He retired, but then he was run over by a mine cart and died from the injuries. They buried him out there, and there’s a nice headstone. It says, ‘Benjamin James Blackman, 1840–1887.’ And there’s an inscription too. It says, ‘He never killed a man who didn’t deserve it.’ What do you think of that?”

“I think that’s a pretty good inscription,” Hunter said.

“There’s an old newspaper, too, in a glass case,” she continued. “I think it’s from Sydney. It’s got his obituary in it. It says, ‘Certain it is that many of his stern deeds were done for the right, as he understood it.’”

The BMW sped along the empty road.

“A fine obituary,” Hunter said, nodding.

“You think so?” she asked.

“About as good as you can get,” Hunter said.

“Would you like an obituary like that?” she asked.

“Not anytime soon,” Hunter replied, smiling slightly.

She smiled back, apologetically. “No, of course not. But do you think that, someday, you’d want to qualify for an obituary like that?”

Hunter considered the question. “I can think of worse things.”

She grew quiet again, but something was clearly on her mind.

"Where is this going?" Hunter asked, breaking the silence.

"This road?" she replied, trying to deflect the question.

"No, this conversation," Hunter clarified.

She took her foot off the accelerator, and the car began to slow. With a slight motion of her wrist, she pulled the BMW off onto a dusty shoulder. The road's edge sloped down into a dry irrigation ditch, causing the car to tilt at a sharp angle. She shifted the car into park, leaving the engine running and the air conditioning still blasting.

"My name is Rosie McMahon," she said, turning toward him. "And I need your help."

CHAPTER 2

"It wasn't by chance that I picked you up," Rosie McMahon said. Hunter's back was pushed firmly against the car door. The BMW was tilted, like a ship about to sink, leaning heavily to the side of the road. The slick leather seat made it difficult for him to sit up. Rosie, one hand on the steering wheel and the other gripping the seatback behind him, loomed over him. Her face was close—only a foot away—but her expression was unreadable, her gaze fixed on the dusty ditch beyond him.

"You think you can get us back on the road?" he asked.

She glanced at the asphalt, glistening in the heat, almost level with her window.

"I think so," she said. "I hope so."

"So do I," he muttered.

She just stared at him.

"So, why'd you stop for me?" he asked.

"What do you think?"

"I don't know. I figured I got lucky. Thought you were just a kind person helping a stranger."

She shook her head.

"No, I was looking for someone like you," she said.

"Why?"

"I've picked up about a dozen guys. Seen hundreds more. That's what I've been doing for the past month—driving around Western Queensland, looking for people who need a ride."

"Why?"

She shrugged off the question, a dismissive gesture.

"The kilometers I've racked up on this car," she said. "You wouldn't believe it. And the money I've spent on fuel."

"Why?" he asked again.

She fell silent, refusing to answer. Hunter shifted

uncomfortably, the armrest digging into his side. He wished someone else had picked him up—someone just driving from point A to point B. He glanced at her.

"Can I call you Rosie?" he asked.

She nodded. "Please."

"Okay, Rosie, what's really going on here?"

Her mouth opened and closed a few times.

"I don't know where to begin," she admitted. "Now that it's time to say it."

"Say what?"

She didn't respond.

"You'd better tell me exactly what you want," he said, "or I'm getting out of this car right now."

"It's thirty-five degrees out there."

"I know."

"You could die in this heat."

"I'll take my chances."

"You can't open the door," she pointed out. "The car's too tilted."

"Then I'll break the windshield."

She paused.

"I need your help," she said again. "I've never met you before."

"Not personally," she said. "But you're the type I was looking for."

"What type?"

She fell silent again, offering a faint, ironic smile.

"I've rehearsed this a million times, but now I'm not sure if it's going to come out right."

Hunter waited.

"Have you ever dealt with lawyers?" she asked. "They don't really do anything for you. Just want a lot of money and time, and then they tell you there's not much that can be done."

"Get a new lawyer," he suggested.

"I've had four," she said. "All in the span of a month. They're all the same. Too expensive. And I don't have the money."

"But you're driving a BMW."

"It's my mother-in-law's. I'm just borrowing it."

"And you're wearing a diamond ring."

She went quiet, her eyes clouding.

"My husband gave it to me," she said.
Hunter studied her.
"So can't he help you?"
"No, he can't."

"Have you ever tried finding a private investigator?" she asked.
"Never needed one. I was a detective."
"They aren't like in the movies," she said. "They just sit in their offices, working the phone or tapping on their computers. They won't actually do anything. I went all the way to Townsville to see one. He said he could help, but he wanted six men on the job and nearly ten thousand dollars a week."
"For what?"
"So, I got desperate. Really desperate. And then I had this idea—what if I looked for hitchhikers? Maybe one of them could help me. Someone who might be the right kind of person. I've been pretty selective. I only stop for men who look tough."
"Thanks for the compliment, Rosie," Hunter said.
"I don't mean it in a bad way," she said. "It wasn't meant to insult you."
"But it could've been dangerous."
She nodded. "It almost was, a couple of times. But I had to take the risk. I needed to find someone. I thought I'd end up with farmhands or men from the mines. Tough guys, out of work, with some time to spare. Maybe even looking to make a little money, but I can't offer much. Is that going to be a problem?"
"So far, Rosie, everything about this is a problem."
She fell silent again.
"I've talked to all of them," she said. "Chatted a bit, like I'm doing with you. I was trying to figure out what kind of people they were inside. Maybe a dozen of them. And none of them were right. But I think you are."
"You think I'm what?"
"I think you're my best shot," she said. "A former major, an ex-soldier, no ties. You're perfect."
"I'm not looking for a job, Rosie."

She nodded. "I know. I already figured that out. But that's even better, really. It keeps things clean. You'd be helping just to help, not for money. And with your background, it obligates you."
"It doesn't obligate me," Hunter replied.
"You were a soldier," she said. "And a peacekeeper. You're supposed to help people."
"We spent more time busting heads than helping anyone. Not much hero work involved."
"But you must've helped people. That's what soldiers do. It's their job."
"We mostly hurt them. Helping wasn't really a priority."
"But it's what you're trained for," she said. "It's your duty."
"If you need a cop, go to the local sergeant. Mount Kalka, or wherever it is."
"Four Ways," she corrected. "I live in Four Ways, north of Mount Kalka."
"Then go to him."
She shook her head. "No, I can't."

Hunter didn't say anything more. He lay pressed against the door, half-reclined, uncomfortable in the tilted car. The engine hummed quietly, and the air conditioning continued to roar. Rosie remained braced above him, silent, staring out the window. Her eyes were blinking, and Hunter could tell she was close to tears, though she fought them back. Disappointment was etched on her face—whether with herself, or with him, he couldn't tell.

"You probably think I'm crazy," she said.
He turned his head to look at her. From her strong legs to her elegant, expensive dress. The hem had ridden up on her thighs, revealing a snow-white bra strap against her tanned skin. She was well-groomed, her hair combed, her nails painted and trimmed, her face intelligent but tired.

"I'm not crazy," she said. Then she looked at him directly, her

expression a mix of desperation and hope.
"I've dreamed about this for a month," she continued. "This is my last chance. It was a ridiculous plan, but it's all I had. There was always the hope it might work, and now I feel like I'm ruining it by coming across as a madwoman."

Hunter paused, thinking of the truck stop diner he'd passed earlier, back in Cloncurry, across from his motel. He could have gone in there, enjoyed a full breakfast—double bacon, lots of coffee, maybe even cake. By the time he'd come out, Rosie would have been long gone.

"Start over," he said at last. "Say what you need to say. But first, get us out of this ditch. I could use a cup of coffee. Is there anywhere nearby where we could get some?"
"I think so," she said. "About an hour from here."
"Then let's head there. We'll talk over coffee."
"You're going to ditch me as soon as we get there," she said.

It was tempting.

She stared at him for a long moment, then nodded. She put the car into drive and pressed the accelerator. The front tires spun, struggling for grip on the loose gravel, sending a cloud of dust around the car. But then they caught traction, and the BMW jerked back onto the road. Rosie straightened it out, then accelerated south.

"I don't know where to begin," she said.
"At the beginning," Hunter replied. "That's usually the best place."

She shook her head, her eyes fixed on the road.

"We don't have that kind of time," she said.

Fifty kilometers southwest of Cloncurry, on a quiet, paved road, a Falcon sat idling on the shoulder. Its hood was slightly open to allow better cooling in the unbearable heat. The landscape around was so flat that the curve of the earth was visible, the dry brush stretching endlessly toward the horizon. The silence was broken only by the faint ticking of the engine and the crackling of the earth under the intense sun.

The driver of the Falcon had adjusted the electric side mirror outward, so he could see the entire road behind him. The dust the car had stirred up earlier had settled, and his view was clear for about a kilometer, all the way to where the blacktop met the shimmering sky. His focus was on that distant point, waiting for a shape to emerge.

He knew what car to expect. The team had been briefed thoroughly. It would be a white Mercedes, driven by a man alone, heading to an appointment he couldn't afford to miss. The man would be driving fast because he was running late—he was always late for everything. They knew the time of his appointment, and with simple math, they'd calculated when he would pass by. That time was rapidly approaching.

"Let's do it," the driver said.

He stepped out into the blazing heat and pressed the hood closed with a click. After sliding back into the seat, he took a blue ball cap from the woman sitting next to him. It was one of three they'd picked up from a souvenir shop at Brisbane Airport, each embroidered with "AFP" in white stitching with the emblem, probably off Temu. He pulled the cap low over his eyes, put the car in gear, and kept his foot on the brake, still watching the mirror.

"Right on time," he said.

The mirage on the horizon wobbled and shimmered before a white shape emerged, heading toward them like a fish leaping from water. It was a white Mercedes sedan, moving fast, crouched low on the road. The driver eased off the brake, and the Falcon crept forward. The Mercedes flew past them, and the Falcon pulled into its slipstream. The driver straightened the wheel, pressed the accelerator, and smiled tightly. The killing crew was ready to work again.

The driver of the Mercedes noticed flashing headlights in his mirror. He glanced again and saw the car behind him. Two peaked caps were visible in the front seat. Instinctively, he checked his speedometer—it was over 120. A cold stab of panic shot through him as he eased off the accelerator. He was already running late, and he had to decide how to handle this. Should he act humble, important, or try to appear like he was just doing his job?

The sedan pulled alongside, and he saw three people inside, one of them a woman. Radio antennas sprouted from the car, but there were no lights or sirens. Not regular cops. The driver was signaling for him to pull over. The woman pressed an ID against her window with "AFP" in bold letters. These people were serious. He relaxed slightly—the AFP didn't pull you over for speeding. It had to be something else, maybe an identity check, which made sense considering how close they were to the northern border of Australia. He nodded and pulled onto the shoulder, braking to a stop in a cloud of dust.

The AFP car pulled in behind him.

The way to handle these situations, the crew knew, was to keep the target calm and compliant for as long as possible. Struggling led to evidence—blood, fibers, fluids. So they moved with a professional air, exiting the car without urgency.

"Mr. Bradley?" the woman called. "Troy Bradley, right?"

The driver of the Mercedes, a man around thirty with dark hair and a soft frame, slid out of his seat. He faced the woman, his southern manners putting him at a disadvantage before he even spoke.

"Yes, love that's me. How can I help you?" he asked.

"Your mobile phone not working?" the woman asked.

Bradley patted his coat pocket.

"It bloody should be," he said.

"May I see it?"

He handed over his phone, and the woman dialed a number, then raised her eyebrows in surprise.

"It seems fine," she said. "Sir, we need just five minutes of your time."

Bradley frowned.

"For what?"

"We have an AFP assistant director a few kilometers up the road. He needs to speak with you urgently. We weren't given all the details, but it seems important."

Bradley checked his watch.

"I have an appointment," he said.

"We know," she replied. "We called ahead and rescheduled it for you. Five minutes is all we need."

Bradley shrugged, starting to feel uneasy.

"Can I see some ID?"

The woman handed over a black leather wallet with a plastic window showing an official AFP badge. Bradley studied it, assuming it was legitimate—after all, he'd never seen an AFP badge before.

"Okay," he said. "I guess I'll follow you."

"We'll drive you," the woman said. "The checkpoint up ahead is very strict about civilian vehicles. We'll bring you right back."

Bradley hesitated but eventually nodded. "Fine."

He followed the group back to the Falcon. The driver held the front passenger door open for him.

"You ride up front, sir," the driver said. "They've listed you as a class-1 individual, and putting someone like you in the backseat would get us in serious trouble."

Bradley swelled with importance at the designation. He slid into the front seat, barely noticing that the woman still had his phone. The driver closed the door, and the others climbed into the back. The Falcon pulled away from the Mercedes and cruised back onto the highway.

"We'll be there soon," the woman said.

The Falcon cruised down the highway, heading toward the destination. The driver kept a steady speed, and Bradley sat in silence, his discomfort growing. In the distance, a plume of dust rose, marking a vehicle on the road several kilometers ahead.

"There it is," the driver said, glancing at the rearview mirror.

The car slowed down as they approached a turnoff. The Falcon left the main road, bumping onto a dirt path that led them behind a tall stand of brush. Hidden from the road, the vehicle came to a stop. The two men in the backseat slid out, drawing handguns and pressing them into Bradley's neck, right behind his ears.

"Don't move," the woman said.

Bradley, terrified, remained perfectly still. His breathing became shallow, and his eyes darted around, but he didn't dare turn his head. A minute later, a large dark vehicle blasted by on the main road. Its dust cloud rustled the nearby brush. The driver got out, approached Bradley's door, and pointed a gun at his throat.

"Get out, carefully," he said.

Bradley barely managed to croak out, "What?"

"We'll tell you what," the woman said. "Now get out."

Bradley obeyed, stepping out of the car with three guns trained on him.

"Walk away from the car," the woman ordered. "Keep walking away from the road."

Bradley hesitated, his eyes searching for an escape, but with three guns aimed at him, he knew better than to run. He took a few steps forward, glancing at the woman. She called his name, "Troy," and the two men jumped back. Bradley's head whipped around to face her just as she raised her gun and fired a single shot through his right eye. The sharp sound of the gunshot echoed across the desert, followed by a cloud of red mist as Bradley collapsed in a heap.

The woman stepped closer, examining his body. Then she stood back, arms outstretched, as if waiting for an airport search.

"Check," she said.

The two men inspected her carefully, searching her hair, clothes, and skin for any trace of blood, bone, or evidence.

"Clear," one man said.
"Clear," the other echoed.

Satisfied, the woman nodded. "Okay."

The two men grabbed Bradley's arms and legs and dragged his body a few feet into the brush. There, they found a narrow limestone crevice, just wide enough to fit a man's corpse. They lowered Bradley's body into the crack, making sure it fit snugly, then let it fall the rest of the way. It wedged into place about seven feet down, out of reach of scavengers.

The bloodstains on the ground had already started to dry and darken. They kicked dirt over the spots, using a eucalyptus branch to sweep away their footprints. Then they climbed back into the Falcon, which bounced back onto the road and cruised away at a steady eighty kilometers an hour. They passed Bradley's abandoned white Mercedes, already covered in a fine layer of dust, and continued down the highway.

"I have a daughter," Rosie McMahon said, breaking the silence. "I told you that, right?"
"You mentioned you were a mother," Hunter replied.

"She's six and a half now," Rosie continued quietly.
Hunter nodded, sensing more was coming.

"They named her Allanah," she said.
"They?"

"My husband's family," she explained. "They chose her name."
"They named your kid?"

"It just happened," Rosie said, her voice distant. "I wasn't in a position to stop it."

Hunter considered that for a moment. "What would you have named her?"

"Hope," Rosie said, her voice soft. "I thought she was my hope."

"But she's Allanah," Hunter said.

Rosie nodded. "Lahni, for short. Sometimes they call her Miss Lahni."

"And she's six and a half?" Hunter asked.
"Yes," Rosie said, hesitating. "We've been married for almost seven years. You can do the math."
"Is that a problem?" Hunter asked, puzzled.
"Is it a problem for you to think about the implications?" she asked in return.

Hunter shook his head. "No, not a problem for me."
"It's not a problem for me either," she said, "but it explains why I wasn't in a position to say no."

Hunter said nothing, waiting for her to continue.

"Warner's family, the McMahons—they're old Queenslanders," she said. "Been here since the early days. They're what you might expect: big money, cattle, mining, old wealth, but a lot of it's gone now. They're not religious, but they act like they are.

And they still hunt for sport."

"Warner McMahon," Hunter said, trying the name out.

Rosie smiled slightly, for the first time since they'd driven out of the ditch. "Warner," she repeated. "It's an old family name."

"Sounds like a movie studio," Hunter quipped. "What's the other brother called—Paramount?"

"Robert," Rosie said. "But everyone calls him Ryan."

"Warner," Hunter said again. "That's a new one to me."

"It was new to me, too," Rosie said. "But I used to like his name. It made him stand out."

"And now?" Hunter asked.

"I met him in Sydney, back in university," Rosie said, her voice trailing off.

"Off his home turf," Hunter observed.

She nodded, the small smile vanishing. "Correct. If I'd met him out here, with his family and everything, it never would have happened."

Rosie fell silent again, staring out at the long road ahead.

I'll continue now, working towards the end of the document!

After a few more minutes, Rosie spotted something ahead in the distance. "There's a diner up ahead," she said. "We can get some coffee there."
"Strange kind of diner if it didn't have coffee," Hunter said dryly.
"There are a lot of strange things out here," she replied.

The diner was isolated, sitting on a slight rise surrounded by an expanse of sunbaked dirt that served as the parking lot. A sign on a tall pole advertised the diner, and there were two utes parked haphazardly, far from each other.

As Rosie slowed the BMW and pulled into the lot, she hesitated.

"Now's the time you're going to ditch me," she said. "You figure one of those guys in the utes will give you a ride."
Hunter didn't respond.
"If you are," she added, "please wait until later. I don't want to be left alone here."

She parked the car next to the signpost, as if it offered some protection from the sun, and turned off the engine. The air conditioner wheezed to a stop. Hunter opened the door, and the oppressive heat hit him like a wall. He stood still for a moment, waiting for her, then they walked toward the diner together. The ground was hard and dry, baked solid by the sun.

Rosie walked half a step ahead of Hunter, her eyes downcast, as if she didn't want to be seen. Her dress had fallen to a modest length at her knees, and she moved with a graceful, dancer-like poise, her upper body still while her legs scissored elegantly beneath her.

Inside the diner's foyer, there was an illegal cigarette machine and a rack filled with flyers for local events—rodeo competitions, shooting ranges, mining jobs. Inside the dining area, it was refreshingly cool. There was a waitress sitting at the counter, a cook in the kitchen, and two men eating in separate booths. All four of them looked up as Rosie and Hunter entered but said nothing.

Hunter took a quick glance around and led Rosie to a booth at the far end of the room. He slid across the sticky vinyl seat and tilted his head back to feel the cool air from the vent overhead. Rosie sat across from him, finally meeting his gaze.

"My daughter looks nothing like me," she said, her voice sad. "That's the cruelest irony in all this. The McMahon genes just steamrolled mine."

Hunter studied her face—her striking green eyes, high cheekbones, thick black curls. Her skin had the rich color of dark coffee, glowing slightly in the diner's dim light.

"Who does Lahni look like?" he asked.

"Them," Rosie said. "The McMahons."

The waitress arrived with ice water, a pad, and pencil, offering no small talk. Rosie ordered iced coffee, while Hunter opted for his black and hot.

"She doesn't look like she's mine at all," Rosie said quietly. "Light brown hair, chubby, but she's got my eyes."
"She's lucky, then," Hunter said.

Rosie offered a brief smile. "Thank you. I hope she stays lucky."

The waitress returned with their drinks. Rosie's iced coffee came in a tall glass, and Hunter's coffee in a plastic carafe with a plain mug. The check was left face down between them, no words exchanged.

"I need you to understand something," Rosie began again. "I loved Warner once. You need to know that. He wasn't hard to love. He was big, handsome, relaxed, always smiling. We were young, in school, and it all seemed so easy back then."

Hunter nodded, saying nothing. Loners like him weren't always comfortable with other people's confessions.

"You told me to start at the beginning," Rosie said.

"Yes," Hunter replied. "I did."

"So I will," she said. "We were in Sydney, both in university. I thought I had everything backward. My biggest worry wasn't whether Warner's family would accept me—I was worried my family wouldn't accept him."

She took a sip of her drink and continued. "I came from wealth. My family's land in Byron Bay goes back generations. We had art, history, money, everything. So I spent my time worrying about how my family would react to me marrying out of our culture."

"And what did they say?" Hunter asked.

"They went insane," Rosie said, taking another sip. "I thought they were being foolish, but now I understand. They were trying to protect me."

"And then?" Hunter prompted.

"I was pregnant," she said flatly. "That made everything a million times worse. My parents disowned me. It was like an old-fashioned story—expelled from the house with nothing but a suitcase."

"What did you do?"

"We got married. No one from either side came. We lived in Sydney for a while, but then Warner couldn't find a job. He wasn't even looking, really. He planned to take over his father's business. I didn't like that idea. I thought we'd start fresh, on our own. But we couldn't make rent, and eventually, I gave in, and we moved back to his family's house in Queensland."

She paused, the weight of her memories heavy in her voice.

"And?" Hunter asked.

"And that was the end," Rosie said softly. "It was like falling straight into hell."

Rosie locked eyes with him. "It was like the ground opened up, and I fell straight into hell. The shock left me numb; I couldn't react at all. They treated me strangely, and on the second day, it hit me—I finally understood. I had always been treated like royalty, even just another cool kid among thousands in Sydney. But now, I had become something else—nothing more than worthless. They didn't say it outright, but it was glaringly obvious. They despised me because I was the dark-skinned woman who had ensnared their precious son.

"They were excruciatingly polite, but it felt like they were simply waiting for Warner to come to his senses and discard me. It happens, you know? Out here, the boys sometimes like a bit of diversity when they're young and reckless. It's like a rite of passage for them. But eventually, they wake up, straighten out, and return to their proper lives. I knew that was what they were thinking and hoping for. It was devastating. I had never viewed myself that way before, not once. I never had to. Suddenly, my whole world was turned upside down. It was like plunging into ice water—I couldn't breathe, think, or even move."

"But he didn't leave you, did he?" Hunter asked.

She lowered her gaze to the table. "No," she murmured. "Instead of leaving, he started hitting me. The first time, he punched me in the face. The next day, Lahni was born."

The Falcon, once used for the job, was transformed back into a regular Avis rental. Hidden behind a stand of trees, miles away from the highway, between Townsville and Big Spring, the car underwent its change. The Victoria plates were swapped out for Queensland ones, and the plastic wheel covers were snapped back on. Cellular antennas peeled from the rear glass were placed neatly in a bag, along with the CB whips, which were detached from the sheet metal. The souvenir ball caps were tucked away with the handguns, now stashed out of sight. Bradley's mobile phone was shattered against a rock, the remnants tossed deep into the brush. A sprinkling of dirt from the roadside was scattered over the front passenger seat, ensuring any stray hairs or fibers would be vacuumed up by the rental company.

The car smoothly rejoined the highway, once again a forgettable sedan with three equally unmemorable passengers inside. They made one last stop at a rest area near the Colorado River, where they sipped sodas and made an untraceable call from a payphone. The call was routed through the Gold Coast, then Brisbane, and eventually to an office in a small Queensland town. The message was simple—mission accomplished, everything going as planned. The response was one of gratitude.

"He busted my lip and knocked my teeth crooked," Rosie continued quietly.

Hunter studied her face closely.

"That was the first time," she said. "He lost control completely. But afterward, he was filled with remorse. He drove me to the emergency room himself. It's a long drive, hours and hours, and during the entire trip, he kept begging for forgiveness. He begged me not to tell the truth about what had happened. He seemed so ashamed, and I agreed to stay quiet. But I didn't have to say anything anyway—by the time we arrived, I had already gone into labor, and they took me straight to the delivery unit. Lahni was born the next day."

"And what happened after that?"

"It was fine for about a week," Rosie said, pausing. "But then it started again. He'd hit me for everything. I wasn't giving enough attention to him, or I didn't want to have sex because I was still in pain from the stitches. He said I'd become fat and ugly after the pregnancy."

Hunter said nothing.

"And after a while, I believed him," Rosie admitted. "For a long time, I thought it was my fault. That's how it happens. You have to have a lot of self-confidence to resist that kind of manipulation, and I didn't. Not in that situation. He destroyed my self-esteem. For years, I tried to do better, thinking I was the problem."

"What about his family?" Hunter asked.

Rosie pushed her half-finished iced coffee away from her.

"They had no idea," she said. "Then his father passed away, and it got worse. His father was the only decent one among them. But after that, it was just his mother and his brother. His brother is awful, and his mother... well, she's a nightmare. But still, none of them know. It all happens in secret. The house is huge, like a compound, so we aren't all living on top of each other. And it's complicated—he's far too proud and stubborn to admit to his family that he made a mistake. So, the more they criticize me, the more he pretends he loves me. He misleads them. He buys me things. This ring, for example."

She held up her right hand, tilting her wrist slightly to show the large diamond set in platinum. It sparkled brightly under the dim diner lights. Hunter glanced at the ring—it was an impressive piece of jewelry, and he could only imagine how much it must have cost.

"He bought me horses, too," she continued. "They all know I love horses, and he bought them for me to look good in front of his family. But really, it's his way of explaining away the bruises. It was his idea of brilliance. A permanent excuse. I'm still learning to ride, so any injury can be blamed on me falling off. And out here, in rodeo country, bruises and broken bones are normal. No one even questions it."

Hunter looked at her more closely. "He's broken your bones?"

She nodded slowly and began touching various parts of her body, twisting slightly in the booth to demonstrate. She hesitated occasionally, as if trying to recall all the injuries.

"My ribs, for starters," she said. "He kicks me when I'm on the floor. He does that a lot when he's really mad. My left arm was twisted out of place. My collarbone was fractured. And my jaw. I've had three teeth reimplanted."

Hunter just stared at her.

She shrugged, attempting to minimize it. "The doctors at the emergency room probably think I'm the worst rider in the history of the West."

"And they believe it?"

"Maybe they just choose to," she said with a hint of bitterness. "And his mother and brother?"

"They don't ask questions," she replied. "There's no chance I'm going to get any sympathy from them."

"Why didn't you leave? Why not get out right after the first time?"

She sighed deeply and closed her eyes, turning her face away from him. She laid her hands flat on the table, then slowly turned them over, palms up, as if trying to find an explanation.

"I can't explain it," she whispered. "No one can. Unless you've lived through it, you can't truly understand. I had no confidence, no money, a newborn baby. I had no friends. I was constantly monitored. I couldn't even make a private phone call."

Hunter remained silent.

She opened her eyes and looked at him directly. "And the worst part? I had nowhere to go."

"What about going home?" he asked gently.

She shook her head. "I never even considered it. Enduring the abuse was easier than crawling back to my family with a mixed-race baby in my arms."

Hunter didn't respond.

"And once you pass up that first chance to leave, it's over," she said softly. "It just gets worse. Each time I thought about it, I still had no money, and Lahni was getting older. First, she was a one-year-old, then a two-year-old, then three. The time is never right. If you stay after the first time, you're stuck forever. And I stayed. I wish I hadn't, but I did."

There was another long silence between them. Rosie looked at Hunter, her eyes pleading for some kind of understanding.

"You have to believe me," she said. "Even if you can't fully grasp it. You're a man. You're big, strong. If someone hits you, you hit them back. You don't like where you are, you move on. It's different for me. Even if you can't fully comprehend it, you have to trust that it's real."

Hunter remained quiet, still listening.

"I could've left if I had abandoned Lahni," Rosie continued. "Warner told me he'd pay for me to go anywhere I wanted, first-class, if I left the baby with him. He even offered to send a limo from Brisbane to take me straight to the airport."

Hunter didn't say a word.

"But how could I do that?" she asked quietly. "Leaving her was never an option. So Warner pretends this is my choice. Like I want to stay. And he keeps on hitting me—punching, kicking, slapping me, humiliating me in every possible way. Even when he's not angry, he does it. And when he is mad? He just loses control completely."

The air in the diner felt thick, punctuated only by the hum of the ceiling vents and the occasional clink of melting ice in her glass. Hunter studied Rosie again, noting the defiance in her posture. Despite everything she had just told him, she sat up straight, head held high, her eyes determined.

"He hits you every day?" Hunter asked after a moment.

Rosie closed her eyes again, exhaling slowly. "Not literally every day, but three or four times a week, usually. Sometimes more. It feels like every day."

Hunter looked at her for a long time, then shook his head slowly.

"You're lying to me," he said.

Rosie turned toward the window, her face flushing red. Hunter wasn't sure if it was anger or embarrassment, or perhaps both.

"Why do you say that?" she asked quietly.

"Because the physical evidence doesn't match your story," Hunter replied. "There's no visible bruising. Your skin looks clear, and the light makeup isn't covering anything significant. I can see you're blushing—you look like you just left a salon. Plus, you moved across that parking lot like a dancer, not someone who's stiff and sore. If he's been hitting you almost every day, he must be using a feather."

Rosie was silent for a moment, then nodded slowly. "There's more I need to tell you."

Hunter looked away.

"The most important part," she said. "The reason I brought you here in the first place."

"Why should I even listen?" Hunter asked, his tone flat.

She unwrapped a drinking straw and began twisting the paper wrapper into a tight spiral between her fingers.

"I had to get your attention," she said, her voice low and apologetic.

Hunter turned his gaze back to the window. He thought back to the morning, to the moment he'd left his motel room, ready to see where the day would take him. The image of the reflection in the rearview mirror flashed in his mind—the cop, and the smooth sound of the BMW's tires as they slowed beside him on the road.

"Well, you've got my attention," he said, still staring outside.

"For five years, it happened exactly as I told you," Rosie said quietly. "Almost every day. But a year and a half ago, it stopped."

Hunter didn't respond.

"I had to tell it to you backward," she admitted, "because I needed you to listen to me."

Hunter said nothing.

"Telling this to a stranger isn't easy," she continued, her voice trembling slightly.

"It's not easy listening to it either," Hunter replied, his tone calm but firm.

Rosie took a deep breath, then asked, "Are you going to leave me now?"

Hunter shrugged. "I almost did a minute ago."

Rosie remained quiet for a long moment. "Please don't," she whispered. "At least not here. Just listen a little longer."

Hunter's eyes met hers. "I'm listening."

"Will you still help me?" she asked softly.

"With what?"

She didn't answer right away.

"What did it feel like?" Hunter asked after a pause.

"What do you mean?" she replied.

"Being hit. What did it feel like, physically?"

Rosie looked away, thinking for a moment. "It depends on where," she finally said.

Hunter nodded, knowing that pain feels different depending on the location. "What about your stomach?"

"I threw up a lot," she admitted. "Sometimes there was blood, and that scared me."

Hunter nodded again. She clearly knew what it felt like to be hit in the stomach.

"I swear, it's true," Rosie said, her voice cracking slightly. "Five whole years. Why would I make that up?"

"So, what changed?" Hunter asked. "Why did he stop?"

Rosie hesitated, glancing around the diner as if she sensed that others might be listening. Hunter noticed the subtle shift, too. He glanced around and caught the eyes of the cook, the waitress, and the two men sitting at distant tables. Their hostility was palpable, but they quickly averted their gazes when he looked their way.

"Can we go now?" Rosie asked quietly. "We need to head back. It's a long drive."

Hunter looked at her. "Am I coming with you?"

"That's the whole point," she said, almost pleading.

Hunter turned his head to the window again, thinking it over.

"Please, Hunter," she continued. "At least hear the rest of the story before you decide. If you don't want to go all the way to Four Ways, I can drop you in Mount Kalka. You can visit the museum or see Benjamin Blackman's grave."

Hunter glanced outside again, watching the shadow on the BMW's hood shift with the movement of the sun. The interior of the car must have been scorching by now.

"You should visit anyway," Rosie added. "If you're really exploring Queensland."

"Okay," Hunter finally said.

"Thank you," she whispered.

He didn't respond.

"I need to use the restroom before we leave," Rosie said, sliding out of the booth with surprising grace for someone who had just shared such a painful story. She walked the length of the room, head down, avoiding eye contact with anyone.

The two men at the tables watched her pass, then their eyes shifted back to Hunter. He ignored them, turned the check over, and left the change on the table. He slid out of the booth and walked toward the door. The two men continued to watch his every step.

Once outside, he stood still for a minute, watching the barren land bake under the intense sun. After a moment, he heard her footsteps approaching from behind. Her hair was freshly combed, and she'd touched up her lipstick.

"I'll use the bathroom too," Hunter said, starting toward the restrooms.

"Wait until I'm in the car," she said nervously, glancing at the men inside the diner. "I don't want to be left alone here. I shouldn't have come in here in the first place."

Hunter watched as Rosie walked quickly to the car, got in, and started the engine. He saw the vehicle shudder slightly as the air conditioner kicked in. Once she was safely inside, he turned and headed for the restroom.

Hunter entered the men's room, a modest space with two porcelain urinals and a single toilet cubicle. The sink was chipped, with a cold water faucet, and a roll of paper towels sat on top of the dispenser instead of inside it. The place wasn't exactly clean.

He stepped up to the left-hand urinal and unzipped, then heard footsteps outside the door. Instinctively, he glanced at the chrome valve above the urinal, which was rounded and reflected a distorted view of the room behind him. Through the reflection, he saw the door open and one of the men from the diner step inside. The door closed again, and the man leaned against it, blocking the exit. He was tall, his head nearly touching the top of the doorframe, and he was fiddling with something behind his back. Hunter heard the soft click of the door lock.

The man shifted, letting his hands fall loose by his sides. He wore a black T-shirt with some sort of logo on it—perhaps a mining company, though the reflection made it hard to read.

"You new around here mate?" the man asked.

Hunter didn't respond, focusing on the reflection.

"I asked you a question," the man repeated.

Hunter still ignored him.

"I'm talking to you," the man insisted, his voice rising.

"Well, that's your first mistake," Hunter said calmly. "For all you know, I could be the polite type, someone who feels obligated to turn around and listen—whereupon I'd be pissing all over your shoes."

The man hesitated, caught off guard. Clearly, he had some kind of prepared speech, but Hunter's interruption threw him off balance. That gave Hunter just enough time to zip up and get ready. The man stood there, still shuffling slightly, deciding how to react.

"So, I guess it's up to me to tell you how things are around here," the man said, regaining some confidence.

"Tell me what?" Hunter asked, buying himself more time.

"How it is around here," the man said, trying to sound authoritative.

Hunter paused for a second. The only downside to drinking coffee was that it had a diuretic effect.

"And how exactly is it around here?" Hunter asked, keeping his tone neutral.

"Around here, you don't bring darkies into decent folks'

places," the man replied bluntly.

"What?" Hunter said, as if he hadn't understood.

"What part don't you get?"

Hunter exhaled slowly, knowing he was just seconds away from making his move. "I didn't understand any of it," he said evenly.

"You don't bring darkies into a place like this," the man repeated.

Hunter narrowed his eyes. "What's a darkie?"

The man stepped forward, his reflection in the chrome valve growing larger. "Islanders," he spat. "People with skin as dark as dirt."

"Pacific Islanders?" Hunter said, his tone sharp. "You don't think calling them 'darkies' is a little outdated? Especially since you probably come out of the mines looking just as dirty. Only difference is, you're a bit slower."

"You some kind of smart cunt?" the man snarled, taking another step closer.

Hunter zipped up and turned to the sink, rinsing his hands under the cold water. "I'm definitely smarter than you," he said, his voice calm but firm. "But then again, that's not saying much. This roll of paper towels here? It's smarter than you. A lot smarter. Each sheet could probably earn a full scholarship to a top university, while you're still struggling to finish high school."

The insult hit the man like a slow-moving truck. He blinked, processing the words. Four or five seconds later, his face twisted in rage, and he swung his right arm in a wide, slow arc, aiming for Hunter's head with a bunched-up fist. The punch could have caused some serious damage, but it never landed.

Hunter caught the man's wrist with his left hand, stopping the swing cold. The smack of their contact echoed off the bathroom tiles.

"The bacteria on this floor are smarter than you," Hunter said, twisting his hips to protect himself while squeezing the man's wrist with his hand. There was a time when he could break bones this way—back then, it wasn't about sheer strength but about pure determination. Now, though, he wasn't sure he had that same fire.

"This is your lucky day," Hunter said through gritted teeth. "For all I know, you could be a cop, so I'm going to let you go."

The man stared at his wrist in desperation as it turned red and began to swell. Hunter could feel the bones clicking and shifting, the radius and ulna coming closer than they should.

"Apologize," Hunter ordered.

The man hesitated for a long moment, then muttered, "I'm sorry. I apologize."

"Not to me, you idiot," Hunter said, increasing the pressure. "To the lady."

The man froze, but Hunter tightened his grip, feeling his thumb sliding over the slick surface of the man's clammy wrist.

"Okay, okay!" the man gasped. "Enough!"

Hunter released him. The man stumbled back, cradling his hand and breathing heavily.

"Give me your keys," Hunter demanded.

The man awkwardly fished them out of his right pocket with his left hand and handed them over. Hunter took the keys and tossed them into the unflushed urinal, then washed his hands again.

"Now go wait for me in the car park," Hunter added.

The man unlocked the bathroom door left-handed and shuffled out. A few minutes later, Hunter walked outside and found the man standing halfway between the diner and the BMW.

"Be real nice now," Hunter called out. "You should offer to vacuum and steam clean her car or something. She'll probably say no, but you know it's the thought that counts. If you're creative enough, you'll get your keys back. Otherwise, you're walking home in stinkin heat."

Rosie, sitting in the car, was watching the interaction through the tinted windows, clearly confused. Hunter made a motion for her to roll down the window, mimicking a circular movement with his hand. She hesitated, then buzzed the window down just a couple of inches, wide enough for her worried eyes to peek through.

"This guy's got something to say to you," Hunter said, stepping back to let the man approach.

The man shifted awkwardly, putting his hand on his chest like he was about to make a formal apology. He bent slightly at the waist to address the narrow gap in the window.

"Ma'am," he began, his voice shaky. "I just wanted to say we'd all be real pleased if you came back soon. And, uh, would you like me to steam clean your car, seeing as you're here?"

"What?" Rosie said, her confusion evident.

Both the man and Rosie looked at Hunter, one pleading, the other astonished.

"Beat it," Hunter said, dismissing the man. "I left your keys in the bathroom."

The man hesitated for a second, then hurried back into the

diner. Hunter walked around the hood of the BMW and opened his door.

"I thought you were ditching me," Rosie said softly. "I thought you'd asked him for a ride."

"I'd rather ride with you," Hunter replied, sliding into the seat.

The Ford Falcon traveled south toward a desolate crossroads town. On one side of the road stood an aging fish and chip takeaway shop, while a vacant lot sprawled across the other. The faded stop line on the asphalt was barely visible. Further down, a crumbling service station sat in contrast to a small, one-room schoolhouse on the opposite side. Dust and heat danced in the air, distorting the view. The car slowed to a crawl as it navigated through the intersection at a leisurely pace. It drifted past the school gate, then suddenly accelerated, its engine roaring as it sped away.

Inside the school, little Lahni McMahon sat by the window, seated in a wooden chair, just about to open the lid of her bright green lunch box. The brief screech of tires caught her attention, and she turned her head, watching the car as it disappeared down the road. Lahni was a thoughtful, observant child, quiet and introspective. Her large, dark eyes remained fixed on the road until the dust finally settled. Then, she returned to her lunch, inspecting its contents and wishing her mum had been the one to pack it, instead of the maid, who worked for the McMahons and wasn't kind.

CHAPTER 3

“What happened a year and a half ago?” Hunter asked.

Rosie stayed silent. They were driving along a long, deserted road, the sun hanging high overhead, almost perfectly aligned with the road. Hunter guessed it was just before midday, and they were headed north. The road itself was patched up in places but relatively smooth, though the shoulders were rough and uneven. Billboards popped up occasionally, advertising fuel, accommodations, and stores several kilometers away. On either side of the road, the landscape stretched out flat and dry, scattered with rusty old windmills that stood still in the distance. Closer to the road were old signs at every other farm gate indicating that the property had been mined and now shut.

“Copper mines,” Rosie explained. “They used to find deposits of it under every other old grazing farm station, now the big mining mob are pulling out cause they’ve got to the bottom of the barrel and it’s not good metal anymore they say.”

The dry land extended as far as the eye could see, dotted with scrub. To the northwest, Hunter thought he could make out distant mountains, but it might have just been the shimmer of heat.

“Are you hungry?” she asked. “If we keep going, we could pick up Lahni from school, and I’d really like that. I haven’t seen her since yesterday."

"Whatever you want," Hunter replied.

Rosie pressed down on the accelerator, bringing the BMW up to a hundred kilometers per hour, the car lurching slightly over the bumps in the road. Hunter adjusted in his seat and tightened his seatbelt. She glanced over at him.

"Do you believe me now?" she asked.

He looked back at her. His years of experience as an investigator had taught him to question everything.

"What happened a year and a half ago?" he asked again. "Why did he stop?"

Rosie adjusted her grip on the steering wheel, flexing her fingers before gripping it tightly again.

"He went to jail," she said.

"For hitting you?" Hunter asked.

"In Queensland?" Rosie gave a bitter laugh, a short burst of disbelief. "Now I know you're not from around here."

Hunter said nothing, watching the hot,dusty red Queensland landscape roll by through the windshield.

"It just doesn't happen here," she continued. "In outback Queensland, a 'country gentleman' would never hit a woman —everyone knows that. Especially not a white gentleman from a family that's been here for generations. So if someone like me—someone dark-skinned—were to make a claim like that, they'd probably lock me away instead."

Hunter remained silent.

"So what did he do?" he asked after a moment.

"He didn't pay his taxes," she replied. "He made a lot of money dealing in mining leases and selling equipment to Papua New

Guinea. But he didn't report any of it to the ATO. They caught up with him eventually."

"They send people to prison for that?"

Rosie pulled a face. "They usually try not to, at least not the first time. They'll let you off with a plan to pay back what you owe, if you come clean. But Warner was too stubborn. He kept hiding things all the way to trial. He refused to pay a cent and even denied that he owed anything, which was absurd. And since his money was tied up in family trusts, they couldn't just take it. That really irritated them."

"So they took him to court?" Hunter asked.

Rosie nodded. "Oh, they did. Made a federal case out of it—literally. His lawyer was an old school friend, and his other best friend, the local prosecutor, tried to help. But it didn't matter. The ATO crushed them. He got sentenced to three to five years. The judge said he had to serve at least thirty months."

Hunter said nothing. The road stretched on as Rosie sped past a truck, the first other vehicle they'd seen in miles.

"I was so happy," she admitted quietly. "I'll never forget it. After the trial, they didn't haul him off in cuffs. They just told him to show up at the prison the next morning. He came home, packed a small bag, and we had a family dinner that night. He hit me for the last time that evening. The next day, his friends drove him to the jail near Townsville—some minimum-security place they jokingly call Tropical Camping. I hear they even have tennis courts there."

"Do you visit him?" Hunter asked.

She shook her head. "I pretend he's dead."

Silence fell between them as the car sped on. In the distance, mountains loomed, shimmering in the heat.

"That's the Great Dividing Range," Rosie said softly. "Watch the light change; it's stunning."

Hunter squinted ahead, but the sun was too bright to notice any real change in color.

"Minimum thirty months," Rosie mused. "That's two and a half years. I figure he's on his best behavior, so he'll probably get out around then."

Hunter nodded. "Most likely."

"So, two and a half years," she repeated. "I wasted the first one and a half."

"You've still got twelve months," Hunter said. "That's plenty of time."

Rosie fell quiet again.

"Help me think through it," she said. "We need to be on the same page. It's important."

Hunter didn't reply immediately.

"Just theoretically," she added. "For now."

He shrugged and then thought it through from her perspective.

"You need to get out," he said after a moment. "In an abusive situation, that's really the only option. You need a place to stay and a way to make money."

"Doesn't sound like much when you put it like that."

"Any major city has shelters. There are organizations that can help."

"What about Lahni?"

"There are child care options at the shelters. Plenty of kids go through those places. Lahni would have friends. And before long, you could get your own place."

"What kind of job could I get?"

"Anything," Hunter said. "You've got an education. You went to college."

"How do I get there?"

"Plane, train, bus—whatever works."

"I don't have any money."

"None at all?"

She shook her head. "I ran out last week."

Hunter glanced at her, confused.

"You dress pretty well for someone without any money," he remarked.

"Online shopping," she said. "I get approval from Warner's lawyer. He signs the gift cards, so I have clothes, but no cash."

"You could sell the diamond," he suggested.

She laughed, but it wasn't a happy sound. "I tried. Turns out it's a fake—stainless steel and cubic zirconia. Worth maybe thirty bucks."

Hunter paused.

"There's probably cash in the house," he said. "You could take some."

"I'd be a fugitive then," Rosie pointed out. "And Lahni—she's Warner's child, too. If I cross state lines with her, they'll say I kidnapped her. They'll put her picture on every news bulletin and social media and find me. They'll take her away, and I'll end up behind bars."

Hunter thought for a moment. "Then don't leave the state. Stay in Queensland. Go to Brisbane."

"I'm not staying in Queensland," Rosie said, her tone final.

Hunter didn't press her further.

"It's not easy," she continued. "His mother keeps an eye on me for him. That's why I didn't sell the ring, even though I could've used the thirty dollars. If she noticed it was gone, she'd be suspicious. She'd figure out what I'm planning. She's smart. So, if I took money and disappeared with Lahni, I might get a few hours head start before she called the police. But a few hours wouldn't be enough, especially in a place as big as Queensland. I wouldn't make it far."

"There's got to be a way," Hunter said, glancing over at her.

Rosie looked toward the back seat, where her bag lay—the one with the legal papers. "There are ways," she said. "Legal processes, protections, making Lahni a ward of the court. But lawyers are slow, and they cost a fortune, and I don't have the money. There are pro-bono lawyers, but they're overloaded with cases. It's all just a huge, complicated mess."

"I can see that," Hunter agreed.

"But a year is a long time," Rosie said. "I should be able to do it in a year, right?"

"So?"

"So, I need you to understand why I wasted the first year and a half. It was overwhelming, so I kept pushing it off. I felt safe. I thought I had plenty of time. You just said it yourself—twelve months is more than enough time. Even if I'm starting from scratch now, I haven't waited too long, have I?"

A soft beep interrupted them, coming from the dashboard. A small orange light shaped like a pump began blinking near the speedometer.

"Low on fuel," Rosie said.

"I saw a billboard for a BP station up ahead, about fifteen kilometers," Hunter noted.

"I need Shell," Rosie replied. "There's a card for Shell in the glove box. I can't pay at BP."

"You don't have money for fuel either?" Hunter asked, incredulous.

She shook her head. "I've been charging everything to my mother-in-law's Shell account. She won't get the bill for a month."

Rosie reached behind her seat and fumbled for her bag. She pulled it forward and dropped it on Hunter's lap. "Go ahead and check it," she said.

Hunter hesitated, the bag sitting heavily on his knees. "I don't feel right looking through a woman's bag."

"I want you to," Rosie insisted. "You need to understand."

After a moment, Hunter opened the bag. A faint scent of perfume and makeup wafted out. Inside, he found a hairbrush tangled with long, dark strands, a nail clipper, and a thin wallet.

"Check it out," she said again.

Hunter opened the wallet. Inside was a single, worn five dollar note. No credit cards. Just a Queensland driver's license with Rosie's startled photo on it, and a small plastic window with a picture of a little girl—Lahni. She was slightly chubby with perfect caramel skin, shiny dark hair, and a bright, radiant smile.

"She's adorable," Hunter said, looking at the picture.

"She really is," Rosie agreed softly.

"Where did you sleep last night?" he asked.

"In the car," Rosie replied. "Motels cost at least forty dollars."

"I found one for under twenty," Hunter pointed out.

She shrugged. "Anything more than five dollars, I can't afford. So, it's the car for me. It's comfortable enough. Then I wait for the morning rush and wash up in a truck stop's bathroom when they're too busy to notice."

"And food?" Hunter asked.

"I don't eat," she said simply.

The car began to slow down as she tried to conserve the little fuel she had left. "I'll pay for the fuel," Hunter offered. "You're giving me a ride, after all."

Another billboard passed on their right, announcing the BP station was ten kilometers away.

"Okay," Rosie said reluctantly. "I'll let you pay. But only because I need to get back to Lahni."

She pressed down on the accelerator again, confident the fuel would last the ten kilometers to the station. It wouldn't take much, Hunter figured, even with a big engine like the BMW's. As the horizon drew closer, he suddenly realized what he needed to do.

"Pull over," he said.

"Why?" Rosie asked, confused.

"Just do it, okay?" he replied.

Though puzzled, Rosie pulled off to the side of the road, leaving two wheels on the asphalt. She kept the engine running and the air conditioning blasting.

"Now wait," Hunter instructed.

They sat in silence for a moment until the truck Rosie had passed earlier rumbled by.

"Stay still," Hunter said, unfastening his seatbelt. He leaned down, grabbed the hem of his shirt, and tore off the front pocket with ease.

“What are you wearing?” he asked.

“What?” she replied, bewildered.

“Tell me exactly what you’re wearing,” he clarified.

Rosie blushed slightly and fidgeted in her seat. “This dress, underwear, bra and shoes,” she said hesitantly.

“Show me your shoes,” Hunter said.

Still confused, Rosie leaned down and slipped off her shoes, handing them to him one by one. He examined them thoroughly before passing them back.

Then Hunter unbuttoned his shirt, took it off, and handed it to her.

“I’m getting out of the car,” he said. “I’ll turn my back. You take off all your clothes and put the shirt on. Leave everything else on the seat.”

“Why?” Rosie asked, clearly baffled.

“Just trust me. If you want my help, you need to do this. All of your clothes, okay?”

Hunter got out of the car and walked a short distance away, turning to face the road they'd traveled. The heat was intense, and he could feel the sun scorching his shoulders. Moments later, he heard the car door open. Turning back, he saw Rosie stepping out, barefoot and now wearing his oversized shirt. She was hopping from one foot to the other, trying to avoid the burning asphalt beneath her feet.

"You can keep your shoes on," he called out.

Rosie quickly leaned in, grabbed her shoes, and slipped them on. "Now step back and wait," he instructed.

She hesitated briefly, then moved about ten feet away from

the car. Hunter returned to the vehicle and began a thorough search. Her clothes were folded neatly on the seat, but he ignored them for now, rummaging through her bag and then the briefcase. Finding nothing of interest, he turned his attention to her clothes. He shook them out—her dress, bra, and underwear—checking for anything concealed. There was nothing. He placed them carefully on the roof of the car and continued his search, this time scouring the rest of the vehicle.

Twenty minutes passed as he meticulously checked every inch—under the hood, inside the cabin, beneath the carpets, and even in the trunk. He looked under the seats and the fenders. After a thorough sweep, he found nothing and felt confident that no civilian could have hidden anything from him in that car.

“All right, you can get dressed now," he called out. "Same routine.”

Hunter turned his back and waited until he heard her approach. She was holding his shirt, which he took from her and slipped back on.

“What was that all about?” Rosie asked, confused.

“Now, I’ll help you,” he replied. “Because now I believe you.”

“Why?”

“Because it’s clear you don’t have any money," Hunter said. "No credit cards either—not in your wallet, and not hidden anywhere else. No one travels three hundred kilometers from home, overnight, with absolutely nothing unless they’re dealing with some serious problems. And someone with serious problems deserves help.”

Rosie remained silent but dipped her head slightly, as if acknowledging his words. They both climbed back into the car, shutting the doors behind them. They sat for a minute in the cool air before she guided the BMW back onto the road.

"So, you've got a year," Hunter said. "That's plenty of time. A year from now, you could be a million miles away, starting fresh. Is that what you want me to help you with? Getting away?"

Rosie didn't respond right away. For the next couple of kilometers, she remained silent as they drove up and down gentle hills. In the distance, buildings began to appear—a service station and possibly a tow truck operation.

"Just agree with me for now," she finally said. "A year is enough. So, it's okay that I waited."

"Yeah," Hunter agreed. "A year is enough. It's okay that you waited."

Rosie didn't say anything more, keeping her focus on the road as they approached the service station, like her life depended on it.

The first building they passed was a junkyard. A long, low shed made of corrugated tin stood in front, its walls covered in old hubcaps. Behind it was an acre filled with wrecked cars, stacked five or six deep, with the oldest ones buried at the bottom like layers of rock. Beyond the shed was the turn for the service station. The station was old, its pumps equipped with pointers instead of digital displays, and it had four public restrooms rather than the usual two. A quiet attendant sat behind the counter inside, keeping cool rather than straying outside into the stifling heat.

The BMW guzzled more than forty liters of fuel, which cost Hunter nearly as much as two nights at a motel. He handed over the notes through the window of the building and waved off the dollar in change, figuring the attendant could use it. The car's dashboard showed the outside temperature at forty-one degrees Celsius when he got back in. Hunter wondered if the attendant's silence was due to the heat—or maybe because he didn't like the idea of seeing a dark-skinned person driving a white man's car.

"Thank you," Rosie said.

"Yu welkam," Hunter replied.

Her eyebrows shot up. "You speak pidgin?"

“I know a little," he said with a nod. "I picked up some Tok Pisin when I served in Timor.”

“We just call it Pidgin," she noted. "Only city folks call it Tok Pisin."

"I'll remember that next time I talk to my mother. Her people are Yolngu," Hunter added.

“So you're not as white as you sound,” Rosie said, eyeing him curiously.

“My dad was about as white as they come," Hunter explained. "But my mom was half Yolngu. Sometimes I feel a lot more than just a quarter Yolngu."

Rosie gave him a faint smile, seemingly unsure whether to believe him. She eased the car back onto the road, and the needle on the fuel gauge jumped up to full, which seemed to give her a sense of relief. She got the car back into its lane and accelerated to a steady cruising speed.

For the next kilometer, Rosie was quiet, lost in thought. She settled back into the seat and rested her hands lightly on the wheel. Then she took a deep breath.

“Here's the problem,” she said. “I don't have a year.”

“Why not?” Hunter asked.

“Because a month ago, Warner's lawyer came to the house,” she began. “He said there was some kind of deal on the table.”

“What kind of deal?”

"I don't know all the details. They didn't tell me. My guess is that Warner's going to rat out some of his business associates in exchange for early release. His friend is probably brokering it with the prosecutor's office."

"Damn," Hunter muttered.

"Exactly," Rosie agreed. "They've been working on this for a while, getting everything in place. I've had to pretend like I'm happy about Warner coming home early, but inside, I'm panicking."

Hunter said nothing.

"I was wrong," she continued. "I thought I was safe, but I wasn't. I did nothing for a year and a half, and now I'm trapped."

"What's the status of the deal?" Hunter asked, watching the road ahead.

"It's done," she said quietly.

"So when's he getting out?"

"Today's Friday. They probably can't do anything over the weekend, so it'll be Monday, I guess. Just a few more days."

"I see," Hunter said.

"I'm scared," Rosie admitted. "He's coming home."

"I understand," Hunter said again.

"Do you?" she asked, her voice trembling. "Monday night, he'll start again. And this time, it'll be worse."

"Maybe he's changed," Hunter offered. "Prison can change people."

But it was a hollow sentiment, and he knew it. From her expression, Rosie wasn't buying it either. In his experience, prison rarely changed anyone for the better.

"No," Rosie insisted. "It's going to be worse. I know it. I'm in real trouble, Hunter. I can feel it."

There was something in her voice that made Hunter pause. "Why?" he asked.

Rosie gripped the wheel tighter and squeezed her eyes shut, even as she continued driving at seventy kilometers per hour.

"Because I was the one who told the ATO about him," she confessed.

****

The Falcon kept moving south, then west, looping back north in a wide, sweeping arc. It diverted near the highway to fuel up at a busy self-service station. The driver slid a stolen Visa card into the machine, then wiped off his fingerprints and tossed the card into the trash next to discarded oil bottles, soft drink cans, and windshield-dirty paper towels. Meanwhile, the woman studied a map, marking their next destination with her finger until the driver returned to the car and twisted around to take a look.

"Now?" he asked.

"Just checking it out," she said. "For later."

****

Rosie spoke again, her voice quiet. "It all seemed like such a solid plan. It felt foolproof. I knew how stubborn and greedy Warner was, so I figured he wouldn't cooperate with the authorities. I was sure he'd end up in jail, at least for a while. Even if he didn't, I thought the whole ordeal would keep him preoccupied. I also hoped it might free up some of the money he'd been hiding. And in a way, it worked—except for the money. But that didn't seem so important at the time."

Hunter looked at her thoughtfully. "How did you do it?"

"I just called them," she said. "The number's in the phone book. They even have a department that deals with tips from spouses—it's one of their main sources of information. Usually, they get those tips during divorces, when people are angry at each other. But I didn't need a divorce to be mad at him."

"So why didn't you go ahead and file for divorce?" Hunter asked. "Wouldn't his imprisonment count as desertion or something?"

Rosie glanced at the briefcase in the back seat, her expression conflicted. "Divorce wouldn't solve anything with Lahni. In fact, it would make things worse. It would put everyone on alert that I might leave the state with her. Legally, Warner could demand to know her whereabouts, and he definitely would."

"You could stay in Queensland," Hunter suggested again.

She nodded slightly but shook her head as if trying to clear her thoughts. "I know. I could. But I can't, Hunter. I know it's irrational, but I just can't stay here. This place—it's not just about Warner. Other things happened here that I need to escape from."

Hunter gave a slight shrug. "It's your decision."

Silence settled in the car again as they continued down the road. The terrain stretched out in front of them, descending from a vast plateau.

"That's the caprock," Rosie said softly. "It's limestone, I think. The water dried up millions of years ago, leaving the rock behind. Geological deposits or something."

Her voice had lost its usual confidence, and her explanation sounded vague, like she was only half-engaged with the present moment.

"So, what exactly do you want me to do?" Hunter asked after a pause.

"I don't know," she said, though Hunter was sure she had a plan. "Help you run? I could do that," he offered. "I'm good at it."

She didn't respond, and Hunter fell into thought. She had mentioned the type of men she had considered for help—out-of-work rodeo riders, roughnecks. None of them seemed equipped to outsmart a federal manhunt. So, perhaps she had chosen wisely by asking for his help—or maybe she just got lucky.

"You need to move fast," Hunter said, turning to face her. "With only two days left, you've got to start now. We should pick Lahni up and hit the road immediately. Head for the Gold Coast, maybe, as the first stop."

"And do what once we're there?" Rosie asked.

"We'll need to get you some new identification," Hunter explained. "A place like the Gold Coast, we could find something, even if it's temporary. I've got some money saved up. I can get more if we need it."

"I can't take your money," Rosie objected. "It wouldn't be right."

"Whether it's fair or not, you're going to need it," Hunter said firmly. "You can pay me back later. After that, maybe you should go back to Sydney. You can start putting together some new paperwork there."

Rosie was quiet for another kilometer before she spoke again.

"No, I can't run," she said with finality. "I can't live as a fugitive.

I can't be illegal. I've never been on the wrong side of the law, and I'm not going to start now. Neither is Lahni. She deserves better than that."

"You both deserve better," Hunter agreed. "But you've got to do something."

"I'm a citizen," Rosie emphasized. "You don't understand what that means to someone like me. I'm not going to throw that away or pretend to be someone I'm not."

"So, what's your plan?" Hunter asked, a bit frustrated.

"You are," Rosie replied.

Hunter thought about that for a moment. Roughnecks, bull riders, and now a six-foot-five, two-hundred-fifty-pound SAS ranger.

"You want me to be your bodyguard?" he asked, watching her closely.

She didn't reply.

"Rosie, I'm really sorry about what you're going through," Hunter said. "I mean it."

But there was no response from Rosie. The silence stretched between them, filled only by the sound of the car speeding southward.

"But I can't be your bodyguard," Hunter said, his voice firm. Rosie didn't respond.

"I'm serious. I can't be," he repeated. "Do you expect me to stay with you every single hour of the day? Twenty-four hours, seven days a week, just to stop him from hitting you?"

Still no reply. In the distance, a massive highway interchange appeared, shimmering in the haze.

"This is ridiculous," Hunter said again. "Maybe I could scare him off. Give him a warning, rough him up a bit to get the message across. But what happens when I leave? Because I will leave, Rosie. I don't plan on staying in one place for too long. And it's not just me, I like going places rather than staying in them. Nobody's going to stick around forever—not for ten years, or twenty, or however long it takes for him to die of old age."

Rosie remained silent, unaffected by his words. She continued driving, calm and steady, as if she was simply waiting for the right moment. The cloverleaf loomed larger as they approached, and she smoothly turned onto the highway, following a green sign that read: **Mount Kalka 75 kilometers**.

"I don't want a bodyguard," she finally said. "I agree, that would be ridiculous."

"Then what do you want from me?" Hunter asked, watching her face for any hint of emotion, but her expression was unreadable. She increased her speed, settling into the center lane.

"What am I supposed to do?" he asked again.

She hesitated for a moment. "I can't say it," she whispered.

"Say what?" Hunter pressed.

Rosie opened her mouth to speak but quickly closed it, swallowing hard without saying a word. Hunter stared at her. Bull riders, roughnecks, an ex-military cop—it all clicked in his mind, and the answer hit him like a punch.

"You're out of your mind," he said.

"Am I?" she shot back, her cheeks turning red.

"Completely insane," he replied. "And you can forget about it."

"I can't forget about it," she said quietly.

Hunter stayed silent, waiting for her to continue.

"I want him dead, Hunter," she finally admitted. "It's the only way out for me, and he deserves it."

"Tell me you're joking," Hunter said, his voice low.

"I'm not. I want him dead."

Hunter turned to stare out of the window, shaking his head. "This is absurd. It's not the Wild West anymore."

"Isn't it?" Rosie challenged. "Isn't it still acceptable to kill someone who needs killing?"

Silence filled the car as they sped toward the distant mountains, the sun casting them in shades of red and purple. The air seemed to change color as the mountains loomed closer.

"Please, Hunter," she said, her voice almost pleading. "Just think about it."

Hunter kept his eyes on the road ahead, watching as Rosie overtook car after car, driving recklessly fast.

"I'm not crazy," she said. "I really tried to do things the right way. As soon as Warner's lawyer told me about the deal, I went to see a lawyer myself—actually, I saw three different lawyers. None of them could help me in less than a month. They all said the same thing: Lahni keeps me trapped here. So I looked for protection. I asked private investigators—they wouldn't take the case. Then I went to a security firm in Townsville. They said they could protect me around the clock, but it would cost nearly ten thousand dollars a week. That's as good as saying no. So I tried, Hunter. I tried everything, but it's impossible."

Hunter remained silent, listening to her.

"So I bought a gun," she added.

"Brilliant," Hunter muttered sarcastically.

“And bullets,” Rosie continued. “I spent all the cash I had on it.”

“You’ve picked the wrong guy,” Hunter said firmly.

“Why? You’ve killed people before, in the army. You told me that.”

“This is different.”

“How?”

“This would be murder, Rosie. Cold-blooded murder. It would be an assassination.”

“No, it’s the same thing as what you did in the army.”

Hunter shook his head. “No, it’s not. This isn’t the same.”

“Didn’t you take an oath? To protect people?”

“It’s still not the same,” Hunter insisted.

Rosie swerved around a large truck, and the car rocked in the turbulent air.

“Slow down,” Hunter warned.

“I can’t slow down,” she replied. “I want to see Lahni.”

Hunter braced himself against the dashboard, the cold air blasting from the vents.

“Don’t worry,” Rosie reassured him. “I’m not going to crash. Lahni needs me. If it weren’t for her, I probably would’ve crashed a long time ago.”

Despite her words, she eased off the accelerator slightly, letting the truck pass them again.

“I know this conversation is hard,” she said.

“You think?” Hunter replied sarcastically.

“But you have to understand my perspective. I’ve thought about this a million times. I’ve gone through every option, every possibility, from A to Z. This is the only solution. I know that. I realize it's difficult for you because you haven't had time to think it through yet. It sounds crazy and cold to you, but I've reached this conclusion after careful consideration. And it's the only way."

"Whatever you say, but I'm not going to kill someone I've never even met."

"He beats me, Hunter," she said, her voice trembling. "He punches me, kicks me, laughs while he does it. I live in fear."

"Go to the police, then."

"There's one cop. He won't believe me, and even if he did, he wouldn't help. They're all friends. You don't understand how it works here."

Hunter said nothing.

"He's coming home," Rosie said softly. "Do you have any idea what he'll do to me?"

Again, Hunter stayed silent.

"I'm trapped, Hunter. Don't you see that?"

Still, Hunter said nothing.

"Is it about money? Is that why you won't help me? Because I can't pay you?" Rosie asked desperately.

Hunter didn't respond.

"I'm begging you," she said. "I have no one else. Why won't you help me? Is it because I'm from PNG? Is it because I'm dark-skinned?"

Hunter remained quiet.

"You'd do it for a white woman, wouldn't you? I bet your girlfriend is white. Probably blonde."

"No, she's a readhead," Hunter admitted.

"If someone was hurting her, you'd kill him."

Yes, he thought. I would.

"And she ran off to Europe without you. Didn't want you to follow her. But you'd still kill for her, wouldn't you?"

"It's not the same," Hunter said for the third time.

"I know," Rosie replied. "Because I'm just some dark-skinned trash, and I'm not worth it."

Hunter said nothing.

"What's her name?" Rosie asked.

"Neve," he replied.

"Okay, imagine Neve is in Europe, trapped in a terrible situation. Some sadist is beating her up every day. She tells you everything. What would you do?"

I'd kill him, Hunter thought.

Rosie seemed to sense his thoughts. "But you won't do the same for me. You'd do it for her because she's white, but not for me."

Hunter's mouth opened halfway before he stopped himself. It was true. He would do it for Neve O'Malley, but not for Rosie McMahon. Why not? Because it was instinct. When it came to Neve, it was a feeling that ran deep, like a drug in his veins. It couldn't be forced. Neve was part of him—or had been. Rosie wasn't, and she never would be. So the impulse just wasn't there.

"It's not about skin color," Hunter said quietly.

Rosie didn't respond.

"Please, Rosie, you have to understand that," he said.

"Then what is it about?" she asked.

"It's about the fact that I know her, and I don't know you."

"And that makes a difference?"

"Of course it does."

"Then get to know me," Rosie said. "We've got two days. You're about to meet my daughter. Get to know us."

Hunter remained silent as the kilometers ticked by. **Mount Kalka 55 kilometers**.

"You used to be in the army," Rosie said. "Aren't you supposed to help people? Or are you scared? Is that it?"

Hunter didn't respond.

"You could do it," Rosie pressed. "You've done it before, so you know how. You could do it and get away clean. Dump his body somewhere no one would find it. You wouldn't get caught."

Hunter remained silent.

"Do you know how? Are you smart enough?" she asked.

"Of course I know how," Hunter replied. "But I won't do it."

"Why not?" Rosie asked, her voice rising.

"Because I'm not an assassin."

"But I'm desperate," she said. "I'll do anything if you help me."

Hunter said nothing.

"What do you want, Hunter? Sex? Is that it?"

"Stop the car," Hunter said firmly.

"Why?"

"Because I've had enough of this."

Rosie slammed her foot on the accelerator, and the car shot forward. Hunter quickly reached over and shifted the gear into neutral. The engine screamed as the car slowed, coasting on its momentum. He took control of the wheel, pulling the car onto the shoulder. Gravel crunched beneath the tires as the car skidded to a halt.

Hunter shoved the gear into park, opened the door, and stepped out into the searing heat. He slammed the door behind him and walked away from Rosie without looking back.

CHAPTER 4

Hunter was drenched in sweat within twenty meters of leaving the car. He was already regretting his decision. Stuck in the middle of nowhere, walking along a major highway where even the slowest vehicles were zipping by at eighty kilometers per hour, it became clear that nobody was going to stop for him. Even if someone wanted to, by the time they reacted, checked their mirrors, and started to brake, they'd be more than a kilometer away, shrugging off the idea and speeding up again. They'd think it was a dumb place to hitch a ride.

But it wasn't just dumb—it was borderline suicidal. The sun was unforgiving, with the temperature easily reaching forty-two degrees. The gusts from passing cars felt like a furnace, and the suction from the trucks was strong enough to almost pull him off his feet. He had no water, and it was getting harder to breathe. Despite the constant flow of traffic just five meters away, he felt completely alone, as if he were stumbling through a desert. If a copper didn't come by and arrest him for jaywalking, he might actually die out there.

He glanced back at the BMW, still sitting on the shoulder of the road. But he kept walking. He made it another fifty meters before stopping and sticking his thumb out, facing east. He knew it was pointless, though. Five minutes and a hundred vehicles later, the only response he'd gotten was a trucker blasting his air horn as he sped by, leaving a whirlwind of dust and grit in his wake. Hunter choked on the dust and felt like he was on fire.

He turned again, just in time to see the BMW start rolling

backward, heading toward him along the shoulder. The steering was erratic—the car was swerving dangerously close to the traffic lanes. Hunter started walking back toward it, then broke into a run. The car fishtailed wildly as it approached, and he reached it just as she slammed on the brakes. The car bounced to a stop, and the passenger window buzzed down.

"I'm sorry," she said, though the noise from the road drowned her words. Hunter caught the shape of her lips, though.

"Get in," she called, her voice barely audible over the din.

His shirt clung to his back, his eyes stung with grit, and the roar of the traffic was deafening.

"Get in," she mouthed again. "I'm sorry."

He climbed in, and the cool blast of air from the vents hit him, making the leather seat feel icy against his overheated skin. She sat at the wheel, small and tense.

"I apologize," she said again. "I'm really sorry. I said some stupid things."

Hunter slammed the door, and the sudden silence was jarring. He held his hand in front of the air vent, feeling the chill.

"I didn't mean what I said," she continued.

"Whatever," Hunter muttered, brushing it off.

"I mean it. I'm just desperate. I don't know what's right or wrong anymore. And I'm really sorry for the thing about... you know, the sex. That was a stupid thing to say."

Her voice softened. "It's just that some of the guys I've picked up... well, I thought that's what it would come down to."

"You were going to sleep with them so they'd kill your husband?" Hunter asked.

She nodded. “I told you, I’m trapped, and I’m scared. I don’t have anything else to offer.”

Hunter didn’t say anything.

“And I’ve seen movies where that happens,” she added.

Hunter nodded. “Yeah, I’ve seen those movies too. They never get away with it.”

Rosie paused for a long moment.

“So, you’re not going to do it,” she said, more as a statement than a question.

“No, I’m not,” Hunter replied firmly.

Another pause, longer this time.

“Okay, I’ll drop you off in Mount Kalka,” she said. “You can’t be out there walking—you’ll die in this heat.”

Hunter thought about it for a long time. Then he shook his head. He had to be somewhere, and when you live on the road, you realize that any place is as good as any other.

“No, I’ll stick around for a couple of days,” he said. “I feel bad for your situation, Rosie. Just because I won’t shoot your husband doesn’t mean I can’t help you in some other way—if you still want me to.”

She hesitated again, then nodded. “Yes, I still want you to.”

“And I’d like to meet Lahni. She seems like a great kid from her picture.”

“She is a great kid.”

“But I’m not going to kill her father,” Hunter reminded her.

Rosie said nothing.

“Is that clear?” he asked.

She nodded again. "I understand. I'm sorry I even asked."

"It's not just me, Rosie. No one would do it. It wasn't a good plan."

Rosie looked small and lost. "I thought anyone would agree if they knew what it was like."

She glanced at the traffic behind them, waiting for a gap. Six cars later, she pulled back onto the highway and floored the accelerator. Within minutes, she was back up to one hundred kilometers per hour, overtaking cars one after another. It took seven minutes to catch up with the trucker who had left Hunter choking in the dust earlier.

****

Meanwhile, the Falcon reached the destination the woman had picked out within eighty minutes. It was an empty brown stain on the map, and in reality, it was a forty-kilometer-wide swath of desolate land. One road cut through it, meandering north and east along the base of distant mountains. It was a hot, barren, and worthless stretch of land, but it had everything she'd expected. She smiled, pleased with her instincts.

"Tomorrow, right here," she said, marking the spot in her mind.

The big car turned south again, kicking up a cloud of dust that lingered long after they had gone.

****

Rosie took an offshoot from the highway just before reaching Mount Kalka, heading south on a small road that led into nothingness. Within five kilometers, it felt like they were on the surface of the moon.

"Tell me about Four Ways," Hunter asked.

She shrugged. "What's there to tell? It's nothing. When they first mapped out Queensland a hundred and fifty years ago, the colonial census mob considered a place settled if it had more than six people per square kilometer. We still don't meet that standard. We're still the frontier."

"But it's beautiful," Hunter remarked.

And it was. The road twisted and turned through a maze of red dirt occasionally broken by green trees and hummock grass, tall and majestic hills to the west, rough and jagged to the north west where ancient rivers had carved their paths. In the distance, the shimmering mirage of the road disappeared under an enormous light blue sky. Even inside the speeding car, Hunter could feel the vast silence of thousands of square kilometers of untouched wilderness.

"I hate it," Rosie said.

"Where will I stay?" Hunter asked.

"On the property, in the bunkhouse, I guess. They're always short a hand. You show up with a pulse, they'll hire you. You can say you're a jackeroo—it'll keep you close."

"I don't know the first thing about cattle."

"Maybe they won't notice," she said dryly. "They don't notice much—not even when I'm being beaten half to death."

An hour later, they were tight on time. Rosie drove fast, the tires squealing around every curve. They reached the top of a long, steep grade, passing between two rocky pillars. Below them stretched flat land as far as the eye could see, a twisted ribbon of road stretching down and intersecting another road twenty kilometers ahead. At the crossroads were a few small buildings, and apart from that and the two roads, there was no sign of human life.

"Four Ways Shire," Rosie said, with a hint of a smile. "Everything you see, and a lot more besides. A thousand square kilometers and about a hundred and fifty people. Well, a hundred and forty-eight now—one of them is sitting here with you, and the other's still in jail."

Her mood had lifted slightly, though she was focused on a plume of dust on the road far below.

"That's the school bus," she said. "We have to beat it, or Lahni will get on, and we'll miss her."

"Town?" Hunter asked, glancing at the small cluster of buildings.

Rosie smiled again. "You're looking at it—uptown Four Ways."

She accelerated down the grade, and the BMW's dust swirled behind them. Despite their speed, the vastness of the landscape made everything feel slower. The bus was about a half-hour away, but Rosie was driving twice as fast, meaning they'd catch up in fifteen minutes. The bus looked close enough to reach out and touch, like a toy on the floor of a room.

"It's good of you to come," Rosie said, her voice sincere. "Thank you."

She sped up again, and just before they caught up to the bus, she swerved into the wrong lane, ready to pass. Hunter figured it was safe enough—there was no chance of oncoming traffic in this empty part of the world.

Rosie passed the bus, kicking up a cone of dust, then pulled back into her lane and slowed as they neared the crossroads.

From ground level, the tiny town looked worn out and defeated, as many small places do under the relentless heat of the sun. Lots that had once been commercially zoned were now overtaken by thorny weeds, bordered by rough block walls but never developed. To the right, on the northwest corner of the crossroads, was a takeaway shop—a long, low shack made of sun-bleached wood. Diagonally across from it stood a one-room schoolhouse, like something from a history book. It seemed to mark the early days of rural education. On the southwest corner was a service station with two pumps and a small yard cluttered with cars that appeared long stalled. Across from the school, the northeast corner was an empty lot, scattered with concrete blocks, as if someone had once planned an ambitious development but abandoned it long ago.

There were four other buildings nearby, all one story and made of plain bricks, set back from the road with thin, rough driveways leading up to them. Hunter guessed they were homes, judging by the junk scattered in their yards—children's bikes, old cars propped up on blocks, and faded living room furniture. The ground was baked hard and dry, fenced off by low chicken wire, maybe to keep snakes out.

The crossroads itself had no stop signs, just thick white lines melting into the blacktop under the heat. Rosie drove straight through, past the school, and then made a wide U-turn, dipping into shallow drainage ditches on either side of the road. She stopped the car close to the school gate, near Hunter's window. The yard was surrounded by a cyclone fence, and the gate was a simple rectangle of galvanized tubing covered in wire.

Rosie stared past Hunter at the school door. Soon after, the bus rumbled down the road and parked across from the BMW, on the other side of the road. The school door swung open, and a woman stepped out, moving slowly, looking tired. Hunter guessed she was the teacher, ready to call it a day. She waved toward the kids, and they poured out in a line—seventeen of them, nine girls and eight boys. Lahni McMahon was seventh in line, wearing a yellow dress and looking overheated. Hunter recognized her instantly from the photograph, and by the way Rosie shifted next to him, catching her breath as she reached for the door handle.

Rosie darted around the front of the car and met her daughter outside on the dusty strip that served as a sidewalk. She scooped Lahni up in a joyful hug, spinning her around and around. Lahni's feet kicked outward, and her green lunchbox swung, thumping against Rosie's back. Hunter could see Lahni laughing while tears glistened in Rosie's eyes. They came back around the rear of the car, holding each other tightly. Rosie opened the door, and Lahni scrambled into the driver's seat, stopping short when she saw Hunter. Her laughter ceased, and her eyes grew wide.

"This is Mr. Hunter," Rosie said gently.

Lahni turned to look at her mother.

"He's my friend," Rosie added. "Say hello to him."

Lahni turned back to Hunter. "Hello," she said shyly.

"Hey, Lahni," Hunter replied. "How was school?"

She paused for a moment. "It was okay."

"Learn anything new?" Hunter asked.

"How to spell some words," she said, then added after another pause, "Not easy ones. Ball and fall."

Hunter nodded seriously. "Four-letter words—that's pretty tough."

"I bet you can spell them," Lahni said, eyeing him curiously.

"B-A-L-L," Hunter spelled out. "F-A-L-L. Like that, right?"

Lahni smiled slightly. "You're a grown-up, so you know. But the teacher said four letters, and really, there's only three, because the L is there twice."

Hunter chuckled. "You're a smart kid," he said. "Now, hop in the back so your mum can get out of the heat."

Lahni scrambled past him, and Hunter caught the familiar scent of primary school. It took him back—he'd gone to at least fifteen different schools, spread across various countries and continents, but they all smelled the same. It had been more than thirty years since he'd last been in one, but the memories were still vivid.

"Mum?" Lahni said, looking at Rosie.

Rosie slid into the driver's seat, looking flushed—whether from the heat, the brief moment of joy, or something else, Hunter wasn't sure.

"Mum, it's hot," Lahni continued. "We should get ice cream spiders—from the takeaway shop."

Hunter saw Rosie start to smile, ready to agree, but then he noticed her glance at her purse, remembering the single five dollar note tucked inside.

"From the takeaway shop, Mum," Lahni repeated. "Ice cream spiders are the best when it's hot, before we go home."

Rosie's smile faltered, and her face fell even more when Lahni mentioned "home." Hunter stepped in to break the silence.

"That sounds like a great idea," he said. "Let's get some ice cream spiders—my treat."

Rosie shot him a grateful yet uneasy glance, but she put the car in drive and headed back through the crossroads, turning left into the shop's parking lot. She pulled into the shade, parking next to the only other car in the lot—a shiny, steel-blue Falcon. Hunter thought it was likely an unmarked police car or maybe a rental.

Inside, the takeaway shop was cool, thanks to an old-fashioned air conditioner venting through the roof. The place was nearly empty, except for three people sitting by a window—a woman with medium-length red hair and two men, one dark and small, the other taller and fairer. They didn't look like locals—probably just a sales team passing through on their way between Mount Kalka and Townsville, Hunter figured. Maybe their heavy samples were keeping them from flying. He quickly looked away and followed Lahni toward a booth at the far end of the shop.

"This is the best table," Lahni said confidently. "The other ones have torn seats, and they sewed them up with thick thread. It can hurt the back of your legs."

"I guess you've been here before," Hunter said with a smile.

"Of course!" Lahni giggled, flashing a grin of small, square teeth. "I've been here lots of times."

She slid across the vinyl bench and patted the seat next to her. "Mummy, sit with me," she said.

Rosie smiled. "I'm just going to use the restroom first. I'll be right back. Stay here with Mr. Hunter, okay?"

Lahni nodded solemnly, and Hunter took a seat across from her. They stared at each other openly for a moment. Hunter wasn't sure what Lahni saw in him, but he saw the living version of the photo from Rosie's wallet—thick black hair tied back in a ponytail, dark eyes wide with curiosity, a little snub nose, and a serious mouth. Her skin was flawless, like deep caramel.

"Where did you go to school?" she asked. "Did you go here, too?"

"No, I went to a lot of different schools," Hunter replied. "I moved around a lot."

"You didn't stay in the same school the whole time?" she asked, clearly surprised.

He shook his head. "Every few months, I went to a new one."

Lahni thought hard for a moment but didn't ask why. Instead, she tried to process the idea of constantly changing schools.

"How did you remember where everything was? Like the bathrooms? Or the teacher's name? You might forget and call her by the wrong one."

Hunter shook his head again. "When you're young, you can remember things pretty easily. It's when you get older that you start to forget."

"I forget things," Lahni said thoughtfully. "I forgot what my daddy looks like. He's in prison. But I think he's coming home soon."

"Yes," Hunter said softly. "I think he is."

"Where did you go to school when you were six and a half, like me?" Lahni asked, her world revolving around school.

Hunter thought back to that time. He had been six and a half when the Gulf War was heating up, and his father had been involved in the conflict. He guessed he had spent part of that year in Darwin, but mostly in Malaysia, based on his memories of the landscape and the places he played.

"Malaysia," Hunter said.

"Is that in Queensland too?" Lahni asked, curious.

"No, it's a group of islands, way out between the Pacific and the South China Sea. Far from here, right in the middle of the ocean," Hunter explained.

"The ocean?" she asked, as though unsure. "Is the ocean in Australia?"

"Do you have a map on the wall at your school?" Hunter asked.

"Yes, we have a map of the whole world," she replied.

"Okay, the oceans are all the blue parts."

"There are a lot of blue parts."

Hunter nodded. "That's for sure."

"My mum went to school in New South Wales," Lahni added.

"That'll be on the map, too. Just find Queensland and look below it."

Hunter noticed her looking down at her hands, as if measuring the distance. Then she glanced up, looking beyond him. He turned to see Rosie making her way back to the table, briefly trapped by the salespeople who were getting up from their booth. She waited until they cleared the aisle before gracefully sitting down beside Lahni, wrapping her in a one-armed hug, playfully tickling her, and drawing a delighted squeal from her daughter.

The waitress, having just finished with the salespeople, approached their table, pad and pencil in hand.

"Three Coke spiders, please," Lahni announced confidently.

The waitress jotted it down. "Coming right up love," she said with a smile as she walked away.

"Is that okay with you?" Rosie asked Hunter.

Hunter nodded. The thought of a Coke spider stirred memories —his first one had been in a military canteen in Korea, inside a long, low concrete building leftover from the post-war occupation. He remembered the warmth of a summer day amongst other expats, with no air conditioning, the feel of heat on his skin, and the fizzing bubbles tickling his nose.

"It's silly," Lahni said. "There are no spiders in the ice cream spider. It just looks lumpy. They should have called them Coke lumps."

Hunter smiled, remembering how as a kid, he too had been puzzled by the little illogicalities of the world.

"Just like primary school," he said. "I found out that 'primary' means easy, so I thought 'primary school' should mean 'easy school.' But I remember thinking it was pretty hard, and that 'hard school' would be a better name."

Lahni looked at him seriously. "I don't think it's hard," she said, considering it carefully, "but maybe it's harder in the ocean."

"Or maybe you're just smarter than I was," Hunter suggested.

Lahni thought about that earnestly. "I'm smarter than some people," she admitted. "Like Mia. She's still stuck on three-letter words. And she thinks you spell zoo with a Z."

Hunter didn't know how to respond to that, and before he could think of something, the waitress returned with a tray holding three tall glasses. She set them down with a touch of ceremony, whispering "Enjoy" to Lahni before stepping back.

But the glasses were tall—almost a foot high—and with the long straws sticking out, they towered above Lahni, whose chin was just about level with the tabletop. She was a long way from reaching the straw.

"You want me to hold it down for you?" Rosie asked. "Or do you want to kneel?"

Lahni thought about it. Hunter began to wonder if this kid ever made quick decisions. He saw a bit of himself in her—he'd always taken things too seriously as a child, often getting teased by classmates for it. But only once.

"I'll kneel," she decided.

It was more than kneeling—she stood on the bench in a crouch, placing her hands flat on the table, one on either side of the glass, and ducked her head down to the straw. Hunter figured it was as good a method as any. As Lahni started slurping her drink, Hunter turned to his own. The ice cream sat like a greasy, round lump in the cola, which tasted far too sweet, as if the syrup had been mixed wrong. The bubbles seemed huge and artificial. It tasted awful—a far cry from that summer's day in Korea.

"Don't you like it?" Lahni asked, spraying some of her own float onto Hunter's sleeve as she spoke with a mouth full.

"I didn't say anything," Hunter replied.

"You're making a funny face."

"Too sweet," he said. "It'll rot my teeth. Yours, too."

Lahni grinned, showing her teeth like she was at the dentist. "Doesn't matter. They're all going to fall out anyway. Mia's already lost two."

She bent back to her straw, vacuuming up the last of the drink, then poked at the leftover sludge in the glass until it was liquid enough to slurp.

"I'll finish yours, too, if you want," she offered.

"No," her mother said firmly. "You'll end up throwing up in the car."

"I won't, I promise," Lahni protested.

"No," Rosie repeated. "Now, go to the bathroom, okay? It's a long way home."

"I already went," Lahni said. "We always go at school, right before we leave. We have to. The bus driver hates it when we pee on the seats."

She laughed, clearly delighted by the idea.

"Lahni," Rosie said, a little sternly.

"Sorry, Mum. But it's only the boys who do that. I wouldn't."

"Go again, anyway, okay?"

Lahni rolled her eyes dramatically, then climbed over her

mother's lap and dashed toward the back of the diner. Hunter placed a ten-dollar bill on top of the check.

"Great kid," he said.

"I think so," Rosie agreed. "Well, most of the time."

"She's sharp as anything," Hunter remarked.

Rosie nodded. "Smarter than me, that's for sure."

Hunter let that comment pass without response. He watched as Rosie's eyes clouded over.

"Thanks for the sodas," she said quietly.

Hunter shrugged. "My pleasure. It's a new experience for me. I don't think I've ever bought a spider for a kid before."

"So, you don't have any of your own, obviously."

"Never even got close."

"No nieces or nephews? No little cousins?"

Hunter shook his head. "I was a kid once—long ago—and that's about all I know about it."

"Stick around a few days," Rosie said with a small smile. "Lahni will teach you more than you ever wanted to know. I'm sure you've already picked up on that."

Just then, Hunter heard Lahni's footsteps coming up behind him. The floor beneath the old, buckled linoleum had air pockets trapped underneath, making hollow slapping sounds as she approached.

"Mum, let's go," she said, her voice urgent.

"Mr. Hunter is coming too," Rosie told her. "He's going to help with the cows."

Lahni gave Hunter a once-over, then said, "Okay, but let's go."

They stepped out into the late afternoon heat. The Falcon was gone from the lot. Lahni climbed into the back seat of the BMW, and Rosie sat for a moment, hand resting on the key, her eyes closed. Then she opened them, started the engine, and pulled away.

Rosie drove back through the crossroads and past the school, heading more than sixty kilometers north. She drove slowly, far more cautiously than before, but Lahni didn't seem to mind. Hunter figured this was how Rosie always drove when heading home.

They passed little along the way. On the left were power lines stretching between weather-beaten poles. Occasionally, there were windmills and oil pumps, most of them rusted and still. There were more of the old abandoned mines and stations. On some parts of the landscape, the earth had been blown clear, leaving nothing but barren caliche ledges. The eastern side of the road was a bit better—patches of mesquite and scraggly grassland stretched out in irregular shapes, suggesting some water ran underground in places.

Every ten or twelve kilometers, they'd pass a ranch gate standing isolated by the roadside. Each gate had a dirt track leading into the distance. Some had names on them, nailed together from wood strips, others had fancy script made from ironwork. Many were adorned with old bleached cattle skulls, their long horns curving outward. Barbed wire stretched from the gates into the distance, marking old property lines. The wooden posts holding up the wire were so weathered and twisted they looked as if they might crumble at the slightest touch.

Occasionally, Hunter could see ranch houses in the distance. Most were two stories, painted white, huddled among barns and sheds with windmills and satellite dishes nearby. The houses looked quiet and weathered under the heat of the late afternoon sun, with the temperature outside still showing over forty degrees Celsius.

"It's the road," Rosie said softly. "It soaks up the sun all day and then gives it back later."

Lahni had fallen asleep, sprawled across the backseat, her head resting on Rosie's briefcase, the edge of the papers detailing her mother's plans for escape brushing her cheek.

"McMahon property starts here," Rosie said, pointing out the left side of the car. "Our track is another eight kilometers down."

The land was flat, rising slightly to the west, where a fragmented plateau stretched into the distance. On the left, the McMahons had a newer stretch of barbed wire fencing that looked like it had been replaced within the last fifty years. The fence ran eastward, enclosing a patchy landscape of green and brown grass. Off in the distance, Hunter spotted a large quarry full of turquoise water, surrounded by tin huts and abandoned equipment.

"McMahon Five," Rosie explained. "That paddock made Warner's grandfather a lot of money, a long time ago. It ran dry about thirty years ago, but it's still a famous family story—the expensive rocks that came out of the ground. Probably the most exciting thing that ever happened to them."

Rosie slowed the car even more as they approached the final few kilometers, clearly reluctant to get home. In the distance, the road climbed into a heat haze, and Hunter saw the barbed wire change abruptly to an odd picket fence painted dull cream. It ran along the shoulder for about half a kilometer, leading to a ranch gate, also painted cream. Beyond the gate, a large house sat much closer to the road than the others they had passed. It had a tall chimney, a two-story core, and sprawling one-story additions. Barns and sheds clustered around it, and all of it—the buildings, the fences—was painted the same dull cream. The low, blazing sun made the cream glow and shimmer, creating horizontal bands of mirage in the heat.

Rosie coasted the last hundred meters, foot off the accelerator, and turned onto the beaten dirt track leading through the ranch gate. A sign above them, cream-painted wood on wood, read *Cream House*. She glanced up at it as they passed underneath.

"Welcome to hell," she muttered under her breath.

The Cream House itself was the main building in a compound of four impressive structures. It had a wide porch with wooden columns and a swinging seat hung from chains. Eighty meters farther on was a barn, but Rosie couldn't drive down to it because a police cruiser was parked diagonally on the track, completely blocking the way. It was an old-model Holden Commodore, black and white with "Four Ways Shire Sergeant" on the door. Hunter figured it had probably been bought secondhand from a bigger city and repainted for rural use. The car was empty, the driver's door standing open, and the light bar on top flashed red and blue, casting colored light across the porch and the front of the house.

"What's going on?" Rosie asked, her hand going to her mouth in panic. "He can't be home already. Please, no."

"The cops wouldn't bring him home," Hunter reassured her. "They're not a limo service."

Lahni was waking up in the back seat. She looked around, wide-eyed, confused by the flashing lights and the silence.

"What's happening?" she asked.

"It's the sergeant," Rosie said.

"Why is he here?" Lahni pressed.

"I don't know."

"Are the lights on because someone called 000? Was there a

burglar? Maybe he wore a mask and stole something."

Lahni scrambled over the armrest and knelt between the front seats, her face full of curious excitement. But then, her expression shifted to fear.

"Maybe he stole my pony, Mum!" she exclaimed.

Before Rosie could respond, Lahni flung the door open and ran across the yard, her arms stiff by her sides, her ponytail bouncing as she sprinted toward the barn.

"I don't think anybody stole a horse," Rosie said. "I think Warner's come home."

"With the lights flashing?" Hunter asked.

Rosie unclipped her seatbelt, got out of the car, and stood next to the open door, her hands resting on the roof. Hunter followed suit, stepping out into the blazing heat. From the police car, he could hear bursts of static-filled radio chatter.

"Maybe they're here looking for you," Hunter suggested. "You've been gone overnight. Maybe they reported you missing."

Across the car roof, Rosie shook her head. "As long as they knew where Lahni was, they wouldn't have cared where I went."

She hesitated for a moment, then stepped away from the car, quietly closing the door behind her. Hunter did the same. Twenty feet away, the house door opened, and a uniformed man stepped onto the porch. It was the sergeant, a heavyset man in his sixties with dark, sun-weathered skin and thinning gray hair. He walked backward, as if taking his leave of someone inside, dressed in blue pants and a khaki uniform shirt with epaulettes and patches on the shoulders. A wide gun belt strapped a wooden-handled revolver to his hip. He stopped short when he saw Rosie, touching his forefinger to his brow in a lazy, almost dismissive salute.

“Mrs. McMahon,” he said, his tone implying something was her fault.

“What happened?” Rosie asked, her voice strained.

“Folks inside will explain,” the sergeant said. “Too damn hot for me to be repeating everything twice.”

His gaze shifted to Hunter. “And who are you?”

Hunter didn’t answer.

“Who are you?” the sergeant repeated, this time more forcefully.

“I’ll tell the folks inside,” Hunter replied. “Too hot for me to be repeating everything twice.”

The sergeant gave him a long, steady look before nodding slowly, as if he’d seen everything before. Then he climbed into his secondhand cruiser, backed it out to the road, and drove off, leaving a cloud of dust that settled over Hunter’s shoes. Rosie started the BMW again and drove it down the track toward the motor barn—a long, low, wall-less farm shed painted red like everything else. Two utes and a Nissan Patrol were parked inside. One ute looked new, while the other was sitting on flat tires, clearly unmoved for a decade. Beyond the barn, a narrow dirt track stretched off into the desert.

Rosie parked next to the Nissan, stepped out, and walked back into the sun. She looked small and out of place in the yard, like a delicate flower blooming in the middle of a wasteland.

“So, where’s the bunkhouse?” Hunter asked.

“Come with me,” Rosie said. “You need to meet everyone anyway and get hired. You can’t just show up at the bunkhouse.”

“Okay,” Hunter agreed.

She led him slowly toward the porch steps. She climbed them cautiously, one at a time, before stopping in front of the door and knocking.

"You have to knock?" Hunter asked, surprised.

Rosie nodded. "They never gave me a key."

They waited in silence, Hunter standing a step behind her, feeling like the hired help. He could hear footsteps approaching from inside, and then the door swung open. A man stood there, gripping the door handle. He looked to be in his mid-twenties, with a big square face, his skin blotched red and white. He was bulky, the kind of school-boy muscle that was starting to turn to fat. He wore dirty denim jeans and a white T-shirt, the sleeves rolled tight over his once-muscular arms. He smelled faintly of sweat and beer, and a red baseball cap, worn backward, sat on his head. A semicircle of forehead peeked above the cap's plastic strap, while a shock of hair —identical in color and texture to Lahni's—spilled out from underneath.

"It's you," he said, glancing at Rosie before quickly looking away.

"Ryan," she acknowledged quietly.

Ryan's eyes then settled on Hunter. "Who's your friend?"

"His name's Hunter. He's looking for work."

Ryan paused for a moment, sizing Hunter up. "Well, come on in, then, I guess," he said. "Both of you. And shut the door—it's hot."

He turned and walked further into the house. As he did, Hunter noticed the letters NQC on his cap. North *Queensland Cowboys*, Hunter thought. A good football club, but not quite good enough. Rosie entered the house like a guest, trailing three steps behind Ryan, and Hunter stayed close behind her.

"Warner's brother," Rosie whispered to Hunter.

Hunter nodded. Inside, the hallway was dim and cool, the red paint from the outside continuing throughout—covering the walls, floors, and ceilings. The paint was worn thin in places, revealing the wood beneath like a faint stain. Somewhere in the house, an old air conditioner hummed slowly, barely cooling the air by a few degrees. The steady rattle of it was peaceful, like the slow ticking of a clock. The hallway itself was large, almost the size of a motel suite, filled with old, expensive furniture. Everything felt like it had been purchased decades ago, back when money flowed more freely. A massive mirror with an ornate red-painted frame hung on one wall, and opposite it, a rack held six bolt-action hunting rifles. The mirror reflected the gun rack, making the hallway seem filled with weapons.

"What did the sergeant want?" Rosie called out.

"Come inside," Ryan called back.

We are inside, Hunter thought, but Ryan was referring to the parlor—a large room at the back of the house, which had once been a kitchen but had been remodeled decades ago. It opened out into an older kitchen that was at least fifty years old. The parlor was painted entirely in worn red, including the large farmhouse table and eight chairs, which were worn down to the wood in places from years of use.

One of the chairs was occupied by a woman who looked to be in her mid-fifties. She wore tight jeans with a belt and a blouse with Western fringe, her hairstyle youthful despite her age. Her bright orange hair was teased up off her scalp above a thin face, making her look like a woman half her age—or perhaps prematurely aged by stress. She appeared preoccupied and slightly confused but still showed signs of vitality and authority. She was rangy and powerful, like the land she lived on, temporarily laid low but not yet defeated.

"What did the sergeant want?" Rosie asked again.

"Something happened," the woman said, her tone heavy with bad news. Hunter noticed a brief flicker of hope in Rosie's eyes before the room fell silent. The woman's gaze shifted to Hunter.

"His name is Hunter," Rosie said. "He's looking for work."

"Where's he from?" the woman asked, her voice hard like rawhide, the authority in the house clear.

"I found him on the road," Rosie replied.

"What can he do?"

"He's worked with cattle. He can tag em, muster, the lot."

Hunter looked out of the window as Rosie lied about his skills. He'd never been near a cow, except for walking past them at an agriculture show as a child. He knew, in theory, that a jackeroo worked on a cattle station and did all manner of jobs to do with the cattle. He knew it involved mustering herds, ear tagging, feeding them, putting them onto the truck to the abbattoir, and lots of cow pies. But he'd never actually touched a cow.

"We'll discuss him later," the woman said. "We have more pressing matters to deal with."

She then gestured across the table. "I'm Judy McMahon," she said, by way of introduction.

"Like the country singer?" Hunter asked.

"I was Judy McMahon before she was born," she replied, pointing to Ryan. "And this is my boy, Robert McMahon. Welcome to Cream House Ranch, Mr. Hunter. Maybe we can find work for you, assuming you're willing and honest."

"What did the sergeant want?" Rosie asked for the third time.

Judy McMahon turned, her gaze hardening as she looked at

Rosie. "Warner's lawyer has gone missing."

"What?" Rosie asked, her voice faint with disbelief.

"He was on his way to see Warner at the state jail but never made it. The shire police found his car abandoned on the road, south of Cloncurry. Just sitting there, empty, with the keys still in it. Miles from anywhere."

"Troy Bradley?" Rosie asked, horrified.

"How many lawyers do you think Warner has?" Judy shot back, her tone laced with scorn.

The room fell into a heavy silence. Rosie went pale, her hand jumping to her mouth as she tried to process the news.

"Maybe the car broke down," she suggested weakly.

"The cops tested it," Judy said. "It was running just fine."

"So, where is he?"

"He's missing, like I told you," Judy replied. "They've searched for him, but they haven't found him."

Rosie took a deep breath, then another. "Does it change anything?" she asked.

"You mean, is Warner still coming home?" Judy asked, her eyes gleaming.

Rosie nodded weakly, her fear evident.

"Don't you worry," Judy said, smiling. "Warner will be back on Monday, just like he was always going to be. Troy being missing doesn't change a thing. The sergeant made that clear. It's all been arranged."

Rosie closed her eyes for a long moment, her hand covering her lips. Then she forced her hand down and gave a shaky smile.

"Well, that's good," she said.

"Yes, it is," Judy agreed with a smug smile.

Rosie nodded vaguely, looking as if she might faint. "What do you think happened to him?" she asked quietly.

"How should I know?" Judy replied dismissively. "Some sort of trouble, I expect."

"But who would make trouble for Troy?"

Judy's smile turned into a sneer. "Take your best guess."

Rosie's eyes widened. "What's that supposed to mean?"

"It means, who would want to cause trouble for their lawyer?"

"I don't know."

"Well, I do," Judy said. "Someone who buys them a fancy Mercedes and still ends up in jail—that's who."

"Well, who would that be?"

"Take your pick. Troy Bradley will take on any client, no matter who they are. He's crooked, maybe halfway, maybe all the way. Most of his clients are the wrong sort."

"The wrong sort?" Rosie asked, her voice trembling.

"You know exactly what I mean."

"You mean dark-skinned people? Why don't you just come out and say it?" Rosie shot back.

Judy's smile widened. "Tell me I'm wrong. Some Aboriginal boy gets sent to jail, and instead of accepting it, he blames his lawyer. Then he gets his brothers and cousins all riled up. And of course, they're all Islanders, and they're all in gangs. You know how that turns out. It's just like what happens up there in Papua New Guinea. And you, of all people, should know what it's like."

"Why should I, of all people? I've never even been to Papua

New Guinea," Rosie replied, her voice shaking with restrained anger.

No one responded to that. Hunter watched as she stood there, proud yet shaken, like a prisoner in enemy territory. The room remained quiet, filled only with the steady thump and click of the old air conditioner.

"You got an opinion on this, Mr. Hunter?" Judy asked, her tone sharp.

It felt like an interview question, one designed to gauge whether he was the right fit for this place. Hunter wished he could come up with something clever to say, some way to divert the conversation. But picking a fight with Judy McMahon on his first day wouldn't do him any good.

"I'm just here to work, ma'am," he replied.

"I'd still like to know your opinion," she pressed.

Definitely like an interview. Clearly, she wanted to make sure the people working for her were of the "right" sort.

"Mr. Hunter used to be a ranger in the SAS," Rosie interjected. "In the army."

Judy nodded. "So, what do you think, ex-army man?"

Hunter shrugged. "There could be an innocent explanation. Maybe he had a nervous breakdown and wandered off."

Judy scoffed. "Doesn't sound likely to me. Now I see why you're an ex-cop."

Silence stretched for a long moment.

"If there was trouble, maybe white folks made it," Hunter said.

"That's not a popular view around here, son," Judy warned.

"I'm not trying to be popular, just right or wrong. And since Queensland's population is about three-quarters white, I figure there's a three-in-four chance white folks were involved—assuming people are more or less the same everywhere."

"That's a big assumption," Judy said coolly.

"Not in my experience."

Judy glanced back at Rosie. "I'm sure you agree with your new friend here."

Rosie took a steadying breath. "I don't claim to be better than anyone else. So, I don't see why I should agree I'm worse."

The room fell silent again.

"Well, time will tell," Judy said with a smile. "One of us is going to end up eating humble pie."

She stretched out the word *pie* into a long drawl, letting it linger in the air before the conversation shifted abruptly. "Now, where's Warner's little girl?" she asked, her voice suddenly bright, as if the previous conversation had never happened. "Did you bring her home from school?"

"She's in the barn, I think," Rosie said. "She saw the sergeant and got worried someone had stolen her pony."

"That's ridiculous. Who would steal her pony?"

"She's just a child," Rosie replied.

"Well, the maid is ready to give the child her supper. Take her to the kitchen, and show Mr. Hunter to the bunkhouse while you're at it."

Rosie nodded, accepting the order like a servant receiving instructions. Hunter followed her out of the parlor and back into the hallway. They stepped outside into the heat and paused in the shade on the porch.

"Lahni eats in the kitchen?" Hunter asked.

Rosie nodded. "Judy hates her."

“Why? She’s her granddaughter.”

Rosie looked away. “She thinks her blood is tainted. Don’t ask me to explain it. It doesn’t make sense, but that’s how it is.”

“So why does she care if you take her away?”

“Because Warner wants her here. She’s his weapon against me. His way of torturing me. And Judy does whatever Warner wants.”

“Does she make you eat in the kitchen too?”

“No, she makes me eat with her. Because she knows I’d rather not.”

Hunter paused at the edge of the porch, where the shadow met the sun. “You should have gotten out of here,” he said. “We should be in Gold Coast by now.”

“I was hopeful for a second,” Rosie said, her voice breaking. “When I heard about Troy Bradley. I thought maybe there’d be a delay.”

Hunter nodded. “So was I. It would have bought us some time.”

Rosie wiped her eyes with the back of her hand and shook her head. “I’m not running,” she said firmly. “I won’t be a fugitive.”

Hunter didn’t say anything.

“And you should have agreed with her,” Rosie added, referring to Judy’s comments. “I would’ve understood you were bluffing. I need her to trust you.”

“I couldn’t,” Hunter replied.

“It was a risk.”

Rosie led him down the porch steps and across the yard toward the barn. Beyond the shed was a horse barn, a massive structure painted the same dull cream as everything else. The big door stood slightly ajar, and a strong, earthy smell wafted out.

“I’m not really a country guy,” Hunter admitted.

“You’ll get used to it,” Rosie replied.

Behind the barn were four corrals, boxed in with white fences. Two were overgrown with scraggly grass, while the other two were filled with desert sand, piled about a foot deep. Striped poles rested on oil drums, creating makeshift jumping courses. Beyond the corrals, a long, low building with small, high windows stood in the distance.

“That’s the bunkhouse,” Rosie said.

She stood still for a moment, lost in thought. Then she shivered, despite the heat, and snapped back to reality. “The door’s around the other side,” she said. “You’ll find two guys in there, Max and Patty. Don’t trust either of them. They’ve been here forever, and they belong to the McMahons. The maid will bring your meals down in about an hour, after Lahni eats but before we do.”

“Okay,” Hunter said.

“Ryan will come by sooner or later to check you out. Watch him closely—he’s a snake.”

“Okay,” Hunter repeated.

“I’ll see you later,” Rosie said.

“You going to be all right?”

Rosie nodded once and walked away. Hunter watched her until she disappeared behind the horse barn. Then he walked around the other side of the bunkhouse, looking for the door.

CHAPTER 5

The boy diligently filled an entire new page in his notebook. The man and the woman with the telescopes called out detailed descriptions, outlining each event in precise order: the sergeant's arrival, the return of the "darkie" along with the kid and a newcomer, the kid rushing off to the barn, the sergeant's departure, and then the darkie and the new guy heading into the house. After a long stretch of inactivity, they reappeared, stepping onto the porch and making their way to the bunkhouse together. The darkie returned alone.

"Who is that?" the boy asked.

"How the hell should we know?" the woman responded.

The boy jotted down: *Tall, heavy, messy clothes—shirt and pants, age unclear.* He added: *Not a jackeroo, wrong shoes. Potential trouble?*

The terrain sloped downward behind the bunkhouse, transforming it into a two-story structure. The lower floor had large sliding doors stuck open on damaged tracks. Inside, there was another ute and a couple of green and yellow tractors. At the far end, a wooden staircase without a handrail led upward through a rectangular gap in the ceiling. Hunter spent a few moments on the ground floor, inspecting the vehicles. The ute had a gun rack visible through the rear window. The air was thick and hot, reeking of petrol and motor oil.

He then ascended the stairs, emerging on the upper level. The interior was painted entirely red—walls, floor, and beams alike. It was even hotter up there, the air stale with little ventilation and no air conditioning. At one end, there was an enclosed area he assumed was the bathroom. The rest of the floor was a wide open space, lined with sixteen simple beds, eight on each side. The beds had iron frames, thin striped mattresses, bedside cabinets, and footlockers.

Two of the beds closest to the bathroom were occupied. Lying half-dressed on the sheets were two small, wiry men. Both wore jeans and fancy boots, with their hands folded behind their heads. As Hunter entered the room, they shifted, unlacing their arms to get a better look at him.

Hunter had spent three years at Campbell Barracks followed by fifteen years in the service, totaling eighteen years of experience walking into unfamiliar dormitories and being stared at by strangers. He had long since learned how to handle such moments. The proper approach was to stride in, pick an empty bed, and remain silent, forcing someone else to speak first. That way, he could assess their temperament before revealing anything of his own.

He selected a bed two places from the top of the staircase, along the north wall, thinking it might be cooler than the south. Back in the army, he would have had a heavy canvas kit bag to claim the bed, its stenciled name and rank offering a silent introduction. But here, the best he could do was take out his folding toothbrush and place it on the bedside cabinet. The gesture was subtle, but the message was clear: *I live here now, just like you. Got something to say about it?*

The two men continued to stare in silence. From their position, it was hard to gauge their physiques, but they were small, likely around five-six or five-seven, weighing about 150 pounds. They were lean but muscular, with the bodies of middleweight boxers. Their tanned arms, faces, and necks contrasted sharply with the pale skin that had been covered by T-shirts. Old fractures stood out on their ribs and collarbones, the kind of marks Hunter recognized—he had a few himself. Rosie did, too.

Hunter walked past them to check out the bathroom. It had a door but was communal inside, featuring four toilets, four sinks, and four showerheads in a single stall. It was reasonably clean and smelled faintly of soap and warm water, suggesting the two men had recently showered, perhaps preparing for a night out. By standing tall, Hunter could peer out the high window and see up to the house, catching a glimpse of the porch and front door.

Returning to the dorm, he saw one of the men sitting up, watching him. His pale back bore more evidence of past fractures. The other man lifted himself onto his elbows, clearly curious about the newcomer.

"Storm's coming," the first man said.

"That's what I heard," Hunter replied.

"Bound to happen with heat like this," the man continued.

Hunter remained silent.

"You hired on?" the man asked.

"I guess," Hunter said.

"So, you're working for us."

Hunter still said nothing.

"I'm Patty," the man said.

The other guy spoke up. "Max."

Hunter nodded. "Hunter. Nice to meet you."

"You'll be doing the dirty work for us," Patty added. "Shoveling manure, hauling bales."

"Whatever," Hunter responded.

"You sure don't look like a jackeroo to me," Patty observed. "Too tall. Too heavy. Center of gravity's all wrong."

"I don't?"

Patty shook his head. "Not a jackeroo, no."

"The Islander woman bring you in?" Max asked.

"Mrs. McMahon," Hunter corrected.

"Mrs. McMahon is Judy," Patty said. "She didn't bring you in."

"Rosie McMahon," Hunter clarified.

Patty said nothing, while Max smiled.

"We're heading to a bar after supper," Patty said. "Couple of hours south. You should come, get to know us."

Hunter shook his head. "Maybe another time, once I've earned something. I prefer to pay my way."

Patty thought for a moment, then nodded. "You got respect mate. Maybe you'll fit in after all."

Hunter stretched out on his bed, fighting the heat as he stared up at the red-painted rafters. After a minute, he closed his eyes.

Forty minutes later, a middle-aged woman who could have been related to Patty brought supper. She handed out metal bowls filled with beef and potatoes, along with cups and utensils. "Water's in the bathroom," she said, directing the comment to Hunter. Then she left.

Hunter dug into the meal, savoring the crispy potatoes and tender beef. Across the room, Patty and Max finished eating and prepared to head out.

"See you later," Patty called as they clattered down the stairs. Hunter heard an engine start, likely the ute, and listened as it drove off.

Afterward, he gathered the dishes and brought them back to the kitchen, where the maid took them with a polite "Thank you." Hunter stepped outside, looking out across the barren landscape. He had no idea what lay to the south, but to the east, there was just more land stretching toward Townsville.

****

Back in his hiding spot, the boy scribbled another note: *New guy stares at us, then looks around. Does he know we're here? Trouble?*

He closed his notebook and pressed himself lower into the ground.

****

"Hunter," a voice called.

Hunter squinted to his right and saw Ryan McMahon sitting in the shadows on the porch swing, wearing the same dirty T-shirt and denims, with his cap still backward.

"Come over here," Ryan said.

Hunter hesitated for a moment before walking back past the kitchen and stopping at the base of the porch steps.

"I want the big mare saddled up," Ryan said. "Bring her out."

Hunter paused again. "You want that right now?"

"When else? I want an evening ride to go check on the cattle," Ryan replied.

Hunter stayed silent.

"And we need a demonstration," Ryan added.

"Of what?" Hunter asked.

"If you want to stay on here, you've got to prove you know what you're doing around the station," Ryan said.

Hunter took a longer pause this time. "Alright."

"Five minutes," Ryan said as he stood and disappeared back

into the house. The door clicked shut behind him. Hunter lingered for a second, feeling the heat radiating off his back, then turned and headed for the barn. He walked toward the big door, the one giving off the bad smell. *A demonstration? This isn't going to go well,* he thought, *in more ways than one.*

Inside the door was a switch in a metal box bolted to the siding. He flicked it, and dim yellow bulbs lit up the massive barn. The floor was beaten dirt, covered in dirty straw. The barn's center was split into back-to-back horse stalls, while the perimeter was packed with floor-to-ceiling hay bales against the outer walls. He walked around the stalls, finding five of them occupied. Each horse was tied to the stall walls with intricate rope halters over their heads.

Hunter examined each horse closely. One was small—clearly a pony. Likely Lahni's. That left four. Two were slightly bigger than the others. He crouched down and looked carefully underneath them, trying to recall what a mare should look like. It was harder to tell than he thought—the stalls were dark, and the horses' tails were in the way. Eventually, he determined the first one wasn't a mare, nor a stallion either—missing parts. A gelding. He moved to the next one. Mare. The third? Also a mare. The last? Another gelding.

He stepped back to get a better look at the two mares. They were large, sleek brown creatures, puffing through their nostrils, shifting slightly, their hooves thudding softly against the straw. Their necks twisted so each could watch him with one eye. Which one was bigger? The one on the left, he decided. A little taller, a bit bulkier. That's the big mare. So far, so good.

Now, the saddle. Every stall had a thick post sticking out from the outer wall, with various pieces of equipment piled on it. A saddle, for sure, but also many straps, blankets, and metal parts. He figured the straps were the reins, and the metal piece must be the bit—it goes in the horse's mouth. Right? He lifted the saddle from the post. It was heavy, but he balanced it on his left arm. Felt good. *Just like a real cowboy. Roy Rogers, eat your heart out.*

He stood in front of the stall gate, the big mare watching him with one eye. She peeled her lips back, revealing big square yellow teeth. *Alright, think. First principles. These teeth mean she's not a predator. Not a biter. She's a herbivore, like antelope on the plains. Timid, a runner when scared. But also a herd animal, looking for leadership.* He opened the gate. The horse moved, ears pinned back, head rising and lowering, testing the rope. Then it swung its massive rear end toward him.

"Hey," he said firmly.

It kept coming. He placed his hand on its side, but it kept moving. *Don't stand behind it. Don't let it kick you,* he thought. *There's a reason for that saying about a horse's kick.*

"Stay still," he ordered.

The horse swung sideways again. Hunter braced his shoulder against its flank and shoved hard, as if breaking down a door. The horse quieted, breathing gently. *I'm in charge,* Hunter thought with a smile. He reached his right hand up near its nose. He'd seen this move in movies: rub the back of your hand on its nose so the horse gets your scent. The nose was soft, dry, and its breath came out strong and hot. Its lips peeled back, and a huge, wet tongue appeared.

"Good girl," he whispered.

Lifting the saddle, he placed it on her back. After some adjusting, he thought it felt solid. *Is it on the right way? Must be. It's shaped like a chair.* Straps hung down on both sides—two long, two short. Two had buckles, two had holes. *These must keep the saddle on,* he thought. He ducked under the horse, trying to grab the far straps. He barely reached them—this was one wide horse. He stretched out, but the saddle shifted.

"Damn," he muttered, straightening it again. The horse

shifted, and the straps slipped further from reach.

"Not like that," a voice called from above.

Hunter turned and looked up. Lahni was lying on top of the hay bales, chin propped on her hands, watching.

"You need the blanket first," she said.

"What blanket?"

"The saddle cloth."

Hunter's horse moved, crowding him against the wall. He pushed it back. The horse stared at him with its big dark eyes and long lashes. *I'm not scared of you,* he thought, holding its gaze. "Does anyone know you're in here?" he called to Lahni.

She shook her head. "I'm hiding."

"Does anyone know you hide in here?"

"My mum might, sometimes. The McMahons don't."

"Do you know how to do all this horse stuff?"

"Of course! I saddle my pony by myself."

"Come help me with this one," Hunter said.

"It's easy," Lahni responded.

"Show me, then."

After a long pause, she finally scrambled down the hay bales and joined him in the stall.

"Take the saddle off," she instructed.

She grabbed a cloth from the equipment post, shook it out, and threw it over the mare's back. Hunter straightened it. Then he placed the saddle on top, and Lahni ducked underneath the horse to fasten the straps with ease.

"You do it," she said. "They're stiff."

Hunter pulled the straps tight.

"Not too tight yet. Wait until she swells up."

"She's going to swell up?"

Lahni nodded seriously. "They do that to stop you. But they can't hold it for long."

Hunter watched as the mare's belly expanded like an oil drum before exhaling through her nose and settling back down.

"Now tighten them," Lahni said.

Hunter pulled the straps tight, and the mare shifted in place. Lahni handed him the reins and told him to remove the rope from the horse's head. He complied, and soon the bridle was in place.

"You did great," Lahni said. "Now just lead her out. Give a yank if she won't move."

"Thanks, kid. Now go hide again," Hunter said.

He led the mare outside, walking her across the yard, matching her pace. She moved smoothly beside him, head bobbing. *McLeod's Daughters, eat your heart out,* he thought again.

Ryan McMahon waited on the porch steps. Hunter brought the horse up to him, holding the leather strap as Ryan checked everything. He nodded, satisfied.

"Not bad," Ryan said. "But you took longer than I expected."

"I like to take it slow, the first time," Hunter said. "Get familiar with them."

Ryan gave another nod. "You're full of surprises. I would've bet the farm you'd never been near a horse outside of TV."

"Well I've been on TV before" Hunter teased.

Ryan smirked. "Double surprise, then. Maybe my sister-in-law wasn't lying for once."

Hunter shrugged. "Why wouldn't she be truthful?"

"She rarely is. Keep that in mind."

Ryan dismissed him, and as Hunter walked away, he heard the creak of leather as Ryan mounted the horse. Hunter didn't look back, heading for the barn and eventually back to his room, where Rosie sat waiting on his bed.

When Hunter climbed the stairs to his room, he found Rosie sitting on his bed, holding a set of folded sheets in her lap. She was still wearing her cotton dress, the white fabric glowing against the warmth of her bare legs.

"I brought you these," she said, lifting the sheets. "From the linen closet in the bathroom. You'll need them. I wasn't sure if you knew where to find them."

Hunter stopped at the top of the stairs, one foot inside the room, the other still on the last step.

"Rosie, this is insane," he said. "You need to leave, right now. They're going to figure out I'm a fraud. I won't last a day. I might be gone by Monday."

"I've been thinking," she said, her voice calm. "All through supper."

"About what?"

"About Troy Bradley. What if this is connected to whoever Warner is supposed to expose? What if they grabbed Troy to stop him?"

Hunter stepped fully into the room, his brow furrowed.

"That doesn't make sense. If that were the case, they would have done something a long time ago."

"Maybe," Rosie conceded, "but what if everyone believed it

was?"

Hunter still didn't follow. "What are you getting at?"

"Think about it," she said. "What if you made Warner disappear the same way Troy did? They'd think it was all related. No one would suspect you. You'd be in the clear."

Hunter shook his head. "We've already talked about this. I'm not a hitman."

Rosie fell silent, her eyes dropping to the sheets in her lap. She began absentmindedly picking at a frayed seam. The sheets looked old, possibly hand-me-downs from the big house. Hunter wondered if they'd once been used by Judy and her late husband. Or maybe by Ryan. Maybe even Warner—and Rosie, together.

"You really should leave, get out of here, right now," Hunter repeated. "I mean it."

"I can't."

"You could stay somewhere in Queensland, just temporarily. Fight it legally. You'd probably win custody, given the circumstances."

"I don't have the money for that," she said quietly. "It could cost a fortune."

"Rosie, you have to do something."

She nodded slowly. "I know what I'm going to do," she said. "Monday night, I'm going to take a beating. And on Tuesday morning, I'll come find you, wherever you are. Then you'll see —and maybe you'll change your mind."

Hunter didn't respond. Rosie tilted her face toward the fading light from the windows, her hair spilling down her shoulders.

"Take a good look," she said. "Come closer."

Hunter stepped forward.

"I'll be covered in bruises," she continued. "Maybe my nose will be broken. Maybe my lips will be split. Maybe I'll lose teeth."

He said nothing.

"Touch my skin," she said softly. "Feel it."

Hesitant, Hunter raised the back of his forefinger and lightly touched her cheek. Her skin was smooth and soft, warm like silk. He traced the curve of her cheekbone.

"Remember this," she whispered. "Compare it to what you feel on Tuesday morning. Maybe it'll change your mind."

Hunter withdrew his hand. Maybe it would change his mind. That was what she was counting on—and that was what he feared most. The difference between acting in cold blood and in hot blood. It was a big difference. For him, a critical one.

"Hold me," she asked quietly. "I can't remember what it feels like to be held."

Hunter sat down beside her and pulled her into his arms. She wrapped her own arms around his waist, resting her head against his chest.

"I'm scared," she murmured.

They sat there for what felt like twenty, maybe thirty minutes. Time slipped away. Rosie's body was warm, her breathing steady. Eventually, she pulled away and stood, her expression somber.

"I have to find Lahni," she said. "It's time for bed."

"She's in the barn," Hunter replied. "She helped me figure out all that horse stuff for Ryan."

Rosie nodded. "She's a good kid."

"She is," Hunter agreed. "Saved me from making a fool of

myself."

Rosie handed him the folded sheets. "Want to go riding tomorrow with me?" she asked.

"I don't know how to ride," Hunter admitted.

"I'll teach you."

"It might take a while."

"It can't," she said, looking away. "We have to make it up to the plateau."

"Why?"

She hesitated before answering. "There's something I need to learn," she said, her voice steady. "Just in case Tuesday doesn't change your mind. I need to know how to handle my gun properly."

Hunter didn't say anything.

"You can't deny me the right to protect myself," Rosie said firmly.

He still didn't respond. Without another word, she quietly descended the stairs, leaving Hunter sitting on the bed, holding the sheets exactly as she had been.

He set to making up his bed. The sheets were old and worn, but that suited the night's sweltering heat. It was still in the low thirties, and even by the middle of the night, it would likely only drop to around twenty-eight degrees. He wasn't going to be looking for extra warmth.

After finishing, Hunter walked back downstairs and stepped outside. Facing east, he saw the black horizon stretch endlessly. He moved around the corner of the bunkhouse to the west, watching as the sunset lit the sky. The southern sun fell quickly, like a giant red ball, flaring briefly against the edge of the plateau before vanishing, leaving the sky glowing red above it.

Footsteps crunched in the dust ahead of him. Squinting into the fading light, he saw Lahni walking toward him, her short steps stiff, her arms at her sides. Her blue halter dress was speckled with bits of straw, her hair glowing a golden brown in the sunlight, like an angel.

“I came to say goodnight,” she said.

Hunter was reminded of days past, when he’d be entertained at family quarters on a base somewhere, the distant sound of taps playing, and polite army children saying goodnight to their fathers’ fellow officers. He smiled at Lahni.

"Good night, Lahni," Hunter said.

"I like you," she replied.

"Well, I like you, too," he said.

"Are you hot?" she asked.

"Very."

"There’ll be a storm soon."

"That’s what everyone keeps saying."

"I’m glad you’re friends with my mummy."

Hunter didn’t respond, just held out his hand. Lahni glanced at it, then looked back at him.

"Aren’t you going to give me a goodnight kiss?" she asked.

"Am I supposed to?" Hunter asked, surprised.

"Of course you are."

"Alright," he said, bending down toward her.

"No, pick me up," she insisted, raising her arms high above her head.

Hunter paused for a second, then scooped her up, settling her into the crook of his arm. He kissed her gently on the cheek.

"Good night," he said again.

"Carry me, please," she said. "I'm tired."

He carried her across the yard, past the paddocks and the horse barn, heading toward the house. Rosie was waiting on the porch, leaning against a column, watching them approach.

"There you are," Rosie said as they got closer.

"Mummy, I want Mr. Hunter to come in and say good night," Lahni said.

"Well, I'm not sure if he can."

"I only work here," Hunter said with a slight shrug. "I don't live here."

"No one will know," Lahni said. "Come in through the kitchen. The maid's in there, and she works here, too. She's allowed in."

Rosie stood, uncertain.

"Please, mummy," Lahni pleaded.

"Maybe if we all go in together," Rosie said hesitantly.

"Through the kitchen," Lahni repeated, this time in a loud whisper that was more obvious than her regular voice. "We don't want the McMahons to see us."

She giggled, nestling her face against Hunter's neck as she rocked in his arms. Rosie glanced at Hunter, as if asking for his opinion. He shrugged. *What's the worst that could happen?* He gently set Lahni down, and she immediately took her mother's hand. Together, they headed for the kitchen door, which Rosie pushed open.

Sunset, the boy wrote, noting the time. The man and the

woman crawled backward from the edge of the gulch, stood, and stretched. *Off duty,* the boy wrote, noting the time again. The three of them worked together, folding the tarp that had covered their ute as neatly as possible without standing, then stowed it in the back. They repacked the cooler, collapsed the telescopes, and climbed into the cab, driving westward across the hardpan toward the glowing red horizon.

Inside the kitchen, the maid was loading a massive dishwasher, an old model covered in white enamel, likely the latest thing when man first walked on the moon. She glanced up at them but said nothing, continuing to stack plates. Hunter noticed the three bowls he had returned earlier, already rinsed and ready.

"This way," Lahni whispered.

She led them through a door into a narrow back hallway. There were no windows, and the air was stifling. Plain wooden stairs, stain faded and worn down to the wood in the shape of crescents, ran along one side. The stairs creaked under Hunter's weight as they ascended.

They emerged into what felt like a closet on the second floor. Lahni pushed the door open, crossed the hallway, and turned right into a narrow corridor. Everything—walls, floor, ceiling—was wood and painted cream. Lahni's room was at the end. It was a small, square space, no more than twelve feet across, and unbearably hot. Facing north, it must have baked in the sun all day. The closed drapes had done little to shield it from the heat.

"We'll go wash up," Rosie said. "Mr. Hunter will wait here, okay?"

Lahni watched him closely to be sure he was staying. He sat down on the edge of the small bed to assure her. Satisfied, Lahni followed her mother to the bathroom.

The bed was narrow, about thirty inches wide, and short—

perfect for a child. It had cotton sheets decorated with small, brightly colored animals of an uncertain species. A night table, bookcase, and small armoire furnished the room. The furniture, crafted from blonde wood, looked new and had been hand-painted with cheerful designs, likely bought from a boutique in Townsville or maybe even as far as Brisbane. Some shelves held books, while others were crammed with stuffed animals. The old air conditioner hummed noisily in the background, rattling from somewhere above. It must have been mounted in the attic, Hunter thought, providing a soothing sound, but little relief from the sweltering heat. Up here on the second floor, it felt like it was well over a forty degrees.

When Lahni and Rosie returned, Lahni seemed suddenly shy, perhaps because she was now in her pajamas—cotton shorts and a T-shirt, printed with small shapes that might have been rabbits. Her hair was damp, and her skin had a rosy glow. She stuck her thumb in her mouth as she climbed into bed, curling up near the pillow, taking up about half the mattress. She was close to Hunter but careful not to touch him.

"Good night, kid," Hunter said softly. "Sleep well."

"Kiss me," she said.

Hunter hesitated for a moment, then leaned down and kissed her forehead. It was warm, damp, and smelled faintly of soap. Lahni snuggled further into the pillow.

"Thank you for being our friend," she whispered.

Hunter stood and stepped toward the door. He glanced at Rosie, silently wondering if she had told Lahni to say that, or if it was heartfelt.

"Will you be able to find your way back down?" Rosie asked quietly.

Hunter nodded.

"I'll see you tomorrow," she said, staying behind in Lahni's room as Hunter found his way to the back stairs. He descended to the hallway and passed through the kitchen, which was now empty. The dishwasher hummed softly. He stepped out into the night, pausing in the quiet darkness of the yard. The air was thicker, hotter than ever. He moved toward the gate. The sunset was gone, leaving the horizon black. The air seemed heavy, charged with pressure. To the southwest, about a hundred kilometers away, faint flashes of heat lightning flickered in the distance, casting brief, random sheets of light across the sky like a giant camera snapping photos.

Hunter looked up. No clouds. No rain. But when he turned around, he caught a glimpse of white in the darkness to his right—a T-shirt, a face, a cap. It was Ryan McMahon.

"Ryan," Hunter said. "Did you enjoy your ride?"

Ryan ignored the question. "I was waiting for you."

"Why?"

"Just making sure you came back out."

"Why wouldn't I?"

"You tell me. Why did you go in? The three of you, like a little family."

"You saw us?"

Ryan nodded. "I see everything."

"Everything?" Hunter echoed.

"Everything I need to," Ryan replied.

Hunter shrugged. "I kissed the kid good night. You got a problem with that?"

Ryan didn't respond immediately. After a pause, he said, "Let me walk you back to the bunkhouse. I need to talk to you."

They walked in silence down the yard. Hunter gazed up at the night sky, filled with countless stars, vivid against the dark void. He liked looking up at the universe, using it as a reminder of how small and insignificant everything was. In the grand scheme of things, maybe nothing mattered at all. Perhaps he should just go ahead and deal with Warner McMahon. What difference would it make in the vastness of space?

"My brother had a problem," Ryan said awkwardly. "I guess you've heard about that."

"I heard he cheated on his taxes," Hunter replied.

Ryan nodded in the dark. "ATO snoops are everywhere."

"That's how they found him?"

"How else?" Ryan asked.

They walked in silence for a few more paces.

"Anyway, Warner went to jail," Ryan said.

"I heard he's getting out on Monday."

"That's right. He won't be happy to find you here, kissing his kid, getting close to his wife."

Hunter shrugged. "I'm just here to work."

"Right, as a jackeroo. Not as a nursemaid."

"I get time off, don't I?"

"Just be careful how you use it," Ryan warned.

Hunter smiled. "You mean I should know my place?"

"Exactly," Ryan said. "And your place isn't next to my brother's wife or cozying up to his kid."

Hunter stopped walking, standing still in the dark. "Tell me, Ryan, why should I care about what makes your brother happy?"

Ryan stopped too. "Because we're family. Things get discussed. You need to understand that, or you won't last here long. You could be run out of town."

"Really?" Hunter asked.

"Yeah," Ryan said.

Hunter smiled again. "Who's going to do that? The sergeant with the beat-up car? That guy might have a heart attack just thinking about it."

Ryan shook his head. "Out here in West Queensland, we handle things ourselves. It's tradition. Law enforcement isn't too strong around these parts, so we've learned to take care of matters personally."

Hunter stepped closer. "So, are you going to do it?"

Ryan stayed silent. Hunter nodded.

"Or maybe you'll send the maid after me with a frying pan."

"Max and Patty will handle it."

"The little guys? Maybe the maid's a better bet. Or you."

"Max and Patty wrestle bulls weighing over a ton. They're not going to be worried about you."

Hunter started walking again. "Whatever, Ryan. I only said good night to the kid. No need to blow this out of proportion. She's lonely. So is her mother. What do you expect me to do?"

"Get smart about it," Ryan replied. "I told you before, she lies about everything. Whatever story she's been feeding you, it's probably bullshit. Don't make a fool of yourself falling for it. You wouldn't be the first."

They turned the corner past the corrals and headed toward the bunkhouse door.

"What does that mean?" Hunter asked.

"Exactly what I said. Ask Max and Patty. They ran off the last guy."

Hunter didn't reply.

Ryan grinned. "Don't believe her. She doesn't tell you the whole truth, and what she does tell you is mostly lies."

"Why doesn't she have a key to the house?"

"She had a key. She just lost it. The house isn't locked anyway—why would it be? We're sixty kilometers from anything."

"So why does she knock?"

"She doesn't have to. But she makes a big show of it, pretending we exclude her. It's all an act. Warner married her, didn't he?"

Hunter said nothing.

"Work if you want," Ryan said, "but stay away from her and the kid. I'm saying that for your sake."

Hunter glanced at him. "Ryan, did you know your hat's on backward?"

"My what?"

"Your cap," Hunter said. "It's on backward. Thought maybe you didn't notice."

Ryan stared at him. "I like it that way."

Hunter nodded. "Well, I guess it keeps the sun off your neck. Keeps it from getting redder."

Ryan's tone hardened. "Watch your mouth. Stay away from my brother's family, and mind your damn mouth."

He turned and walked back toward the house. Hunter watched him until he disappeared behind the barn. In the distance, lightning flickered on the far northwest horizon, and the sound of Ryan's boots in the dust slowly faded away.

CHAPTER 6

Hunter went straight to bed, even though it was still early. His personal rule was simple: sleep whenever you can, so you won't need to when you can't. He had never followed a standard schedule. To him, there was no real distinction between a Tuesday or Sunday, a Monday or Friday, or night and day. He could easily sleep for twelve hours, then work thirty-six straight. And if nothing required his attention after that, he'd sleep another twelve hours, repeating the cycle as long as possible.

The bed was short, the mattress lumpy. The room's air hung over him like a thick, hot blanket, making the thin sheet feel almost suffocating. Outside, the night was alive with the sound of insects—countless clicking and whining noises that merged into a single piercing hum if he let his mind drift. Occasionally, he heard the distant, mournful cries of dingos or wild cats. The horses were restless, too, shifting uneasily in the barn, momentarily settling before stirring again with each distant call. He imagined the flutter of bat wings, sensing their leathery beats against the night air. Slowly, his eyes grew heavy as he watched stars flicker through a small window high above him.

****

Meanwhile, the road from Mount Kalka to Yabbie Creek stretched over two hundred kilometers, lined with scattered motels, service stations, and fast-food spots. The crew had driven an hour west, covering about seventy kilometers, before stopping at the second place they passed. This had become a habit for the woman leading them—never stop at the first place, always the second, and always arrive very late. She justified it as smart security, though it had started feeling almost superstitious.

The second stop had a service station big enough for semi-trucks, a two-story motel, and a 24-hour restaurant. The tall fair man paid cash for two rooms—one on the first floor far from the office, and another upstairs, halfway down the row. The woman took the upper room.

"Get some rest," she instructed. "We've still got work ahead."

Hunter woke around two in the morning when Max and Patty returned. The air was still as hot as before, the cicadas still loud. He heard the ute's engine a couple of kilometers out, growing louder as it neared, before slowing and turning in at the gate. The springs squealed as it bounced across the yard, pulling into the shed beneath the bunkhouse. After the motor switched off, there were only the sounds of cooling metal and footsteps on the stairs—heavy and unsteady. He feigned deep sleep, tracking the sounds as they moved past him, to the bathroom, and finally to their bunks. The bedsprings creaked as they collapsed onto the mattresses. Soon, there was nothing but the hum of the cicadas and the deep, steady breaths of men who had worked hard and drunk even harder. Hunter was used to this sound—he had spent many years in dormitories.

When he woke again, the insects had fallen silent, and the stars had faded. Through the high window, streaks of dawn began to color the sky. Summer this far south—it had to be around six in the morning, he thought. The air was already warm. He checked his watch: ten past six, Saturday morning. His thoughts drifted to Neve in London. It was ten past noon there; she would have been awake for hours, likely visiting a museum or thinking about lunch in a quaint tearoom. Then his mind shifted to Rosie McMahon, over in the main house, just two days away from the day her world would change again when Warner returned. And Lahni, perhaps restless in her tiny bed, unknowingly inching closer to the same day.

Hunter got up, tossed the crumpled sheet aside, and headed naked to the bathroom with his clothes balled in his hand. Max and Patty were still fast asleep, sprawled out in their clothes, Max's boots still on. The air reeked faintly of stale beer, the smell of a long night.

He set the shower to warm, scrubbing the sweat from his body, before turning it to cold to wake himself up. But even the cold water felt warm, likely heating up as it pumped through the baked earth. Afterward, he filled the sink with water and soaked his clothes—a trick he had learned long ago from Pacific sentries on midday watch. Wearing wet clothes provided a kind of built-in air conditioning, cooling him down as they dried. Dressed in a damp cotton shirt, he headed downstairs and stepped out into the dawn. The sun was already climbing over the horizon, the sky turning purple overhead. The red dust beneath his feet was still warm from the day before.

The watchers regrouped in stages, as they had five times before. It had become routine. The man drove the ute to the boy's place, where he found him waiting outside. Then they headed to pick up the woman. But when they arrived, things had changed.

"He just called," the woman explained. "New plan. We need to head up to the Carpentaria Gulf for face-to-face instructions."

"Face-to-face with who?" the man asked. "Not him, right?"

"No, some new people we'll be working with."

The boy remained silent, and the man just shrugged. "Fine by me."

"We're getting paid, too," the woman added.

"Even better," the man replied.

They squeezed into the ute, and it turned north.

Hunter walked around the corner of the bunkhouse, past the paddocks, and toward the barn. The entire place felt stifled by the heat, eerily quiet. He found himself wondering about the horses—did they lie down to sleep? Stepping into the barn, he got his answer. They were standing, heads bowed, knees locked, dozing on their feet. The big mare he had dealt with the night before sensed his presence, opened one eye lazily, and then shifted slightly before closing it again.

He scanned the barn, thinking through the work he might be expected to do. The horses would need to be fed, surely. There must be a food supply somewhere. Hay, he figured. The bales stacked everywhere must be for that, or maybe just for bedding. In a corner, he found a room filled with sacks of feed supplement, waxed-paper bags from a supplier down in Warwick. The horses probably got a mix of hay and the supplement to balance out their diet. They'd need water, too—there was a brass tap with a long hose attached, and each stall had a trough.

Leaving the barn, he walked up toward the house. Peeking through the kitchen window, he saw no one. The room looked just as it had the night before. He continued toward the road but heard the front door creak open behind him. Turning, he saw Ryan McMahon stepping out onto the porch. He was wearing the same T-shirt and Maroons cap, though now the cap was facing the right way. A rifle was slung over his shoulder—one of the .22 bolt-action guns from the hallway rack. He rested it on his shoulder and stopped a few paces away.

"I was just about to come get you up," Ryan said. "I need a driver."

"For what?" Hunter asked.

"Hunting," Ryan replied. "We'll take the ute."

"You can't drive?"

"Of course I can, but it takes two. You drive while I shoot."

"You shoot from the ute?"

"I'll show you," Ryan said.

He led Hunter over to the newer ute, which had a roll bar built into the bed.

"You drive," Ryan explained. "I'll ride in the back, leaning on the bar. It gives me a full range of fire."

"While we're moving?"

"That's the skill of it. It's fun. Warner came up with the idea. He was good at it."

"What are you hunting?" Hunter asked.

"Dingo," Ryan said, pointing down the track into the desert. "The best hunting country is south of here. They're all out there—nice big ones. Dingo steak makes a fine lunch."

Hunter said nothing.

"You've never eaten dingo?" Ryan asked. Hunter shook his head.

"Good eating," Ryan continued. "During the Depression, that's about all people had around here. Kept them alive. Now, the tree-huggers have them protected. But if they're on our land, they're ours to shoot. That's how I see it."

"I'm not a fan of hunting," Hunter said.

"Why not? It's a challenge."

"For you, maybe. I already know I'm smarter than a dingo."

"You work here, Hunter. You'll do what you're told."

"We need to talk about formalities before I do anything," Hunter replied.

"Like what?"

"Like wages."

"Seven hundred a week," Ryan said. "Room and board included."

Hunter stayed quiet.

"Is that fine with you?" Ryan pressed. "Or are you just here for Rosie?"

Hunter shrugged. Seven hundred a week wasn't much, but then, he wasn't here for the money.

"Fine," he said.

"And you'll do whatever Max and Patty ask."

"Alright," Hunter agreed. "But I won't go hunting. Not today, not ever. It's a matter of conscience."

Ryan was quiet for a moment. "I'll find ways to keep you away from her, you know. Every day, I'll make sure of it."

"I'll be in the barn," Hunter said, walking away.

Lahni brought him his breakfast where he was sitting. She wore a small pair of blue denim overalls, with her hair still wet and hanging loose. In her hands was a plate of scrambled eggs, and silverware was tucked neatly into her breast pocket like pens. She was focused on remembering a message.

"My mummy says, don't forget your riding lesson," she recited carefully. "She wants you to meet her here in the barn after lunch."

Without saying anything more, she dashed back toward the house. He sat on a bale of hay, quietly eating his breakfast. When he was done, he took the empty plate to the kitchen, then headed over to the bunkhouse. Max and Patty weren't around to give him any tasks, which was fine by him. He didn't bother to seek them out either, just lay down to nap in the heat.

The Carpentaria Gulf lies off northern Queensland's coast, bordered by both Queensland and the Northern Territory, stretching up toward Papua New Guinea. Its tropical, unpredictable climate made it sparsely inhabited. Scattered along the coast were abandoned farms, isolated and far from any towns. One such place had an old house, its structure bent with age and sun-faded to gray. In front of it stood an empty barn, open on one side facing west toward the house. The way the barn and house were positioned, the interior of the barn was hidden unless you were directly in front of it.

Inside the barn, the Falcon waited, engine running to keep the air cool. A staircase on the barn's exterior led up to a small platform in front of a hayloft door. A woman stood on the platform, out in the heat, watching the dusty road that wound its way toward the property. She spotted the approaching ute two kilometers away, moving quickly and raising a trail of dust behind it. Once certain the vehicle was alone, she descended the stairs and signaled the others.

They exited the car and stood outside in the heat, listening for the ute as it drew nearer. When it rounded the barn, they signaled it to slow down, guiding it into position like traffic controllers. One of them led the ute on foot, directing it until it was backed up tightly against the barn's rear wall. With a thumbs-up, the driver was signaled to stop. One man moved to the driver's window while his partner approached the passenger side.

The driver switched off the engine and relaxed, as was human nature. After a fast drive to a secret meeting point, with the promise of new instructions and a big payday, it was easy to let his guard down. He rolled down the window. On the passenger side, the woman did the same. Seconds later, both were dead, shot through the head with nine-millimeter bullets. The boy sitting in the middle had just enough time to realize what had happened before he, too, was killed—two shots to the chest from the small, dark man who leaned in after him. The woman then stepped forward, adjusting the windows on both sides to leave them slightly cracked—just enough to let insects in, but keep larger scavengers out. Insects would assist decomposition, but they didn't want any scavengers carrying body parts away, which might attract attention.

Meanwhile, Hunter napped for a few hours before Max and Patty returned. They didn't give him any directions either, only cleaned up for lunch. They informed him they had been invited to eat in the house, and he wasn't included because he'd refused to drive.

"Ryan told me you chased someone off," Hunter said.

Max just grinned.

"Who?" Patty asked.

"Some guy who came down here with Rosie."

"The Islander?"

"Some friend of hers."

Patty shook his head. "We didn't chase anyone off. Who do you think we are, the police?"

"You're the cop," Max replied.

"Am I?"

Max nodded. "Ryan said so. Said you used to be a military man."

"You guys talking about me?"

Max shrugged and went quiet.

"Anyway, gotta go," Patty said.

About twenty minutes later, Rosie brought Hunter his lunch, a covered dish with a strong bacon smell. She hurried away nervously without saying a word. He tasted the meal—it was a blend of sweet potato and savory bacon pieces, with shredded beef meat mixed with spinach and some BBQ sauce (the one in the brown bottle with the yellow lid), slightly overcooked in a warm oven. It wasn't great, but he'd eaten worse, and hunger helped. He ate slowly, then returned the dish to the kitchen. Ryan was standing on the porch steps like a guard.

"The horses need more feed supplements," Ryan called out. "You're going with Max and Patty to get it after lunch. Fill the ute with as many bags as it'll hold."

Hunter nodded, dropped the dish off with the maid, thanked her, and walked down to the barn. He sat on a bale of straw, waiting, while the horses in their stalls watched him lazily. One of them chewed slowly, bits of hay stuck to its lips.

Ten minutes later, Rosie came into the barn. She had changed into faded jeans and a sleeveless plaid shirt, carrying a straw hat and her purse. She looked small and frightened.

"Ryan doesn't know you called the ATO," Hunter said. "He thinks they were just snooping randomly, and maybe Warner does too."

She shook her head. "Warner knows."

"How?"

"He doesn't really know," she admitted. "But he convinced himself it was me. He needed someone to blame, and I was the obvious target. No evidence, but in this case, he's right. It's ironic, isn't it?"

"But he didn't tell Ryan."

"No, he wouldn't. He's too proud to agree with them. They hate me, he hates me, but he keeps their secret, and they keep it from him. They make sure I know it, though."

"You need to leave. You've got forty-eight hours."

"I know," she said. "Forty-eight hours exactly. They'll get him out at seven in the morning and drive all night to be there. It's about a seven-hour drive, so by this time on Monday, he'll be back home."

"Then leave now."

"I can't."

"You should," Hunter insisted. "This place is like a trap. It's as if the outside world doesn't even exist."

She gave a bitter smile. "Tell me about it. I've been stuck here almost seven years. Pretty much my whole adult life."

She hung her hat and bag on a nail in the wall and started saddling the horses, quick and efficient. Her small muscles rippled as she lifted the saddles, her fingers deftly securing the buckles. In no time, she had both horses ready.

"You're good at this," Hunter commented.

"Thanks," she replied. "I've had plenty of practice."

"Then how do they think you keep falling off so often?"

"They assume I'm clumsy."

Hunter watched as she led his horse out of its stall. The animal was one of the geldings, and she looked even smaller beside it. He realized he could probably span her waist with one hand in those jeans.

"You don't seem clumsy to me," he said.

She shrugged. "People believe what they want to believe."

He took the reins from her, and the horse snorted softly, shifting its feet and moving its head up and down. His hand moved with it.

"Walk him out," she said.

"Don't we need leather pants and gloves for this?" he asked.

She laughed. "Are you kidding? We never wear that stuff here. It's way too hot for that."

He waited while she got ready. Her horse was a smaller mare. She put her straw hat on and slid her purse into one of the saddlebags. Then she led her horse confidently out into the yard, stepping into the bright sun and heat.

"Okay, watch this," she instructed. Standing beside the mare, she placed her left foot in the stirrup, grabbed the saddle horn with her left hand, and with a couple of small bounces on her right foot, she smoothly lifted herself into the saddle.

Hunter mimicked her movements. He put his left foot into the stirrup, gripped the horn, and hoisted himself up with a pull from his arm. He leaned his weight forward and to the right, suddenly finding himself seated high on the horse. It felt surprisingly wide, and the height made him feel like he was riding on top of a tank.

"Put your right foot in the stirrup," she said.

He did, squirming until he found a somewhat comfortable position. The horse waited patiently beneath him.

"Now gather the reins in your left hand and rest them on the horn."

That part was easy enough; it was just like in the movies. He let his right hand hang loosely, imagining he was holding a Browning rifle or a coiled lasso.

"Relax now," she added. "And give him a light kick with your heels."

He did, and the horse lurched forward into a walk. He grabbed the saddle horn to steady himself and, after a few steps, started to get a feel for the rhythm. The horse's movements swayed him from side to side, forward and back with every alternate step. Using his legs for balance and gripping the saddle horn helped keep him steady.

"Good," she said. "I'll lead, and he'll follow. He's gentle."

I'd be gentle too, he thought, if I had to carry a hundred and twenty kilos in forty-degree heat. Rosie clicked her tongue and gently kicked her heels, and her horse moved gracefully ahead of his, leading the way through the yard and past the house. She swayed effortlessly in the saddle, her muscles flexing as she adjusted to the motion. Her hat shaded her face, and her left hand held the reins while her right hand hung loosely at her side. He caught a glimpse of the fake diamond on her finger flashing in the sunlight.

Rosie led them out through the gate and across the road without pausing to look. Hunter, out of habit, glanced both ways, seeing nothing but shimmering heat and distant mirages. On the other side of the road, the ground rose about a foot onto a sandstone ledge. He leaned forward in the saddle as the horse climbed, trying to stay balanced. Ahead, the rock stretched out in gentle slopes, rising maybe fifty feet over the next kilometer. There were deep cracks and holes, some of them as large as craters, and the horses picked their way between them with surprising surefootedness. So far, Hunter hadn't had to steer at all, which suited him just fine since he wasn't entirely sure how to.

"Watch out for death adders," Rosie called back to him.

"Great," he replied.

"Horses spook easily at anything that moves. If they bolt, just hang on and pull the reins hard."

"Great," he said again, less enthusiastically.

There were a few hardy shrubs growing in the cracks of the sandstone, and smaller holes in the rock, some only a couple of feet wide. Perfect for a snake, Hunter thought. At first, he kept an eye on them, but soon gave up—it was too hard to see anything in the harsh shadows, and the saddle was already beginning to chafe.

"How far are we going?" he asked.

She turned her head slightly, as if she'd been expecting the question.

"We need to get over the rise," she said. "Down into the gullies."

The rocky surface leveled out into smoother, unbroken sections, and Rosie slowed her pace, letting Hunter's horse catch up to hers. But it stayed just behind, not quite even with her, keeping her face hidden from view.

"Ryan told me you had a key," Hunter said.

"Did he?"

"He said you lost it."

"That's not true," she replied. "They never gave me one."

Hunter stayed quiet, waiting.

"They made a big show of not giving me a key," she continued. "Like it was some kind of symbol."

"So, Ryan was lying?"

She nodded, facing away. "I told you not to believe a word he says."

"He also said the door's never locked."

"Sometimes it is, sometimes it isn't."

"He said you don't have to knock, either."

"That's another lie," she said. "Since Warner's been gone, if I don't knock, they grab a rifle. Then they pretend it's no big deal, saying strangers make them jumpy. All for show."

Hunter said nothing.

"Ryan's a liar," Rosie repeated. "I've told you that."

"I'm starting to believe you," Hunter admitted. "Because he also told me you brought another guy down here, and Max and Patty ran him off. But when I asked them, they didn't know anything about it."

Rosie was silent for a long moment.

"No, that part's true," she finally said. "About a year ago, I met someone in Mount Kalka. We had an affair. At first, we only saw each other at his place. But he wanted more."

"So you brought him here?" Hunter asked.

"It was his idea. He thought he could find work and be close to me. I thought it was a terrible idea, but I went along with it. It actually worked for a little while—two or three weeks. Then Ryan found out."

"And then what?"

"That was the end of it. My friend left."

"So why would Max and Patty deny it?"

"Maybe it wasn't them who made him leave. Maybe Ryan dealt with it himself. My friend wasn't as big as you—he was a schoolteacher, between jobs."

"And then he just disappeared?"

"I saw him once after that, back in Mount Kalka. He was scared, didn't want to talk to me."

"Did Ryan tell Warner?"

"He promised me he wouldn't. We made a deal."

"What kind of deal?"

Rosie fell silent again, riding without speaking for a long moment.

"The usual kind," she eventually said. "If I did something for him, he'd stay quiet."

"What kind of something?"

She hesitated again before answering.

"Something I really don't want to talk about."

"I see."

"Yeah, you see."

"And did he keep his promise?"

"I have no idea," she said bitterly. "He made me do it twice, and it was disgusting. He's disgusting. But he swore he'd keep quiet. Of course, he's a liar, so he probably told Warner anyway. I always knew it was a gamble I'd lose, but what choice did I have?"

"Ryan thinks that's why I'm here," Hunter said. "He's convinced we're having an affair, too."

She nodded. "I'd assume so. He doesn't know Warner hits me. Even if he did, he wouldn't expect me to do anything about it."

They rode in silence again for a while, the horses plodding slowly along.

"You need to leave," Hunter said eventually. "How many times do I have to tell you?"

"I'm not running," she replied firmly.

They reached the top of the rise, and Rosie made a small sound to stop her horse. Hunter's horse halted just beside hers. From this vantage point, they could see the land sloping back down, broken by dry, rocky gullies the size of sports fields. Behind them, the compound lay about a kilometer away, the cream-colored house and outbuildings looking small and flat against the baked ground. The road stretched north and south like a thin gray ribbon, and a dirt track wound off through the desert beyond the motor barn. The air was painfully clear, but turned hazy at the horizons. The sun beat down relentlessly, and Hunter could feel his skin burning.

"Be careful going down," Rosie said. "Keep your balance."

She nudged her horse forward, letting it find its way down the slope. Hunter followed, losing the rhythm as his horse took shorter steps, making for a bumpy descent.

"Follow me," she called back.

She guided them toward a dry gully with a flat, sandy floor. Hunter tried to figure out which rein to pull, but his horse made the turn on its own. Its hooves crunched on gravel, and it slipped occasionally, but soon stepped down into the gully, jolting him sharply forward. Ahead, Rosie had dismounted and was stretching her legs, waiting for him. His horse came to a stop beside hers, and he dismounted awkwardly, the opposite of how he'd gotten on earlier.

"So, what do you think?" she asked.

"Well, now I know why cowboys always walked funny in those old movies."

She gave a brief smile and led both horses to the rim of the gulch, securing the free ends of their reins with a large stone. The heat shimmered in the silence, the only sound being the faint hum of the air. Rosie opened her saddlebag and took out her pocketbook. She unzipped it, slipped her hand inside, and pulled out a small chrome handgun.

"You promised you'd teach me," she said.

"Hold on," he replied.

"What?"

He didn't answer immediately, stepping to the left, then to the right. He crouched, then stood tall again, eyes focused on the ground as he moved around, using the sunlight and shadows to help him see.

"What is it?" she asked again.

"Someone's been here," he said, his voice low. "There are tracks —three people, and a vehicle coming from the west."

"Tracks?" she asked, confused. "Where?"

He pointed to the ground. "Tire marks. Looks like a ute stopped here. Three people crawled on their knees to the edge."

He positioned himself where the tracks ended, lying down on the hot ground, pulling himself forward on his elbows. He raised his head.

"They were watching the house," he said.

"How do you know?"

"There's nothing else they could have been watching from here."

Rosie knelt beside him, still holding the chrome pistol in her hand. "It's too far away," she remarked.

"They probably used binoculars or telescopes," he replied.

"Are you sure?"

"Ever notice any reflections? Like sunlight bouncing off glass in the mornings when the sun was rising in the east?"

Rosie shuddered. "No," she said. "Never."

"These tracks are fresh—no more than a day or two old." His voice was steady as he spoke.

She shuddered again. "It's Warner," she whispered. "He thinks I'm going to take Lahni. Now that he knows he's getting out, he's having me watched."

Hunter stood up and returned to the center of the gulch. "Look at these tire marks," he said. "They've been here four or five times."

He pointed to the ground where several overlapping tracks formed a crisscrossing pattern. The tire treads were clearly impressed in the powdery sand, the outer edge of the front right tire almost completely bald.

"But they're not here now," Rosie pointed out. "Why not?"

"I don't know," Hunter replied. And the silence between them passed for a moment.

Rosie turned away, offering him the gun. "Please, show me how to use this."

He shifted his gaze from the tracks to the gun. It was a small Makarov .22 automatic with a two-and-a-half-inch barrel, chrome-plated, with pink plastic grips designed to look like mother-of-pearl. It appeared practically unused, as if it had never been fired.

"Is it a good one?" she asked.

"How much did you pay for it?"

"Over two hundred dollars."

"Where?"

"In a gun shop in Mount Kalka."

"Is it legal?"

She nodded. "I did all the paperwork. Is it any good?"

"It's decent enough, I guess," he said. "For two hundred bucks, it'll do the job."

"The guy in the store said it was perfect."

"For what?"

"For a woman. I didn't tell him why I needed it."

Hunter hefted the gun in his hand. It was small but felt solid, neither too light nor too heavy. Definitely not loaded, though.

"Where are the bullets?" he asked.

She walked back to the horses, fetched a small box from her bag, and returned, handing it to him. It was filled with tiny .22-caliber bullets, probably about fifty in total.

"Show me how to load it," she said.

Hunter shook his head. "You should leave it out here," he said. "Just ditch it and walk away."

"But why?"

"Because this whole situation is out of control. Guns are dangerous, Rosie. Keeping one around Lahni is a bad idea—there could be an accident."

"I'll be very careful," she promised. "Besides, the house is already full of guns."

"Rifles are different," he explained. "She's too small to pull the trigger while it's pointing at her. But this..."

"I keep it hidden. She hasn't found it yet."

"She will eventually. It's only a matter of time."

Rosie shook her head. "It's my decision," she said firmly. "She's my daughter."

Hunter said nothing.

"She won't find it," Rosie continued. "I keep it by my bed, and she doesn't come in there."

"And what if you end up using it? What happens to her then?"

She nodded. "I know. I think about that all the time. I just hope she's too young to understand. And if she's older, maybe she'll see it was the lesser of two evils."

"No," Hunter said gravely. "What happens to her in that moment? While you're in jail?"

"They don't lock you up for self-defense," she insisted.

"Who says it's self-defense?"

"You know it would be."

"It doesn't matter what I know. I'm not the prosecutor or the judge."

She fell silent.

"Think about it, Rosie," he pressed. "You'll be arrested, charged with first-degree murder. You've got no bail money, no funds for a proper lawyer. You'll get a public defender, and the case will drag on for months. Even if everything goes your way, it'll be a year before you're free. What happens to Lahni in that time?"

Rosie didn't respond.

"She'll spend that year with Judy," Hunter said. "Because that's who the court will leave her with. Her grandmother. The perfect solution, right?"

"Not if they knew what the McMahons are really like."

"Okay, then maybe halfway through the year, Child Protective Services steps in and takes her to a foster home. Is that what you want for her?"

Rosie winced. "Judy would send her there anyway. If Warner

weren't around, she wouldn't keep her."

"Then leave the gun here," Hunter urged. "It's not worth it."

He handed it back to her. She cradled it in her hands, turning it over like it was something precious. The fake pearl grips flashed in the sunlight.

"No," she said quietly. "I need to learn how to use it. For my own peace of mind. That's my decision, not yours."

Hunter was silent for a moment, then he shrugged. "Alright. It's your life, your child, your choice. But guns are serious, so pay attention."

She handed the gun back to him. He placed it flat in his left palm. It stretched from the base of his thumb to the middle of his finger.

"Two things," he said. "First, this is a very short barrel—only two and a half inches. Did the guy at the store explain that?"

She nodded. "He said it would fit easily in my bag."

"It makes it inaccurate," Hunter explained. "The longer the barrel, the straighter it shoots. That's why rifles are so long. If you use this, you need to be right next to your target. Ideally, touching them. Across the room? You'll miss by miles."

"Okay," she said.

"Second, this bullet is tiny and slow." He showed her a shell from the box. "It's not going to do a lot of damage. You'll need to be close, and you'll need to keep pulling the trigger until the gun is empty."

"Got it."

"Now watch."

Hunter clicked the magazine out of the gun and loaded nine bullets into it. He slid it back in, pulled the first round into the chamber, and removed the magazine to reload the empty slot. He clicked it back in and cocked the gun, leaving the safety on.

"It's cocked and locked," he said. "You do two things: flip the safety off and pull the trigger ten times. There's one bullet in the chamber and nine more in the magazine."

He handed the gun back to her. "And don't point it at me."

She took it, carefully holding it away from him.

"Try it," he said. "Safety off, then the trigger."

She flipped the safety with her left hand, pointed the gun, and closed her eyes as she pulled the trigger. The shot rang out, the gun jerking downward in her grip. A chunk of rock and a puff of dust flew up ten feet away. The metallic sound of the shell casing ejecting echoed, and the horses shuffled nervously. Silence settled in again.

"Well, it works," she said.

"Put the safety back on," he reminded her.

She clicked the safety back, and he checked on the horses. They were calm, still standing in place, watching warily. He didn't want to chase them in the heat. Satisfied, he turned back, removed his shirt, and walked over to the rim of the gulch, laying it out flat like a man's torso.

"Shoot my shirt," he said. "Always aim for the body—biggest and most vulnerable target."

She hesitated. "I can't do that. You don't want holes in your shirt."

"I'm not too worried about that," he replied. "Go ahead."

She forgot to release the safety at first, pulling the unyielding trigger twice before realizing her mistake. She clicked it off, aimed, and fired. The shot went high and wide, missing by at least twenty feet.

"Keep your eyes open," Hunter instructed. "Picture you're angry at the shirt, like you're pointing at it and shouting."

Rosie kept her eyes open this time, raising her arm level and aiming. She fired again, but the bullet flew six feet to the left and a little low.

"Let me show you," Hunter said, taking the gun from her. It felt tiny in his hand, the trigger guard barely big enough for his finger. He closed one eye, aiming. "I'm aiming for where the pocket used to be."

He fired twice in quick succession. The first shot hit the shirt under the armpit, the second lower down, but still on target. He relaxed, handed the gun back to Rosie, and said, "Your turn."

She fired three more shots, each one missing. The last hit the dirt, seven feet short of the shirt. She lowered the gun, staring at the shirt with disappointment.

"So, what have you learned?" Hunter asked.

"I need to be close," she said quietly.

"Exactly. Very close. And it's not entirely your fault. Short-barrel handguns are for close-range use. See how I missed by twelve inches at fifteen feet? The shots didn't even land in the same place. And I'm a good shot—I won competitions in the army."

"Okay," she said.

He knelt in the dust, reloaded the gun, then handed it back. "If you're not sure, leave it here. If you pull that gun, you have to be ready. No hesitation."

Rosie nodded, understanding the gravity of his words. "Last resort."

"Exactly. From the moment you pull that gun, it's all or nothing."

She stood still for a long time before finally bending down to pick up the gun and placing it back in her bag. Hunter retrieved his shirt and put it on, noting that neither bullet hole was visible—one under his arm, the other tucked below his waistband. He walked around the gulch, collecting the eight spent shell casings, jingling them like loose change in his pocket.

As they rode back, the conversation turned to fear. Rosie was quiet as they ascended the rise, pausing again at the top to look down at the cream-colored house compound in the distance. She clasped both hands on her saddle horn, her eyes distant and contemplative. Hunter's horse, as usual, stayed slightly behind hers, giving him the same view but framed by her neck and shoulder.

"Do you ever get scared?" she asked after a long silence.

"No," he said.

She was quiet for a few moments before asking, "How is that possible?"

Hunter glanced at the sky. "I learned how to deal with fear when I was a kid."

"How?"

He looked down at the ground. "I had an older brother. He was always ahead of me, always doing things I wanted to do. He had scary comics, and when we had access to Australian TV, he'd watch it. There was this show, something about space adventures—I don't remember the name. It was in black-and-white. They had this spaceship that looked like a small submarine with spider legs, and they'd land somewhere to explore. I remember one episode where they were chased by this monster—it was hairy, like an ape, maybe like Bigfoot. It chased them back to the ship, and they barely slammed the hatch shut in time."

"And you were scared?"

Hunter nodded, though she couldn't see him. "I must have been around four years old, and I was terrified. I was convinced that thing was under my bed. I had this old, high bed, and I was sure the monster was living underneath it, waiting to grab me. I couldn't sleep for days. If I fell asleep, I knew it would get me."

"What happened?" she asked.

"I got mad. Not at myself for being scared, because that monster was totally real to me. I got mad at it for making me afraid. One night, I just lost it and yelled out, 'Fine, come out and try it! I'll beat the crap out of you!' I faced it down, turned the fear into anger."

"And that worked?"

"I've never been scared since. I made a habit of it. Those space explorers shouldn't have run—they should've stood their ground and fought. That's how I see it now. If you face something scary, you should step toward it, not away."

"Is that what you do?"

"Always."

"Is that what I should do? With Warner?"

"I think it's what everyone should do."

Rosie stayed quiet, her gaze fixed on the house below, then the distant horizon beyond it. She clicked her tongue, and the horses moved forward again, down the slow slope toward the road. She shifted to maintain her balance, and Hunter mirrored her movements, staying safely in the saddle, though not comfortably. He figured riding horses would be one of those things he'd only do once.

"So, what did Ryan say about us?" she asked.

"He said you've been away a lot recently, sometimes at night, and he thinks we've been having an affair in some motel in Mount Kalka. Now he's outraged that you've brought me here, so close to Warner coming back."

"I wish that were true," she said. "That we were just having an affair in some motel. I wish that's all it was."

Hunter stayed silent.

"Do you wish it was true?" she asked after a pause.

He watched her as she rode, her slim hips swaying gently with the horse's gait. Her arms were sun-kissed and lithe, her hair hanging down to the middle of her back.

"I can think of worse things," he said.

It was late afternoon when they returned. Max and Patty were waiting, leaning against the barn wall, casting long shadows. Their ute was ready for the trip to pick up feed, parked in the yard.

"Do all three of you have to go?" Rosie whispered.

"It's Ryan," Hunter whispered back. "He wants me away from you, trying to spoil the fun we're supposed to be having."

She rolled her eyes. "I'll take care of the horses. They need to be brushed."

They dismounted at the barn door, and Max and Patty peeled themselves off the wall, their body language showing impatience.

"You ready?" Patty called out.

"He should've been ready half an hour ago," Max grumbled.

Hunter made them wait. He walked slowly to the bunkhouse, not letting them rush him, partly because he was stiff from the ride. After using the bathroom and rinsing the red dust off his face, he splashed cold water on his shirt before heading back, still at a slow pace. The ute had been turned to face the gate, engine running. Rosie was brushing the horse, thin clouds of dust rising from its chestnut coat. Max sat in the driver's seat, and Patty stood by the passenger door.

"Come on, let's go!" Patty called.

Hunter climbed into the middle seat. Max swung his feet inside and slammed his door shut. Patty crowded in on the other side, and Max drove off toward the gate. When they reached the road and Max made a left turn, Hunter realized the situation was far worse than he had imagined.

CHAPTER 7

Hunter had seen the feed bags stacked in the storeroom. There were at least forty of them, piled head-high, made of waxed paper and likely weighing about fifteen kilos each. That was over six hundred kilos of feed—more than half a ton. How long could four horses and a pony possibly take to eat through all of that?

He had always figured the trip to buy more feed was Ryan's way of getting him away from Rosie for a while. Buying more feed when there was plenty left seemed like a convenient excuse. But they weren't actually going to buy more feed, because they had turned left. Each bag was stamped with the name of the supplier in Warwick, a town southeast of Four Ways Shire. Warwick. He had seen that name at least forty times, printed clearly on every bag. And Warwick was southeast, not northwest. They should have turned right.

Ryan's plan was becoming clear. He wasn't just getting Hunter out of Rosie's life for a short while—he was planning something permanent. Max and Patty had been told to take care of him, and Hunter knew they would follow orders. But they didn't realize he had seen the feed bags, or that he had spent the past week studying maps of Queensland. The left turn hadn't gone unnoticed.

How would they try to handle it? Rosie had hinted that her former teacher friend had been scared off, scared so badly that he wouldn't even speak to her later in Mount Kalka. Maybe they thought they could scare him, too. If so, they were in for a surprise. Hunter could feel the aggression building inside him, and as he had learned to do, he used that energy to control his reactions. The adrenaline eased the stiffness in his legs and pumped him up. He flexed his shoulders, pressing against Max on one side and Patty on the other.

"How far is it?" he asked, playing innocent.

"Couple hours," Patty replied.

They were driving at about a hundred kilometers per hour, heading south on a long, straight road. The landscape was monotonous—dry red scrubland to the left, sunbaked sandstone to the right, broken into ledges and layers. The sun beat down relentlessly, and there was no other traffic. It looked like the kind of road that only saw a few vehicles each day. Maybe their plan was to drive far enough away, pull over, throw him out, and leave him to die of thirst or exhaustion. Or maybe he'd step on a death adder.

"No, less than a couple of hours," Max corrected. "Only about a hundred kilometers."

Maybe they were taking him to the bar they had mentioned the day before. Maybe they had friends there. They'd need them, Hunter thought. Two third-rate cowboys wouldn't stand a chance against him. He exhaled slowly, trying to relax as he weighed his options. The thing about the kind of undiluted rage he'd described to Rosie was that it tended to come out in an all-or-nothing way. He recalled his first day at high school. After finishing primary school, his family had returned to the Australia for a six-month stay, and he had been enrolled at a large high school off-base, somewhere near Seymour, close to Pucka Base. He had been ready for it. High school, he'd reasoned, would be bigger and tougher in every way—including the locker-room scuffles.

His plan, as always, had been to make a strong first impression by hitting the first person who challenged him. It had worked for him before—hit hard, hit early, and get your retaliation in first. But this time, he had taken it too far. A tough kid had shoved him that morning, and ten minutes later, the kid was on his way to the hospital for a three-week stay. That was when Hunter realized he had overreacted. It turned out to be a very genteel school in a nice neighborhood, and his behavior had shocked everyone. They had looked at him like he was some sort of brute, and he had felt ashamed. Since then, he had learned to be calmer, to assess situations before acting, and sometimes even to give warnings.

"We coming straight back?" he asked, keeping things casual.

It was a smart question. They couldn't say no without giving something away, but they also couldn't say yes if they weren't really heading to the feed store.

"We're going for a couple of beers first," Patty said.

"Where?" Hunter asked.

"Where we went yesterday," Patty replied.

"I'm broke," Hunter said. "I haven't been paid yet."

"We're buying," Max said.

"Is the feed store open late on a Saturday?" Hunter pressed.

"They'll accommodate us for a big order," Patty said.

Maybe they had switched suppliers, or maybe this was a different location.

"Do you use them a lot?" Hunter asked.

"Been going there for years," Max replied.

"Then we're heading back right after?"

"Of course," Patty assured him. "You'll be back in time for your beauty sleep."

"That's good," Hunter said, pausing for effect. "Because that's how I like it." His voice carried a warning: mess with me, and you'll regret it.

Patty said nothing. Max just smiled and kept driving.

The landscape gradually flattened as they moved north. Hunter, having studied the maps, knew they were approaching the Leichhardt River basin, where ancient waters had scoured the land flat. Max maintained a steady speed of a hundred kilometers per hour, while Patty stared out the window. The road remained straight and featureless. Hunter leaned back, resting his head on the gun rack behind him, and waited. Waiting was something he was used to. In the SAS, many high-stakes actions had been preceded by long periods of calm, waiting on your stomach or squatting for hours or sometimes days. He had learned to wait.

As they drove farther north, the road became rougher, and the ute labored over it, the rear wheels bouncing and skipping over the uneven surface. Vultures perched on the telephone poles, and the sun hung low in the western sky. A sign appeared by the road: "Four Ways, 10 kilometers." It was riddled with bullet holes.

"I thought Four Ways was south," Hunter said. "Where Lahni goes to school."

"It's split," Patty explained. "Part of it's up here, part of it's down there. A hundred and sixty kilometers of nothing in between."

"The world's biggest town, end to end," Max added. "Bigger than Sydney."

He slowed the ute around a long curve, and a cluster of low buildings came into view in the distance, silhouetted by the setting sun. There were tin signs along the roadside, announcing what lay ahead: a service station, a country store, and the Great Northern Truck Stop Restaurant, owned by someone named Kenny. The diner was the first building they reached. It sat about a hundred feet from the road, a low, wooden structure with an iron roof, surrounded by two acres of dry, parched earth. Ten or twelve utes were parked in front, their noses lined up against the building like airplanes at a terminal. Nearest to the door was the sergeant's secondhand police car, parked as if it had been abandoned.

Max pulled into the lot, parking in line with the other vehicles. The bar had neon beer signs in the windows, trapped between dirty glass and faded gingham curtains. Max switched off the engine, pocketed the keys, and in the sudden quiet, Hunter could hear the sounds of the bar—fans whirring, the low hum of a radio playing classic rock, chatter, the clink of bottles and glasses, and the crack of pool balls. It seemed like a decent-sized crowd inside.

Max and Patty opened their doors and got out simultaneously. Hunter slid out through the passenger side, feeling the heat radiating from the ground, from the back of his neck down to his heels.

"Alright," Patty said. "We're buying."

They stepped inside a small lobby with a pay phone on the wall, surrounded by scrawled numbers and old messages. A second door, with a frosted glass pane reading "Bar", led into the bar itself. Patty pushed it open.

For a ex-SAS ranger, walking into a bar is like stepping onto a playing field—it's his place of business. In the military, about ninety percent of low-level trouble happens in bars. Put a bunch of young men trained for combat in a room with unlimited alcohol, throw in unit rivalries and civilian women, and it's a recipe for chaos. Just like a batter sizing up the field as he steps to the plate, an SAS ranger scans the bar for trouble spots. Hunter immediately counted the exits: there were three —the front door, a back door by the restrooms, and a private door behind the bar. The windows were too small to be useful for an escape.

Then he scanned the crowd, looking for signs of trouble. Who was staring? Who went silent? But there was nothing to worry about here. The place was crowded with about twenty or twenty-five men, all lean and tanned, dressed in denim. They glanced at Max and Patty with casual recognition, but none seemed concerned about Hunter's presence. The sergeant was nowhere to be seen, though there was an empty stool at the bar with a fresh beer bottle in front of it. It could be his usual spot.

Next, Hunter scanned for weapons. There was an old revolver mounted above the bar, fixed to a wooden plaque with a message branded into it: "We don't call 000." There were probably a few modern handguns scattered around the room, too. Long-neck bottles were everywhere, but Hunter wasn't worried about those. Contrary to what movies suggest, real bottles are too thick to shatter easily—they just make a loud bang. Pool cues, however, were a different story. The pool table in the middle of the room had four men playing, and there were at least a dozen more cues lined up in a rack on the wall. A pool cue, short of a shotgun, is the best barroom weapon ever—sturdy, long enough to give an advantage, and perfectly balanced.

The bar was unnaturally cold, the air thick with the smell of beer and cigarette smoke. The radio near the pool table played over the low rumble of conversation. Beyond the table, there were small round lounge tables surrounded by stools padded in green vinyl. Patty held up three fingers to the bartender, and soon they had three cold bottles in hand. He led the way to the tables, but Hunter stepped ahead of him, wanting to choose his seat. His rule was always to sit with his back to the wall, with a clear view of all exits, if possible. He weaved through the tables and sat down. Max took a seat to his right, and Patty to his left. A bottle slid across the scarred tabletop toward him, its surface marked with cigarette burns.

The sergeant reappeared, coming from the direction of the restrooms, checking that his pants were zipped. He froze for a moment when he saw Hunter, his face betraying nothing, then moved to the bar, taking the empty stool with his back to the room.

Patty raised his bottle in a mock toast. "Good luck," he said.

You're the one who'll need it, Hunter thought, taking a long sip of the cold, fizzy beer. It had a strong, hoppy taste.

"I need to make a phone call," Patty said, pushing back from the table and standing. Max leaned in, trying to fill the space left by his absence. Patty walked through the crowd and out into the lobby. Hunter took another sip of beer, silently counting the seconds. He tallied up the people in the room—twenty-three in total, including the bartender, who he assumed was Kenny.

Two minutes and forty seconds later, Patty returned. He bent over and whispered something into the sergeant's ear. The sergeant nodded. Patty spoke again, and the sergeant nodded once more, drained his bottle, and stood up. He turned to face the room, glanced briefly in Hunter's direction, then walked out through the door. Patty watched him go, then made his way back to the table.

"The sergeant's leaving," he announced. "Suddenly remembered some urgent business."

Hunter said nothing.

"Did you make your call?" Max asked, the question sounding rehearsed.

"Yeah, I made my call," Patty replied.

Then he sat down and picked up his bottle again. "Don't you want to know who I called?" he asked, looking directly at Hunter.

“Why would I care who you called?” Hunter replied.

“I called the ambulance,” Patty said, his voice casual. “Best to call it ahead of time, since it’s coming all the way from Normanton. It can take hours to get here.”

“We’ve got a confession to make,” Max added. “We lied before. There was a guy we ran off—a schoolteacher who was fooling around with the Islander woman. Ryan didn’t think it was appropriate with Warner in prison, so we took care of it. Brought him down here.”

“Want to know what we did?” Patty asked.

“I thought we were going to the feed store,” Hunter said.

“The feed store’s in Warwick,” Max said.

“So why are we all the way out here?”

“We’re telling you,” Patty said. “This is where we brought the other guy.”

“What’s that got to do with me?”

“Ryan thinks you’re in the same situation,” Max said.

"He thinks I’m involved with Rosie?" Hunter asked.

Max nodded. “That’s right.”

“What do you think?”

“We agree. Why else would you be hanging around? You’re not exactly a horseman, are you?”

“Suppose I told you we’re just friends?”

“Ryan doesn’t think so,” Patty said.

“And you believe him?”

“Sure we do. She comes on to him, he told us that himself. So why should you be any different? Can’t say we blame you. She’s a fine-looking woman. I'd probably take a shot myself if she weren't Warner's. You've got to respect family, even if they're Islanders."

Hunter didn't respond.

"We brought the other guy here," Patty continued. "He was a schoolteacher, got too bold. So we took him out back, told him we were going to cut it off. He started crying, begging for mercy. We cut him a little anyway, just for fun. There was blood everywhere, but we let him go. Told him if we saw him again, we'd finish the job. Never saw him again after that."

"So it worked," Max said with satisfaction. "Only problem was, he almost bled out. Should've called the ambulance then, too. But you live and learn, right? This time, we called ahead. Just for you."

"You cut him?" Hunter asked.

"Sure did," Patty said, pride in his voice.

"Sounds like you're proud of yourselves."

"We do what's needed. Got to look after the family."

"And you're telling me all of this?"

Max nodded. "Why not? Who the hell are you?"

Hunter shrugged. "Well, I'm not a schoolteacher."

"What's that supposed to mean?"

"It means if you try to cut me, you'll be the one in the ambulance."

"You think so?"

Hunter nodded. "The horse I was riding could cause more trouble than you two."

He looked at each of them in turn, his serene confidence filling the space between them. Confidence, born from years of experience, can work wonders in a situation like this. And Hunter felt very sure of himself. It had been a long time since he'd lost a two-on-one bar fight.

"Your choice," he said calmly. "Back off now, or end up in the hospital."

"Well, you know what?" Max said, smiling. "I think we'll stick to our plan. Whatever kind of guy you think you are, we're the ones with all the friends here. And you've got none."

"I didn't ask about your social life," Hunter said.

But it was true—they had friends in the bar. He could feel the atmosphere shift. Conversations were quieting, and people were starting to watch. The pool game had slowed down. Tension hung in the air. Maybe it wouldn't just be two against one. Maybe this would turn into something much worse.

Patty grinned. "We don't scare easy," he said. "Call it a professional thing."

They're rodeo riders, Hunter thought. Ryan had told him they rode bulls that weighed a ton and a half. A man like that wouldn't be easily intimidated. Hunter had never been to a rodeo, but he knew enough from TV and movies. The riders sat on a fence, jumped on a bull as it was released, and had to stay on for what—eight seconds? If they didn't, they risked getting kicked, stomped, or gored. These guys had a dumb kind of courage, plenty of strength, and they were used to pain and injury. But they were also used to a structured buildup, a countdown before the action began. Maybe three, two, one. Maybe ten, nine, eight.

"Let's do it," Hunter said. "Right now, out in the yard."

He stepped out from behind the table, catching Max off guard, and moved quickly toward the exit by the restrooms, past the radio and the pool table. Groups of men blocked his path but quickly parted to let him through. Max and Patty were right behind him, counting down in their heads, getting ready for the fight. Maybe twenty paces to the exit, maybe thirty seconds until they were outside. Hunter kept his stride even, falling into the rhythm. Twenty-seven, twenty-six.

As he neared the door, he snatched a pool cue from the rack, reversing it in his hands, and swung in a complete arc, smashing it against the side of Patty's head. One. There was a sickening crunch of bone, followed by a spray of blood. Patty dropped like he'd been shot. Hunter swung again, this time at Max, aiming for his head. Max's arm came up to block the blow, but his forearm broke clean in half. He screamed. Hunter swung again, hitting him in the head. Three. Max staggered, and Hunter jabbed him in the face, knocking out a couple of teeth. Four. He backhanded the pool cue with all his strength, smashing Max's upper arm and breaking it. Five. Max collapsed beside Patty, and Hunter stood over them, raining down four more blows on ribs, collarbones, knees, and skulls. Six, seven, eight, nine. Nine powerful swings in six or seven seconds of sheer fury. Hit hard, hit early, get your retaliation in first.

The other men in the bar had turned away from the fight, but now they were cautiously edging closer again. Hunter turned in a slow circle, holding the cue at the ready, daring anyone to come at him. No one did. He bent down and took the ute keys from Max's pocket, then dropped the cue, letting it clatter to the floor. He shoved his way through the crowd and out the door, breathing hard. No one tried to stop him. Clearly, friendship had its limits here in Four Ways Shire.

Outside, the searing heat hit him like a wall, immediately bringing a sweat to his skin. He reached the ute, slid inside, started the engine, and backed out. He peeled away, heading south back towards scrublands and red dirt. No one followed.

The sun had already dipped below the horizon about an hour into his drive back, and by the time he passed beneath the ranch gate, it was fully dark. Every light in the Cream House was on, and two cars were parked in the yard. One belonged to the sergeant, a well-worn cruiser, while the other was a striking lime green Mercedes. The sergeant's car had its red and blue lights flashing, casting flickers across the yard. The Mercedes, illuminated by the porch light's harsh yellow glow, took on a sickly hue, almost like a corpse's skin. Swarms of moths fluttered everywhere, their paper-like wings filling the air and clustering around the porch bulbs in chaotic waves, resembling mini snowstorms as they constantly shifted and regrouped. Beneath their restless fluttering, the steady rhythm of night insects had already begun, their chorus filling the air.

The front door stood wide open, and the sound of lively conversation spilled from the foyer, indicating a small group inside. Hunter stepped closer and peered into the room. He saw the sergeant, Judy McMahon, Ryan, and Rosie, who was standing alone near the gun rack. She had changed out of her usual jeans and shirt, now dressed in a red and black sleeveless dress that ended at her knees. Her expression was blank, though it was clear from the tension in her features that she was overwhelmed by a mix of emotions. Across the room, a man in a suit stood by the red-framed mirror, allowing Hunter to see him from both the front and back. He was the likely driver of the Mercedes. Sleek and slightly pudgy, he wasn't particularly tall or short, dressed neatly in a pressed seersucker suit. He looked to be around thirty, with light hair that was carefully combed but noticeably receding from his high forehead. His complexion was pale, except for patches of sunburn on the higher parts of his face, as if he'd been out golfing in the early afternoon. His face was lit up with a broad, politician-like smile, the kind that suggested he had just been showered with compliments he was humbly pretending not to deserve.

Hunter lingered on the porch, deciding not to step inside. His weight caused the floorboards to creak loudly, and Ryan immediately noticed. He did a quick double-take, staring into the darkness before rushing out. He grabbed Hunter by the elbow and pulled him against the wall, out of sight from the foyer.

"What are you doing here?" Ryan asked.

"I work here, remember?" Hunter replied.

"Where are Max and Patty?"

"They quit."

Ryan stared at him, stunned. "They what?"

"They quit," Hunter repeated.

"What does that mean?"

"It means they chose to leave. They didn't want to work here anymore."

"Why would they do that?"

Hunter shrugged. "How should I know? Maybe they were just exercising their right to quit in a free labor market."

"What?"

Hunter didn't answer. Ryan's absence and the sound of voices on the porch drew people to the door. Judy McMahon was the first to appear, followed by the sergeant and the man in the seersucker suit. Rosie remained inside, standing near the rifles, still looking numb. The group fell silent when they saw Hunter. Judy wore the expression of someone facing an awkward social situation, the sergeant seemed confused, and the new guy, clearly the one in the suit, looked like he was trying to figure out who this newcomer was.

"What's going on?" Judy asked.

"This guy says Max and Patty quit on us," Ryan said.

"They wouldn't do that," Judy responded. "Why would they?"

The man in the suit stepped forward as though expecting an introduction.

“Did they give a reason?” Judy asked.

The sergeant focused on Hunter, his expression unreadable. Hunter said nothing, simply waiting.

“Well, I’m Tom Peacock,” the man in the suit announced, extending his hand. “I’m the Prosecutor up in Mount Kalka, and a friend of the family.”

“Warner’s oldest friend,” Judy added absently.

Hunter nodded and shook the man’s hand. “Mick Hunter,” he introduced himself. “I work here.”

Peacock clasped Hunter’s hand with both of his and gave a politician's smile, part genuine, part knowing.

“Are you registered to vote yet?” he asked. “If so, just letting you know I’m running for QLD Supreme Court judge in January. Would love to have your support.”

He chuckled, self-deprecating, the laugh of someone secure among friends, joking about how politics sometimes intrudes on politeness. Hunter withdrew his hand and gave a silent nod.

“Tom has worked so hard for us,” Judy chimed in. “And now he’s brought us some wonderful news.”

“Troy Bradley showed up?” Hunter asked.

“No, not yet,” Judy replied. “Something else entirely.”

“And nothing to do with the election,” Tom said. “You all understand that, right? Sure, it’s election season, but I’d do this for you anyway.”

“And you know we’d all vote for you anyway, Tom,” Judy added with a smile.

The group exchanged beaming smiles, but Hunter’s gaze

drifted to Rosie, who stood alone in the foyer, not smiling at all.

"You're getting Warner out early," Hunter said. "Tomorrow, I assume."

Tom Peacock ducked his head modestly, as if accepting a compliment. "That's right. They said weekend administration was impossible, but I managed to change their minds. First Sunday release in the system's history, but hey, there's a first time for everything."

"Tom's driving us up there," Judy said. "We're leaving soon, going to drive all night."

"We'll be there at seven in the morning, waiting right outside the prison gates," Tom added. "Old Warner's going to get a warm welcome."

"Is everyone going?" Hunter asked.

"I'm not," Rosie said quietly.

She had slipped out onto the porch, her hands gripping the railing as she leaned forward, staring into the dark horizon.

"I have to stay and look after Lahni," she explained.

"There's plenty of room in the car," Tom suggested. "Lahni can come along too."

Rosie shook her head. "I don't want her to see her father walking out of a prison door."

"Well, it's your choice," Judy said, her tone indifferent. "He's only your husband, after all."

Rosie didn't respond. She shivered slightly, as though the warm night air had suddenly turned cold.

"Then I guess I'll stay, too," Ryan said. "Keep an eye on things. Warner will understand."

Hunter watched him closely. Rosie abruptly turned and went back into the house, with Judy and Tom following behind her. The sergeant and Ryan remained on the porch, stepping closer together, subtly blocking the doorway to prevent Hunter from entering.

"So why did they quit?" Ryan asked.

Hunter glanced at both men and shrugged.

"Well, they didn't exactly quit," he said. "I was trying to soften the blow for the family. Truth is, we were in a bar, and they picked a fight with someone. You saw us there, right, sergeant?"

The sergeant nodded cautiously.

"It happened after you left," Hunter continued. "They picked a fight and lost."

"Who with?" Ryan asked. "Who was the guy?"

"The wrong guy."

"But who was he?"

"Some big guy," Hunter said. "Beat them up pretty bad. I think someone called an ambulance for them. They're probably in the hospital now. Maybe even dead. They lost, and they lost bad."

Ryan stared at him. "Who was the guy?"

"Just some stranger, minding his own business."

"Was it you?" Ryan asked.

"Me?" Hunter said, raising an eyebrow. "Why would they pick a fight with me?"

Ryan said nothing.

"What reason would they have to pick a fight with me, Ryan?"

Hunter asked again. "Think about it."

Ryan remained silent before finally turning and storming back into the house, slamming the door behind him. The sergeant stayed behind.

"So they got hurt bad," the sergeant said.

Hunter nodded. "Seems that way. You might want to make some calls and check. Then let people know—this is what happens when you pick fights with the wrong strangers."

The sergeant nodded again, still cautious.

"Maybe it's something you should remember, too," Hunter said. "Ryan told me folks around here settle things on their own. He said they don't like getting law enforcement involved. Said it's a tradition around here."

The sergeant was quiet for a moment.

"I suppose it could be," he said.

"Ryan said it definitely is. A real tradition."

The sergeant turned slightly.

"Well, you could put it that way," he said. "And I'm a man of tradition."

Hunter nodded.

"Glad to hear it," he said.

The sergeant paused briefly before heading down the porch steps, walking toward his car. He turned off the flashing lights, started the engine, and carefully maneuvered past the midnight black Mercedes before driving off through the gate. Hunter caught a whiff of unburned fuel in the air and heard the muffler popping as the car disappeared into the night. Soon, all he could hear were the cicadas chirping in the quiet.

Hunter stepped off the porch and made his way around to the

kitchen door, which was left open—either for ventilation or so the maid could listen in on the action. She stood just inside, near the coloured plastic strips that hung down in place of an insect screen.

"Hey," Hunter greeted her, recalling his long-held belief that being friendly with the kitchen staff was key to eating well. But she didn't respond, just eyed him warily.

"Let me guess," he said. "You only made two dinners for the bunkhouse."

Her silence was answer enough.

"Ryan told you I wasn't coming back, didn't he?"

She gave a small nod.

"Well, he was wrong," Hunter said. "It's Max and Patty who didn't come back. I'll have their dinners then—both of them. I'm hungry."

She hesitated before shrugging. "I'll bring them down in a minute."

He shook his head. "No need. I'll eat here. Save you the walk."

He pushed aside the plastic strips with the backs of his hands and stepped into the kitchen. The faint scent of chili from lunchtime still lingered.

"What's for dinner?" he asked.

"Steaks," she replied.

"Perfect," he said. "I prefer beef to dog."

"What?" she asked, confused.

"I like beef better than dingo," Hunter clarified with a grin.

"So do I," she muttered, before using pot holders to pull two plates from the warming oven. Each held a rib-eye steak, mashed potatoes, and a pile of fried greens. She placed them side by side on the kitchen table, setting a fork to the left of one plate and a knife to the far right of the other. It looked like a feast built for two.

"Patty was my cousin," she said quietly.

"He probably still is," Hunter said. "Max got it worse."

"Max was my cousin too," she added.

"I'm sorry to hear that," Hunter replied.

"Different branch of the family," she explained. "More distant. But they were both idiots."

Hunter nodded. "Not the sharpest tools in the shed."

"But the McMahons are sharp," she warned. "Whatever you're up to with the Islander woman, keep that in mind."

With that, she left him alone to eat.

When he finished, Hunter rinsed the plates and left them stacked in the sink. He walked down to the horse barn, wanting to stay near the house, and sat down on a hay bale in the stifling heat. The horses were restless at first but soon grew used to his presence, eventually falling asleep. He could hear the soft shuffling of hooves cease and the slow, rhythmic breaths of slumber.

Then he heard footsteps on the porch, followed by the sound of someone descending the steps and crossing the yard. He listened as car doors opened and shut, and the engine of the black Mercedes rumbled to life. Hunter got up and stepped to the barn door just in time to see the Mercedes turning in front of the house, lit by the porch lights. Tom Peacock was behind the wheel, with Judy McMahon seated next to him, her teased hair glowing under the lights, revealing the outline of her skull beneath the layers.

The big car drove out through the gate, turning right without stopping, its headlights bouncing through the dark as it accelerated down the road. Once it disappeared, the night insects resumed their familiar hum, and the only movement left was the fluttering of moths & mozzies around the porch lights.

Hunter waited by the barn door, wondering who would come for him first. He figured it would be Rosie, but it was Ryan who emerged from the house about five minutes after his mother had left to fetch Warner. Ryan walked down the steps and across the yard, heading toward the bunkhouse, his baseball cap worn backward again. Hunter stepped out of the barn, cutting him off.

"Horses need watering," Ryan said. "And their stalls need cleaning."

"Do it yourself," Hunter replied.

"What?"

"You heard me."

Ryan stopped in his tracks. "I'm not doing it."

"Then I'll make you," Hunter said, his tone low.

"What the hell is this?" Ryan asked, growing tense.

"It's a change," Hunter said calmly. "A big change for you, Ryan. The moment you sent Max and Patty after me, you crossed a line. Now, you're in a different situation. You do exactly what I tell you to do from here on out."

Ryan said nothing, his eyes locked on Hunter.

Hunter leaned in, his voice firm. "When I say jump, you don't ask how high—you just start jumping. Got it? I own you now."

Ryan remained still, his face set. Hunter raised his right hand, swinging a slow, deliberate slap. Ryan flinched, ducking into Hunter's left hand, which swiftly knocked the ball cap from his head.

"Now go look after the horses," Hunter ordered. "And after that, you can sleep in the barn with them. If I see you before breakfast, I'll break your legs."

Ryan stood frozen.

"Who are you going to call?" Hunter asked mockingly. "The maid? The sergeant?"

Ryan didn't answer. The oppressive night closed in around them, the vast isolation in the outback of Four Ways Shire stretching out in all directions. A small town of only a hundred and fifty souls, most of them scattered kilometers beyond the dark horizon.

"Okay," Ryan whispered, finally giving in.

He turned and walked toward the barn. Hunter tossed his ball cap into the dirt and strolled back to the house. The porch lights blinded him for a moment, and the large moths flitted out to greet him, swarming the light like paper clouds.

****

Two-thirds of the group that had been watching him knew he was on the move. They had made improvements compared to their previous attempts. The woman had checked the map and dismissed the idea of approaching from the west, knowing the Ford Falcon wouldn't survive the desert terrain. Besides, hiding a kilometer away made no sense, especially in the dark. It was much smarter to drive directly to the house, stopping just a hundred meters shy, long enough for two men to jump out, then turn back north while the others moved toward the ranch gate, sneaking into the small ditches close to the road.

It was the two men on foot. They had night-vision gear, nothing fancy, just commercial-grade binoculars equipped with infrared technology, bought from a camping catalog. The devices picked up the heat rising from the ground, making Hunter appear like a shimmering figure as he walked through the night.

CHAPTER 8

Hunter found Rosie sitting alone in the parlor. The room was dim, with thick, stifling air. She was seated at a heavy stained table, her posture perfect—back straight, forearms resting lightly on the wooden surface. Her eyes were fixed on a point on the wall, where there was nothing to see.

"Twice," she said. "I feel cheated twice. First it was supposed to be a year, and then it was nothing. Then they said forty-eight hours, but it's really only twenty-four."

"You can still leave," Hunter suggested.

"Now it's less than twenty-four," she continued. "Sixteen hours, maybe. I'll have breakfast alone, but he'll be back for lunch."

"Sixteen hours is plenty of time," he said. "You could be anywhere in sixteen hours."

"Lahni's asleep," she said softly. "I can't wake her, throw her in a car, and run forever, being chased by the cops."

Hunter didn't respond.

"I'm going to try to face it," she said. "Start fresh. I plan to tell him that enough is enough. If he lays a hand on me again, I'll divorce him. However long it takes."

"That's the way to go," Hunter encouraged.

"Do you think I can?" she asked.

"I believe anyone can do anything if they want it badly enough," he replied.

"I want it," she said firmly. "Believe me, I want it."

Silence settled between them. Hunter glanced around the room, taking in the atmosphere.

"Why is everything painted cream?" he asked.

"Because it was cheap," she replied. "In the fifties, everyone was painting their houses and fences creams and ivories. It was the cheapest paint in the store with little colour added to it beyond the base white."

"I thought they were rich, back then, with the oil."

"They were rich. They still are—richer than you could imagine. But they're stingy."

Hunter nodded, noticing the spots where the staining had worn away to reveal the wood underneath. "I can see that."

Rosie nodded again but said nothing.

"Last chance, Rosie," he said gently. "We could leave right now. No one's here to call the coppers. By the time they get back, we could be anywhere."

"Ryan's here," she reminded him.

"He's staying in the barn."

"He'd hear the car."

"We could take his phone."

"He'd chase us. He could reach the sergeant in two hours."

"We could disable the other cars."

"He'd hear us."

"I could tie him up," Hunter said lightly. "Or drown him in a horse trough."

She gave a bitter smile. "But you won't drown Warner."

Hunter shrugged. "Figure of speech."

Rosie was quiet for a moment, deep in thought, before scraping back her chair and standing up. "Come see Lahni," she said. "She looks so beautiful when she's asleep."

She passed by him and took his hand, leading him through the kitchen and into the rear lobby. They walked up the back stairs, past the sound of a slowly turning fan, down a long, hot hallway to Lahni's door. Rosie eased it open with her foot, positioning Hunter so he could see inside.

A night-light plugged into a low outlet cast a soft orange glow across the room, revealing the child sprawled on her back, arms thrown above her head. The sheet had slipped off, and her rabbit-print T-shirt had ridden up, exposing a small band of caramel skin at her waist. Her hair was a tousled mess across the pillow, her long dark lashes resting on her cheeks, her mouth slightly open.

"She's six and a half," Rosie whispered. "She needs this—her own bed, in her own place. I can't make her live like a fugitive."

Hunter said nothing.

"Do you understand?" she asked softly.

He shrugged. Not really. At six and a half, he'd lived like a fugitive his whole life, moving from one military town to another with little notice depending on where his fathers consultancy took their family. He remembered mornings when he got ready for school only to end up on a plane halfway around the world hours later. He'd fallen asleep in strange bedrooms, not knowing where he was until his mother told him the next morning. It hadn't hurt him.

Or maybe it had.

"It's your decision," he said.

Rosie pulled him back into the hallway and gently closed Lahni's door behind them. "I'll show you where I hid the gun," she said. "Tell me if you approve."

She led him down the hallway, the sound of the air conditioner loud around them. As they walked, a warm breeze blew from a nearby vent, and Hunter watched Rosie's dress sway with each step. Her heels made the tendons in the back of her legs more defined. Her hair flowed down her back, blending with the dark pattern of her dress. She turned left, then right, leading him through an archway and down another set of stairs.

"Where are we going?" Hunter asked.

"Separate wing," she explained. "It was added later—by Warner's grandfather, I think."

The staircase led them to a narrow ground-floor hallway that connected to a large master suite, as big as a small house. There was a walk in wardrobe, a spacious bathroom, and a sitting room with a sofa and two armchairs. Beyond the sitting room, an archway led to a bedroom.

"In here," she said, guiding him into the bedroom.

"See what I mean?" she asked. "We're far from anywhere. No one hears anything. And I try to stay quiet. If I scream, he hits harder."

Hunter nodded, glancing around the room. The window faced east, with the sound of insects buzzing beyond the screen and bouncing off the glass. The king-sized bed stood close to the window, flanked by side tables, and across from it stood a chest-high dresser, likely made of hardwood from a hundred years ago.

"Queensland red mahogany," Rosie explained motioning towards the furniture. "It's what happens when eucalyptus grows near the coast."

"You could have been a teacher," Hunter said. "You're always teaching me things."

Rosie gave a faint smile. "I thought about it, back in my uni days. It was an option in my other life."

She opened the top-right drawer.

"I moved the gun," she said. "I took your advice. Keeping it in the bedside table was too risky—Lahni could have found it. This is too high for her."

Hunter stepped closer, glancing into the drawer. It was wide and deep, filled with neatly folded, delicate items of lingerie. The pistol lay on top of them, the mother-of-pearl grips looking right at home.

"You could have just told me where it was," Hunter said. "You didn't have to show me."

She was silent for a moment. Then she asked, "He's going to want sex, isn't he?"

Hunter didn't reply.

"He's been locked up for a year and a half," she continued. "But I'm going to say no."

Hunter remained quiet.

"That's a woman's right, isn't it?" she asked. "To say no?"

"Of course," he said.

"Even if she's married?"

"In most places, yes," he replied.

There was another pause.

"And it's also her right to say yes, right?" she asked.

"Equally," Hunter agreed.

"I'd say yes to you," she said.

"I'm not asking," he replied.

Rosie hesitated. "Can I ask you?"

Hunter met her gaze. "Depends on why."

"Because I want to," she said simply. "I want to go to bed with you."

"Why?"

"Honestly? Just because I want to," she admitted. "And maybe to hurt Warner a little. In secret. In my heart."

Hunter said nothing.

"Before he gets back," she added.

Still, Hunter didn't respond.

"And because Ryan already thinks we're doing it," she said. "I figure, why take the blame without getting the fun?"

Hunter stayed silent.

"I just want a little fun," she said softly. "Before it all starts again."

He remained quiet.

"No strings attached," she said. "I'm not asking for anything to change. Not with your decision. Not with Warner."

"It wouldn't change anything," Hunter said.

Rosie looked away. "So what's your answer?"

Hunter studied her profile, her face blank. It was as though she had run out of options, leaving only raw instinct. He'd seen this look before, in people faced with an inevitable disaster. When the warning sirens blared in their minds, they often turned to this as their last, instinctive choice.

"No," he said.

Rosie stayed quiet for a long moment. Then she spoke again.

"Will you at least stay with me?"

****

The killing crew moved fifty kilometers closer to Mount Kalka in the dead of night. They did so discreetly, hours after booking a second night at their initial location. This was the woman's preferred method—using six false names and two overlapping sets of motel records to create enough confusion to keep them safe.

They drove east along the highway, passing the interchange, and continued toward Normanton until they spotted the first group of motels catering to the Kalka state recreation area. These motels were far enough from the tourist spot to be affordable and anonymous, the kind of places where décor wasn't a priority and service was impersonal—but they were clean, decent, and filled with people just like themselves. That was exactly what the woman wanted. Blending in was her specialty. She had an instinct for choosing the right places. They stopped at the second motel they came across, where the small dark man paid cash for two rooms.

Hunter awoke on Warner McMahon's sofa as Sunday's dawn began to break. The bedroom window faced east, and the night insects had already fallen silent as the sky brightened. The bed sheets were damp and tangled, but Rosie wasn't under them. He could hear the shower running in the bathroom and the smell of freshly brewed coffee hung in the air.

He stood up, stretched, and wandered through the archway into the bedroom. Rosie's dress was still on the floor. Hunter moved to the window to check the weather—it hadn't changed. The sky remained hazy with heat. He strolled back to the sitting area, where a built in nook in the corner held a small coffee machine. Two mugs sat nearby, upturned and accompanied by spoons, much like a hotel setup. The bathroom door remained closed, and the sound of the shower was still loud behind it.

Hunter filled a mug with coffee and wandered into the wardrobe. There were two large open areas, one on each side. Long alcoves with row after row of hangers and shelves. He looked into the left alcove first—it was Rosie's. Dresses, pants, blouses, and shoes filled the space. He turned to the right, which must be Warner's closet. Inside, he found a dozen suits, rows of denim jackets, jeans, stacks of T-shirts, folded button-up shirts, neckties, and belts with fancy buckles. Dusty shoes lined the floor, appearing to be around size eleven. Hunter shifted his coffee cup to the other hand and examined one of Warner's suit jackets—it was a forty-four long, meant for someone about six feet two or three, weighing around one hundred ninety to two hundred pounds. Warner wasn't especially large, but he was a foot taller and twice the weight of his wife—not exactly a fair matchup.

Hunter's eyes landed on a photo frame lying face-down on a stack of shirts. He turned it over to reveal a five-by-seven color photograph under a cream-colored mat, encased in a lacquered wooden frame. The photo showed three young men, somewhere between boyhood and adulthood, probably seventeen or eighteen years old. They were standing close together, leaning against the fender of an old ute, gazing expectantly at the camera as if waiting for the self-timer to snap the shot. They looked full of youthful energy, with their whole lives ahead of them. One of them was Tom Peacock, slimmer and more muscular than he was now, with a lot more hair. Hunter assumed the other two were Troy Bradley and Warner McMahon. Bradley was shorter and stockier, while Warner resembled a younger version of Ryan.

He heard the shower turn off, placed the photo back on the stack, and closed the closet door. Moving back to the sitting area, he waited a moment before Rosie emerged from the bathroom in a cloud of steam. She was wrapped in two towels, one around her body and the other like a turban around her hair. Hunter watched her, unsure of what to say.

"Good morning," she greeted him.

"To you too," he replied.

She unwrapped the towel from her hair, letting it fall wet and straight around her shoulders.

"But it's not a good morning, is it?" she said. "It's a bad morning."

"I guess," Hunter agreed.

"He could be walking out of the gate right now."

Hunter checked his watch—it was almost seven.

"Any minute now," he said.

"You can use the shower if you want," she offered. "I need to see to Lahni."

"Okay."

He stepped into the bathroom, which was large and decorated with reconstituted marble that had a gold tint. It reminded him of a place he had once stayed in Gold Coast. After using the toilet and rinsing his mouth, Hunter stripped off his clothes and stepped into the enormous shower stall, which was enclosed by frost-tinted glass. A hubcap-sized showerhead was positioned above him, with additional water jets in each corner aimed directly at him. When he turned the faucet, the water roared to life, hitting him from all directions like a waterfall. The side jets pulsed hot and cold, making it impossible to hear himself think. He washed quickly, soaped his hair, and rinsed off, then shut it down.

Grabbing a towel from a nearby stack, he dried off as best as he could in the humidity before wrapping the towel around his waist and stepping into the dressing area. Rosie was there, buttoning her white shirt. She was dressed in white pants with gold jewelry, her skin dark and her hair already curling in the heat.

"That was fast," she remarked.

"Hell of a shower," Hunter replied.

"Warner chose it," she said. "I hate it. There's so much water, I can barely breathe in there."

She closed her closet and twisted slightly, examining her reflection in the mirrored doors.

"You look good," Hunter said.

"Do I look Islander enough?" she asked, gesturing at her white clothes.

Hunter didn't reply.

"No jeans today," she said. "I'm tired of pretending I was born a cowgirl in Mount Kalka."

"You look good," Hunter repeated.

"Seven hours," she said, glancing at the clock. "Six and a half if Tom drives fast."

Hunter nodded. "I'm going to find Ryan."

She stretched up on her toes and kissed him on the cheek.

"Thanks for staying," she said softly. "It helped me."

He didn't reply.

"Join us for breakfast in twenty minutes," she said, before walking out of the room to wake her daughter.

Hunter dressed and made his way back into the house, taking a different route. The place was like a maze. He ended up walking through a living room he hadn't seen before, which led him into the foyer with the mirror and the rifles. He opened the front door and stepped out onto the porch. The heat was already intense. The sun hung low on his right, casting harsh shadows that made the yard look uneven and pocked.

He walked down to the barn and pushed through the door. The heat and the stench inside were as bad as ever, but the horses were awake and restless. They had been well cared for, with clean stalls, fresh water, and full feed troughs. Hunter found Ryan asleep in one of the empty stalls, curled up on clean straw.

"Rise and shine, little brother," Hunter called.

Ryan stirred, sitting up, disoriented and tense as the memories of the previous day returned. His clothes were dirty, and hay clung to him.

"Sleep well?" Hunter asked.

"They'll be back soon," Ryan said. "What do you think will happen then?"

Hunter smiled. "You mean, am I going to tell them I made you clean the barn and sleep in the straw?"

"You wouldn't dare."

"No, I guess I wouldn't," Hunter said. "So are you going to tell them?"

Ryan stayed silent, and Hunter smiled again.

"No, I didn't think you would," Hunter said. "Stay here until noon, then I'll let you into the house so you can clean up for the big event."

"What about breakfast?"

"You don't get any."

"But I'm hungry."

"Then eat the horse food. Turns out there's plenty of it."

Hunter left the barn and headed back to the kitchen, where the maid was brewing coffee and heating a skillet.

"Pancakes," she said. "That's all I can manage. They'll want a big lunch, so that's where my morning's going."

"Pancakes are fine," Hunter replied.

He walked into the silent parlor, listening for any sounds from above. Rosie and Lahni should have been stirring by now, but the house remained eerily quiet. Hunter tried to picture the house's layout in his head, but it was too chaotic. It seemed like the original ranch house had been expanded haphazardly over time, resulting in a disjointed maze of rooms and hallways.

The maid came in with a stack of plates—four of them, along with silverware and napkins piled on top.

"You're eating in here, I assume," she said.

Hunter nodded. "But not Ryan. He's staying in the barn."

"Why?"

"I think a horse is sick."

The maid sighed, annoyed, and removed one of the plates from the stack. "So I'll have to bring it down to him, then?"

"I'll take it," Hunter said. "You're busy."

He followed her back to the kitchen, where she flipped four pancakes onto a plate, added some butter, mango chunks and maple syrup, and handed it to him. Hunter wrapped the utensils in a napkin, grabbed the plate, and headed back out into the heat. He found Ryan exactly where he'd left him, sitting up, doing nothing.

"What's this?" Ryan asked.

"Breakfast," Hunter said. "I had a change of heart. Because you're going to do something for me."

"Yeah? What?"

"There's going to be a big lunch for Warner's homecoming," Hunter said.

Ryan nodded. "I suppose so."

"You're going to invite me as your guest. Act like I'm your buddy."

"I am?"

"Yep, if you want those pancakes—and if you want to walk without a limp for the rest of your life."

Ryan stayed quiet.

"And dinner, too," Hunter added. "You get it?"

"Her husband's coming home," Ryan said. "It's over, isn't it?"

"You're jumping to conclusions, Ryan. I'm not interested in Rosie. I just need to talk to Warner."

"About what?"

"Just do it, okay?" Hunter said.

Ryan shrugged. "Whatever."

Hunter handed him the plate of pancakes and headed back to the house.

Rosie and Lahni were seated at the table. Lahni's hair was damp from her shower, and she was dressed in a yellow seersucker dress.

“My daddy’s coming home today,” Lahni said. “He’s on his way right now.”

Hunter nodded. “I heard.”

“I thought it was going to be tomorrow, but it’s today.”

Rosie stared blankly at the wall, saying nothing. The maid brought in pancakes on a platter, serving two to Lahni, three to Rosie, and four to Hunter. Then she took the platter back to the kitchen.

“I was going to stay home from school tomorrow,” Lahni said. “Can I still?”

Rosie didn’t respond.

“Mum? Can I still?”

Rosie turned her gaze to Hunter, as though he had spoken. Her face was blank, reminding him of a guy he once knew who had gone to the eye doctor for trouble reading. The doctor had spotted a tumor, arranging for him to have his eye removed the next day. Knowing the certainty of what was to come had haunted him—the dread and anticipation were worse than the actual event.

“Mummy? Can I?” Lahni asked again.

“I guess,” Rosie said.

“What?”

“Mummy, you’re not listening. Are you excited too?”

“Yes,” Rosie said.

“So can I?”

“Yes,” Rosie repeated.

Lahni turned to her food, eating hungrily. Hunter picked at his pancakes, watching Rosie, who barely touched hers.

"I'm going to see my pony now," Lahni announced.

She scrambled off her chair and dashed out of the room. Hunter heard the front door open, then the sound of her footsteps on the porch. He finished his meal, while Rosie sat there, holding her fork in midair as though she had forgotten how to use it.

"Will you talk to him?" she asked. "Warner, that is."

"Sure."

"I think he needs to know it's not a secret anymore."

"I agree."

"Will you look at him while you talk to him?"

"I guess so."

"Good. You should. You've got gunfighter's eyes—maybe like Benjamin Blackman had. Let him see them. Let him know what's coming."

"We've been over this," Hunter reminded her.

"I know."

Rosie got up and left the room, and Hunter set about killing time. It felt like waiting for an air raid. He walked out onto the porch and looked down the road where it disappeared into the horizon. The morning air was still clear, and there was no heat shimmer over the asphalt yet.

He sat down on the porch swing, positioning himself sideways so he faced the ranch gate. He put one leg up on the seat, the other on the floor, and did what most soldiers do when they're waiting for the action—he fell asleep.

Rosie woke him about an hour later, touching his shoulder. Hunter opened his eyes and saw her standing over him. She had changed into pressed blue jeans, a checked shirt, and croc-skin boots with a matching belt. Her hair was tied back, and she had applied pale powder and blue eye shadow.

"I changed my mind," she said. "I don't want you to talk to him. Not yet."

"Why not?"

"It might set him off if he knows someone else knows."

"You didn't think that before."

"I've thought about it more. I think it'll be worse if we start that way. It's better coming from me—at least at first."

"You sure?"

She nodded. "Let me talk to him first."

"When?"

"Tonight," she said. "I'll tell you tomorrow how it went."

Hunter sat up, planting both feet on the ground.

"You were pretty sure you'd have a busted nose by tomorrow," he said.

"I think this is best."

"Why did you change your clothes?"

"These are better," she said. "I don't want to provoke him."

"You look like a cowgirl born in Mount Kalka."

"He likes me like this."

"And dressing like yourself would provoke him?"

She made a defeated face.

"Don't chicken out, Rosie," Hunter urged. "Stand and fight."

"I will," she promised. "Tonight, I'll tell him I won't take it anymore."

Hunter said nothing.

"So don't talk to him today, okay?" she asked.

He looked away. "It's your call."

"It's better this way," she said, heading back inside.

Hunter stared south at the road. Sitting down, he couldn't see as far as before, and the heat shimmer had begun to rise from the asphalt.

Rosie woke him again an hour later. She hadn't changed her clothes, but the makeup was gone.

"You think I'm doing this wrong," she said.

Hunter rubbed his face. "I think it would be better if it was all out in the open. He should know that someone else knows. If not me, then his family."

"I can't tell them."

"No, I guess you can't."

"So what should I do?"

"Let me talk to him."

"Not right away. It'll make things worse. Promise me you won't."

Hunter nodded. "It's your call. But promise me something too—talk to him tonight. For sure. And if he starts anything, get out of the room and scream. Make sure we all hear you. It'll embarrass him. It'll change the dynamic."

"You think so?"

"He can't pretend nothing's happening if everyone hears you."

"He'll deny it. He'll say I was having a nightmare."

“But deep down, he’ll know we know.”

Rosie stayed silent.

“Promise me, Rosie,” Hunter insisted. “Or I’ll talk to him first.”

After a moment, she agreed. “Okay, I promise.”

Hunter settled back on the swing, trying to sleep for another hour. But his internal clock told him the time was drawing near. Warner would have been released by seven, and the drive from Townsville to the ranch wouldn’t take more than six or seven hours—especially for someone like Tom Peacock, who likely wasn’t worried about speeding tickets.

It was almost noon, and Hunter saw Ryan leaving the barn, walking stiffly in the bright sunlight. He was carrying his breakfast plate, his movements slow. He passed Hunter without a word, heading into the house.

At twelve-thirty, Lahni returned from the paddocks. Her yellow dress was dirty, and her hair matted with dust.

“I’ve been jumping,” she said proudly. “I pretend I’m a horse and run around the jumps as fast as I can.”

“Come here,” Hunter said.

She stood close, and he brushed the dirt from her dress.

“Maybe you should shower again,” he suggested. “Get your hair clean.”

“Why?”

“So you look nice for your daddy when he gets home.”

She thought about it for a moment, then nodded. “Okay.”

“Be quick.”

She stared at him for a second before running into the house.

By a quarter to one, Ryan came back outside, clean and wearing fresh jeans and a new T-shirt. He had on snake-skin boots with silver accents and a backwards maroon cap with a "State of Origin 2005" flash on the side.

“They lost, right?” Hunter said.

“Who?”

“The Maroons. In 2005.”

“So?”

“So nothing, Ryan.”

The door opened again, and Rosie came out with Lahni. Rosie was still in her cowgirl outfit, with makeup back on. Lahni’s hair was clean and tied back with a ribbon, and she was still in her yellow seersucker dress. Rosie held her daughter’s hand, looking shaky as if her legs were weak.

Hunter stood up and gestured for her to sit down. Lahni climbed up beside her. No one spoke. Hunter walked over to the porch rail, scanning the road. In the distance, a dust cloud appeared—a long, red teardrop of dust rising and falling with the curves of the road.

The dust cloud grew until Hunter could make out the lime green Mercedes leading it. It shimmered through the heat, slowing as it neared the gate. The car braked sharply, its front end dipping low before turning in. The dust drifted southward, as if confused by the sudden change in direction.

The Mercedes crunched over the gravel, and sunlight flashed off the windshield. Inside, Hunter could see three figures—Tom Peacock at the wheel, Judy McMahon in the back, and a large, pale man in the front passenger seat. He had short, fair hair and wore a plain blue shirt, craning his neck and smiling broadly.

Warner McMahon had arrived home.

CHAPTER 9

The Mercedes rolled to a stop by the porch, the suspension settling as the engine went quiet. No one moved inside the car at first. Then, in unison, three doors opened, and the passengers emerged. Ryan and Lahni hurried down the steps of the porch to meet them, while Hunter stepped back, and Rosie slowly rose and took his place by the rail.

Warner McMahon left his door ajar and stretched in the sun, as anyone would after a year and a half in a cell and six hours on the road. His skin was pale from his time in prison, and he had gained weight from the starch-heavy meals, but it was clear he was Ryan's brother. The resemblance was unmistakable—the same hair, the same face, the same build and posture. Ryan walked right up to him, arms wide, and embraced him tightly. Warner returned the hug, and they staggered, laughing and slapping each other's backs, as though celebrating a victory on a suburban lawn after a local footy game.

Lahni, unsure, hesitated in the background, her movements uncertain amid the noise and activity. Warner let go of Ryan and knelt, arms open, inviting her closer. Hunter noticed Rosie's expression—closed off and unreadable. Lahni stood frozen, her hands in her mouth, but after a moment, she made a decision and ran into Warner's arms. He lifted her into the air, kissed her cheek, and spun her in circles. Rosie let out a soft sound, barely audible, and turned her gaze away.

After setting Lahni back down, Warner glanced up at the porch, a triumphant smile on his face. Behind him, Ryan was chatting with their mother and Tom Peacock, the three of them huddled near the car. Warner, however, extended his hand, beckoning his wife to come closer. She withdrew further into the shadows of the porch.

"You should talk to him," she whispered to Hunter.

"Make a decision," Hunter replied, keeping his voice low.

"I'll see how it goes," she said, taking a deep breath and forcing a smile. She then skipped down the steps, took Warner's hands, and folded into his arms. Their kiss was long enough to clarify their relationship but brief enough to avoid any display of deep passion. Meanwhile, Ryan and Judy had finished their conversation with Tom and were now walking toward the porch. Ryan looked anxious, and Judy, fanning herself, gave Hunter a hard, meaningful look.

"I understand Ryan invited you to lunch," she said as she reached the top of the steps.

"That was kind of him," Hunter responded.

"Yes, very thoughtful. But today is strictly a family affair."

"Oh, really?" Hunter replied.

"Even Tom isn't staying," she added, as though it confirmed some unspoken fact.

Hunter remained silent.

"I'm sorry," Judy continued, "but the maid will bring your meal down to the bunkhouse, as usual. You can all get together tomorrow."

Hunter paused, then nodded. "Alright," he said, "I wouldn't want to intrude."

Judy smiled, while Ryan avoided Hunter's gaze. The two of them entered the house, and Hunter made his way down the porch steps and into the searing midday heat. It felt like a furnace. Tom Peacock stood alone by the Mercedes, ready to leave.

“Hot enough for you?” he asked with a politician’s practiced grin.

“I’ll manage,” Hunter replied batting at some persistent flies.

“There’s a storm coming.”

“So I’ve heard.”

Tom nodded. “Hunter, right?”

Hunter nodded in return. “I guess things went smoothly in Townsville?”

“Like clockwork,” Tom said. “But I’m beat. Queensland is a huge place—you forget that until you’re driving across it. You could drive for days. I’m letting them have their celebrations and heading off to bed.”

Hunter nodded again. “Maybe I’ll see you around.”

“And don’t forget to vote in January—preferably for me,” Tom added with a familiar bashful smile before he waved at Warner. Warner, in response, mimicked a gun with his fingers, pretending to shoot Tom. Tom climbed into the Mercedes, started it up, and drove off, leaving a cloud of dust in his wake.

Hunter watched as Warner strolled back across the yard, holding Lahni’s hand in one and Rosie’s in the other. His eyes were squinted against the bright sun. Rosie was quiet, but Lahni chattered away as they passed Hunter and walked up the steps, side by side. At the door, Warner allowed Lahni to enter first, then guided Rosie in after her. The door closed behind them with a firm thud, raising a small puff of dust from the porch.

For the next few hours, Hunter saw no one except the maid, who brought him lunch and later collected the empty plate. From time to time, he glanced at the house from the bathroom window, but it remained sealed and silent. Late in the afternoon, he heard voices near the horse barn and went to investigate, finding Warner, Rosie, and Lahni outside. The heat was stifling, and Warner looked restless, scuffing his feet in the dirt. Rosie appeared tense, her face slightly flushed, either from stress or the intense heat. There was also the possibility she had been slapped.

“Lahni, let’s go see your pony,” Rosie said.

“I saw him this morning, Mum,” Lahni replied.

“But I didn’t,” Rosie insisted, extending her hand. “So let’s go see him again.”

Lahni hesitated, confused, but eventually took Rosie’s hand. They walked away, Rosie mouthing the words *talk to him* as they passed Warner, who turned to face Hunter, as if noticing him for the first time.

“Warner McMahon,” he said, offering his hand.

Up close, Warner resembled an older, sharper version of Ryan—perhaps more intelligent, though not in a kind way. It wasn’t hard to imagine a streak of cruelty behind those eyes. Hunter shook his hand, feeling its softness and size, more suited to a bully than a fighter.

“Mick Hunter,” he said. “How was prison?”

For a split second, surprise flashed in Warner’s eyes before he quickly regained control. Impressive, Hunter thought.

“It wasn’t great,” Warner replied. “Ever been inside yourself?”

Hunter smiled. “Thankfully no, but I’ve been on the otherside of the bars before.”

Warner nodded. “Ryan said you were a ranger. Now you’re a drifter.”

"I have to be. I didn't have a wealthy father."

Warner paused. "You were in the military, right? SAS?"

"That's right."

"Never had much respect for the military myself."

"Yeah, I gathered that."

"How's that?"

"Well, you didn't seem too keen on paying for it."

Warner's eyes flickered briefly with annoyance before calming again. "It's a shame you gave in and got out early."

"If you can't handle the time, don't commit the crime," Hunter said.

"You got out of the army, didn't you? Maybe you couldn't handle it either."

Hunter smiled. "I didn't have a choice—they kicked me out."

"Why?"

"I broke the law, too," Hunter said. "A colonel was beating his wife—a good woman, but he was the sneaky type, did it in secret. I couldn't prove it, but I wasn't going to let him get away with it. So I caught him alone one night. He's in a wheelchair now, drinks through a straw."

Warner was silent, his expression hardening. But after a long pause, he said, "Well, at least I can feel better knowing my taxes didn't go to you."

"You don't approve?"

"Of either of you," Warner said coldly, and then turned and walked away.

Hunter returned to the bunkhouse, where the maid brought him dinner and later came back for the plate. Darkness fell outside, and the air was filled with the usual chorus of night insects. He lay on his bed, sweating as the temperature stayed a solid hundred degrees. From time to time, he heard distant dingo howls, the screams of wild cats, and the faint flapping of bat wings.

Then he caught the sound of light footsteps on the stairs. He sat up just as Rosie appeared in the doorway. Her hand was pressed against her chest as if she was out of breath, panicked, or both.

"Warner talked to Ryan," she said. "For a long time."

"Did he hit you?" Hunter asked, his tone sharp.

Rosie's hand moved to her cheek. "No," she said.

"Did he?"

She looked away, her voice dropping. "Well, just once. But not hard."

"I should go break his arms," Hunter muttered.

"He called the sergeant."

"Who did?"

"Warner. Just now, after he talked to Ryan."

"About me?"

She nodded. "He wants you gone."

"It's fine," Hunter said calmly. "The sergeant won't do anything."

"You sure?"

Hunter nodded. "I handled things with him before."

Rosie hesitated. "I have to get back now. He thinks I'm with Lahni."

"Want me to come with you?"

"Not yet. Let me talk to him first."

"Don't let him hit you again, Rosie. Come get me if you need to—or make noise, scream and shout if it comes to that."

Rosie turned to leave, pausing at the top of the stairs. "I will, I promise. You're sure about the sergeant?"

"Don't worry," Hunter reassured her. "He won't do a thing."

But that reassurance proved wrong. About ninety minutes later, Hunter learned that the sergeant had escalated the matter to the Mount Kalka regional command. He heard it when a police cruiser turned under the gate, heading down the road toward the bunkhouse. The sound of the engine and tires crunching on the dusty track grew closer. Hunter got up from his bed and went downstairs, just in time to be caught in the beam of the spotlight mounted on the car's windshield. It illuminated him clearly, casting a bright cone of light across the parked farm tractors.

Two officers stepped out of the car, and Hunter immediately sensed they were a different breed from the sergeant. Younger, fitter, more professional. Both were of medium height, their builds a balance between lean and muscular. Their uniforms were immaculate, and they carried themselves with a military precision. One was a senior constable, the other an Aboriginal constable armed with a shotgun.

"What's this?" Hunter called out.

"Step over to the car," the senior constable ordered.

Hunter kept his hands visible as he approached. "What's going on?"

"A property owner has requested we remove a trespasser."

"I'm not trespassing. I work here."

"Well, I guess you're fired now. So that makes you a trespasser, and we're here to remove you."

"That's a job for the Mount Kalka police?" Hunter asked, incredulous.

"In a rural community like this, we assist the local guys on their days off or with serious crimes."

"Trespassing is a serious crime?"

"No," the constable replied dryly. "But today's the Four Ways sergeant's day off."

The moths had gathered around the spotlight, flitting in the heat from the bulb and occasionally bumping against Hunter's arm. He could feel their papery wings brushing against his skin.

"Fine, I'll leave," Hunter said. "I'll walk out to the road."

"If you do, then you'll be a vagrant on a Shire highway—that's illegal too, especially at night."

"So where are you taking me?"

"You're leaving the Shire. We'll drop you off in Mount Kalka."

"They owe me wages. I never got paid."

"We'll stop at the house first."

Hunter glanced over at the constable with the shotgun, who stood at the ready, professional and alert. Then he looked to the senior constable, whose hand rested on the butt of his gun. In his mind, he pictured Ryan and Warner, both smug and triumphant, grinning at each other. But it was Judy he could almost see, silently mouthing the word *checkmate*.

"There's an issue," Hunter said. "The daughter-in-law is being abused by her husband. It's been going on for a while, and he just got out of prison today."

"Has she filed a complaint?"

"She's too scared. The sergeant is a good ol' boy, and she's an Islander from New South Wales."

"There's nothing we can do without a formal complaint," the senior constable said.

Hunter glanced at the constable, who just shrugged. "He's right. We can't act unless the victim comes forward."

"I'm telling you now," Hunter pressed.

The constable shook his head. "It needs to come from her."

"Step into the car," the senior constable said firmly.

"You don't have to do this."

"Yes, we do."

"I need to stay—for her sake."

"Look, we've been informed you're no longer welcome here. That's all there is to it."

"The woman wants me here, as a protector."

"Is she the property owner?"

"No."

"Are you officially employed by her?"

Hunter didn't respond.

"So get in the car."

"She's in danger."

"If we get a call, we'll respond."

"She can't call. And even if she does, the sergeant won't pass it on."

"Then there's nothing more we can do. Now, into the car."

Hunter remained silent.

The senior constable opened the back door and paused. "You could always come back tomorrow," he said quietly. "No law against trying to get rehired."

Hunter glanced once more at the shotgun, admiring its wide, formidable barrel, then at the Glock on the senior constable's hip. In his mind, he saw the same smug grins on the faces of Ryan and Warner. And Judy, still silently mouthing *checkmate*.

"Alright," Hunter said. "But I'm not happy about it."

"Most of our passengers aren't," the constable replied.

With that, he guided Hunter into the back seat, pressing down on his head as he ducked into the car. The interior was cold, with a heavy wire barrier separating the back from the front. The door handles and window controls had been removed, and small aluminum panels were riveted over the gaps. The seat was covered in vinyl, and the car smelled strongly of disinfectant, mixed with the sharp odor of an air freshener shaped like a pine tree hanging from the rearview mirror. A radar device was mounted on the dash, and quiet chatter came through the radio.

The two officers climbed into the front seats, and the car rolled toward the house. The McMahon family—Judy, Ryan, Warner, and Rosie—stood lined up on the porch, watching Hunter go. They were all smiling, except for Rosie. The car stopped at the foot of the steps, and the senior constable buzzed his window down.

"This man says you owe him wages," he called out.

There was a brief silence, broken only by the sound of insects.

"Tell him to sue us," Ryan replied coldly.

Hunter leaned forward against the wire barrier. He called out, "Rosie, sapos i gat hevi, ringim ol dispela man stret!"

The senior constable turned his head. “What did you say?”

“Nothing,” Hunter replied.

“So, what about your money?” the constable asked.

“Forget it,” Hunter said.

The window buzzed back up, and the car pulled away, heading for the gate. As they left, Hunter craned his neck, watching them all turn back into the house, all except Rosie, who stood still, staring straight ahead at the spot where the car had been. The car accelerated down the road, and soon they were out of sight.

“What was that you called out?” the senior constable asked.

Hunter said nothing, but the constable answered for him. “It was Pidgin, for the woman. He said, ‘Rosie, if there’s trouble, call these men directly.’ Terrible accent, though.”

Hunter stayed silent.

They drove back the same sixty kilometers Hunter had previously covered in the white BMW, back to the small crossroads town where Lahni’s school, the service station, and the old takeaway shop were located. The senior constable maintained a steady eighty kilometers per hour the whole way, and the drive took just over an hour. By the time they arrived, everything was shut down for the night, with only a few lights on in a couple of houses. They passed the area where Rosie had chased after the school bus, the silence inside the car unbroken. Hunter sprawled on the vinyl bench, gazing out at the darkness.

Another twenty minutes north, they passed the turn where Rosie had descended from the hills. They didn’t take it, continuing straight toward the main highway and Mount Kalka beyond. But they never made it. About a kilometer before the Shire line, ninety-five minutes into the journey, a call crackled over the radio. The dispatcher's voice was bored and staticky.

"Blue Five, Blue Five," she called.

The constable stretched for the microphone. "Blue Five, copy. Over."

"Report to the cream house Ranch immediately, sixty kilometers north of Four Ways crossroads. Domestic disturbance, over."

The constable glanced at his partner. "Copy. Nature of the incident? Over."

"Unclear at this time. Believed to be violent. Over."

The senior constable muttered, "Well, damn."

"Copy. En route. Out," the constable said, then replaced the microphone. He turned toward Hunter. "Seems your Pidgin wasn't so bad after all. She must've understood you."

Hunter stayed silent as the senior constable spun the car into a wide U-turn, heading back south. He pushed the cruiser to a hundred twenty kilometers per hour on the straights and held it steady at a hundred through the curves, not bothering with the lights or siren. He didn't even slow down at the crossroads—there was no need; the odds of encountering another vehicle on this road were next to none.

They arrived back at the ranch exactly two hours and thirty minutes after they'd left—ninety-five minutes south, fifty-five minutes back north. The first thing they saw was the sergeant's old cruiser, parked haphazardly in the yard with its door open and light bar flashing. The senior constable swerved through the dust and slammed the cruiser to a stop behind it.

"What's he doing here?" the senior constable grumbled. "It's his day off."

No one was in sight. Both officers stepped out, heading toward the porch steps. Hunter called out, "Let me out."

"No chance," the senior constable replied curtly. "You stay right where you are."

They moved up the porch steps, across the floorboards, and pushed the door open. It swung shut behind them, leaving Hunter alone. He waited—five minutes, then seven, then ten. The car grew increasingly warm in the still air, with only the occasional crackle from the radio and the steady hum of insects outside breaking the silence.

After about twelve minutes, the constable returned alone, walking slowly to his side of the car. He reached in for the microphone.

"Is she okay?" Hunter asked.

The constable nodded, but his expression was sour. "She's fine. Physically, at least. But she's in a heap of trouble."

"Why?"

"The call wasn't about her getting attacked. It was the other way around. She shot him. He's dead. So we've just arrested her."

CHAPTER 10

The constable clicked the microphone and called for backup and an ambulance, relaying an interim report to the dispatcher. He mentioned "gunshot wounds" twice and used the term "homicide" three times.

“Hey,” Hunter called over. “Stop calling it homicide on the radio.”

“Why?” the constable asked.

“Because it was self-defense. He was beating her. We need to make that clear from the start.”

“It’s not for me to decide. Not for you, either.”

Hunter shook his head. “It is for you to say, because what you report now influences what happens later. If you put it in people’s minds that it’s a homicide, it’ll be tough for her. Better for everyone to know what really happened.”

“I don’t have that kind of pull.”

“Yes, you do.”

“How would you know what influence I have?”

“Because I was in your shoes once. I was a ranger, in the military. I know how these things work.”

The constable remained silent.

“She has a child,” Hunter continued. “You should keep that in mind. She needs a low bail, and she needs it tonight. You can help make that happen.”

"She shot him," the constable said. "She should have thought about that before."

"He was beating her. It was self-defense."

The constable didn't reply.

"Come on, give her a break. Don't make her a victim twice."

"The victim? Her husband's the one lying there dead."

"You should have some sympathy. You know what it's like for her."

"And why should I feel a connection to her?" the constable asked.

Hunter didn't respond.

"Do you think I should cut her some slack just because she's Indigenous and so am I?"

"You wouldn't be cutting her slack," Hunter replied. "You'd just be being fair. She needs your help."

The constable hung up the microphone. "Now you're offending me," he said, stepping out of the car and slamming the door behind him. He walked away toward the house. Hunter glanced out the window to the rocky terrain west of the compound, regret gnawing at him. He knew how this would go. *I should've made her leave the gun up there on the plateau,* he thought. *Or taken care of the whole thing myself.*

The state police remained inside the house for over an hour before Hunter saw any movement. Eventually, another cruiser arrived, identical to the first, with a different pair of officers —this time, a white constable and an Aboriginal senior constable. They entered the house immediately, and once again, the heat and stillness settled in. Animal cries echoed in the distance, while the hum of insects and the beating of wings filled the air. Some lights flicked on in the house's windows and then turned off again.

After about twenty minutes, the Four Ways sergeant stumbled out of the house, looking disoriented and exhausted, his shirt dark with sweat. He clumsily maneuvered his cruiser out from the police vehicles and drove off.

An hour later, an ambulance pulled in, its emergency lights cutting through the night. Hunter saw the red flashing far to the south before the boxy vehicle, marked with "Normanton Paramedics," approached the gate. It might have been the same one Patty had called the previous night. It circled the yard and backed up to the porch steps. The paramedics emerged, moving slowly, stretching and yawning, knowing their medical expertise wasn't needed here. They retrieved a rolling gurney and were met by the backup sergeant, who led them into the house.

Hunter sat sweating in the airless car, imagining the medics walking through the hallways to the bedroom, attending to the body, and maneuvering it onto the gurney. It wouldn't be easy, with narrow stairs and tight corners. But before long, they emerged, carrying the gurney down the porch steps. Warner McMahon was nothing more than a large, heavy shape wrapped in a white sheet. The medics aligned the gurney with the rear of the ambulance, collapsed the wheels, and slid it inside. Then they shut the doors.

The paramedics stood around with three of the officers. The constable Hunter had argued with earlier was nowhere to be seen—he was likely guarding Rosie inside. The remaining officers in the yard appeared relaxed, the adrenaline of the night having drained away. They seemed a bit deflated, as though they were supposed to have prevented the outcome. Hunter understood exactly how they felt.

After a few minutes of conversation, the ambulance crew climbed back into their cab and drove off. The officers watched it until it disappeared from view, then they returned inside. Five minutes later, they came back out, this time with Rosie. She was dressed in the same jeans and shirt, her hair damp with water. Her hands were cuffed behind her back, her face pale and sweaty, her eyes vacant. The officers escorted her down the steps awkwardly, their movements out of sync. Once they reached the dirt, they regrouped and led her to their cruiser. The constable opened the door while the sergeant placed a hand on her head, helping her inside. She didn't resist, moving passively. Hunter watched as she slid sideways on the seat, uncomfortable with her hands trapped behind her. She briefly pointed her toes, looking elegant again for a moment. The constable hesitated before shutting the door. Then, Judy and Ryan appeared on the porch to watch her leave.

Judy's hair was disheveled as if she had gotten out of bed in a hurry. She wore a short satin robe that shimmered under the porch lights, its whiteness contrasting with the pale skin of her legs. Ryan stood behind her in jeans and a T-shirt, barefoot. Both of their faces were pale and stunned, their wide eyes staring blankly.

The backup officers climbed into their cruiser, while the constables from Hunter's car did the same. They followed the backup vehicle out to the gate. As Hunter turned to look, he saw Judy and Ryan watching them go. The cruisers turned right and accelerated north. The last thing Hunter saw as he glanced back was Lahni stumbling onto the porch, dressed in kangaroo-print pajamas, clutching a small bear in her left hand while pressing the knuckles of her right into her mouth.

As the police car drove away, the interior cooled down rapidly. There was a small opening in the wire grille in front of Hunter, and if he sat in the middle of the seat and ducked his head, he could see out of the windshield. It was like watching a film play out in real time—the backup car swaying in the headlights, almost unreal against the backdrop of black, dusty night. He couldn't see Rosie, but he guessed she was slumped down, hidden behind the police lights stacked along the rear shelf.

"Where are they taking her?" Hunter called out.

The sergeant shifted in his seat and answered after a moment. "Mount Kalka. Shire jail."

"But this is Four Ways," Hunter said. "Not Mount Kalka."

"There are only about 150 people in Four Ways Shire. You think they have their own separate jail and court?"

"So, how does it work?"

"Mount Kalka handles everything for all the small shires nearby—administration, courts, jails, everything."

Hunter was quiet for a moment. "That's going to be a big problem."

"Why?" the sergeant asked.

"Because Tom Peacock is the prosecutor in Mount Kalka, and he was Warner McMahon's best friend. He'll be prosecuting the person who shot his friend."

"Worried about a conflict of interest?"

"Wouldn't you be?"

"Not really," the sergeant replied. "We know Tom. He's not an idiot. If he thinks defense counsel might nail him for impropriety, he'll step aside. He'd have to. What's the word, excuse himself?"

"Recuse," Hunter corrected.

"Whatever. He'll hand it off to an assistant. Both Mount Kalka prosecutors are women, actually. So, the self-defense argument might get some sympathy."

"It doesn't need sympathy," Hunter said. "It's obvious."

"And Tom's running for judge in January," the sergeant continued. "Lots of Aboriginal and Islander votes in Mount Kalka Shire. He's not going to risk anything that makes him look bad in the papers. Rosie's lucky, really. An Islander woman shoots a white guy in Four Ways, gets tried in Mount Kalka by a woman prosecutor—she couldn't ask for better."

"She's from New South Wales, not an Islander."

"But she looks like one," the senior constable said. "That's what counts to a guy who needs votes."

The police cruisers drove on in convoy, passing the ambulance just before the crossroads. Hunter didn't respond. The sergeant added, "The morgue's in Mount Kalka, too. It's one of the oldest buildings in town—Mount Kalka was that kind of place."

Hunter nodded. "Rosie told me. It was like the Wild West."

"You planning to stick around?"

"I think so. I need to make sure she's alright. She said there's a museum in town—some gunslinger's grave."

"Benjamin Blackman's," the sergeant said. "Famous outlaw."

"Never killed a man who didn't need killing."

The sergeant nodded in the rearview mirror. "That could be Rosie's defense."

"Why not?" Hunter said. "It was a justified killing."

The sergeant stayed quiet for a moment. "Bail might be tricky, though. Dead body and all. Who's her lawyer?"

"She doesn't have one."

"She got money for one?"

"No."

"Well, that's a problem," the sergeant said.

"How old's the kid?"

"Six and a half."

The sergeant grew silent again.

"What's the issue?" Hunter asked.

"No lawyer is a big issue. That kid could be seven and a half before her mom even gets a bail hearing."

"Surely she'll get a lawyer soon, right?"

"Sure, eventually. But this is Queensland. You don't get one immediately. Takes time. You get one when the indictment comes back. And that's where Tom will avoid his conflict—he'll just delay it. Lock her up and forget about her. By the time she's indicted, he'll be a judge. No more conflict of interest."

"Recuse," Hunter corrected.

"Whatever. No lawyer changes everything."

The constable in the passenger seat finally spoke up. "See? Didn't matter what I called it on the radio."

The sergeant added, "Forget the museum. You want to help her? Get her a lawyer."

The rest of the ride into Mount Kalka was silent. They followed the backup cruiser off the highway, crossing under an overpass and traveling through the darkness. When they neared the cloverleaf, the sergeant slowed and pulled over onto the shoulder.

"We're back on patrol now," he said. "Time to let you out."

"Can't you take me to the jail?"

"You're not going to jail. You haven't done anything. And we're not a taxi service."

"So where am I?"

"Downtown Mount Kalka," the sergeant replied, pointing ahead. "Couple kilometers that way."

"Where's the jail?"

"At the crossroads before the railroad, in the courthouse basement."

The sergeant got out, stretched, and opened Hunter's door. Hunter slid out and stood in the warm humid night air, hazy stars hidden overhead. He could hear occasional cars on the highway. The dusty roadside was littered with crushed beer cans tangled in wildflowers and scrubby bushes.

"Take care now," the sergeant said, climbing back into the cruiser. The car rolled back onto the road, curving up onto the highway, the taillights vanishing into the east.

Hunter began walking north, under the overpass, toward the neon glow of Mount Kalka. He passed through pockets of light from streetlamps, walking by a string of motels that became fancier the farther he went from the highway. A rodeo arena sat back from the street, posters still advertising an event from a month ago. *There's a rodeo here in July,* Rosie had said. *But you've missed it for this year.*

Hunter walked in the street, as the sidewalks were crowded with empty tables like outdoor market stalls. The sweet scent of mangoes hung in the air—*the best in Queensland,* Rosie had told him. *So, in their opinion, the best in the world.* He imagined old trucks arriving at dawn, loaded with ripe mangoes, the families ready to sell, their winter prosperity hanging in the balance. But Hunter knew nothing about farming. His ideas of agriculture came from movies. Maybe it was all different—government subsidies, corporations in charge.

Beyond the mango stalls, there were two eateries—a bakery and a pizza place, both dark and closed. It was late Sunday night, far from anywhere. At the end of the strip, a crossroads appeared, with a sign pointing to the museum straight ahead. But just before the turn, to the right, stood the courthouse. It was a decent-looking building, but Hunter didn't linger. He slipped around the side to the back, where no jail he'd ever seen had its main entrance. There was a lit doorway at semi-basement level, with two cement steps leading down from the parking lot. A dusty Toyota sat in the corner, and the lot was fenced with razor wire, warning unauthorized parkers they'd be towed. Yellow bulbs glowed over the fence posts, swarming with insects. The asphalt was still warm underfoot.

The jail door was steel, scarred and faded, with "No Admittance" stenciled on it. Above the door, a small camera pointed down, its red light glowing. Hunter knocked hard and stepped back, waiting for the camera to see him. When nothing happened, he knocked again. After a moment, a woman opened the door. She wore a remand centre officer's uniform—white, maybe fifty, with sand-colored gray hair. A wide belt held a gun, a nightstick, and pepper spray. She moved slowly but looked alert.

"Yes?" she asked.

"Do you have Rosie McMahon in here?"

"We do."

"Can I see her?"

"No."

"Not even for a minute?"

"Not even."

"When can I?"

"Are you family?"

"I'm a friend."

"Not a lawyer, right?"

"No."

"Then Saturday. Visiting is two to four."

Hunter sighed. Almost a week.

"Can you write that down for me?" he asked, hoping to get inside. "Maybe give me a list of what I can bring her?"

The bailiff shrugged and stepped inside. Hunter followed her into the cool, dry air. A small lobby greeted him, with a high desk like a lectern serving as a barrier. Behind the desk were cubbyholes, and Hunter spotted Rosie's croc-skin belt rolled into one of them, along with a small Ziploc bag holding her fake ring. To the right was a barred door, with a tiled corridor stretching beyond.

"How is she?" Hunter asked.

The bailiff shrugged. "Not happy."

"About what?"

"Mainly about the cavity search. She was screaming, but rules are rules. Not like I enjoy it either."

She pulled a laminated sheet from a stack and slid it across the desk.

"Saturday, two to four," she repeated. "And don't bring anything not on the list, or you won't get in."

"Where's the prosecutor's office?"

"Upstairs, second floor. Enter through the front."

"When do they open?"

"Eight-thirty, more or less."

"What about legal aid?"

She smiled. "Ever seen a courthouse without them? Take a left at the crossroads."

"Lawyers?"

"Cheap or expensive?"

"Free."

Her smile widened. "Same street. It's all legal aid and community lawyers."

"Can I see her?"

"Saturday, like I said."

"Not even for a minute?"

"Not even."

"She has a daughter," Hunter said, though it didn't seem relevant.

"Breaks my heart," the bailiff replied dryly.

"When will you check on her?"

"Every fifteen minutes. Suicide watch, but I doubt she's the type. You can tell. Tough woman. That's my guess. But rules are rules."

"Tell her Hunter was here."

"Who?"

"Hunter. Tell her I'm sticking around."

The woman nodded, as if she'd heard it all before. "I'm sure she'll be thrilled."

Hunter left, walking back toward the strip of motels, thinking about all the jail duty he'd done early in his career in Kosovo, wishing he could honestly say he'd done it better than the woman he'd just met.

He walked nearly the entire way back to the highway, stopping when the prices dropped below eighty dollars. He chose a place, roused the night clerk, and paid for a room toward the end of the row. The room was shabby, showing signs of wear and neglect, with a layer of grime that suggested the staff wasn't overly concerned with cleanliness. The bedding was limp, and the air was stuffy and hot, likely because they turned off the air conditioning when the room wasn't occupied. Still, it was functional. Being ex-military, he found that almost any place was manageable—there was always somewhere worse to compare it to.

He slept fitfully until seven the next morning, then took a lukewarm shower and headed out for breakfast at a bakery located about halfway back to the courthouse. It opened early and boasted about its Queensland-sized doughnuts, which were larger and more expensive than usual. He had two doughnuts and three cups of coffee before going to find some clothes. Since giving up on the idea of owning a house while he travelled around Australia, he'd returned to his old habit of buying inexpensive clothes and discarding them instead of bothering to wash them. It worked for him—it kept the burden of permanence at bay.

He found a discount store that had already been open for an hour, selling a bit of everything from cheap plastic plates to work boots. He found a rack of light cream chinos with the brand labels removed—perhaps they were defective or stolen. He picked out his size and paired it with a loose-fitting dark khaki shirt that looked like something from Fiji, but plain. The shirt cost less than one of those oversized doughnuts. He also grabbed some plain underwear. There were no fitting rooms in the store, so he persuaded the clerk to let him use the staff bathroom. He changed into the new clothes and transferred his belongings from one pocket to another. The eight shell casings from Rosie's Makarov clinked around like loose coins. He weighed them in his hand for a moment before dropping them into his new pants pocket.

He balled up his old clothes and stuffed them into the trash bin in the bathroom. Then, he paid fifty dollars in cash at the register. He figured the new clothes would last him about five days, which worked out to ten dollars a day. It seemed like a lot to spend on clothes until he considered that a washing machine would cost around eight hundred dollars, a dryer another eight hundred, and you'd need a house with a basement to put them in, which could easily cost six hundred grand, plus thousands more in taxes, maintenance, and insurance every year. Suddenly, ten bucks a day for clothes didn't seem so unreasonable.

He waited on the sidewalk until eight o'clock, leaning against a wall under an awning to avoid the sun. He figured the courthouse bailiffs would switch shifts at eight, and five minutes past, he saw the heavyset woman drive out of the lot in her dusty Toyota. She made a left turn and passed right by him. He crossed the street and walked around the courthouse again, thinking maybe the day shift would be more cooperative. The night workers were always tougher, with less public interaction and supervision, making them feel like they ran the place.

But the day shift wasn't any better. The day bailiff, a younger and thinner man, gave him the same responses: No, you can't see her. When can I? Saturday. Is she alright? As well as can be expected. It sounded like a canned response you'd hear outside a hospital from a cautious spokesperson. The man confirmed that only lawyers were allowed unrestricted access to the prisoners. So Hunter walked back up the steps, resolved to find a lawyer.

****

The events of the previous night had left the house in shock, quiet and mostly empty, which was just fine for the killers. The ranch hands weren't around, the tall stranger had disappeared, and Rosie McMahon and her husband were gone. Only the old woman, the second son, and the granddaughter remained. The girl hadn't gone to school, even though the bus came and went. She wandered aimlessly around the barn, looking confused and lethargic, as did the others. This made them easier to watch—more vulnerable targets.

The two men were hidden behind a rock across from the ranch gate, positioned about twenty meters up the slope for a good view. The woman had dropped them off three hundred meters to the north and driven back toward Mount Kalka. "When do we do this?" they had asked her. "When I say," she had replied.

****

Hunter turned left at the crossroads in the center of Mount Kalka and followed a street parallel to the railroad tracks. He passed the bus depot and reached a strip that was now filled with low-end businesses serving the courthouse crowd—duty lawyers and storefront legal clinics, just like the night shift bailiff had mentioned. The legal clinics had rows of desks facing the windows, with chairs for customers and waiting areas inside the doors. They were all dingy, cluttered with piles of files and memos taped to the walls. At 8:30 in the morning, they were already busy, with knots of people waiting inside and anxious clients perched on the customer chairs. Most were with their families, and many had children in tow. All the clients were Aboriginal, though the lawyers were a mixed bunch—men and women, young and old, some bright-eyed, others looking defeated. The one thing they all had in common was the harried look of people at their wits' end.

He chose the only office with an empty chair in front of a lawyer. The seat was toward the back, and the lawyer was a young white woman, maybe twenty-five, with thick, short dark hair. She had a deep tan and wore a white sports bra instead of a shirt, with a leather jacket draped over her chair. She was nearly hidden behind two towering stacks of files and was on the phone, clearly upset.

He approached her desk and sat down, even though she hadn't invited him to. She glanced at him briefly before returning her focus to the phone, speaking slow, accented Pidgin. She was explaining, with growing frustration, that they had won the case but the other party still refused to pay. As the conversation continued, she became more upset, blinking back tears of embarrassment. Eventually, she ended the call, saying she would follow up later, and then sat silently, trying to calm herself.

When she finally turned her attention to Hunter, she asked, "Problem?" with a mixture of resignation and irritation.

Hunter could see she was struggling. "Winning the case is only half the battle," she said, sighing. "Sometimes, it's a lot less than half, to be honest."

"So what happened?" he asked.

She shook her head. "We don't need to get into it."

"Some guy refusing to pay?" Hunter guessed.

She shrugged, her expression both defeated and irritated. "A farmer. He crashed his car into my client's truck, injuring the man, his wife, and two of their kids. It was early in the morning, and the guy was driving back from a party, drunk. My clients were on their way to market. It was harvest time, and because of the accident, they couldn't work the fields and lost their entire crop."

"What were they farming?"

"Tomatoes," she replied. "They rotted in the fields. We sued the rancher and won fifty thousand dollars. But he won't pay. He's just sitting back, waiting them out. His plan is to starve them out of the country and back to Papua New Guinea. And it's working because going back to court will take at least another year, and my clients can't survive that long on nothing."

"They didn't have insurance?" Hunter asked.

She shook her head again. "The premiums are way too high. These families are barely getting by as it is. The best option we had was to sue the rancher directly. We had a strong case, presented it well, and we won. But the old man is just stalling."

"Tough break," Hunter said, sympathetically.

"Unbelievable," she muttered. "You wouldn't believe the things these people go through. This family I'm talking about, the border patrol killed their eldest son."

"Seriously?" Hunter asked, surprised.

She nodded. "Twelve years ago. They were illegal immigrants back then. They paid everything they had to a guide who abandoned them in the tropics. They were out there with no food or water, walking south at night to avoid the heat, and the border patrol chased them down with rifles and shot their eldest boy. They buried him in the mangroves and kept walking."

"And no one did anything about it?"

"They couldn't. They were illegals. And it happened all the time. Every one of them has a story like that. Now they're legal, but when I try to convince them to trust the law, something like this happens, and I feel like an idiot."

"Not your fault," Hunter said.

"It feels like it is. I should've known better," she replied, looking away, clearly upset.

Hunter watched as she composed herself. After a few moments, she shifted back to business. "Anyway, how can I help you?"

"It's not for me," Hunter explained. "It's for a woman I know."

"She needs a lawyer?" she asked, straightening up.

"She shot her husband. He was abusing her," Hunter said plainly.

"When did it happen?"

"Last night. She's in jail, across the street."

"Is he dead?"

Hunter nodded. "Yeah, he's gone."

She sighed and pulled out a yellow notepad. "What's your name?" she asked.

"My name?" Hunter raised an eyebrow.

"You're the one talking to me," she replied, jotting down notes.

"Hunter," he said.

"I'm Sally," she introduced herself. "Sally Strong."

"You should go into private practice," Hunter said. "Name like that, should have it's own billboard."

She smiled faintly. "One day, maybe. Right now, I'm serving a five-year sentence with my conscience."

"Paying your dues?"

"Atoning," she clarified. "For my privilege. For getting a law degree from USYD and coming from a family where twenty grand is just a monthly maintenance fee for their Potts Point apartment, rather than a matter of life or death during a Queensland winter."

"Good for you, Sally," Hunter said.

"So, tell me about this woman," Sally prompted.

"She's Papuan, her husband was white. Her name is Rosie McMahon, and he was Warner McMahon," Hunter explained.

"Warner, like the movie studio?" Sally quipped as she scribbled down the names.

Hunter nodded. "The abuse stopped for a while because he was in prison for tax evasion. He got out yesterday and started again. She shot him last night."

"Okay," Sally said, making notes. "But getting solid evidence and witnesses will be tricky. The abuse was mostly hidden."

"Pretty bad injuries, but she always said they were accidents, usually involving horses," Hunter explained.

"Horses?" Sally asked, puzzled.

"Yeah, like she fell off of them," Hunter said, shrugging. "I don't know why. Maybe shame, coercion, or fear."

"But you're sure the abuse was real?" she asked.

"In my mind, no doubt," Hunter replied.

Sally stared at her notes for a moment, deep in thought. "It's not going to be easy. The laws here aren't too far behind when it comes to spousal abuse, but we'll need solid evidence. His prison sentence helps our case—he wasn't exactly a model citizen. We could aim for involuntary manslaughter and push for time served, followed by probation. We might have a shot."

"It's justifiable homicide, not manslaughter," Hunter argued.

"I'm sure it is, but the question is what can work, not what's ideal," Sally countered.

"And she needs bail today," Hunter pressed.

Sally looked up at him, stunned. "Bail? Today? Forget it."

"She has a little girl, six and a half," Hunter added.

Sally jotted it down. "It won't help. Everyone in here has kids."

She ran her fingers through the files on her desk. "All these cases involve families, kids of all ages—six, seven, ten. It's the same story over and over."

"The girl's name is Lahni," Hunter said. "She needs her mother."

Sally wrote "Lahni" on the pad and connected it to "Rosie McMahon" with an arrow.

"There are only two ways to get bail in a case like this," she explained. "First, we'd have to essentially hold the entire trial during the bail hearing. And we're nowhere near ready for that. My schedule is packed, and even if I could start now, it would take months to prepare properly."

"What's the other way?" Hunter asked.

"We convince the prosecutor not to oppose bail. If he doesn't object, then it's just up to the judge to decide if it's appropriate. And the judge is likely to follow the prosecutor's lead."

"Tom Peacock was Warner McMahon's best friend," Hunter said grimly.

Sally slumped in her chair. "Great. He'll recuse himself, obviously. But his office will still push back hard. So no, bail isn't happening."

"But will you take the case?" Hunter asked.

"Of course, I will. That's what we do here. I'll call Tom's office and go see Rosie. But that's all I can do right now. You understand? Taking the case and not taking the case amount to the same thing at this point."

Hunter shook his head. "That's not good enough, Sally. I need you to get to work on this now. Make something happen."

"I told you, I can't. Not for months," Sally said, her frustration rising.

Hunter stayed quiet for a moment, thinking. Then he asked, "You interested in a deal?"

"A deal?" she repeated.

"I help you, you help me."

She looked at him, skeptical. "How could you help me?"

"I can recover that fifty grand for your tomato farmers. Today. And in exchange, you start working on Rosie's case today."

"What are you, a debt collector?"

"No, but I'm a fast learner," Hunter said with a shrug. "How hard can it be?"

She hesitated. "I can't let you do that. It's probably illegal unless you're registered."

"Just suppose, next time you see me, I've got a check for fifty grand in my pocket," Hunter suggested.

"How would you pull that off?"

"I'd just ask the guy for it," Hunter said casually.

She shook her head, torn. "It would be unethical."

"As opposed to what?" he countered.

She didn't answer right away, staring off into the distance. Then she glanced at the phone, imagining what it would feel like to make that victory call. "Who's the farmer?" Hunter asked.

She shook her head again, conflicted. "I can't tell you. I'm worried about the ethics."

"I'm offering," Hunter said. "You're not asking."

After a long pause, Sally sighed. “I have to go to the bathroom.”

She was taller than Hunter had expected, her long legs tanned and well-toned. As she walked away in her denim shorts, Hunter noted she looked just as good from the back as she had from the front. Once she disappeared through a door at the rear, Hunter quickly leaned over her desk, opened the drawer, and pulled out the top file. Flipping it around, he scanned the pages until he found a deposition. There, typed neatly in a box labeled “Defendant,” was the name and address he needed. He folded the paper into quarters and slipped it into his shirt pocket before closing the file and putting it back in the drawer. He clicked the drawer shut and sat back down just as Sally returned.

She walked back to her desk and settled in. “Anywhere around here I can borrow a car?” Hunter asked casually.

“You don’t have one?” she asked, raising an eyebrow.

He shook his head.

Sally hesitated, then pulled a set of keys from the pocket of her jacket slung over the back of her chair. “You can borrow mine, I guess. It’s parked in the lot behind the building.”

She handed him the keys.

“It’s a Hyundai,” she said. “There are maps in the glove compartment if you’re not familiar with the area.”

Hunter pocketed the keys, pushing his chair back. “Maybe I’ll catch you later,” he said as he stood up.

Sally didn’t reply. He gave her a quick nod and walked out through the crowded office and into the sunlight outside.

CHAPTER 11

Sally's Hyundai was the only one in the parking lot behind the building, parked directly under the blazing sun. It was a relatively new red N line hatchback, about eighteen months old, with New South Wales plates. The glove compartment contained more than just maps; there was also a handgun inside.

It was a sleek, nickel-finished SIG Sauer P7M10 with a four-inch barrel and ten rounds of .40 caliber ammunition. Back in Hunter's day, the military had considered the 9mm version, but the cost had been prohibitive—likely sixteen times more expensive than Rosie McMahon's affordable eighty-dollar Makarov. It was a top-tier weapon, one of the finest available. Maybe it had been a gift from her family in Sydney, possibly along with the car itself. He could picture the scenario: the Hyundai, a perfect graduation present, but the gun? That might have caused some concern. Her parents, perched high in their city apartment, probably worried about their daughter's safety working with the underprivileged. They likely did thorough research before buying her the best gun they could find, just as they would have purchased a Rolex if she needed a watch.

Out of habit, he dismantled the gun, inspected the parts, and reassembled it. It was in excellent condition, though it had been fired a handful of times and cleaned meticulously afterward. It suggested she had spent some time at a shooting range—perhaps an exclusive one in Double Bay. Smiling, he tucked the gun back under the maps in the glove compartment. Then, after reclining the seat and starting the car, he cranked the air conditioning. He spread the maps on the passenger seat and checked for the farmers address. It looked like the place was north and east of town, probably about an hour's drive if he pushed the pace.

The Hyundai had a sporty automatic transmission with paddle shifters on the steering wheel. Hunter quickly shifted out of first gear as he left the parking lot, getting used to the car's feel. It was a firm ride, and there was an odd little vase on the dashboard, holding a pink flower that perked up as the interior cooled. A subtle fragrance filled the car. He hadn't driven in over twenty-five years, not since learning illegally as a teenager behind the wheel of a massive SAS truck, and this was about as far from that experience as possible.

The map displayed seven ways to exit Mount Kalka. He had come in from the southernmost route, but it didn't lead where he needed to go, so he was left with six options. His instincts told him to head west. The town seemed to be concentrated to the east of the crossroads, so going east would almost certainly be wrong. He drove away from the lawyers' offices and bondsmen, in the direction of Yabbie Creek, and soon found what he was searching for: a cluster of auto dealerships on the outskirts of town, a feature common to any sizable town.

He cruised up and down the strip, examining his options. Two places stood out, both offering flashy signs advertising cheap car services and free loaners. He chose the dealership farther from town. The front lot displayed used cars draped in flags, each windshield boasting low prices. The office was in a portable unit, and behind it stood a long, low shed with hydraulic lifts. The floor was a dirt-stained mess. Four mechanics were visible—three of them idle while one worked under a Kia SUV. It was a slow start to a hot Monday morning.

Hunter drove the Hyundai into the shed, and the three idle mechanics wandered over. One appeared to be the foreman.

Hunter asked him to adjust the clutch to make it smoother. The foreman gladly accepted the fifty-dollar job. Hunter agreed to the price and requested a loaner. The man led him to an old, faded Ford Mustang convertible parked behind the shed. It had once been white but had turned khaki from age and sun exposure. Hunter took the gun from Sally's car, wrapped it in the maps, and placed it on the Mustang's passenger seat. Then he asked the mechanic for a tow rope.

"What do you need to tow?" the mechanic asked, puzzled.

"Nothing. Just the rope," Hunter replied.

The mechanic raised an eyebrow but fetched the rope. Hunter tossed it into the Mustang's footwell, then headed back into town and out again, this time going north and east. He felt much better about driving the Mustang—only a fool would attempt unlicensed debt collecting in a bright red car with out-of-town plates and a flower vase on the dash.

He made one stop in the countryside to remove the Mustang's plates, using a coin to unscrew them. He stashed the plates on the floor beside the coil of rope and kept the bolts in the glove compartment before driving on toward his destination. The landscape looked familiar, like the area around the McMahon property, but better irrigated, with green crops sprouting in cultivated fields. He saw wildflowers and prickly pear cacti along the roadside but no people. The sun was high, and the horizon shimmered in the heat.

The farmers name, Bobby K. Peterson, was listed on the legal papers, but the address was just a route number. According to Sally's map, it was a stretch of road running about 40 kilometers before vanishing into the Northern Territory. It was much like the road that led south from Four Ways to the McMahon property—a dusty ribbon of blacktop with drooping power lines and large ranch gates every fifteen kilometers or so. The ranch names weren't always a clue to the owners, much like how the McMahon house had no identifying signage. Finding Peterson in person might have been difficult.

But it wasn't. The road intersected with another, and the crossroads had a line of mailboxes nailed to a weathered plank. The names on the boxes were neatly written in black paint. Peterson's name was clear, along with "Big Horns Station" just below it.

The entrance to Big Horns Station was about fifteen kilometers north. A black iron arch marked the entrance, like something from a gothic story. Hunter drove past it and parked by a power pole on the roadside. Getting out, he gazed up at the lines above. A transformer was perched at the top where the power line split, running toward the ranch house. A phone line hung just below it, running parallel.

Hunter retrieved Sally's gun and the rope from the car, tying one end of the rope to the trigger guard in a neat knot. After measuring out twenty feet of rope, he swung the gun like a weight, aiming to throw it between the phone line and the power line. He missed on the first attempt, but on the second, the gun sailed through the gap and caught. He lowered it back to himself, untied the rope, and tossed the gun back into the car. Then, gripping the rope, he yanked it sharply. The phone line snapped at the junction box and slithered down the pole, coming to rest a hundred meters away.

After coiling the rope again, he got back into the car and drove down the long driveway. The house at the end looked like something from a period film—white with four massive columns supporting a second-story balcony. The steps led up to double front doors, and a well-kept lawn spread out beside a gravel parking area. Hunter parked on the gravel and shut off the engine. He tucked his shirt into his waistband, recalling how some personal trainer had once told him it made his torso look more triangular. Slipping the gun into his right hip pocket, he noted how its shape showed through. Then he rolled up the sleeves of his new shirt to his shoulders, grabbed the Mustang's steering wheel, and squeezed until his biceps bulged, veins standing out prominently. When you had arms as big as most people's legs, it made sense to use what nature had given you.

He climbed out of the car and went up the steps, ringing the bell beside the door. Somewhere deep in the house, he heard a distant chime. He was about to ring again when the left door opened, revealing a maid who barely reached halfway up the frame. She wore a gray uniform and looked like she was from the Philippines.

"I'm here to see Bob Peterson," Hunter said.

"Do you have an appointment?" the maid asked, her English impeccable.

"Yes, I do."

"He didn't tell me."

"He probably forgot," Hunter replied. "I've heard he can be a bit of an asshole."

The maid fought back a smile.

"Who should I say is here?"

"John J. Curtin," Hunter replied.

The maid hesitated for a moment, then smiled. "You mean the fourteenth Prime Minister? He succeeded Arthur Fadden, born in 1885 in Victoria, and served from 1941 until 1945. He was one of nine prime ministers from Victoria and died in office."

"He's a distant relative," Hunter said. "I'm from Victoria, too, but politics isn't my thing. Tell Mr. Peterson I'm from a bank in Sydney, and we've just found some stock in his grandfather's name. It's worth about a million dollars."

"That will certainly catch his interest," the maid replied.

She disappeared up a wide staircase in the back of the foyer, moving gracefully with one hand gliding along the railing. The foyer was enormous, cool, and paneled in polished golden hardwood. A grandfather clock taller than Hunter ticked softly, marking each second. There was a velvet-covered chaise like the ones you'd see in portraits of high-society women. Hunter wondered if it would collapse under his weight. He pressed a hand down on the velvet, feeling the firmness of horsehair padding beneath it. Just then, the maid returned, descending the stairs as gracefully as she had gone up.

"He'll see you now," she said. "He's on the balcony at the back of the house."

Hunter followed her upstairs to a large landing, where French doors led out onto a balcony that ran the entire width of the house. The shaded area offered a view of endless grassland, and ceiling fans spun lazily overhead. White-painted wicker furniture formed a seating area where a man sat with a pitcher and a glass, perhaps filled with lemonade. The man looked to be around sixty, with a bull-like neck and a sun-etched face. His white hair was thick, and he wore a completely white outfit: pants, shirt, and shoes. He looked like he belonged at a fancy country club, ready for lawn bowling.

"Mr. Curtin?" Peterson called.

Hunter walked over and sat down without waiting for an invitation. "Do you have kids?" he asked.

"I have three sons," Peterson replied.

"Any of them home?"

"They're all away, working."

"Your wife?"

"She's visiting Brisbane."

"So it's just you and the maid here today?"

Peterson was puzzled but polite, his expression that of someone about to receive a million-dollar windfall. "Why do you ask?"

"I'm a banker," Hunter said. "I have to ask."

"Tell me about this stock," Peterson said, his curiosity piqued.

"There isn't any stock," Hunter said bluntly. "I made that up."

Peterson's face shifted from surprise to disappointment, then irritation. "Then why are you here?"

"It's just a method we use," Hunter explained. "In reality, I'm a loan officer. Sometimes, people need to borrow money, but they might not want their household staff to know."

Peterson raised an eyebrow. "I don't need to borrow money, Mr. Hayes."

"You sure about that?"

"Positive."

"That's not what we've heard."

"I'm a wealthy man. I lend money—I don't borrow it."

"Really? Word is, you've been having trouble keeping up with your obligations."

The realization slowly dawned on Peterson. His body stiffened as the shock traveled up to his face. He glanced at the bulge of the gun in Hunter's pocket, as though seeing it for the first time. His hand instinctively reached for a small silver bell on the table beside him. He shook it vigorously, its tinkling sound cutting through the stillness.

"Maria!" he shouted. "Maria, come here!"

The maid appeared almost immediately, stepping quietly onto

the balcony.

"Call the police," Peterson ordered. "Dial 000. I want this man arrested."

She hesitated.

"Go ahead," Hunter said. "Make the call."

The maid hurried inside, disappearing into the room directly behind Peterson's chair. It was dark and masculine, likely a private study. Moments later, they heard the clicking of buttons, followed by her voice calling out, "The phones aren't working! Even my mobile it has no WiFi Mr Peterson"

Hunter's earlier sabotage had done the trick. "Wait downstairs," he instructed the maid.

Turning his attention back to Peterson, Hunter said, "I want you to honor your legal obligation."

"You're not a banker," Peterson said, growing more agitated.

"No, I'm not. Took you long enough to figure that out."

"So what are you, really?"

"I'm a guy looking for a check. Fifty thousand dollars, to be precise."

"You're working for *those* people?" Peterson began to rise from his chair, but Hunter extended his arm, pushing him back down hard enough to make a point.

"Stay seated," Hunter said firmly.

"Why are you doing this?"

"Because I care," Hunter replied calmly. "There's a family in trouble. They're going to spend the entire winter worried sick, waiting for disaster to strike. I don't like to see people living in fear, no matter who they are."

"If they don't like it, they should go back to Papua New Guinea,"

Peterson spat out.

Hunter looked at him, surprised. “I’m not talking about them. I’m talking about *you*—your family.”

Peterson frowned. “My family?”

Hunter nodded. “If I stay mad at you, they’re going to suffer. A car accident here, a mugging there. Maybe you’ll fall down the stairs and break a leg—or maybe it’ll be your wife. The house could catch fire. One disaster after another. You’ll never know when the next one’s coming, and it’ll drive you crazy.”

“You couldn’t get away with that,” Peterson challenged.

“I’m getting away with it right now, aren’t I? I could start today—with you.”

Peterson stayed silent.

“Hand me that pitcher,” Hunter said, gesturing to the crystal jug on the table.

Peterson hesitated but eventually passed it over, moving like an automaton. The pitcher was fancy, probably old crystal, maybe even imported from Ireland. It likely cost a thousand dollars. Hunter balanced it in his hand, sniffing the contents—lemonade. Without warning, he tossed the pitcher over the edge of the balcony. The yellow liquid arced through the air, followed by the sharp crash of the crystal shattering on the patio below.

“Oops,” Hunter said casually.

“I’ll have you arrested,” Peterson said, his voice quivering with anger. “That’s criminal damage.”

“Maybe I’ll start with one of your sons,” Hunter replied coldly. “Pick one at random and throw him off the balcony, just like that.”

“You’ll pay for this,” Peterson warned again, but his voice

lacked conviction.

"Why? Because the law suddenly matters to you? Or does it only matter when it's convenient for *you*?"

Peterson said nothing. Hunter stood up and lifted his chair, throwing it over the railing. It smashed onto the stone below, splintering into pieces.

"Give me the check," Hunter demanded. "You can afford it. You're a rich man, remember? You just told me so."

"It's about principles," Peterson muttered, his voice weak. "They don't belong here."

"And you do? Why? They were here before you were."

"They lost—to us."

"And now you're losing—to me. What goes around, comes around."

Hunter reached for the silver bell on the table, examining the intricate filigree pattern on its surface. It was likely an antique, maybe Scottish. He squeezed it hard between his thumb and fingers, crushing it out of shape. Then, without a word, he flattened it further and slipped it into Peterson's shirt pocket.

"I could do the same thing to your head," Hunter said quietly.

Peterson made no response.

"Now give me the check," Hunter continued, his voice low and controlled. "Before I lose my temper."

Peterson paused for a long moment, then finally sighed. "Okay."

He led Hunter inside to the study and over to the desk. Hunter stayed close, wary of any sudden moves. He didn't want to risk Peterson pulling a revolver from a drawer.

"Make it out to cash," Hunter instructed.

Peterson wrote the check, making sure the date and amount were correct, then signed it.

“This better not bounce,” Hunter warned.

“It won’t.”

“If it does, you’ll follow it—off the patio.”

“I hope you rot in hell,” Peterson muttered, handing over the check.

Hunter folded it carefully and slipped it into his pocket. As he walked out of the study, he passed by the grandfather clock in the foyer. With a quick tilt, he overbalanced it, and the heavy clock fell like a tree, smashing on the floor. The ticking stopped.

****

The two men withdrew from the property after nearly three hours. The heat was unbearable, and they didn’t need to stay any longer. It was obvious that no one was going anywhere. The old woman and her son mostly stayed inside, while the kid hung around the barn, occasionally venturing out until the sun forced her back indoors. Once, she slowly walked back to the house when the maid called her for a meal. With nothing more to see, the men gave up and moved north, staying hidden behind the rocks. When they were far enough away from the house, they made their way to the dusty roadside. Right on time, the woman arrived in a Ford Falcon, the air conditioning blasting. She had bottles of cold water for them. They drank, and then gave her their report.

“Alright,” the woman said. “Looks like it’s time to move forward.”

“Sooner the better,” the darker-skinned man agreed.

“Let’s get it done,” the fairer man said.

****

Hunter reattached the plates to the old Mustang once he was well away from Peterson's property. Then he drove back to Mount Kalka and retrieved Sally Strong's Hyundai from the mechanics. He paid them the fifty dollars without argument, though he wasn't entirely sure they had done anything to the car. The clutch felt just as stiff as it had before. He shifted from first to second gear and quickly concluded that they hadn't touched it at all.

After leaving the car in the lot behind the building, complete with the maps and the handgun in the glove compartment, Hunter entered the old store from the front and found Sally at her desk in the back. She was on the phone, busy with clients —a family group of three generations sat quietly in front of her, their faces anxious. Sally had changed her clothes; she now wore black, high-waisted pants made from a thin cotton or linen fabric, along with a matching black jacket. The jacket made her white sports bra look like a formal top, giving her a professional, attorney-like appearance.

Seeing Hunter, she covered the mouthpiece of the phone and excused herself from the clients. She twisted in her chair and leaned toward him, lowering her voice.

"We've got big problems," she whispered. "Tom Peacock wants to see you."

"Me?" Hunter asked. "Why?"

"Better you hear it from him."

"Hear what? Did you meet with him?"

She nodded. "Yeah, I went straight over. We talked for about half an hour."

"And? What did he say?"

"Better you hear it from him," she repeated, a note of concern creeping into her voice. "We'll talk later, okay?"

Hunter looked at her, sensing the worry in her tone. She turned back to her phone call as the family group in front of her desk leaned in, listening attentively. Hunter pulled the fifty-thousand-dollar check from his pocket and unfolded it, smoothing it out on the desk in front of her. Sally glanced at it and paused mid-sentence. She covered the phone again and took a deep breath.

"Thanks," she said softly, though her tone was laced with embarrassment. It seemed she might have been reconsidering her end of the bargain.

Hunter placed her car keys on the desk, then left the office and headed out to the sidewalk. He turned right and made his way toward the courthouse.

The Mount Kalka Queensland State Prosecutor's office occupied the entire second floor of the courthouse. A door from the stairwell led into a narrow corridor that opened up into a wooden gate and a secretarial area. From there, three doors led into three offices: one for the prosecutor and one for each of the assistants. The interior walls were glass from the waist up, with old-fashioned venetian blinds covering the glass. The whole setup looked outdated and cramped. The windows had bulky air conditioning units, all running at full blast, adding a deep, low hum to the building's structure.

The secretarial area housed two cluttered desks. One was occupied by a middle-aged woman who appeared to be a permanent fixture there, and the other by a young man who might have been a college intern working over the summer. The intern looked up as Hunter entered, a bright, eager expression on his face, clearly doubling as the office receptionist.

"Tom Peacock wants to see me," Hunter said.

The intern's eyes widened. "Mr. Hunter?" he asked, confirming his identity.

Hunter nodded, and the young man pointed to the corner office. "He's expecting you," he said.

Hunter threaded his way through the cramped space to the door marked with an acetate plaque reading, *Thomas F. Peacock, State Prosecutor*. The window was covered from the inside by closed blinds. Hunter knocked once and entered without waiting for an invitation.

Peacock's office was a mess of filing cabinets, piles of paperwork, and multiple telephones. The man himself sat behind a large desk, leaning back in his chair, holding a photograph frame in both hands. His expression was somber as he stared at the picture.

"What can I do for you?" Hunter asked.

Peacock shifted his gaze from the photograph to Hunter. "Please, sit down," he said, sounding unusually weary. The booming, hearty voice of the politician was gone, replaced by a tired, ordinary tone.

Hunter picked up a chair and angled it sideways for more legroom. "What's going on?" he asked again.

"You ever have your life turned upside down overnight?" Peacock asked, his voice heavy.

Hunter nodded. "Yeah, happens now and then."

Peacock placed the framed photograph on the desk where both of them could see it. It was a color photo of three young men leaning against the fender of an old Ford ute—Warner McMahon, Troy Bradley, and Peacock himself. They looked carefree, young, and full of potential, frozen in a moment of youthful exuberance.

"Me, Warner, and Troy," Peacock said softly. "Now Warner's dead, and Troy's missing."

"Any news on Bradley?" Hunter asked.

Peacock shook his head, his face clouded with worry. "Nothing. Not a word."

Hunter remained silent, letting the weight of the situation settle.

"We were inseparable back then," Peacock continued, his voice distant. "In a place like this, friendships go deeper than normal. It was us against the world."

"Was Warner his real name?" Hunter asked.

Peacock looked up. "Why do you ask?"

"Well, I assumed your name was Tom, but the sign on your door says Thomas."

Peacock offered a tired smile. "Yeah, it's Thomas on my birth certificate. My family always called me Tom. But when I was little, I couldn't pronounce it, so it came out as Tom. The nickname stuck."

"So Warner was really Warner?"

Peacock nodded. "Plain and simple. Warner McMahon."

Hunter leaned back. "So what can I do for you?"

Peacock seemed lost in thought for a moment. "I'm not really sure," he admitted. "Maybe I just need someone to listen, maybe help me sort things out."

"What kind of things?"

Peacock looked troubled. "I don't know, really. Like, when you look at me, what do you see?"

“I see the State Prosecutor,” Hunter said plainly.

“And?”

“I don’t know what else to say.”

Peacock was quiet for a while, the only sound coming from the hum of the air conditioners. “You like what you see?” he asked, his voice subdued.

Hunter shrugged. “Less and less, to be honest.”

“Why?”

“Because I walk in here and find you getting all nostalgic over your friendship with a crooked lawyer and a wife-beater.”

Peacock looked away, clearly pained by the blunt statement. “You don’t mince words, do you?”

“Life’s too short.”

There was a moment of silence between them, broken only by the soft roar of the air conditioners, their motors humming in and out of sync with one another.

“Actually, I’m three things,” Peacock said finally. “I’m a man, I’m a Prosecutor, and I’m running for judge.”

“So?”

“Troy Bradley isn’t a crooked lawyer. He’s far from it. He’s a good man, and he’s a crusader. He needs to be. The truth is, the legal system in Queensland isn’t known for protecting the rights of the accused—especially not the poor. You know that because you had to find a lawyer for Rosie McMahon yourself. That can only mean she wasn’t going to get court-appointed representation for months. And even with a lawyer, she’s still facing a long delay. It’s a bad system. I know it, and Troy knows it.”

Peacock paused, his voice growing more urgent. “The law

guarantees everyone the right to counsel, and Troy takes that responsibility seriously. He makes himself available to anyone who can find their way to his door, and he gives them fair representation, regardless of who they are. Sure, some of his clients are bad guys, but the law applies to them, too. Most of his clients, though, are just ordinary people—people who are poor, white or Aboriginal."

Hunter stayed quiet, letting Peacock speak.

"He does what he does because he believes in the law, not because he's trying to defend criminals. The legal system's flawed, but Troy doesn't pick and choose who deserves justice. That's not how it works. And now that he's missing... well, it leaves a lot of questions. Warner's gone, and Troy's disappeared without a trace."

Peacock exhaled heavily, his expression haunted. "What am I supposed to do? I'm running for judge in this mess."

Hunter considered his words for a long moment before responding. "You can't fix everything, and you sure as hell can't change the past. But if you care about this case, you'll figure out what needs to be done."

Peacock looked at him, clearly searching for reassurance.

"Look," Hunter said, standing up. "You wanted me to listen. I've listened. Now you need to make a choice. You can either do your job or get out of the way."

Peacock stared at the photograph on his desk, then nodded slowly. "You're right," he said. "It's just hard to see things clearly when you're in the middle of it."

"That's life," Hunter said, heading toward the door. "Good luck with your campaign."

"So, let me take a wild guess," Peacock said, leaning back in his chair. "I don't know who told you that Troy was crooked, but

I'd bet it was an older, wealthy white person with some sort of status."

Hunter thought of Judy McMahon.

"Don't tell me who it was," Peacock continued. "But I'll bet you I'm right. Someone like that sees a lawyer helping out poor folks or people of color, and they don't like it. First, it's just an annoyance, then they see it as an insult to their race or class, and from there, it's an easy leap to calling it crooked."

"Okay," Hunter admitted. "Maybe I'm wrong about Bradley."

"I can guarantee you're wrong about him. You could look all the way back to the day he passed the bar exam and not find a single crooked thing in his past," Peacock said, pointing to the photograph, his finger just below Troy Bradley's chin. "He's my friend, and I'm proud of that—as both a man and a Prosecutor."

"What about Warner McMahon?" Hunter asked.

Peacock nodded. "We'll get to Warner, but let me first tell you about being a Prosecutor."

"What's there to explain?"

"It's the same idea as with Troy. I believe in the constitution, the rule of law, and fairness. You could turn this office upside down and not find a single case where I've been anything less than fair. Yes, I've been tough, and I've put plenty of people in prison, some on death row, but I've never done anything without being sure it was the right thing."

"Sounds like you're campaigning," Hunter said dryly. "But I'm not registered to vote in this state."

Peacock gave a small smile. "I know. I checked. That's why I'm speaking plainly now. If this was a political speech, it'd sound way too cheesy. But this is real. I want to be a judge because I know I can do some good. You know how the system works here in Queensland?"

"Not really."

"Judges here are elected, and they hold a lot of power. It's a strange state—there's plenty of wealth, but a lot of poverty, too. Poor people need court-appointed lawyers, but here's the problem: there's no public defender system in Queensland. The judges pick the defense lawyers, and they can pick anyone they want from any law firm. It's pure patronage. The judge decides the fees, too. So, naturally, the judge appoints a lawyer from a firm that's supported his election campaign. It's all cronyism, not based on talent. The judge hands over thousands in taxpayer money to these firms, and they assign a junior lawyer who does almost no work. Meanwhile, some poor guy ends up in jail for a crime he might not have committed."

Peacock leaned forward, his voice growing more intense. "I've seen it happen too many times. Defense lawyers meet their clients for the first time in the courtroom. We've had drunk lawyers, and lawyers who fall asleep during trials. They don't do their jobs. A year before I got here, a guy was convicted of raping a child and sentenced to life in prison. Later, some pro bono group discovered the man had actually been in jail at the time of the crime—fifty kilometers away. There was plenty of evidence proving it, all in black and white in the public record. His original lawyer didn't even bother to check."

"Not exactly a stellar system," Hunter remarked.

"That's why I want to be a judge," Peacock explained. "So I can fix things. But for now, in this office, we make sure that no one falls through the cracks. Every time we put together a prosecution case, one of us plays the defense and tries to tear it apart. We do it thoroughly because we know no one else will, and I wouldn't be able to sleep if we didn't."

"Rosie McMahon's defense should hold up," Hunter said.

Peacock's expression darkened. "No, it's a nightmare. It's a complete disaster for me—as a man, as a Prosecutor, and as someone running for judge."

"You'll have to recuse yourself."

"Of course I will," Peacock agreed. "But that doesn't change the fact that it's personal. It's still my office, and whatever happens will reflect on me."

"You want to explain what the problem is?"

Peacock sighed. "Don't you see? Warner was my friend. I'm an honest prosecutor, and I want to see justice served. But I'm looking at the possibility of sending a woman of color to death row. If I do that, I can kiss my election chances goodbye. This Shire has a large Aboriginal population, and asking for the death penalty for a minority woman is political suicide. It won't just stay local either. The national media will have a field day. Headlines will paint us as backward, redneck barbarians, and it'll follow me forever."

"Then don't prosecute her. It wouldn't be justice anyway—it was self-defense, plain and simple."

Peacock looked unconvinced. "She's got you believing that?"

"It's obvious."

"I wish it were obvious," Peacock said, his voice heavy. "For the first time in my career, I'm willing to bend the rules to make this go away."

"You don't need to bend the rules," Hunter said, narrowing his eyes. "Do you?"

"Let's walk through it," Peacock suggested. "Step by step. The spousal abuse defense can work, but it has to be an act of passion—spur of the moment. The law doesn't allow premeditation. And Rosie was prepared. The fact is, she bought that gun as soon as she knew Warner was coming home. I've seen the paperwork—it came through this office. She was ready for him."

Hunter stayed silent.

"I know her," Peacock said, his voice softening. "Warner was my friend, so I've known her for almost as long as he did."

"And?"

Peacock hesitated. "There are... complications."

"What kind of complications?"

Peacock looked conflicted. "I don't know how much I should say, legally speaking. So let me just guess, and you don't respond. That way, you're not put in a tough spot."

"Okay."

"She probably told you she came from a wealthy wine-growing family, right?"

Hunter said nothing.

"She met Warner while they were students at USYD, got pregnant, and had to get married. That led her parents to cut her off."

Hunter remained silent.

"She probably also told you that Warner hit her, starting when she was pregnant. And she made you believe that she tipped off the ATO, which got her even more frightened about Warner coming home."

Again, Hunter said nothing.

Peacock sighed. "I get it. She told you a lot of things, but most of it is hearsay and won't hold up in court. Even if the lawyer tries to get it admitted to support her mental state, it's risky. But say they let you testify. You'd paint a picture of serious abuse, and maybe the jury would be sympathetic enough to overlook the premeditation."

"So where's the issue?"

"The problem is, if you take the stand, you'd be cross-examined, too."

"And what if I am?" Hunter asked.

Peacock leaned forward, looking uncomfortable. "Let me take a few more guesses. Don't answer, and don't take offense if I'm wrong."

"Go ahead."

"My guess is Rosie's premeditation was more extensive than you think. She thought about it for a long time, and I'd even bet she tried to get you to do it for her."

Hunter didn't react.

"My next guess is that she didn't just stumble across you by accident. She picked you, somehow, and probably worked hard to convince you to get involved."

Hunter stayed silent.

Peacock swallowed hard, clearly uneasy. "And another guess: she offered you something in return—sex, as a bribe."

Hunter still said nothing.

"And I'd bet that, at some point, she tried again to get you into bed."

Hunter remained quiet, though his gaze grew more focused.

Peacock sighed. "If I'm right, all of this would come out under cross-examination. It would damage the entire defense. Probably beyond repair."

Hunter's expression didn't change.

"And it gets worse," Peacock continued grimly. "Much worse. If Rosie told you things, then her credibility is what matters most, right? The big question becomes: was she telling you the truth about the abuse or not? To test that, the cross-examination would start with innocent questions—who she is, where she's from—and you'd repeat what she told you."

"And then?"

"And then her entire credibility would fall apart. From there, it's straight to death row."

"Why?"

"Because I know her, and she's a compulsive liar, Hunter. She makes things up."

"What kind of things?"

"Everything. I've heard her stories over and over again. For instance, did she tell you she came from a wealthy wine-growing family?"

Hunter nodded. "She mentioned a thousand acres in the Hunter Valley. That's not true?"

Peacock shook his head. "She's from a public housing block in southwest Sydney. No one really knows much about her parents. She probably doesn't either."

Hunter paused before shrugging. "It's not a crime to disguise a humble background."

"She wasn't a student at USYD, either. She was a stripper. A prostitute, actually. She worked at university parties, among other things. Warner met her during one of her performances—he was entranced by her. I think she did some kind of trick with a long-neck beer bottle. Somehow, he fell for her, saw her as someone he could rescue. 'Let me take you away from all this,' that kind of thing. And I get it—she was stunning back then. Smart, too. She saw Warner as her ticket out. She went off birth control without telling him, got pregnant, and forced his hand. Warner did the gentlemanly thing and married her."

"I don't believe you."

Peacock shrugged. "It doesn't matter whether you do or don't. I'll explain why in a moment. But the sad truth is, it's all true. She's smart. She knew that a life of prostitution only gets worse with time. She wanted a way out, and Warner was it. She took him for everything—diamonds, horses, you name it."

Hunter shook his head. "I still don't believe you."

Peacock gave a slight nod. "I get it. She's very convincing. But even if it's true, it doesn't justify him hitting her, right?"

Peacock paused, then answered his own question. "No, of course not. But here's the real problem: he never hit her. Warner was a lot of things—lazy, a bit dishonest in business, sure. He was born into wealth, and it made him a little arrogant. But he saw himself as a Queensland gentleman, and a true gentleman would never hit a woman. Not ever. She's making it all up. I promise you, Warner never laid a hand on her."

Hunter's jaw tightened. "Your promise doesn't prove anything. What else would you say? He was your friend."

Peacock nodded, conceding the point. "Fair enough. But the fact is, there's no other evidence. No witnesses, no whispers of abuse, nothing. I was around them countless times, and every story I heard about horseback riding accidents seemed genuine. We'll check the medical records, of course, but I don't expect to find anything ambiguous."

"You said yourself that abuse can be covert."

"Covert? Sure. But *that* covert? Come on. I've seen it all, Hunter. Abusive couples who live in isolation, maybe. But Warner and Rosie weren't isolated. They were surrounded by family and friends. Before this, there wasn't a single rumor about abuse between them—nothing from me, Troy Bradley, or anyone else. So do you get what I'm saying? All we have is her word. And if you take the stand to back her up, your testimony will show she's a pathological liar."

Peacock leaned back in his chair. "Did she tell you she tipped off the ATO?"

"Yeah. She said she called some special unit."

Peacock shook his head. "That's not true. The ATO caught Warner through his bank records during an unrelated audit. Rosie didn't know anything about it. I know this for a fact because Warner came to Troy for legal advice, and Troy came straight to me. I've seen the indictment. Black and white. Rosie made up that story."

Hunter was silent for a long moment. "Maybe she is a liar," he said finally. "But liars get abused, too. Abuse can be covert—you don't know for sure it wasn't happening."

Peacock nodded slightly. "You're right. I don't know for sure. But I'd bet my life it wasn't."

"She convinced me."

"She probably convinced herself. She lives in her own fantasy world, Hunter. She's a liar, through and through, and she's guilty of premeditated murder."

"So why are we having this conversation?" Hunter asked, his tone sharp.

Peacock paused, clearly struggling with his thoughts. "Can I trust you?" he asked quietly.

Hunter raised an eyebrow. "Does it matter?"

Peacock stared at the wall, deep in thought. The hum of the air conditioners filled the silence as seconds ticked by.

"Yes," Peacock finally said. "It matters. It matters a lot—to Rosie, and to me. Because you're misreading me right now. I'm not some angry friend trying to protect Warner's reputation. I'm looking for a way to defend Rosie. I want to save her, even if that means stretching the truth a little. Do you understand that? I'm seriously tempted to pretend the abuse was real and downplay the premeditation. I'm desperate to make this go away—because then I won't have to charge her, and I might save my shot at becoming a judge."

The room fell silent again, filled only by the noise of the air conditioners and faint chatter from outside.

"I want to see her," Hunter said finally.

Peacock shook his head. "I can't let you. You're not her lawyer."

"You could bend the rules," Hunter suggested.

Peacock sighed and dropped his head into his hands. "Please, don't tempt me. Right now, I'm considering throwing the rulebook out the window."

Hunter stayed quiet, watching as Peacock stared into space, clearly strained.

"I need to figure out her real motive," Peacock said finally. "If it was cold and calculated—about money or something like that—then I don't have a choice. She'll have to go down for it."

Hunter remained silent, listening carefully.

"But if it wasn't about something like that, I want your help," Peacock admitted. "If her medical records show anything that backs up the abuse, I want to try saving her with that defense."

Hunter still said nothing.

"Okay," Peacock added with a grimace. "What I really mean is, I want to save myself. I need to salvage my chances in the election. Maybe even save both of us—her and me. Lahni too. She's a great kid. Warner loved her."

"What do you want from me?" Hunter asked cautiously.

"If we go down that road."

Hunter nodded slightly. "If."

"I'd need you to lie on the stand," Peacock said, his voice low. "I'd want you to repeat what she told you about the beatings and adjust her other stories to keep her credibility intact."

Hunter didn't respond, taking in the weight of what was being asked.

"That's why I need to trust you," Peacock explained. "And that's why I had to lay everything out for you—so you know exactly what you're getting into with her."

Hunter took a deep breath. "I've never done something like that before."

"Neither have I," Peacock said, clearly struggling with the situation. "Just talking about it is tearing me apart."

Hunter was silent for a moment before asking, "Why do you think I'd even want to do this?"

Peacock gave a small, knowing smile. "I think you care about her. I think you feel sorry for her. You probably want to help, and by helping her, you'd be helping me."

"How would you make it work?"

Peacock shrugged. "I'll be recused from the case from the start, so one of my assistants will handle it. I'll find out exactly what can be proven for certain, and I'll coach you so you don't trip up. That's why I can't let you see Rosie right now. They keep records downstairs, and it would look like prior collusion."

Hunter sat back, uncertain. "I don't know."

"I'm not sure either," Peacock admitted. "But maybe it won't even have to go to trial. If the medical evidence is somewhat supportive, and we take depositions from both Rosie and you, we might have a chance to justify dropping the charges altogether."

"Lying in a deposition would be just as bad," Hunter pointed out.

Peacock nodded. "Think about Lahni."

"And your judgeship," Hunter added.

Peacock didn't shy away from the comment. "I'm not hiding my ambitions from you. I want to get elected, no question about it. But it's for an honest reason—I want to make things better. That's always been my goal, to work my way up and improve the system from within. It's the only way to create real change. For someone like me, anyway. I don't have political influence or the right connections."

Hunter said nothing, deep in thought.

"Let me think it over," Peacock said, after a long pause. "Give me a day or two, and I'll figure out what to do next."

"Are you sure?" Hunter asked, raising an eyebrow.

"No, of course I'm not sure," Peacock replied with a heavy sigh. "I hate everything about this situation. But Warner's gone, and nothing's going to bring him back. Yes, this would damage his memory, but it could save Rosie. And Warner loved her—more than anyone else ever could. He took on all the criticism from his family and society for her. I think he'd be willing to sacrifice his reputation to save her life. His life, really, for hers."

Silence settled over them once more, heavy and thick.

"She needs bail," Hunter said after a moment.

Peacock shook his head firmly. "That's out of the question."

"Lahni needs her mother."

"That's a much bigger issue than just bail," Peacock said

quietly. "Lahni can handle a few more days with her grandmother. It's the rest of her life that we need to be thinking about. Give me time to work this out."

Hunter shrugged, accepting that he wouldn't get any further for now. He stood up to leave.

"This conversation is completely confidential, right?" Peacock asked, his voice urgent. "I should've made that clear from the beginning."

Hunter nodded. "Of course."

"Get back to me," Peacock said.

Without another word, Hunter nodded again and walked out of the room.

CHAPTER 12

"One simple question," Sally began. "Is it even possible for domestic abuse to be so hidden that close friends wouldn't notice?"

"I'm not sure," Hunter replied. "I don't have much experience in that area."

"Neither do I."

They sat across from each other at Sally's desk, tucked away in the back of the legal office. It was midday, and the heat was stifling, enforcing an unspoken curfew on the town. Only those who absolutely had to be out were braving it. The office was mostly empty—just Sally, Hunter, and another lawyer twenty feet away. Inside, it was easily over forty degrees, with the humidity rising, and the old air conditioner above the door doing little to help. Sally had changed into shorts again, leaning back in her chair with her arms raised above her head, her back lifted off the sticky vinyl. Sweat glistened on her skin, giving it an oiled appearance against her tan. Hunter's shirt was soaked through, making him reconsider its five-day life expectancy.

"It's a catch-22," Sally said. "If you know about the abuse, it's not really covert. If it's truly hidden, you might think it's not happening at all. Like, I assume my dad doesn't beat my mum, but what if he does? Who would know? What about your family?"

Hunter smiled. "Unlikely. My dad was a big guy, Australian SAS captain—not exactly the gentle type. But then again, you didn't know my mum. She might've been the one beating him."

"So, yes or no when it comes to Rosie and Warner?"

"She convinced me," Hunter said firmly. "No question about it."

"Even after everything?"

"She convinced me," he repeated. "She may lie about other things, but I believe he was hitting her. That's my take."

Sally gave him a long look, her lawyer instincts kicking in. "You're absolutely sure?"

"No doubt at all," Hunter affirmed.

"Well," Sally sighed, "a tough case just got even tougher. And I hate when that happens."

"Same here," Hunter agreed. "But tough doesn't mean impossible."

"Do you understand the legal situation?" she asked.

Hunter nodded. "It's not that complicated. Either way, she's in deep trouble. If the abuse was real, she undermined her case with all the premeditation. If it wasn't real, it's a straight-up murder charge. Plus, with her history of lying and exaggeration, she's got no credibility. The only reason she's got a shot is because Peacock wants that judgeship so badly."

"Exactly," Sally said.

"Are you comfortable riding that kind of luck?"

"Not really."

"Neither am I."

"Morally or practically," Sally added. "Anything could happen. For all we know, Tom might have some secret love child out there, and it could come out, forcing him to step back. Maybe he has weird habits no one knows about. November is a long way off. Counting on him to stay electable is a gamble. Rosie needs a solid defense, not a lucky break."

Hunter chuckled. "You're smarter than I thought."

"I was waiting for you to say 'smarter than I look.'"

"I think more lawyers should dress like you," he joked.

"You need to stay off the stand," Sally said, changing the subject. "It's safer for her if you do. No deposition either. Without you, the only thing tying her to premeditation is the gun. We can argue that buying the gun and using it weren't directly connected. Maybe she bought it for another reason."

Hunter didn't respond.

"They're running tests on it now," Sally said. "Ballistics and fingerprints. They found two sets of prints. I'm guessing hers, and maybe his, too. Could've been a struggle. Maybe it was an accident."

Hunter shook his head. "The second set of prints is mine. She asked me to show her how to use it. We went to the plateau and practiced."

"When was that?"

"Saturday. The day before he came home."

Sally stared at him, her eyes wide. "Christ, Hunter. You definitely need to stay off the stand."

"That's the plan."

"And if they subpoena you?"

"I'll lie, I guess."

"Can you?"

"I was a bloke in uniform of sorts for thirteen years. It's not that big of a leap."

"What would you say about your prints on the gun?"

"I'd say I found it somewhere, returned it to her. Make it seem like she'd had second thoughts about using it."

"You're comfortable lying about that?"

"If it helps her, I am. And I think it would. She's made her case harder to prove, that's all. You?"

Sally nodded. "In a case like this, I think so. Her lies about her background don't bother me. People lie about things all the time, for all kinds of reasons. The real issue is premeditation. In other states, premeditation wouldn't be such a big deal. They understand the reality—sometimes a battered woman has to wait for the right moment, when he's drunk or asleep. Other places have seen plenty of cases like that."

"So, where do we start?"

"We start where we have to," Sally said. "And it's not a great place. The circumstantial evidence is overwhelming. The thing speaks for itself. Her room, her gun, her husband dead on the floor. It screams murder. If we leave it like that, they'll convict her in a heartbeat."

"So?"

"So, we backtrack on the premeditation and prove the abuse through her medical records. I've already started the paperwork. We filed a subpoena with the prosecutor's office, requesting records from all Queensland hospitals and neighboring states. It's standard in domestic violence cases—people often drive far to hide their injuries. Hospitals usually respond quickly, so we should have the records by tomorrow. If the injuries were caused by violence, the records will show it's at least possible. Then Rosie takes the stand and talks about the abuse. She'll have to own up to her lies about her past, but if we spin it right, she might even gain some sympathy. Being an ex-hooker trying to reform could work in her favor."

"You sound like a good lawyer," Hunter said.

She smiled. "For someone so young?"

"Well, what are you? Two years out of law school?"

"Six months," she corrected. "But you learn fast up here."

"Clearly."

"With careful jury selection, we could end up with a mixed jury—some undecided, some leaning toward not guilty. The not-guiltys will wear down the undecideds after a couple of days, especially if it's this hot."

Hunter peeled his shirt away from his sweaty skin. "It can't stay this hot forever."

"I'm talking about next summer," Sally said. "If she's lucky. Maybe the summer after that."

"You're kidding."

She shook her head. "The record here is four years in jail between arrest and trial."

"What about Lahni?"

Sally shrugged. "We'll just have to pray the medical records look good. If they do, we might be able to convince Tom to drop the charges altogether. He's got a lot of flexibility."

"It wouldn't take much to push him," Hunter said. "Not with the mood he's in."

"Exactly. This could all be over in a few days if we're lucky."

"When are you going to see her?"

"Later today. But first, I'm heading to the bank to cash a fifty-thousand-dollar check. Then I'm putting the money in a Woolies grocery bag and delivering it to some very happy people."

“Okay,” Hunter said.

“I don’t want to know how you got it,” she added.

“I just asked for it.”

“I still don’t want to know,” she repeated. “But you should come with me. Be my bodyguard. I don’t usually carry fifty grand around in a green plastic bag. Plus, it’ll be cool in the car.”

“Okay,” Hunter said again.

The bank teller showed no particular surprise at handing over fifty thousand dollars in mixed notes. She treated it like just another part of her day, counting the money three times before carefully stacking it into the lime green Woolies grocery bag that Sally had brought. Hunter carried the bag back to the car for her, though there wasn’t much danger of them getting robbed— the oppressive heat had cleared the streets, and the few people still outside moved slowly and lethargically.

The interior of Sally’s Hyundai was blistering, too hot to sit in immediately. She started the car, cranked up the air conditioning, and left the doors open until the temperature dropped enough for them to get inside. Even after the cool-down, it was still over thirty-five degrees, but it felt almost refreshing. Everything was relative. Sally drove, heading north and east, handling the car with ease—better than Hunter had.

“There’s going to be a storm,” she said.

“Everyone keeps telling me that,” Hunter replied. “But I don’t see it.”

“Ever experienced heat like this before?”

“Maybe,” he said. “Once or twice—in Saudi Arabia and the Pacific. But Saudi’s drier, and the Pacific’s wetter, so not exactly like this.”

The sky ahead was a harsh, light blue, so hot it seemed almost white. The sun was an intense, diffuse glare that felt like it was coming from everywhere at once. Hunter squinted so hard that the muscles in his face began to ache.

"This is all new to me," Sally said. "I expected it to be hot, but this is unbelievable."

She asked him about his time in the Middle East and Pacific, prompting Hunter to launch into the expanded version of his life story. He found that he was enjoying her company. The first thirty-six years of his life were easy to recount, a neat linear progression from childhood to adulthood, achievement to achievement, all underscored by military promotions and medals. The last few years were harder to explain—more aimless, drifting. He saw them as a triumph of disengagement, but he knew others wouldn't. So, he told the story as plainly as he could, letting her fill in the blanks for herself.

In return, Sally offered up her own biography. In many ways, it mirrored his, though through a different lens. She was the daughter of a lawyer, just as he was the son of a soldier. She hadn't really considered doing anything outside the family trade, just as he hadn't. Like him, she had watched people walk the walk, and then followed in their footsteps. She'd spent seven years at the University of Sydney, while he'd spent four at Campbell Barracks. Now, at twenty-five, she was the legal world's version of an ambitious lieutenant. Hunter had been an ambitious lieutenant at that age, too, and he remembered exactly what it felt like.

"So, what's next for you?" he asked.

"After this?" she said, pausing to think. "Probably to Melbourne. Maybe Canberra—I'm getting interested in policy."

"You won't miss this hands-on stuff?"

"I probably will," she admitted. "But I won't give it up completely. Maybe I'll volunteer for a few weeks each year, and I'll definitely try to help fund it. That's how we get all our money, you know—big firms in the big cities, with a conscience."

"I'm glad to hear that. Somebody needs to do something."

"That's for sure."

"What about Tom Peacock?" Hunter asked. "Will he make a difference?"

She shrugged while keeping her eyes on the road. "I don't know him very well. His reputation's good, though. And, honestly, he can't make things any worse. The system is so broken. I'm a Labor voter, so in theory, I'm fine with the idea of electing judges. But in practice, it's out of control. Do you know how much it costs to run a campaign here?"

"No idea."

"Well, think about it. We're talking about Mount Kalka Shire, mostly. Some posters, newspaper ads, a few local TV commercials. In a market this small, you'd struggle to spend more than five figures. Yet these candidates are collecting hundreds of thousands, maybe even millions. And if they don't spend it all, they get to keep what's left—for 'future expenses.' Basically, they're collecting their bribes in advance. Law firms, mining interests, special interest groups—they're all paying for future favors. It's a rigged system. You can get filthy rich running for judge in Queensland. And once you're elected and play your cards right, you retire into a cushy partnership with a big law firm and land a spot on a few corporate boards. It's not about becoming a judge—it's about becoming royalty."

"So, will Peacock make a difference?" Hunter asked again.

"He will if he wants to. It's as simple as that. And right now, he'll make a big difference to Rosie McMahon. That's what we need to focus on."

Hunter nodded as Sally slowed the car, searching for a turn. They were back in farming country, not far from the Peterson place, though Hunter didn't recognize the landscape. It was a dry, harsh stretch of land, so hot it felt like the parched vegetation could burst into flames at any moment.

"Does it bother you that Rosie lied so much?" Sally asked.

Hunter shrugged. "Yes and no. No one likes being lied to, but from her perspective, she saw a problem and did what she needed to solve it."

"So, she was definitely planning it for a while?"

"Should I be telling you this?" Hunter asked with a wry smile.

"I'm on her side," Sally reassured him.

Hunter nodded. "She planned it. She told me she looked at a hundred different guys and scoped out a dozen before deciding on me."

Sally seemed oddly reassured. "Somehow, that makes me feel better. It proves how desperate she was. Nobody would go that far without real cause."

"I agree," Hunter said. "I feel the same way."

Sally slowed the car again, turning onto a narrow farm track. After about ten meters, they passed beneath a makeshift farm gate—just a rectangle of weathered sleepers nailed together and leaning slightly. The crossbar bore a name that had been so scorched and faded by the sun it was now indecipherable. Beyond the gate, a few acres of cultivated ground lay dry and barren. Rows of turned dirt stretched out, an irrigation system pieced together from salvaged parts standing idle. Piles of fieldstone were scattered here and there, along with wooden frames once meant to support crops that no longer grew. The whole scene spoke of months of exhausting labor, all leading to bitter disappointment.

About a hundred meters beyond the last row of dry earth stood a small, low wooden house, painted a dull, sun-bleached white. A windmill creaked behind it, and a barn stood nearby, an irrigation pump venting through the roof. A rusted Holden HQ ute sat idle outside. The house's front door was closed. Sally parked the Hyundai next to it.

"The family's called Longman," she said, "and I'm sure they're home."

Fifty thousand dollars in a grocery bag had an effect unlike anything Hunter had ever seen. It was, quite literally, a gift of life. The Longman family consisted of five people—two from the older generation and three from the younger. They were all small and wiry, clearly hardened by difficult circumstances. The parents were likely in their early fifties, and the oldest child, a daughter, looked to be about twenty-five. The two younger sons were probably somewhere in their early twenties. They stood quietly together inside the doorway as Sally greeted them cheerfully, walking straight past them and dumping the money onto their kitchen table.

"He changed his mind," she said in Pidgin. "He decided to pay up, after all."

The Longmans formed a semicircle around the table, staring at the pile of cash in stunned silence, as if it represented such a dramatic turn of fortune that they couldn't react at first. There were no questions, just a quiet acceptance that it had finally happened. Then, after a moment, they erupted into a stream of excited plans. First, they would get the internet reconnected so they wouldn't have to walk eight kilometers to their neighbor's house. Then, they'd restore their electricity so they wouldn't have to run a generator. After that, they'd repay what they had borrowed from friends. And then they would buy a tank of diesel fuel, so they could run the irrigation pump again. Next, they would fix their ute and drive into town to get seed and fertilizer. The room fell silent once more as it dawned on them that they could plant, harvest, and sell a whole crop before winter arrived.

Hunter stayed back, observing the room. It was a live-in kitchen that opened into a small, hot parlor. The parlor was stuffy and airless, with a yard-long set of encyclopedias and a collection of religious statuettes on a low shelf. A single picture hung on the wall: a photograph of a boy, probably about fourteen, sporting the first signs of a mustache. He was dressed in a white confirmation robe and wore a shy smile. The picture was framed in black, with a small square of black cloth draped over the frame.

"That's my eldest son," a voice said softly. "The picture was taken just before we left our village in Papua New Guinea."

Hunter turned to see the Longman mother standing behind him.

"He was killed on our journey here," she added quietly.

"I know," Hunter said gently. "I heard about it. The border patrol. I'm so sorry."

"It was twelve years ago. His name was Ratu Longman."

The way she said her son's name carried the weight of memory, a small act of honor.

"What happened?" Hunter asked.

The woman was silent for a moment. Then, with a heavy sigh, she explained, "It was horrible. They hunted us for three hours in the night. We were walking and running, while they had a ute with bright lights. We got separated in the dark. Ratu was with his sister—she was twelve at the time. He sent her one way and went the other, straight into the lights. He knew it would be worse if they captured her. He gave himself up to protect her. But they didn't try to arrest him or ask any questions. They just shot him down and drove away. They passed right by me as I hid. I heard them laughing, like it was a game."

"I'm so sorry," Hunter said again, his voice barely a whisper.

She gave a small shrug. "It was common then. A bad time, a bad place. We found out later that more than twenty people had been killed on that route in just a year. Some were tortured in horrible ways. Ratu was lucky—he was only shot. Some were made to suffer for hours. You could hear their screams echoing across the tropics. And some girls were taken away, never to be seen again."

Hunter remained silent, letting the weight of her words settle over the room. She gazed at the picture of her son for a moment longer before turning away with immense effort. She forced a smile and gestured for Hunter to return to the kitchen with her.

"We saved some rum for this day," she said softly.

On the kitchen table, shot glasses were lined up, and the daughter—the same girl Ratu had saved—was pouring from a bottle. The younger son handed the glasses around. Hunter took his and waited. The father, Longman, raised his glass in a toast, directing it toward Sally.

"To our lawyer," he said, "for standing up for those who cannot stand up for themselves to be heard in the courtroom.'"

Sally blushed a little. Longman smiled at her and then turned to Hunter.

"And to you, sir, for your generous help in our time of need."

"No problem," Hunter said quietly. "Anytime."

The rum was harsh, and Ratu's mind was scattered, so they declined a second drink and left the Longmans to their celebration. Once again, they had to wait for the car's air conditioning to cool down the Hyundai's interior. Then, they drove back to Mount Kalka.

“I really enjoyed that,” Sally said. “It feels like I finally made a difference.”

“You definitely did,” Hunter replied.

“Even though you were the one who made it happen.”

“You handled the hard work,” he said.

“Still, thank you.”

“Did the border patrol ever face an investigation?” he asked.

She nodded. “Yes, thoroughly, according to the records. There was enough commotion that something had to be done. Nothing concrete, of course, but plenty of vague rumors to push it forward.”

“And?”

“And nothing. It was a cover-up. No one was even charged.”

“But did it stop?”

She nodded again. “As abruptly as it started. So, clearly, they got the message.”

“That’s how it goes,” he said. “I’ve seen it before, in other places, different circumstances. The investigation isn’t really to find anything. It’s more like a warning, saying ‘You can’t keep doing this, so knock it off, whoever you are.’”

“But justice wasn’t served, Hunter. Over twenty people died, some in horrific ways. It was a year-long massacre. Somebody should have been held accountable.”

“Did you catch that quote back there form the father?” he asked.

“Of course,” she replied. “I went to USYD.”

"Remember Adam Smith?"

"I think so, he lived in another era, right? An economist?."

He nodded. "Born in the 1700's. He was an economist *and* political philosopher. He said, 'No society can surely be flourishing and happy, of which the far greater part of the members are poor and miserable.'

"That's awful."

"It is," Hunter said. "But that's reality."

They reached Mount Kalka in under an hour. Sally parked on the street, right outside the legal mission, so they only had to walk a few meters in the heat. But even those few steps felt like trudging through a furnace with a hot towel wrapped around their heads. Once inside, they found Sally's desk cluttered with little handwritten notes scattered across it. She gathered them up, read them one by one, and then tossed them into a drawer.

"I'm going to check in with Rosie at the jail," she said. "The prints and ballistics results are back from the lab. Note says Tom Peacock wants to talk to you about them. Sounds like he's got a problem."

"I'm sure he does," Hunter said.

They paused briefly before stepping outside again. Then, they parted ways in front of the courthouse. Sally headed toward the jail, and Hunter climbed the steps inside. The public areas had no air conditioning, and by the time he made it to the first floor, he was drenched in sweat. The intern at the desk silently pointed to Tom Peacock's office. Hunter went straight in and found Peacock poring over a technical report, the kind of man who believes reading something enough times might eventually change its content.

"She killed him," Peacock said. "The ballistics match perfectly."

Hunter took a seat across from the desk.

"Your prints were on the gun, too," Peacock added.

Hunter said nothing. If he was going to lie, he'd save it for when it mattered.

"You're in the national fingerprint database," Peacock continued. "You knew that, right?"

Hunter nodded. "All military personnel are."

"So, maybe you found the gun discarded," Peacock said. "Maybe you handled it because you didn't want a family with a kid finding a stray firearm. Maybe you picked it up and put it somewhere safe."

"Maybe," Hunter said.

Peacock flipped a page in the file. "But it's worse than that, isn't it?"

"Is it?"

"Are you a praying man?"

"No," Hunter replied.

"You should be. You should get on your knees and thank someone."

"Like who?"

"Maybe the QLD police. Maybe Warner himself for calling the sergeant."

"Why?"

"Because they just saved your life."

"How?"

"You were in a squad car when this went down. If they'd left you in the bunkhouse, you'd be our prime suspect."

"Why?"

Peacock turned another page. "Your prints were on the gun. On the shell cases. On the magazine. Even on the ammo box. You loaded that gun, Hunter. Probably test-fired it, too. She bought it, technically it was hers, but the fingerprint evidence makes it look like it was really your weapon."

Hunter stayed quiet.

"So you see?" Peacock said. "You should be grateful to the state police. Without them, I'd be coming after you. You could've easily sneaked up from the bunkhouse to the bedroom and done it. You knew where the bedroom was, didn't you? Ryan told me you spent the night there."

"I didn't sleep with her," Hunter said. "I was on the sofa."

Peacock smirked. "Think a jury would believe you? Or an ex-prostitute? I wouldn't. It'd be easy to suggest some kind of jealous motive. But luckily for you, you were in a police car at the time."

"So, you're a lucky man, Hunter. Right now, having a white male suspect would be priceless to me. You'd be the perfect candidate for death row, standing out among the other inmates. A big white fella like you, thrown in with a bunch of black and Aboriginal guys—I'd look like the most impartial prosecutor in Queensland. The election would be over before it even started."

Hunter said nothing.

Peacock sighed. "But you didn't do it, unfortunately. She did. And now my case for premeditation is falling apart. It's almost completely gone. Clearly, she thought it through—she even found an ex-army ranger to train her with weapons. We pulled your record after we got your prints. You were a rifle-shooting champion seven years in a row. You even served as an instructor. You loaded her gun. What am I supposed to do?"

"Stick to your plan," Hunter said. "Wait for the medical reports."

Peacock went quiet again, then sighed heavily. He nodded. "We'll have them tomorrow. I did something out of the ordinary, though. I hired a defense expert to take a look. You know, the kind that usually works for the defense. Normally, we wouldn't touch them, but I want someone who can convince me there's even a slim chance Rosie's telling the truth so I can let her go without looking like I've lost my mind."

"So relax," Hunter said. "It'll be done tomorrow."

"I hope so," Peacock replied. "It might be. Troy Bradley's office is sending over some financial records. He handled all of Warner's affairs. If there's no financial motive and the medical reports check out, maybe I can breathe easy."

"She didn't have any money," Hunter said. "That was one of her biggest problems."

Peacock nodded. "Good. Her problems solve mine."

The room went quiet, the air conditioner humming in the background. Hunter felt cold sweat on the back of his neck.

"You should do something proactive," he suggested. "For the election."

"Like what?" Peacock asked.

"Something popular. Like reopening an inquiry into the border patrol. People would appreciate that. I just met a family whose son was killed by them."

Peacock was silent for a moment before shaking his head. "That's old news."

"Not for the families," Hunter said. "There were over twenty homicides in a year. The survivors likely still live here—and they're probably voters by now."

"The border patrol was investigated," Peacock said. "That was before my time, but it was a thorough one. I reviewed the files years ago."

"You have the files?"

"Of course. Most of it happened in or near Four Ways, so it's all here. It looked like a few rogue officers acting on their own. The investigation likely served as a warning. They probably left the patrol. It has a high turnover rate. Those guys could be anywhere by now—probably out of the state. It's not just immigrants who move south."

"It would still make you look good."

Peacock shrugged. "I'm sure it would, but I have some standards. It'd be a waste of public funds—just political grandstanding. It wouldn't lead anywhere. Those people are long gone. It's ancient history."

"Twelve years ago isn't ancient."

"It is around here. Things move fast. Right now, I'm focused on what happened last night, not twelve years ago."

"Fair enough," Hunter said. "It's your call."

"I'll get in touch with Sally tomorrow when we have everything we need. It could all be over by lunch."

"Let's hope so."

"Yeah, let's," Peacock agreed.

Hunter walked back out into the stairwell, the trapped air suffocatingly hot. It was even worse outside. The heat was so intense that it felt like the oxygen had been burned out of the air. He crossed the street and made his way back to the mission, sweat stinging his eyes. When he walked inside, he saw Sally sitting alone at her desk.

"You're back already?" he asked, surprised.

She nodded.

"Did you see her?"

She nodded again.

"What did she say?"

"Nothing at all," Sally replied. "Except that she doesn't want me to represent her."

"What do you mean?"

"Exactly what I said. The only thing she told me was, 'I refuse to be represented by you.'"

"Why?"

"She didn't give a reason. That was the only thing she said, over and over. After that, she just went silent."

"What the hell?"

Sally shrugged. "I've got no idea."

"Has anything like this happened before?"

"Not to me, or anyone else I know. Usually, clients here are either so desperate they'll bite your hand off for help, or they're falling over themselves to thank you."

"So, what went wrong?"

"I don't know. She seemed pretty calm, fairly rational."

"Did you try to convince her?"

"Of course. I did what I could without pushing her too far. I didn't want to risk her starting to yell and making things worse. If a guard overhears her, I'll lose my standing with the court, and then she'll really be in trouble. I plan to try again later."

"Did you mention I sent you?"

"Yeah, I used your name. Didn't change a thing. All she kept saying was that she refused representation, and then she clammed up."

"Any idea why?"

Sally shrugged again. "No clue. I mean, I'm not exactly Harvey Specter, but I didn't think I came across as incompetent. I was sweating like a pig and half-naked from this heat, sure, but this isn't Sydney. We're in Mount Kalka. She's Aboriginal, and I'm a breathing lawyer. She should've been thrilled I even showed up."

"So what now?"

"Now, I have to convince her to accept representation before anyone hears her refuse."

"And if she still doesn't?"

"Then I move on, and she's on her own. Eventually, some court-appointed lawyer will step in, but that won't be until much later—probably when the indictment comes in."

Hunter paused. "I'm sorry, Sally. I didn't expect this."

"It's not your fault."

"Try again at seven, alright?" he suggested. "When the upstairs offices are empty and before the night shift begins. The woman coming on duty seemed nosier than the guy there during the day. He might not notice much. You'll have a better chance to press her. Let her yell if she wants to."

"Okay," she agreed. "Seven it is. What a day. It's been a rollercoaster."

"Just like life," Hunter said.

She smiled briefly. "Where will you be?"

"I'm staying at the last motel before the highway."

"You enjoy traffic noise?"

"I enjoy cheap rooms. Number eight, under the name Frank Forde."

"Why?"

"Habit," he replied. "I like aliases. I like staying under the radar."

"Who's Frank Forde?"

"Prime Minister. Shortest serving PM after Curtin died in office, lasted a week."

Sally was quiet for a moment. "Should I dress more like a lawyer? Do you think it would help with Rosie?"

Hunter shrugged. "I doubt it. Look at me—I'm dressed like a scarecrow, and she didn't say anything about it."

Sally smiled again. "You do look a bit like that. When I saw you this morning, I thought you were a homeless bloke in trouble."

"This is a new outfit," Hunter said. "Fresh today."

She gave him another glance but stayed silent. He left her to her paperwork and walked to the pizza place south of the courthouse. It was packed with people, probably because the giant air conditioner above the door was dumping cool mist onto the sidewalk. Clearly, it was the coldest spot in town. He got the last table and gulped down ice water as fast as the waiter could refill his glass. He ordered a large meat lover's pizza, loaded with bacon, figuring he needed the salt.

****

While he ate, a new description was being relayed by phone to a hit squad. The call, routed through Brisbane and the Gold Coast, went to a motel about a hundred kilometers from Mount

Kalka. The man spoke clearly, providing an exact description of a new target, a male, including his full name, age, physical appearance, and likely movements over the next forty-eight hours.

The woman on the receiving end made no notes, relying on her well-trained memory. She had no issue speaking on the phone, using a device from a military surplus shop that disguised her voice. After the man finished, she named her crew's price. There was a pause on the other end—he was deciding whether to negotiate. He didn't. Just said okay and hung up. She smiled to herself. Smart guy. They didn't work for cheapskates.

****

Hunter finished his pizza, had an ice cream, more water, and coffee, lingering as long as possible. Eventually, he paid at the counter and walked back towards his motel. The heat outside was even more unbearable after being in the air-conditioned restaurant. Once in his room, he took a long, cool shower, rinsed his clothes in the sink, and hung them to dry. He cranked the air conditioning up and lay down on the bed to wait for Sally. Checking his watch, he figured if she arrived after eight, it'd be a good sign. It meant she'd spent time with Rosie. He closed his eyes and tried to sleep.

CHAPTER 13

Sally arrived around seven-twenty. He awoke from a restless, overheated nap, hearing a soft knock at the door. He rolled out of bed, wrapped a damp towel around his waist, and padded across the worn carpet, barefoot, to open the door. There she stood. He looked at her, but she just shook her head. He glanced outside at the fading light of dusk and saw her red car parked in the lot. Turning, he stepped back into the room, and she followed him inside.

"I tried everything," she said.

She had changed back into her professional clothes—the black pants and jacket. The pants were high-waisted, nearly touching the bottom of her sports bra, leaving an inch of tanned skin exposed. Aside from that, she looked every bit the part of a lawyer. He couldn't imagine that inch of skin being significant to someone in Rosie's position.

"I asked her if it was something about me. Maybe she wanted someone older, a man, or an Aboriginal person?" Sally continued.

"What did she say?"

"She said she didn't want anyone at all."

"That's insane."

"It is," Sally agreed. "I explained her situation, in case she wasn't fully grasping it. It didn't change anything."

"Tell me exactly what she said."

"I already did."

Hunter shifted uncomfortably, adjusting the too-small towel. "Let me put my pants on."

He grabbed them from the chair and ducked into the bathroom. They were still damp and clammy, but he pulled them on and zipped them up before returning to the room. Sally had taken off her jacket and placed it on the chair next to his wet shirt. She sat on the bed, elbows on her knees.

"I tried everything," she repeated. "I even asked to see her arm. When she asked why, I told her I wanted to check how good her veins were, for the lethal injection. I described how she'd be strapped down, the drugs they'd use, and the people watching her die from behind the glass."

"And?"

"It didn't matter. It was like talking to a brick wall."

"How hard did you push?"

"I raised my voice a bit, but she just waited for me to finish and then repeated herself. She's refusing representation, Hunter. We have to accept that."

"Is that legal?"

"Of course. There's no law that says you have to have a lawyer. Only that one must be offered."

"Isn't it a sign of insanity or something?"

Sally shook her head. "Not by itself. Otherwise, every murderer could refuse counsel and claim an incapacity defense."

"She's not a murderer."

"She doesn't seem eager to prove that."

"Did anyone overhear her?"

"Not yet, but I'm worried her next move will be to put it in writing. If that happens, I won't even be able to talk to her—no one will."

"So, what do we do?"

"We have to work around her. Keep dealing with Peacock behind the scenes. If we can get him to drop the charges, she'll be free whether she wants us to help or not."

Hunter shrugged. "Then that's the plan. But it's all completely bizarre, isn't it?"

"It sure is," Sally agreed. "I've never seen anything like it."

****

Meanwhile, about a hundred kilometers away, the two male members of the hit squad returned to their motel after dinner. They had opted for pizza, too, but with pitchers of cold beer instead of water and coffee. Inside their room, their female partner was pacing, a clear sign that she had news.

"What's up?" the taller man asked.

"A side job," she replied.

"Where?"

"Mount Kalka."

"Is that wise?"

She nodded. "Mount Kalka's still safe enough."

"You sure?" the dark-haired man asked.

"Wait until you hear what he's offering to pay."

"When?"

"Depends on the other job we've got."

"Okay," the taller man said. "Who's the target?"

"Just some guy. I'll give you the details after we've handled the first job."

She moved to the door. "Stay in now. Get some rest. We've got a busy day ahead."

****

Sally glanced around the room. "This place is terrible."

Hunter looked around as well. "You think?"

"It's awful."

"I've stayed in worse."

There was a brief pause. "You hungry?"

Hunter had already eaten pizza and ice cream, but the sliver of midriff showing was tempting. So was the inch of her back, exposed by her high-waisted pants. A cleft there was bridged by the waistband, like a tiny span over a valley.

"Sure," he said. "Where?"

She hesitated. "My place? It's hard for me to eat out around here. I'm a vegetarian, so I usually cook for myself."

"A vegetarian in Queensland? You must feel out of place."

"I do," she said. "So, how about it? I also have better air conditioning than this."

He smiled. "Home-cooked food and cool air? Sounds good to me."

"Do you eat vegetarian?"

"I eat anything."

"Great, let's go."

He pulled on his damp shirt, and she grabbed her jacket. After locking the room, he followed her to the car.

She drove a few kilometers west, to a small residential complex on a patch of dry land between two busy roads. The buildings had sand-colored gyprock walls with dark wooden beams for accents, though the place looked worn down from the heat. Her unit was in the middle, a townhouse flanked by others. She parked on a cracked concrete slab with withering desert weeds sprouting from the gaps.

Inside, it was wonderfully cool. The central AC was running hard, creating a noticeable pressure in the air. The narrow living room had a kitchen in the back and a staircase to the left. The furniture was cheap and secondhand, and there were lots of books, but no television.

"I'm going to take a shower," she said. "Make yourself comfortable."

She disappeared upstairs while Hunter looked around. The books were mostly law texts—Queensland civil and criminal codes, constitutional commentary. A phone on a side table had four numbers programmed: Work, R Home, R Work, and M & D. On a bookshelf sat a photo in a silver frame, showing a middle-aged couple, probably in their fifties, in a casual outdoor setting, possibly Sydney. The man had gray hair and a long, aristocratic face. The woman looked like an older version of Sally, same hair, minus the color. They were likely her parents, labeled M & D on the phone. He assumed R was a boyfriend, though there was no picture of him. Perhaps there was one upstairs, by her bed.

He sat down, and within ten minutes, Sally came back downstairs. Her hair was wet and combed, and she had changed into shorts and an old, faded USYD soccer T-shirt. The writing was barely legible from so many washes. The shorts were short, and the T-shirt clung tightly, showing she'd ditched the sports bra. She was barefoot and looked stunning.

"You played soccer?" he asked.

"My partner did," she said.

He smiled at the hint. "Still does?"

"She's a she. Rhiannon. I'm gay. And yes, she still plays."

"Is she any good?"

"As a partner?"

"As a soccer player."

"She's pretty good. Does that bother you?"

"That she's good at soccer?"

"No, that I'm gay."

"Why would it?"

Sally shrugged. "It bothers some people."

"Not me."

"I'm Jewish, too."

Hunter smiled. "Did your parents buy you the handgun?"

She glanced at him. "You found that?"

"Yeah. Nice piece."

She nodded. "A gay Jewish vegetarian from Sydney's Eastern suburbs. My parents thought I needed it."

"I'm surprised they didn't get you a machine gun."

She laughed. "I'm sure they considered it."

"You really take your self-defense seriously. It must feel like walking around Lebanon."

She laughed again. "It's not that bad here. Queensland has some great people."

"What does Rhiannon do?"

"She's a lawyer, too. In the Northern Territory right now."

"Same reasons?"

Sally nodded. "A five-year plan."

"There's still hope for the legal profession, then."

"So, it doesn't bother you? That it's just dinner with a friend and back to the motel on your own?"

"I never expected anything else," he lied.

The meal turned out to be fantastic, even though he wasn't really hungry. It was some kind of dark, chewy concoction made from crushed nuts mixed with cheese and onions—probably packed with protein and maybe some vitamins, too. They drank a bit of wine, but mostly stuck to water. Afterward, he helped her clean up, and they talked until eleven.

"I'll give you a ride back," she offered.

But she was barefoot and looked comfortable, so he shook his head. "I'll walk. A couple of kilometers will do me good."

"It's still hot out," she warned.

"Don't worry. I'll be fine."

She didn't insist. They made plans to meet at the mission in the morning, and he said goodnight. The outside air was thick, like walking through soup. The forty-minute walk left him drenched in sweat again by the time he reached his motel.

He woke early the next morning, rinsed his clothes in the sink, and put them on wet. By the time he arrived at the law offices, they had dried stiff in the hot, dry desert air. The sky was clear and brilliantly blue.

Sally was already at her desk, wearing a sleeveless black A-line dress. An Aboriginal man was sitting in one of the client chairs, speaking softly to her as she scribbled on a yellow notepad. Behind him, waiting patiently, was the young intern from Tom Peacock's office, holding a thin, brightly colored AusPost Express packet in his hand. Hunter took a spot just behind him. Sally, sensing the growing group around her, glanced up and made a quick "just a minute" gesture before returning to her client. After a few more quiet words, the man stood and shuffled away. The intern stepped forward and placed the packet on Sally's desk.

"These are Rosie McMahon's medical reports," he said. "The originals. Mr. Peacock made copies. He wants to meet at nine-thirty."

"We'll be there," Sally replied.

She pulled the packet toward her as the intern left with the Aboriginal man. Hunter sat in the client chair. Sally looked at him, her fingers resting on the packet, a puzzled look crossing her face. Hunter shrugged in response. He had expected the packet to be thicker too.

Sally opened the packet, pressing its edges inward so it gaped like a mouth, then tipped out the contents onto the desk. There were four individual manila folders, each marked with Rosie's name, her Medicare number, and a reference code. The dates on the reports stretched back over six years. The older the report, the more faded the manila cover, as if time had leeched the color out of the paper. Hunter moved his chair closer to Sally's, and she arranged the reports in chronological order, placing the oldest on top. She opened it and nudged it between them so they could both see. Then, she shifted her chair slightly until her shoulder brushed against his.

"Okay, let's see what we've got," she said.

The first report detailed Lahni's birth, timed down to the minute. There were pages of gynecological notes, covering dilation and contractions. At thirteen minutes past three in the morning, Rosie had received an epidural, which was deemed fully effective by three-twenty. There was a shift change at seven. Labor dragged on until lunchtime. Accelerants were administered. At one o'clock, an episiotomy was performed, and Lahni was born at twenty-five minutes past. No complications. The placenta was delivered normally, and the episiotomy was stitched up immediately. The baby was pronounced completely healthy.

There was no mention of facial bruising, a split lip, or loosened teeth.

The second report, dated fifteen months after the birth, covered two cracked ribs. An X-ray was attached, showing the left side of her torso. Two ribs were visibly fractured. Her left breast appeared as a dark shape in the image. The attending doctor had noted that Rosie claimed to have been thrown from a horse and landed against the top rail of a fence. As with most rib injuries, there wasn't much to be done aside from binding them tightly and recommending plenty of rest.

"What do you think?" Sally asked.

"Could be something," Hunter said.

The third report was dated six months later, at the end of summer. It dealt with severe bruising on Rosie's lower right leg. The same doctor noted that she reported falling off a horse during a jump and hitting her shin on the pole of the obstacle. The report contained a lengthy technical description of the contusion, along with measurements. The bruise was an oval shape, tilted, about four inches wide and five inches long. X-rays had been taken, and the bone was unbroken. Painkillers had been prescribed, with an initial supply provided by the emergency room.

The fourth report was dated two and a half years later, about nine months before Warner went to prison. It detailed a broken collarbone on the right side. There were no familiar names on this report—apparently, the entire emergency room staff had changed. The new doctor recorded no comment on Rosie's claim that she had fallen from her horse onto the rocky plateau. The notes on the injury were extensive, and an X-ray showed the bone cleanly snapped in the middle.

Sally stacked the four reports together and turned them upside down on the desk.

"Well?" she asked.

Hunter didn't answer right away, just shook his head.

"Well?" she asked again.

"Maybe she went to another hospital sometimes," he suggested.

"No, we would've found that. We check all the hospitals as a matter of routine."

"Maybe they went out of state."

"We checked that, too," she said. "For domestic violence cases, we cover all states and territories. Routine procedure."

"Maybe she used a different name."

"They're tracked by Medicare number."

He nodded. "This isn't enough, Sally. She told me about more injuries. We've got the ribs and the collarbone, but she said he broke her arm, too. And her jaw. She even said she had three teeth replaced."

Sally stayed silent. Hunter closed his eyes, trying to think the way he used to—like a seasoned investigator with thirteen years of experience and a naturally suspicious mind.

"There are two possibilities," he said finally. "Either the hospital records system screwed up."

Sally shook her head. "Highly unlikely."

He nodded again. "Agreed. So that leaves the second option—

she was lying."

Sally was quiet for a long moment.

"Maybe she exaggerated," she suggested. "You know, to make sure you'd help her."

He nodded vaguely and checked his watch. It was twenty past nine. He leaned over and slid the reports back into the AusPost packet.

"Let's see what Tom thinks."

Meanwhile, two-thirds of the hit squad were heading south out of Mount Kalka, unusually silent. The third member stayed behind at the motel, lost in thought. They were taking risks now—twelve years in the business, and they'd never stayed in one area this long. It had always seemed too dangerous. In and out, fast and clean, had been their method. Now, they were breaking that rule. Radically. So, there was no chatter that morning. No jokes, no excitement before the mission. Just a lot of nervous, private thoughts.

Still, they had the car ready on schedule, along with everything they needed. They ate a half-hearted breakfast and sat quietly, checking their watches.

"Nine-twenty," the woman said finally. "It's time."

When they entered Peacock's office, there was already someone else there. He was a man around seventy, overweight and flushed, clearly struggling with the heat. The air conditioners were working so hard the air was audible over the hum of the motors, and papers fluttered off the desk. Yet, the temperature still hovered around thirty-five degrees. The man was mopping his face with a large white handkerchief. Peacock, seated behind his desk, had removed his jacket and sat perfectly still, his head in his hands. Copies of Rosie McMahon's medical reports were spread out before him, but he stared at them as if they were written in another language.

When he looked up, his gaze was blank, and he gestured vaguely toward the stranger.

“This is Art Macalister,” he said. “A well-known professor of forensic medicine from the University of Queensland, among other things. One of the top defense experts around. I’d say this might be the first time he’s ever set foot in a prosecutor’s office.”

Sally stepped forward and shook the man’s hand. “It’s a pleasure to meet you, sir. I’ve heard a lot about you.”

Art Macalister remained silent. Sally introduced Hunter, and they all arranged their chairs in a loose semicircle around the desk.

“The reports came in early this morning,” Peacock began. “They include everything on record from Queensland—just one hospital. Nothing from the Northern Territory, New South Wales, Victoria, or anywhere else. I photocopied everything and sent the originals to you right away. Dr. Macalister arrived about thirty minutes ago and has been reviewing the copies. He’s asked to see the X-rays, which I couldn’t copy.”

Hunter handed the AusPost Express packet to Macalister, who spilled its contents just as Sally had earlier. He carefully pulled out the three X-rays—of the ribs, the leg, and the collarbone—and held each one up to the light coming through the window, studying them for several minutes. When finished, he neatly returned them to their folders, showing the precision of a man used to order.

Peacock leaned forward. “Dr. Macalister, are you ready to give us a preliminary opinion?”

He sounded tense and formal, as if already in court. Macalister picked up the first folder, the oldest one detailing Lahni’s birth.

“There’s nothing of interest here,” Macalister said in a deep, resonant voice, the kind you’d expect from a wise old uncle in an old movie. It was the perfect voice for a witness stand. "This is standard obstetrics, notable only for the fact that a rural Queensland hospital was operating at a state-of-the-art level for its time, about ten years ago."

"Nothing suspicious?" Peacock asked.

"Nothing at all. Aside from the fact that the husband was likely involved in the pregnancy, there's no evidence he did anything to her."

"And the other reports?"

Macalister moved to the next file, the one about the ribs. He pulled out the X-ray film and held it at the ready.

"Ribs serve an important purpose," he explained. "They form a protective cage around the internal organs, but not a rigid one—rigidity would cause the bones to shatter under any severe impact. Instead, the rib cage is flexible, thanks to the complex ligaments at each end of the bones, allowing it to absorb and spread out force."

He held the X-ray up and pointed to various points on the image.

"That's exactly what we see here," he continued. "The ligaments are stretched and torn. This was caused by a broad, blunt force. The flexibility of the ribs dissipated the impact, but even then, two ribs cracked."

"What kind of blunt object?" Peacock asked.

"Something long, hard, and rounded—probably around five or six inches in diameter. A fencing rail, for example."

"Could it have been a kick?"

Macalister shook his head. "Definitely not. A kick delivers a lot of force through a small surface area—the toe of a boot, for instance, is about fives centimeters by a centimeter. That's more of a sharp impact than a blunt one, and it would result in fractured bones without any ligament stretching."

"What about a knee?"

"A knee would produce a circular impact, similar to a punch. The ligament stretching would show a completely different pattern."

Peacock drummed his fingers on his desk, sweating now. "So, there's no way a person could have done it?"

Macalister shrugged. "Unless they were some kind of contortionist who could keep their leg perfectly rigid and hit her in the side like a fence rail. I'd say it's impossible."

Peacock was quiet for a moment. "What about the bruised shin?"

Macalister switched to the third file, reading the description of the bruise before shaking his head.

"The shape is crucial. It's exactly what you'd see if something long, hard, and rounded—again, like a fence rail or maybe a sewer pipe—hit her shin at an angle."

"Couldn't he have hit her with a pipe?"

"In theory, yes," Macalister conceded. "But it would require him to be positioned almost behind her, swinging the pipe two-handed from above, and landing the blow at just the right angle. It's highly unlikely."

"But possible?"

"No," Macalister said firmly. "Not possible. I'd testify to that under oath."

Peacock fell silent again. "What about the collarbone?"

Macalister opened the last report. "These notes are very thorough," he commented. "Clearly, the physician was excellent."

"But what do they tell you?"

"It's a classic injury," Macalister said. "The collarbone acts like a circuit breaker when a person falls. They throw out their hand to break the fall, but the force travels through the arm and shoulder until the collarbone snaps, preventing more serious damage to the neck or brain. It's inconvenient and painful, but it's not life-threatening. Generations of cyclists, skaters, and horseback riders have a lot to thank evolution for."

"Falling isn't the only cause, though?"

"No, but it's the most common. In rare cases, I've seen it caused by downward blows, like a missed swing with a cricket bat or beams falling in a burning building."

Peacock looked deflated. "Rosie McMahon wasn't in a burning building, and no one's mentioned a cricket bat."

Silence fell over the room, broken only by the roar of the air conditioners.

"Okay," Peacock said slowly. "Let me ask it this way—do we have any evidence of violent abuse against this woman?"

Macalister hesitated before shaking his head. "No. Not within the bounds of reasonable likelihood."

"None at all? Not even a sliver?"

"No, I'm afraid not."

"Not even if we stretch those bounds as far as they'll go?"

"There's nothing there. She had a normal pregnancy and was an unlucky horseback rider. That's all I see."

Peacock's shoulders sagged. "No reasonable doubt? I only need the smallest amount."

"It's not there."

Peacock paused. “Doctor, with all due respect, you’ve been a thorn in my side and my colleagues’ across the state for years. You’ve come up with some of the most bizarre explanations I’ve ever heard. So, please—is there any way you could see this differently?”

Macalister remained silent.

“I’ve offended you,” Peacock said.

“Not in the way you think,” Macalister replied. “I’ve never given a bizarre explanation in my life. If I see a possibility for exoneration, I speak up. But when there’s no merit, I remain silent, and I’ve advised many defense teams to plead out their cases. This is one of those cases.”

“So, you’re saying this case has no merit?”

Macalister nodded. “Exactly. If Ms. Strong had hired me directly, I’d have told her that her client’s word can’t be trusted. And believe me, I hate to say it.”

Peacock’s expression darkened.

“I’m sorry, Mr. Peacock,” Macalister said, standing and gathering the reports back into the packet. “I really am. It would have been immensely satisfying to help, but there’s nothing here.”

Peacock didn’t respond, and Macalister left, the door slamming shut behind him in the gust from the air conditioners. Sally and Hunter watched as Peacock slumped at his desk, head in his hands.

“Go away,” he muttered. “Just leave me alone.”

The air in the stairwell was stifling, and it only got worse when they stepped onto the sidewalk. Hunter switched the AusPost Express packet into his left hand and gently caught Sally’s arm with his right, stopping her at the curb.

"Is there a good jeweler in town?" he asked.

"I think so. Why?"

"I want you to sign out Rosie's personal belongings. You're still her lawyer, at least officially. Let's get her ring appraised and see if she's been honest about anything."

"You still have doubts?"

"I was an SAS ranger. First, we check. Then we double-check."

"Alright," she said. "If that's what you want."

They turned and headed down a narrow alley. Sally signed a form at the courthouse, taking possession of Rosie's lizard-skin belt and her ring, both listed as material evidence. Afterward, they walked away from the cheaper part of town, searching for a jeweler. About ten minutes later, they found one nestled among a row of upmarket boutiques. The shop window was too crowded to be called elegant, but judging by the prices, the owner had an eye for quality—or perhaps for sheer optimism.

"How do we handle this?" Sally asked.

"Say it's part of an estate sale. Maybe it belonged to your grandmother."

The jeweler was an elderly man, slightly stooped. He might have looked sharp several decades ago, but he still had the keen gaze of someone who missed little. Hunter watched as a flash of suspicion crossed the man's face—police? But then he seemed to decide otherwise. Sally didn't look like a cop, and Hunter knew from experience that people often misjudged him too. The man's next calculation was whether his new customers were sharp or not. Hunter was used to watching people weigh him up. Eventually, the jeweler decided to proceed cautiously.

Sally produced the ring, telling him it was a family heirloom she might sell if the price was right.

The jeweler positioned the ring under a desk lamp and inserted a jeweler's loupe into his eye.

"Color, clarity, cut, and carat," he said. "Those are the four Cs we look for."

He turned the ring left and right under the light, watching it flash. Then, he picked up a small card with circular holes punched into it, each one slightly larger than the last. He slipped the diamond into the holes until he found the perfect fit.

"Two and a quarter carats," he said. "The cut is excellent. The color is good, though just a hint of yellow keeps it from being exceptional. The clarity isn't flawless, but it's close. This stone is very nice. Quite nice indeed. How much are you looking for?"

"Whatever it's worth," Sally replied.

"I could offer twenty," the man said.

"Twenty what?"

"Thousand dollars."

"Twenty thousand?" Sally repeated in disbelief.

The man raised his hands defensively. "I know, I know. Someone probably told you it's worth more. And maybe it is—if you sold it retail at a big shop in Brisbane or Sydney. But this is Mount Kalka, and you're selling, not buying. I have to make a profit too."

"I'll think about it," Sally said.

"Twenty-five," the jeweler offered. "Twenty-five thousand dollars."

Sally hesitated. "That's your best offer?"

"It's the highest I can go and still be fair to myself. I have to make a living."

"I'll think about it," Sally repeated.

"Well, don't think too long," the man warned. "The market changes quickly, and I'm the only jeweler in town who'll deal with a piece like this."

Once outside, Sally held the ring as though it were burning her fingers. Then, she carefully tucked it into a zippered pocket in her bag, pushing it down with her fingertips.

"If that guy says twenty-five, it's probably worth sixty," Hunter said. "Maybe more. He didn't exactly scream 'honest business.'"

"Definitely worth more than thirty bucks," Sally muttered. "It's not a fake. She's pulling the wool over our eyes."

Hunter nodded faintly. He knew she really meant *your eyes*l, but she was too polite to say it outright.

"Let's go," he said.

They walked westward through the oppressive heat, back toward the cheaper part of town, beyond the courthouse, near the railroad tracks. It was about a kilometer, and they took their time, the heat making any attempt to hurry impossible. Hunter stayed quiet the whole way, fighting his usual internal battle over when to give up on a lost cause.

He stopped her again just before they entered the legal mission.

"I want to try one more thing," he said.

"Why?" she asked, a hint of impatience in her voice.

"Because I was in the army. First, we double-check. Then we triple-check."

She sighed. "What do you want to do?"

"I need you to drive me."

"Where to?"

"There's an eyewitness we can talk to."

"An eyewitness? Where?"

"Down in Four Ways. She's at school."

"The kid?" Sally asked, incredulous.

Hunter nodded. "Lahni. She's smart. Sharp as a tack."

"She's six years old."

"If anything was going on, she'll know."

Sally stood still for a moment, glancing through the windows of the legal mission. Inside, the place was packed with clients, all worn down by the heat and the hardships of life.

"I need to get back to work," she said. "It's not fair to them."

"Just this one last thing."

"I'll lend you the car again. You can go alone."

"I need your opinion. You're the lawyer, and I won't get into the school without you. You've got authority. I don't."

Sally looked at him for a long moment before nodding. "Alright. A deal's a deal."

"This is the last thing. I promise."

"Why, exactly?" Sally asked.

They were driving south in the little red Hyundai, heading out of Mount Kalka along the empty road. The landmarks were unfamiliar to Hunter; it had been dark when he traveled the other way, in the back of a police car.

"Because I'm a ranger," he said simply.

"Okay," Sally replied slowly. " You're going to have to help me as I'm not picking up what you're putting down?"

"Rangers never really know what they're being deployed into, we're a special unit who are deployed first when there's trouble," he said. "Our time from alert to deployment is a maximum of eighteen hours anywhere globally, but with that you need to be able to move quickly and read situations and people extremely well."

"I thought they dealt in combat and just shooting people."

"They do, eventually. But ninety-nine percent of the time, it's about intuition. A good ranger has a feel for people and situations."

"Feelings don't change facts."

"No, they don't."

"Have you ever been wrong before?"

"Plenty of times."

"But?"

"But I don't think I'm wrong this time."

"So why, exactly?" she asked again.

"Because I understand people, Sally."

"I do too," she said. "Like, I know Rosie McMahon pulled one over on you, just like she did on everyone else."

Hunter said nothing more. He stared out the window at the distant mountains, where Rosie had once chased the school bus. The AusPost packet rested on his knees, and he idly fanned himself with it. After a moment, he threw it onto the back seat.

"She had no money with her," he said.

Sally didn't reply, just drove on, her hands steady on the wheel at nine and five o'clock. Hunter could sense her pity for him, radiating in waves.

"What?" he asked.

"We should turn back," she said. "This is a complete waste of time."

"Why?"

"Because what is Lahni really going to tell us? I get your logic—if Rosie broke her arm, she'd have been in a cast for six weeks. And Lahni's smart; she'd remember that. Same with the broken jaw—Rosie would've been wired up, and Lahni would have noticed. But we know neither of those things happened. We've got her medical records in the car with us. If she'd broken any bones, it would've been in there. Or do you think she had them set in the barn by a blacksmith? So, at best, Lahni will just confirm what we already know. And at worst, she won't remember anything because she's only six. This trip is a complete waste."

"Let's just do it anyway," Hunter said. "We're halfway there, and she might remember something useful. Besides, I want to see her again. She's a great kid."

"I'm sure she is," Sally said. "But spare yourself, okay? What are you going to do—adopt her? She's caught in the middle of this, and you need to accept that."

They drove in silence the rest of the way until they reached the crossroads with the takeaway shop, school, and service station. Sally parked where Rosie had, and they stepped out into the heat.

"I'd better come with you," Hunter said. "She knows me. We can talk to her in the car."

They walked through the gate and into the school, but emerged again a minute later. Lahni McMahon wasn't there, and she hadn't been there the day before either.

"Understandable, I suppose," Sally said. "She's been through a lot."

Hunter nodded. "Let's keep going. It's only another hour north."

"Great," Sally replied, sarcasm in her voice.

They got back into the Hyundai and drove the next hundred kilometers of barren land in silence. It took less than an hour since Sally was driving faster than Rosie had. Hunter recognized the landmarks—he spotted the old mines far off on the horizon to the left. McMahon Three.

"It's just ahead," he said.

Sally slowed down. The cream-painted picket fence appeared, replacing the wire fence, and the gate emerged through the heat haze. Sally braked and turned in, the small car bouncing uncomfortably across the yard. She stopped near the bottom of the familiar porch steps and switched off the engine. The place was silent. No signs of activity, though people were clearly home—he could see all the cars lined up in the vehicle barn: the white BMW, the Nissan Patrol, the new ute, and the old ute, all crouched in the shadows.

They stepped out of the car and stood behind the open doors for a moment, as if the doors offered some protection. The air was utterly still and hotter than ever, easily over a hundred and ten degrees. Hunter led the way up the porch steps into the shade of the roof and knocked on the door. It opened almost immediately. Judy McMahon stood there, holding a .22 rifle in one hand. She said nothing for a long moment, just looking him over.

"It's you," she said finally. "I thought it might be Ryan."

"You lost him?" Hunter asked.

Judy shrugged. "He went out. Hasn't come back yet."

Hunter glanced toward the vehicle barn. "All the cars are still here."

"Someone picked him up," Judy said. "I was upstairs. Didn't see them, just heard them."

Hunter said nothing.

"I didn't expect to see you again," Judy added after a pause.

"This is Rosie's lawyer," Hunter said, nodding toward Sally.

Judy turned her gaze to Sally, unimpressed. "This is the best she could do?"

"We need to see Lahni," Hunter said.

"What for?"

"We're interviewing witnesses."

"A child can't be a witness," Judy said dismissively.

"I'll decide that," Sally said firmly.

Judy just smiled. "Lahni's not here," she said.

"Where is she?" Hunter asked. "She wasn't in school."

Judy remained silent.

"Mrs. McMahon, we need to know where Lahni is," Sally said, her voice calm but insistent.

Judy smiled again. "I don't know where she is, lawyer girl."

"Why not?" Sally asked.

"Because Child Protective Services took her," Judy replied.

"When?"

"This morning. They came for her."

"And you let them take her?" Hunter asked, incredulous.

"Why wouldn't I? I don't want her, not now that Warner's gone."

Hunter stared at her. "But she's your granddaughter."

Judy made a dismissive gesture, the rifle moving slightly in her hand. "That's a fact I was never thrilled about."

"Where did they take her?" Hunter asked, his voice tightening.

"A foster home, I guess," Judy said indifferently. "Then she'll get adopted—if anyone wants her. I hear half-breeds are hard to place. Decent folk don't usually want Islander trash."

Silence followed, broken only by the faint sounds of the earth baking in the heat.

"I hope you get a tumor," Hunter said, turning sharply and heading back to the car without waiting for Sally. He got in, slammed the door, and sat, staring straight ahead, his face burning with anger. His hands clenched and unclenched, massive fists opening and closing. Sally got in beside him and started the car.

"Get me out of here," he said.

She took off, leaving a cloud of dust behind. Neither of them spoke during the drive back south to Mount Kalka.

It was three in the afternoon by the time they returned, and the legal mission was half-empty due to the oppressive heat. Sally's desk was covered in the usual pile of messages, five of them from Tom Peacock, each progressively more urgent than the last.

"Shall we go?" Sally asked.

"Don't mention the diamond," Hunter said. "It's over now, can't you see?"

And it was. Hunter could see it immediately in Peacock's face. There was a kind of relaxation, a sense of finality—some closure, a form of peace. Peacock was sitting behind his desk, which was covered in papers, arranged in two piles—one larger than the other.

"What?" Hunter asked.

Peacock ignored the question and handed a single sheet of paper to Sally.

"Waiver of her rights," he said. "Read it carefully. She's declined legal representation and stated it's entirely voluntary. She's also added that she refused your help from the start."

"I questioned her competency," Sally said.

Peacock nodded. "I'll give you that. But there's no doubt now. So, you're both here purely as a courtesy, okay?"

Then, he handed over the smaller pile of papers. Sally took them, fanning them out, and Hunter leaned closer to look. They were computer printouts, filled with numbers, dates, and financial details—bank records, balance statements, and transaction listings. There were five separate accounts—two regular checking accounts and three money-market deposits—all under the name of the McMahon Non-Discretionary Trust, numbered one through five. The balances were substantial, adding up to nearly two million dollars.

"Troy Bradley's office sent these over," Peacock said. "Now, check the bottom sheets."

Sally rifled through the papers, reaching the bottom where the sheets were paper-clipped together. Hunter read over her shoulder. It was dense legal text, outlining the formal minutes of a trust agreement. A notarized deed was attached, stating that the sole trustee in full control of all of Warner McMahon's funds was his legal wife, Rosie.

“She had two million bucks in the bank,” Peacock said. “Effectively all hers.”

Hunter glanced at Sally. She nodded. “He’s right.”

“Now, take a look at the last clause,” Peacock said.

Sally turned the page. The final clause concerned reversion—the trusts would revert to Warner’s control at a future date unless he became mentally incapacitated or died, at which point the funds would transfer to Rosie entirely, either by prior agreement or through inheritance.

“Is that clear?” Peacock asked.

Sally nodded, while Hunter remained silent.

Peacock handed her the larger pile. “Now, read this,” he said.

“What is it?” she asked.

“A transcript,” Peacock replied. “Of her confession.”

Silence fell over the room.

“She confessed?” Sally asked, her voice incredulous.

“We videotaped it,” Peacock said.

“When?”

“Noon today. As soon as we got the financial records, my assistant went to see her. We tried to contact you first, but we couldn’t reach you. She told us she didn’t want a lawyer, so she signed the waiver. Then she confessed. We brought her up here and recorded the whole thing. It’s not pretty.”

Hunter half-read, half-listened as Peacock spoke. It certainly wasn’t pretty. The transcript began with the usual legal assurances—Rosie confirming her free will and the absence of coercion. Then she told her story, starting from her days in Sydney. She had been an illegitimate child, then a prostitute—*street stroller*, she called it, some slang Hunter didn’t recognize.

Eventually, she became a stripper, upgrading her title to sex worker. She admitted to latching onto Warner—*my meal ticket*, she called him. From there, the confession became a story of boredom and greed. She had grown restless in Queensland and wanted out, with money in her pocket. The more money, the better. Warner's ATO troubles were a golden opportunity, and the trusts were too tempting to resist. She even admitted to trying to have him killed in prison, but found it impossible in a federal minimum-security facility. So, she waited. When she heard he was being released, she bought the gun and started recruiting people to help her, fabricating stories of domestic violence to cover her tracks. Hunter was mentioned as a last resort. When he refused, she carried out the plan herself. Realizing her medical records would reveal no abuse, she confessed and threw herself on the mercy of the prosecutor. Her signature appeared at the bottom of every page.

Sally finished reading a full minute after Hunter. "I'm sorry, Hunter," she said quietly.

There was a long silence.

"What about the election?" Hunter asked, as a last hope.

Peacock shrugged. "Under Queensland law, it's a capital crime —murder for remuneration. We have more than enough evidence. And I can't ignore a voluntary confession, can I? A couple of hours ago, I was feeling down about it. But then I realized something. A confession actually helps me. No trial means we save taxpayer money, and it justifies me asking for a life sentence instead. With a story like hers, she'll come off looking terrible, no matter who you are. So, if I back off the death penalty, I'll look like the magnanimous one. The whites might grumble a little, but the darker-skinned voters will love it. See what I mean? The whole situation has flipped. She was the victim, and I was the villain. Now, she's the villain, and I'm the good guy. I think I'm in the clear."

No one spoke for a minute. The air conditioners droned on.

"I've got her personal belongings," Sally said. "A belt and a ring."

"Take them to storage," Peacock replied. "We'll be transferring her later."

"Where?"

"The penitentiary. We can't keep her here."

"And where's storage?"

"Same building as the morgue. Make sure you get a receipt."

Hunter followed Sally over to the morgue, barely aware of the heat, dust, or noise of the streets. It felt like he was floating, insulated from everything around him. Sally spoke to him occasionally, but he couldn't hear her. All he could hear was the voice in his head telling him, *you were wrong*. It was a voice he'd heard before, though not often. And it was no easier to hear now than it had been then.

"Hunter?" Sally called. "You're not listening, are you?"

"What?" he replied.

"I asked if you wanted to get something to eat."

"No," Hunter said. "I want to get a ride."

Sally stopped walking. "What now? Quadruple-check?"

"No, I mean I want to leave. Go somewhere else. I hear Fiji's nice this time of year."

"The bus depot's on the way back to the office."

"Good. I'll take a bus. I'm done hitchhiking. You never know who's going to pick you up."

The morgue was a low industrial building in a paved yard. It looked like it could have been a tire shop or a garage, with metal siding and a roll-up door for vehicles. The personnel entrance had two small steps framed by steel-pipe handrails. Inside, it was freezing, with industrial air conditioners blasting full force. The room felt like a meat locker, which it essentially was. To the left was a set of double doors leading directly into the morgue, standing open. Hunter could see autopsy tables and gleaming stainless steel equipment under harsh fluorescent lights.

Sally placed the lizard-skin belt on the reception counter and fished in her bag for the ring. "These are for Queensland vs. Rosie McMahon," she told the attendant.

He left and returned with an evidence box.

"No, this is personal property," she corrected. "Not evidence. I'm sorry."

The attendant gave her a look that said *why didn't you say so*, and turned back to the shelves.

"Wait," Hunter called. "Let me see that."

The attendant hesitated, then slid the box across the counter. It had no lid—just a shallow cardboard tray with *McMahon* scrawled on the front in marker. Inside was the Makarov in a plastic bag, labeled with an evidence number. Two brass shell casings were in another bag, along with two tiny .22 bullets, gray and slightly deformed, each in its own bag labeled *Intercranial #1* and *Intercranial #2*. Both had reference numbers and signatures.

"Is the pathologist here?" Hunter asked.

"Sure," the attendant said. "He's always here."

"I need to see him. Right now."

Hunter expected some resistance, but the attendant simply pointed toward the double doors. "In there."

Sally hung back, but Hunter walked through. At first, the room seemed empty, but then he saw a glass door in the corner. Behind it, a man in green scrubs was sitting at a desk, doing paperwork. Hunter knocked on the glass, and the man looked up, mouthing *come in*.

"Can I help you?" the pathologist asked.

"There were only two bullets in Warner McMahon?" Hunter asked.

"Who are you?"

"I'm with the defense," Hunter said. "The lawyer's outside."

"The defense?" the pathologist repeated, a little surprised.

"No, the lawyer," Hunter clarified.

"Alright," the man said. "What about the bullets?"

"How many were there?"

"Two," the pathologist said. "Took a lot of effort to get them out."

"Can I see the body?"

"Why?"

"I'm worried about a miscarriage of justice."

That was a line that usually worked with pathologists. They knew they'd be called as witnesses, and the last thing they wanted was to be embarrassed on cross-examination. It wasn't good for their reputation—or their ego. They preferred to clear up any doubts beforehand.

"Okay," the pathologist agreed. "He's in the freezer."

He led Hunter through another door at the back of his office and down a dim corridor to a steel door, like the entrance to a meat locker.

"It's cold in there," he warned.

"I'm glad somewhere is," Hunter muttered.

The pathologist opened the door, and they stepped into a bright, fluorescent-lit room. A wall of twenty-seven stainless steel drawers lined the far side, arranged in three rows of nine. Eight of them were occupied, each marked with a tag, like a filing cabinet. The air was frosty, and Hunter's breath clouded in front of him. The pathologist slid one of the drawers open on its smooth runners.

"I had to take off the back of his head," the pathologist said. "Practically had to scoop his brains out with a ladle to find the bullets."

Warner McMahon lay on his back, naked, his body shrunken in death. His skin was a cold, gray color, like unfired clay. His eyes were open and blank, staring at nothing. Two bullet holes marred his forehead, about three inches apart—neat, ridged wounds, like they'd been drilled with precision.

"Classic .22 gunshot wounds," the pathologist remarked. "The bullets go in, but they don't have enough power to come out. They just rattle around inside. But they get the job done."

Hunter closed his eyes for a moment, then smiled—wide and genuine. "They get the job done, alright."

There was a soft knock at the door. Hunter opened his eyes to see Sally standing there, shivering.

"What are you doing?" she called.

"What comes after quadruple-check?" Hunter asked, his breath hanging in the cold air.

"Quintuple-check," she replied. "Why?"

"And after that?"

"Sextuple-check," she said, stepping further into the room. "What's going on?"

"Because we're going to be doing a whole lot of checking now."

"Why?" she asked, confused.

"Because something's very wrong here, Sally. Come take a look."

CHAPTER 14

Sally slowly made her way across the tile floor. "What's the problem?" she asked.

"Tell me what you notice," Hunter replied.

She hesitated before glancing at the body, as though it took real effort.

"Shot in the head," she said, "twice."

"How far apart are the entry wounds?"

"About three inches."

"What else do you see?"

"Nothing," she said.

Hunter nodded. "Exactly."

"So?"

"Take a closer look. The wounds are clean, right?"

Sally moved a step closer to the body, leaning slightly forward.

"They look clean," she confirmed.

"That's significant," Hunter explained. "It means these aren't contact wounds. A contact wound is when the gun's muzzle is pressed right against the skin. You know what happens in that case?"

She shook her head but stayed quiet.

"The first thing that comes out of a gun is a burst of hot gas. If the gun was pressed against the forehead, that gas would get trapped under the skin and have no place to go because of the bone. It forces its way back out, tearing a large, star-shaped hole. Right, doc?"

The pathologist nodded.

"We call it star-burst splitting," he said.

"That's not what we see here," Hunter pointed out. "So, it

wasn't a contact shot. If it had been a close-range shot, say two or three inches away but not quite touching, we'd see burn marks on the skin."

"Burn rim," the pathologist added.

"And that's missing too," Hunter continued. "Next thing out of the gun is soot. If the shot had come from six or eight inches, we'd see a smudge of soot on the forehead, maybe a couple of inches wide. But there's none of that here either."

"So?" Sally pressed.

"Then there's the gunpowder," Hunter went on. "Tiny, unburned particles. No gunpowder burns perfectly; some of it gets ejected from the gun in a spray. If the shot was fired from about a foot, maybe a foot and a half away, we'd see little black specks embedded in the skin. It's called tattooing. Do you see any?"

"No," Sally replied.

"Exactly. All we have are the bullet holes. No other signs. Based on the lack of close-range evidence, I'd say the shots were fired from at least a meter away, at the very least."

"Two metres, fifty one centimetres," the pathologist estimated.

Hunter looked over at him. "You measured the powder pattern?"

The pathologist shook his head. "Crime scene sketches. The victim was found on the far side of the bed, near the window. The bed gave him about half a metre of space on that side. He was found near the bedside table, close to the head of the bed, right by the window. There's no way she could've been next to him; otherwise, we'd see the close-range indicators you just mentioned. So, the closest she could've been was across the bed, likely at the foot. Based on the bullet trajectories, he was probably backing away. It was a king-size bed, so my best guess is that the shooter was about two and a half metres away, maybe a little more."

"Great work," Hunter said. "You'd be willing to testify to that?"

"Of course. That's the minimum distance. It could've been

farther."

Sally frowned. "What does this mean?"

"It means Rosie didn't do it," Hunter said.

"Why not?"

"How big is a man's forehead? Twenty centimetres across, maybe ten high?"

"And?"

"There's no way she could've hit such a small target from over eight feet away."

"How can you be so sure?"

"Because I watched her shoot yesterday. It was her first time ever firing a gun. She was awful. Absolutely hopeless. She couldn't have hit the broad side of a barn from two metres away, let alone twice in a row. I told her that if she wanted to hit anything, she'd have to press the gun against him and empty the clip."

"You're digging her grave," Sally warned. "That's not the kind of testimony you should offer freely."

"She didn't do it, Sally. She couldn't have."

"She could've just gotten lucky."

"Maybe once. But not twice. Two shots that close together? And horizontally aligned? No way. He'd have started to fall after the first shot, so the second one had to come immediately after. That's skilled shooting."

Sally was silent for a moment.

"She could've been pretending," she suggested. "Maybe she was an expert all along and just lied about needing to learn so you'd do it for her."

Hunter shook his head.

"She wasn't faking. I've been around people shooting all my life. If someone can shoot, it shows. And if they can't, you can't hide that either."

Sally said nothing.

"It wasn't Rosie," Hunter repeated. "Even I wouldn't have been able to pull that off with the gun she had, not from that distance. A quick double-tap to the head? Whoever did this is a better shot than I am."

Sally smiled faintly. "That's saying something?"

"It is," Hunter said, without a hint of modesty.

"But she confessed. Why would she do that?"

"I have no idea."

Lahni wasn't entirely sure she understood everything. She had hidden on the stairs above the foyer when her grandmother spoke with the strangers. She heard them mention a "new family," and she knew what that meant. She already knew she needed a new family. The McMahons had told her that her father had passed away, and her mother had left, never to return. They had also made it clear they didn't want to keep her. That was fine with her, though; she didn't want to stay with them either. They were cruel. They had already sold her pony, along with all the other horses. A big truck had come for them early that morning. She hadn't cried. Somehow, she knew it was all connected. No more Daddy, no more Mummy, no more pony, no more horses. Everything had changed.

So when the strangers came, she went with them because she didn't know what else to do. Later, the strangers let her talk to her mother over the phone. Her mother had cried, and in the end, she told Lahni to be happy with her new family. But Lahni wasn't sure if these strangers were her new family or if they were just taking her to them. She was too scared to ask, so she stayed silent. Her hand was sore where she had been biting it.

"It's a mess," Tom Peacock said. "You understand? It's best to leave it alone. If we open it up, things could spiral out of control fast."

They were back in Peacock's office, which was at least twenty degrees hotter than the morgue. Both of them were sweating heavily.

"You get what I mean?" Peacock asked. "It'll only make things worse."

"You think so?" Sally asked.

Peacock nodded. "It'll confuse everything. Let's say, just for argument's sake, that Hunter's right. Though, honestly, he's working off a highly subjective theory. He's guessing, more or less. And what's his guess based on? It's based on Rosie giving him the impression she couldn't shoot. But we already know every other impression she gave him was a total pile of horse shit from start to finish. But let's assume he's right. What do we get from that?"

"What?"

"A conspiracy, that's what. We already know she tried to rope Hunter in. Now you're talking about her roping in someone else. She tells them where to go, where to find the gun, and they show up, take the weapon, and do the job. If that's true, we're looking at conspiracy to commit murder. That's premeditated, cold-blooded stuff. We go down that road, and she's heading straight back to the lethal injection. That's way worse than a lone act of murder, trust me. At least with a single shooter, you could argue it was a crime of passion. A conspiracy? That's real, deliberate evil. We leave things as they are, with her guilty plea, and I'm comfortable pushing for a life sentence. But if we start talking conspiracy, we're putting her right back on track for death row."

Sally didn't say a word.

"So do you get where I'm coming from?" Peacock said. "There's no upside here. None. It only makes things worse. Besides, she already confessed to doing it herself. I think she's telling the truth. But if not, then her confession was a calculated lie meant to cover her tracks, knowing a conspiracy would look far worse. And we couldn't ignore that. It'd make us look like fools."

Sally stayed silent. Hunter shrugged.

"So, leave it alone," Peacock said firmly. "That's my advice. If it would help her, I'd look into it. But it won't. So, we should leave it alone, for her sake."

"And for your shot at being a judge," Hunter remarked.

Peacock nodded. "I'm not hiding that."

"You okay with leaving it alone?" Sally asked Hunter. "As a prosecutor, don't you worry someone might be getting away with something?"

Peacock shook his head. "That's a lot of ifs. If it happened the way Hunter thinks. If, if, if. That's a big word. Honestly, I think it's highly unlikely. I'm all for prosecuting criminals, but I'm not about to build a case on one person's subjective opinion about how well someone else can shoot, especially when that someone is as good a liar as Rosie. For all we know, she's been shooting since she was a kid. A rough upbringing in Sydney? Any rural Queensland jury would have no trouble buying that."

Hunter didn't respond.

Sally gave a small nod. "Okay," she said. "I'm not her lawyer anyway."

"And what would you do if you were?"

Sally shrugged. "Probably leave it, like you said. Getting tangled up in a conspiracy charge wouldn't do her any good."

She stood slowly, like the heat was weighing her down. She tapped Hunter on the shoulder, gave him a look that said, *What can we do?*, and headed for the door. He followed her. Peacock watched them go halfway out the room, then dropped his gaze back to an old photograph of three boys leaning on the fender of a ute.

Together, Sally and Hunter crossed the street to the bus depot. It was only about fifty meters from the courthouse and legal mission. The depot was quiet, no buses in sight, just a patch of blacktop stained with diesel and surrounded by shaded benches. A small white fiberglass roof provided some relief from the afternoon sun. The office there had a tiny air conditioner humming away, and inside, a woman sat on a high stool, reading a magazine.

"Peacock's right, you know," Sally said. "He's doing her a favor.

It's a dead-end case."

Hunter said nothing.

"So, where are you headed?" she asked.

"I'll take the next bus out," he replied. "That's my rule."

They looked at the schedule posted on the wall. The next bus was headed to Brisbane, via Roma, arriving in about half an hour from Normanton, taking the long route.

"Ever been to Roma?" Sally asked.

"I've been to Charleville. It's not far," he answered.

He tapped on the office glass, and the woman sold him a one-way ticket. He slipped it into his pocket.

"Good luck, Sally," he said. "Four and a half years from now, I'll look for you in the lawyers section of the Pacific Highway billboards."

She smiled.

"Take care, Hunter," she said.

She hesitated, like she wasn't sure whether to hug him, kiss him on the cheek, or just walk away. In the end, she smiled again and walked off. He watched her until she disappeared from sight. Then he found the shadiest bench and sat down to wait.

****

She still wasn't sure. The strangers had taken her to a nice place, one that felt like a house, with beds and everything. Maybe this was her new family. But they didn't seem like a family. They were busy, constantly doing things she didn't understand. They reminded her of doctors. They were kind, but always preoccupied, much like people at the doctor's office. Maybe they really were doctors. Maybe they could tell she was upset and were going to make her feel better. She thought about it for a long time before finally asking.

"Are you doctors?"

"No," they replied.

"Are you my new family?"

"No," they said again. "You'll meet your new family soon."
"When?"
"In a few days, okay? But for now, you'll stay with us."
They still seemed very busy.

The bus arrived more or less on schedule. It was a large white coach with an Irish name brightly written down the side, dirty from the road, shrouded in a cloud of diesel smoke, with heat visibly rising from its air conditioner vents. It came to a stop about ten metres away, the engine rumbling loudly. The door hissed open, and three passengers got off. Hunter stood and walked over to board. He was the only one getting on. The driver took his ticket.

"Two minutes, okay?" the driver said. "Just need a quick break."

Hunter nodded silently and made his way down the aisle, finding an empty double seat on the left. That side would face the setting sun after they turned south at Cloncurry, but the windows were tinted dark blue, and the air inside the bus was cool, so he figured he'd manage. He sat sideways, stretched out, and rested his head against the window. The eight spent shells in his pocket pressed uncomfortably against his leg. He shifted slightly, moving them through the fabric of his pants before pulling them out and rolling them in his hand. They were warm, making a dull metallic sound as they clicked together.

Cloncurry, he thought.

The driver returned, climbed back into his seat, and checked both ways like an old train conductor. Then he settled in, and the door closed with a sigh behind him.

"Wait," Hunter called.

He stood up and made his way back down the aisle to the front.

"I've changed my mind," he said. "I'm getting off."

"I already cancelled your ticket," the driver replied. "If you want a refund, you'll have to send in a claim."

"I don't need a refund," Hunter said. "Just let me off, please."

The driver looked at him blankly for a moment, then operated the mechanism to open the door again. Hunter stepped down into the heat and walked away. He heard the bus pull off behind him, turning right as he went left. Its rumbling faded as it drove off into the distance.

Hunter kept walking until he reached the law office. The working day had ended, and the place was bustling again with small groups of worried-looking people, some talking to lawyers, others waiting their turn. Sally was at her desk, speaking with a woman who had a baby on her lap. When she saw Hunter, she looked up, surprised.

"The bus didn't come?" she asked.

"I need to ask you a legal question," Hunter said.

"Is it quick?"

He nodded. "It's about civilian law. If a guy tells his lawyer about a crime, how far can the cops push the lawyer to spill the details?"

"It's privileged information," Sally replied. "Between lawyer and client. The cops can't press at all."

"Can I use your phone?"

She gave him a puzzled look but then shrugged. "Sure," she said. "Have a seat."

He pulled a spare chair up beside hers, behind the desk.

"Got a phone book for Cloncurry?"

"Bottom drawer," she answered. "It covers all of Queensland."

Sally turned back to her conversation, and Hunter found the phone book in the drawer. He flipped to the emergency services page near the front, where all the important numbers were listed. He dialed the state police office in Cloncurry. A woman answered, asking how she could help.

"I have information about a crime," Hunter said.

The woman put him on hold. After about thirty seconds, another voice picked up, the background full of ringing phones and distant conversations.

"Sergeant Patterson," the man said.

"I have information about a crime," Hunter repeated.

"Your name, sir?"

"Joseph Cook," Hunter said. "I'm a lawyer from Mount Kalka Shire."

"Okay, Mr. Arthur, what's the information?"

"You found an abandoned car south of Townsville on Friday—a Mercedes Benz that belonged to a lawyer named Troy Bradley, who's currently listed as missing."

Hunter heard the sound of a keyboard clicking on the other end.

"Got it," Patterson said. "What can you tell me?"

"I have a client who claims Bradley was abducted from that car and killed near the scene."

"What's your client's name?" Patterson asked.

"I can't tell you that," Hunter replied. "It's privileged information. And frankly, I'm not sure I believe him myself. But I need you to check his story. If it checks out, I might be able to convince him to come forward."

"What's he telling you?"

"He says Bradley was flagged down and forced into another vehicle. He was driven north to a hidden spot on the left side of the road, where he was shot, and the body was hidden."

Sally had paused her conversation and was now staring at Hunter with wide eyes.

"So, I need you to search the area," Hunter continued.

"We've already searched the area," Patterson said.

"How far out?" Hunter asked.

"Just the immediate vicinity."

"No, my guy says it's a kilometer or two north. You'll need to look under bushes, in cracks in the rocks, any pumping houses—anywhere a car could pull off the road."

"A kilometer or two north of the abandoned car?" Patterson clarified.

"That's what he says. Not less than one, not more than two kilometers," Hunter confirmed.

"On the left side?"

"That's what he's pretty sure of," Hunter replied.

"Do you have a number we can reach you at?"
"I'll call you back," Hunter said. "In about an hour."

He ended the call. The woman with the baby had disappeared. Sally continued to gaze at him.

"What is it?" she asked.

"We should've concentrated on Bradley earlier."

"Why?"

"What's the one undeniable fact we have here?"

"What's that?"

"Rosie didn't kill Warner, that's what."

"That's just your opinion, not a fact."

"No, it *is* a fact, Sally. Trust me, I know these things."

She gave a small shrug. "Okay, so what?"

"So, someone else killed him. Which brings up the question—why? We know Bradley has vanished, and we know Warner's dead. They were linked, lawyer and client. Let's assume, for argument's sake, that Bradley's dead too, not just missing. They were working on some deal that got Warner out of jail—a big one, because that doesn't happen easily. Getting a remission isn't simple; it likely involved some serious information. Something valuable. Something that could spell trouble for someone. Suppose that someone decided to take them both out—either for revenge or to stop that information from leaking?"

"Where'd you come up with this?"

"From Rosie, actually," he said. "She suggested that's what I should do. Take Warner out and pretend it was to halt the deal."

"So Rosie followed her own advice."

"No, Rosie's a parallel here," Hunter replied. "She hated him, had a motive, and is definitely a liar, but she didn't kill him. Someone else did."

"For her."

"No," Hunter said firmly. "That's not how it went down. She just got lucky. It was a coincidence. Like if he'd been hit by a truck somewhere else. She might be happy with the outcome, but she didn't cause it."

"How certain are you?"

"Very certain. Anything else is ridiculous. Think about it, Sally. Whoever shot Warner was a professional. Professionals plan ahead, at least a few days in advance. And if she'd hired someone days ago, why would she be wandering around Queensland picking up guys like me for rides? And why would she let Warner get killed in her own bedroom, making her the prime suspect? With her own gun?"

"So what do you think happened?"

"I think a hit team took out Bradley on Friday and made sure the body stayed hidden until it couldn't be found until much later, once the trail had gone cold. Then, on Sunday, they killed Warner, setting it up to look like Rosie did it. In her bedroom, using her own gun."

"But she was with him. Wouldn't she have noticed? Wouldn't she have said something?"

He hesitated. "Maybe she was with Lahni at the time. Maybe she walked back into the room and found it already done. Or maybe she was in the shower. Her hair was wet when they arrested her."

"But she'd have heard the shots."

"Not with that shower. It's like Niagara Falls. And a .22 is a quiet gun."

"How do you know where they'll find Bradley's body? Assuming you're right?"

"I thought about how I'd do it. They obviously had their own vehicle out there, in the middle of nowhere. Maybe they staged a breakdown or a flat tire. Flagged him down, forced him into their car, then drove him off. But they wouldn't have kept him in there long. Too risky. I'd say two to three minutes tops, which is about a kilometer or two from where they started."

"Why north? Why the left side?"

"I would've driven north first, scouted the left-side shoulder, found a good spot, then backtracked, set up, and waited for him."

"Possible," she said. "But the Warner thing? That's hard to believe. They went to that house in Four Ways, in the middle of nowhere, hid out, and snuck in? While she was in the shower?"

"I could've done it," he said. "And I'm assuming they're as good as me. Maybe even better, especially if they shoot better."

"You're insane," she said.

"Maybe," he replied.

"No, definitely," she said. "She confessed to it. Why would she do that if she had nothing to do with it?"

"We'll figure that out later. First, we wait an hour."

He left Sally to work and went outside into the heat. He decided it was time to check out the Wild West museum. When he arrived, it was already closed. Too late in the day. But he spotted an alley leading to a courtyard behind the buildings. A locked gate stood in the way, but it was low enough for him to step over. Behind it was a small collection of restored artifacts from the old days—a one-cell jailhouse, a replica of Judge Roy

Bean's courthouse, and a hanging tree. They were arranged in a neat sequence—arrest, trial, and punishment. Nearby was the grave of Benjamin Blackman. Well-tended, with a handsome headstone. His full name was James Benjamin Blackman, born in 1840 and died in 1887. The inscription read: "Never killed a man that didn't need killing." Hunter didn't have a middle name. It was just Mick Hunter. Born in 1960, not dead yet. He wondered what his headstone might say. Probably nothing, since no one would be around to arrange it.

He walked back up the alley, stepped over the gate again, and saw a long, low, two-story concrete building. The ground floor housed retail shops, while the upper floor contained offices. One window bore the name "Troy C. Bradley, Attorney at Law" in gold lettering. There were two other law firms in the building, which was within sight of the courthouse. These were probably the cheap lawyers, Hunter thought, as they were separated from the free lawyers on Sally's row and the expensive ones on another street. Although Bradley drove a Mercedes-Benz, so maybe he did a lot of volume, or perhaps he was just vain and struggling with lease payments.

He paused at the crossroads. The sun was low in the west, and clouds were gathering on the southern horizon. A warm breeze brushed his face, strong enough to tug at his clothes and stir the dust on the sidewalk. He stood for a moment, letting the breeze press his shirt against his stomach. Then it died, and the oppressive heat returned, but the clouds remained, like dark smudges in the sky.

He returned to Sally's office, where she was still at her desk, facing an endless stream of problems. A middle-aged Aboriginal couple sat in her client chairs, with patient, trusting expressions. The stack of paperwork on her desk had grown. She gestured vaguely toward his chair, still next to hers. He squeezed in and sat down, then dialed a number from memory, asking for Sergeant Patterson under the alias Joseph

Cook.

After a minute on hold, Patterson answered, and Hunter immediately knew they had found Bradley's body. The urgency in Patterson's voice made it clear.

"We need your client's name, Mr. Arthur," Patterson said.

"What did your team find?" Hunter asked.

"Exactly what you said: a kilometer and a half north, on the left side, in a deep limestone crevice. One shot, right through the eye."

"Was it a .22?"

"No chance. From what I've been told, it was something bigger. Nine millimeter, at the very least. Some big, messy cannon. Most of his head is gone."

"Any idea when he died?"

"That's a tough one, considering the heat out here. And the dingoes got to him—ate some of the parts the pathologist would usually work with. But if someone said Friday, we wouldn't argue."

Hunter remained silent.

"We need names," Patterson pressed.

"My guy's not the one who did it," Hunter replied. "I'll speak to him, and maybe he'll give you a call."

He hung up before Patterson could push the issue any further. When he looked up, Sally and her clients were staring at him. Apparently, they understood enough to follow the conversation.

"Joseph Cook? Which prime minister was that?" Sally asked.

"The one wedged between Fishers second and third terms"

Hunter answered. "One of two who lost at double dissolution elections."

"Who was the other?"

"Fraser in eighty three."

"So, they found Bradley?" she asked.

"They sure did."

"So, what now?"

"Now we go warn Tom Peacock."

"Warn him?"

Hunter nodded. "Think about it, Sally. Maybe this isn't two for two—maybe it's two out of three. Tom, Troy, and Warner—they were a trio. Rosie said all three worked on the deal together. She said Tom brokered it with the feds, so he knew what they knew. He could be next."

Sally turned to her clients. "I'm sorry, I have to go," she said.

Tom Peacock was packing up for the day, standing with his jacket on and his briefcase snapped shut. It was past six o'clock, and the daylight outside his office windows was dimming. When they told him that Bradley was dead, they watched the color drain from his face. His skin seemed to contract and wrinkle under a layer of sweat. He stumbled back around his desk and collapsed into his chair. He was silent for a long moment, then slowly nodded.

"I guess I always knew," he said. "But I was hoping, you know?" He glanced down at a photograph on his desk.

"I'm really sorry," Hunter said.

"Do they know why?" Peacock asked. "Or who did it?"

"Not yet."

Peacock paused again. "Why'd they tell you before me?"

"Hunter figured out where they should look," Sally said. "He gave them the location, essentially."

She then laid out Hunter's two-out-of-three theory: the deal, the dangerous knowledge, and the possibility that Tom was next. Peacock sat quietly, listening. His color returned slowly as he processed what she was saying. After a long silence, he shook his head.

"That can't be right," he said. "The deal was nothing at all. Warner caved and agreed to pay the taxes and penalties. That's it—nothing more. He got desperate and couldn't handle the jail time. Happens all the time. Troy contacted the ATO, made the offer, and they didn't even flinch. It was routine. The branch office handled it with junior personnel. That's how ordinary it was. The federal prosecutor just needed to sign off on it, which is where I came in. I pushed it through a bit quicker than normal, that's all. It was just a standard ATO issue. And believe me, nobody gets killed over a routine ATO matter."

He shook his head again. Then his eyes widened, and he went still.

"I think you should leave now," he said.

Sally nodded. "We're very sorry for your loss. We know you were close."

But Peacock looked confused, as if that wasn't what he was concerned about.

"What is it?" Hunter asked.

"We shouldn't be talking anymore," Peacock said.

"Why not?"

"Because we're going in circles, and we're heading toward a conclusion we don't want to reach."

"We are?"

"Think about it—nobody gets killed over a routine ATO matter. Or do they? Warner and Troy were planning to take the trust money away from Rosie and give most of it to the government. Now Warner and Troy are dead. Two plus two makes four. Rosie's motive just got a whole lot bigger. If we keep talking like this, I'm going to have to think there's a conspiracy. Two deaths, not just one. I won't have a choice. And I really don't want to do that."

"There was no conspiracy," Hunter insisted. "If she'd hired someone already, why would she pick me up?"

Peacock shrugged. "Maybe to throw off suspicion? To distance herself?"

"Do you really think she's that smart?"

"I think she might be."

"Then prove it. Show us she hired someone."

"I can't do that."

"Yes, you can. You have her bank records. Show us a payment."

"A payment?"

"You don't think these people work for free, do you?"

Peacock grimaced. He pulled out a set of keys and unlocked a drawer in his desk, retrieving a pile of financial documents. The McMahon Non-Discretionary Trust, numbers 1 through 5. Hunter held his breath as Peacock flipped through the pages. After a few moments, Peacock squared the documents and set them back on the desk, his face expressionless.

Sally leaned forward and picked them up, skimming through the fourth column on each page—the debit column. There were plenty of debits, but they were small and random. Nothing larger than $399, several under $100.

"Add up the last month," Hunter said.

She scanned backward. "Roughly $950."

Hunter nodded. "Even if she saved every penny, $950 doesn't buy you much—certainly not someone who operates the way we've seen."

Peacock remained silent.

"We need to talk to her," Hunter said.

"We can't," Peacock replied. "She's already on her way to the prison outside of the city."

"She didn't do it," Hunter said. "She's completely innocent."

"Then why did she confess?"

Hunter closed his eyes, thinking for a moment.

"She was forced to," he said. "Someone got to her."

"Who?"

Hunter opened his eyes. "I don't know who, but we can find out. Get the bailiff's log from downstairs. See who visited her."

Peacock's face remained blank and sweaty, but he picked up the phone and dialed an internal number, requesting the visitor's log to be brought up immediately. They waited in silence. Three minutes later, they heard footsteps in the outer office, and the bailiff entered. He was out of breath, carrying a thick book.

Peacock took the log from him, scanned through it quickly, then placed it on the desk, pointing to a specific entry. Rosie McMahon had been logged in early Monday morning and out two hours ago, into the custody of the Queensland Department of Corrections. In between, she had received only one visitor, twice: the same Assistant Prosecutor, once at nine on Monday morning and again at noon on Tuesday.

“Preliminary interview, followed by the confession,” Peacock said.

There were no other entries.

“This is accurate?” Hunter asked.

The bailiff nodded. “Guaranteed.”

Hunter studied the log again. The first interview with the prosecutor had lasted just two minutes—Rosie must have refused to speak. The second interview took twelve minutes, after which she was escorted upstairs to record her confession.

“No one else?” he asked.

“There were phone calls,” the bailiff said.

“When?”

“All day Monday, and Tuesday morning.”

“Who was calling her?”

“Her lawyer.”

“Her lawyer?” Sally asked.

The bailiff nodded. “It was a pain. I had to keep bringing her back and forth to the phone.”

“Who was the lawyer?” Sally asked.

“We’re not allowed to ask. Confidentiality rules—lawyer-client discussions are private.”

“Was it a man or a woman?”

“It was a man.”

“Aboriginal?”

“I don’t think so. He sounded like a regular guy. His voice was a bit muffled—probably a bad line.”

"Was it the same person every time?"

"I think so."

The office fell silent. Peacock nodded slightly, signaling to the bailiff, who took it as a dismissal. They listened as he walked out through the outer office, and the lobby door closed behind him.

"She never told us she had legal representation," Peacock said. "She told us she didn't want a lawyer."

"She told me the same thing," Sally added.

"We need to figure out who this person was," Hunter said. "We need the phone company to trace those calls."

Peacock shook his head. "That's not possible. Conversations between a lawyer and their client are privileged."

Hunter fixed his gaze on Peacock. "Do you really think it was a lawyer?"

"Don't you?"

"Of course not. It was someone threatening her, forcing her to lie. Think about it, Peacock. When the Assistant Prosecutor first interviewed her, she didn't say a word. But twenty-seven hours later, she's confessing. The only thing that happened in between was a series of calls from this mystery man."

"But what kind of threat could make her confess to something she didn't do?"

****

The killing crew was unsettled in their new role as babysitters. Every member felt the same unease, for the same reasons. Taking a child hostage wasn't part of their usual skill set. The initial abduction had been simple—deception and lure, a standard operation. The woman and the tall man had arrived at the cream-colored house together, their pairing designed to match the public's image of social workers. They arrived in a large, official-looking sedan and spoke in a brisk, professional tone, adding a touch of self-righteous concern for the child's welfare. They carried a stack of fake documents that looked like legitimate warrants and authorizations from the Department of Social Services.

But the grandmother barely even glanced at them. She didn't resist at all, which struck the crew as strange. She handed the child over without hesitation, almost as if she was relieved to be rid of her. The child didn't resist either—no tears, no screaming. She was quiet and cooperative, as if she was trying her best to please the new adults. They simply placed her in the car and drove away. It had gone as smoothly as the Troy Bradley operation—almost too smoothly.

But from that point on, everything diverged from the usual routine. Normally, they would've driven straight to a remote location and eliminated the target, concealing the body before making their getaway. But this job was different. They had to keep the child hidden—alive and unharmed. For how long? Maybe days, maybe longer. It wasn't something they'd ever done before, and that made them nervous. Professionals always feel uneasy when they step outside their expertise. It's part of what makes them professionals.

"Call Social Services," Hunter said. "Right now."

Peacock just stared at him.

"You asked what kind of threat could make her confess," Hunter continued. "Don't you see? They must've gotten to her kid."

Peacock remained frozen for a moment before springing into action. He yanked open another drawer and pulled out a large black binder, quickly thumbing through it. He picked up the phone and dialed a number, but no one answered. He hung up and dialed again, this time reaching an after-hours emergency contact. He asked the question, using Lahni's full name, Alannah McMahon. After a long pause, he received an answer. His face paled as he slowly and carefully set the phone down, as if it were fragile.

"They've never heard of her," he said.

Silence filled the room as Peacock closed his eyes, then opened them again.

"Alright," he said. "We've got a problem with resources. We'll need the Queensland police, of course, and the AFP, since this is a kidnapping. But we've got to act immediately. Speed is crucial in cases like this. They could be taking her anywhere. So, I want you two to head up to Four Ways right now. Talk to Judy, get the full story—descriptions and everything."

"Judy won't talk to us," Hunter said. "She's too hostile. What about the sergeant up in Four Ways?"

"That guy's useless. He's probably drunk right now. You'll have to handle it yourselves."

"Waste of time," Hunter muttered.

Peacock opened another drawer and pulled out two QLD state police badges. He tossed them onto the desk.

"Raise your right hands," he said. "Repeat after me."

He mumbled through some kind of oath. Hunter and Sally repeated what they could catch. Peacock nodded.

"Congratulations, you're now reserves of the Four Ways Shire."

Hunter stared at him, incredulous.

"What?" Peacock asked.

"You can still do that? Just make people reserves?"

"Of course I can," Peacock said. "Just like the Wild West out here. Now get moving, alright? I've got a ton of calls to make."

Hunter picked up his star, feeling the weight of it in his hand. It was the first time in over five years that he'd held a badge of authority. Sally rose to her feet beside him.

"Meet back here as soon as you're done," Peacock called. "And good luck."

Eight minutes later, they were back in the red Hyundai, driving north toward the cream-colored house for the second time that day.

****

The woman took the call. She let the phone ring four times as she retrieved the voice-altering device from her bag and switched it on. But it turned out she didn't need it. There was no need to speak. It was a one-way message, long and complicated but clear and concise in its meaning. The message repeated twice before the call ended. She hung up and placed the device back in her bag.

"It's happening tonight," she said.

"What is?" the tall man asked.

"The extra job. The Mount Kalka situation. Seems things are starting to unravel up there. They found Bradley's body."

"Already?"

"Yeah," she said. "So we move on the extra job right away—tonight—before things spiral further out of control."

"Who's the target?" the tall man asked.

"His name is Mick Hunter. Some drifter, ex-military. I've got a description. There's also a lawyer involved. She'll need to be dealt with too."

"We're handling this alongside the babysitting gig?" the tall man asked.

The woman shrugged. “As we’ve always said, we keep the babysitting going as long as possible. But we reserve the right to end it if necessary.”

The two men exchanged uneasy glances. Lahni watched them closely from her bed.

CHAPTER 15

Hunter wasn't much of a companion on the drive north. He stayed silent for the first hour and a half as evening set in quickly. He kept the Hyundai's dome light on and was absorbed in the maps from the glove box, particularly focusing on a detailed topographical one that depicted the northern region of Four Ways Shire. The Shire's boundary was a perfectly straight line running east to west, just fifty kilometers from the Gulf of Carpentaria at its closest point, which didn't make sense to him.

"I don't get why she lied about the diamond," he finally said.

Sally gave a small shrug, pushing the car to its limits.

"She lied about everything," she replied.

"The ring was different," he insisted.

"Different in what way?" she asked.

"It's a different kind of lie. Like the difference between apples and oranges."

"I don't get it."

"The ring is the one thing I can't explain."

"That's the only thing?"

"Everything else fits, but the ring is a problem."

They drove on in silence for another kilometer, the power line poles flashing briefly in the headlights as they passed.

"You know what's really happening, don't you?" Sally asked.

"Ever used AI to design something?" he asked in response.

"No."

"Me neither."

"So?"

"Do you know what it is?"

She shrugged again. "Sort of."

"It can build a whole house, car, whatever you ask it to. It can paint it, decorate it, even walk through it. Rotate it, look at it from every angle—day, night, crash-test it. It's like it's real, but it's not. It's virtual."

"And?"

"I see this whole situation in my head, like that. Except for the ring. The ring throws it all off."

"You want to explain that?"

"No point, not until I figure it out."

"Is Lahni going to be okay?"

"I hope so. That's why we're on this trip."

"You think her grandmother can help?"

He shrugged. "I doubt it."

"Then how does this help Lahni?"

He didn't respond. Instead, he returned the maps to the glove compartment and pulled out a SIG Sauer handgun. He checked the magazine—still fully loaded with ten rounds. He inserted the magazine, chambered a round, and carefully tucked the pistol into his pocket.

"You think we'll need that?" Sally asked.

"Eventually," he said. "Got any more ammo in your bag?"

She shook her head. "I didn't think I'd ever use it."

He didn't respond.

"You okay?" she asked.

"I'm good," he replied. "Probably how you felt before that big trial, the one before the guy refused to pay."

She nodded. "Yeah, it felt good."

"That's your thing, isn't it?"

"Guess it is."

"This is mine," he said. "It's what I'm made for. The chase. I'm a ranger, always have been, always will be. I'm a hunter, more than just by name. When Peacock handed me that badge, it kicked my mind into gear."

"You know what's going on, don't you?"

"Besides the ring," he added.

"Tell me."

He stayed quiet.

"Tell me," she repeated.

"Ever ridden a horse?"

"No. I'm a city girl. Biggest open space I've seen is the Sydney Botanical Gardens."

"I rode one with Rosie. First time."

"So?"

"They're tall. You feel really high up."

"So?"

"Ever ride a bike?"

"In Sydney?"

"Skateboard?"

"Yeah, a bit, back when it was trendy."

"Ever fall?"

"Once, pretty badly."

He nodded. "Tell me about that meal you cooked for me."

"What about it?"

"It was homemade, right?"

"Of course."

"You measured the ingredients?"

"You have to."

"So you have a scale in your kitchen?"

"Obviously."

"The scales of justice," he said.

"What are you talking about, Hunter?"

He glanced out the window, watching the red picket fence blur past in the headlights.

"We're here," he said. "I'll explain later."

Sally pulled in under the gate and steered toward the motor barn as instructed, leaving the headlights on. "I want to check out that old ute," he said.

She parked, aiming the headlights at the barn, illuminating half of the new ute, part of the Nissan Patrol, and all of the old one parked between them.

"Stay close," he instructed.

They stepped out into the humid night air, which felt heavier than before. The yard was eerily quiet, only disturbed by insects. Together, they approached the abandoned ute. It looked like an old Toyota, maybe two decades old, still bearing resemblance to the newer ute beside it. Its fenders were round, the paint faded, and a roll bar was attached to the bed. The ute looked like it hadn't moved in years, its tires flat and springs sagging under the relentless heat.

"So?" Sally asked.

"I think it's the ute from the photo," Hunter said. "The one in Peacock's office, with Warner and Bradley leaning on it?"

"They all look the same to me," Sally replied.

"Warner had the same photo."

"That mean something?"

Hunter shrugged. "They were good friends."

They turned back toward the house. Sally switched off the headlights, and Hunter led her up to the porch. He knocked, and Ryan McMahon answered, looking surprised.

"So, you came back," Hunter said.

Ryan frowned. "My mates took me out to help me deal with things."

Hunter flashed his newly acquired badge. "Police. We need to talk to your mother."

"Police? You?"

"Peacock called us up as reserves. It's valid in Four Ways Shire. Where's your mother?"

Ryan hesitated, then glanced at the sky. "Storm's coming in from the south."

"Where's your mother, Ryan?"

Ryan gave in. "Inside."

Hunter led Sally past him into the foyer, which was a bit cooler than outside. The air conditioner thumped methodically loudly from somewhere upstairs. They moved into the parlor where Judy McMahon sat at the table, dressed similarly to before. Tight jeans and a country blouse. Her hair was stiff with hairspray.

"We're here on official business," Hunter said, showing her the badge. "We need answers."

"Or what?" Judy asked. "You going to arrest me?"

Hunter sat across from her, staring her down. "You've done everything wrong."

"Like what?"

"My grandmother would've died before she let anyone take her grandkids. She'd have said 'over my dead body,' and meant it."

There was a brief silence before Judy spoke. "It was for her own good. I had no choice. They had papers."

"You've given grandchildren away before?"

"No."

"Then how do you know the papers were legitimate?"

Judy shrugged. "They looked right. Full of legal words, references to Queensland."

"They were fake," Hunter said. "It was a kidnapping, Mrs. McMahon. They took your granddaughter to pressure your daughter-in-law."

He studied her face for a reaction, searching for any hint of realization, guilt, or remorse. Something flickered there, though he couldn't quite identify it.

"How many people were there?"

"Two," she finally answered. "A man and a woman."

"White?"

"Yes."

"What did they look like?"

"Ordinary," she said. "Like social workers. They had a big car."

"Details?"

"Fair hair. Cheap suits. Blue eyes. The man was tall."

"What about the car?"

"It was a big sedan, but nothing fancy. Gray or blue, maybe."

"You have any humble pie in the kitchen?"

"Why?"

"Because I should stuff it down your throat. Those people—those 'social workers'—are the ones who killed Troy Bradley. And you handed your granddaughter to them."

Judy stared at him, her face pale. "Troy's dead?"

"Two minutes after they took him out of his car."

She stammered, trying to ask about Lahni but unable to form the words.

"Not yet," Hunter said. "That's my hope. It should be yours too, because if they hurt her, you know what I'll do?"

She didn't respond, just shook her head.

"I'll come back here and break your spine. Snap it like a twig."

****

They made her take a bath, and it was awful. One of the men stood inside the bathroom, watching her the entire time. He wasn't tall—short, actually—with black hair on both his head and his arms. Her mother had always told her, "Never let anyone see you without clothes, especially not a man," but here he was, standing there, staring at her. She hadn't even brought pajamas with her. In fact, she hadn't brought anything at all.

"You don't need pajamas," the man said, his voice matter-of-fact. "It's too warm for them."

He continued to watch her as she dried off with a small white towel. She really needed to use the bathroom, but she wasn't about to do that in front of him. She had to squeeze past him to get out of the bathroom. Outside, the other two—the taller man and the woman—were waiting, watching her all the way to the bed. They were all horrible. She hated them all.

She crawled into the bed and pulled the covers over her head, trying her hardest not to cry.

****

"What now?" Sally asked.

"We head back to Mount Kalka," Hunter replied. "I want to stay on the move. There's still a lot to take care of tonight. But take it slow, okay? I need some time to think."

She drove out to the gate, turning south into the darkness. She switched the fan on high to clear the hot night air.

"Think about what?" Sally asked.

"About where Lahni is."

"Why do you think the same people who killed Bradley are involved?"

"It's all about deployment," Hunter explained. "I can't see them using separate teams for a hit and a kidnapping, not out here in the middle of nowhere. It's probably the same group. Either a hit team doing the kidnapping on the side, or a kidnapping team moonlighting as killers. My guess is it's a hit team, because the way they took out Bradley was pretty professional.

If that's how they moonlight, I wouldn't want to see them doing what they're really good at."

"All they did was shoot him. Anyone could do that."

"No, not just anyone. They got him to stop his car, they talked him into getting into theirs, and they kept him quiet the whole time. That takes skill, Sally—more than you might think. Then they shot him through the eye. That's important."

"Why?"

He shrugged. "It's a tiny target. In a situation like that, it's a quick shot. Raise the gun, pull the trigger. One, two. There's no logical reason to aim at something so small. It's a sign of confidence, almost like showing off, or maybe just enjoying their precision and skill. It's a thrill for them."

The car was quiet for a moment, the only sounds coming from the engine and the tires on the road.

"And now they've got the kid," Sally said.

"And they're uneasy about it, because it's not their usual job. They're used to working just with each other, following their usual methods. Having a live kid around makes them nervous—they're more visible and vulnerable."

"They could look like a family, though. A man, a woman, and a little girl."

"No, I think there's more than two of them."

"Why?"

"If it were me, I'd have three people. In the service, we usually worked in threes—a driver, a shooter, and someone watching the rear."

"You shot a lot of people? In the SAS?"

He gave a small shrug. "A lot is subjective."

She went quiet for a moment, clearly considering whether to scoot away from him just a bit. In the end, she decided to stay where she was.

“So why didn’t you do it for Rosie?” she asked. “If you’ve done it before?”

“She asked me that too. I still don’t know.”

Another kilometer passed in silence.

“Why are they still holding Lahni?” she asked. “I mean, they’ve already gotten the confession. What’s left for them to gain?”

“You’re the lawyer,” he said. “You tell me. When does it become set in stone? When is it truly irrevocable?”

“Well, technically, never. A confession can be withdrawn at any time. But practically speaking, if she pleads guilty to the charges, that would be a significant step.”

“And how soon could that happen?”

“Tomorrow, easily. The sentencing judge is basically always in session. It would take ten, fifteen minutes tops.”

“I thought the legal process moved slowly in Queensland.”

“Only if you plead not guilty.”

The car sped on in silence for several kilometers. They passed through a small crossroads with a school, a service station, and a takeaway shop, all of which were briefly illuminated by the headlights as they flashed by. The sky ahead was still clear, stars twinkling, but the clouds were rapidly building behind them in the north.

“So maybe tomorrow they’ll let her go,” Sally said.

“And maybe tomorrow they won’t. They’ll worry she could identify them. Lahni’s sharp. She’s quiet, but she’s always watching and thinking.”

"So what's the plan?"

"We try to figure out where they're holding her."

Hunter opened the glove compartment and pulled out the maps again, spreading out a large-scale one of Mount Kalka Shire on his knee. He clicked the dome light on.

"How do we start?" Sally asked. "I mean, they could be anywhere—abandoned buildings, farmhouses. There must be a million places to hide."

"No, I think they're using motels."

"Why?"

"Appearances are crucial to them. It's part of their method. They convinced Troy Bradley somehow, and Judy McMahon didn't find them suspicious. They need the right look —running water, showers, closets, working electricity for hairdryers and shavers."

"There must be tens of motels, though," she said. "Hundreds, maybe."

He nodded. "And they're moving constantly, I'm sure of it. They change motels every day for security."

"So how do we find the right one tonight?"

Hunter held the map up to the light. "We find it by thinking like them. We figure out what we'd do, and that should lead us to what they've done."

"That's a big gamble."

"Maybe, maybe not."

"So are we starting now?"

"No, we're going back to your office for now."

"Why?"

"I don't like direct assaults, not against professionals like these, especially not when a kid's involved."

"So what's the plan?"

"We split them up. Draw two of them out, maybe get one of them to talk."

"Get one to talk? How?"

"We decoy them. They know we're onto them, so they'll come after us to control the damage."

"They know we know? How?"

"Someone just told them."

"Who?"

Hunter didn't answer. He just stared down at the map, studying the faint red lines representing roads stretching across thousands of empty kilometers. He closed his eyes, trying to picture what those roads looked like in reality.

Sally parked in the lot behind her law office. She had a key to the back door, and as they walked, Hunter was on high alert, scanning the shadows. They made it inside without incident. The old building was quiet, dusty, and hot. The air conditioning had been turned off at the end of the day.

Hunter stood still for a moment, listening carefully for any sign that someone else might be there—an ancient instinct buried deep in the brain. But there was nothing.

"Call Peacock and give him an update," Hunter said. "Tell him we're here."

He made her sit back-to-back with him at another desk in the middle of the room, positioning them so that he could watch the front entrance while she watched the rear. He rested the pistol on his lap with the safety off and then dialed Sergeant

Patterson's number in Townsville. Patterson answered, clearly frustrated to still be on duty.

"We checked with the bar association," Patterson said. "There are no lawyers licensed in Queensland under the name Joseph Cook."

"I'm from Tasmania," Hunter replied smoothly. "Just volunteering here, pro bono."

"Yeah, right," Patterson scoffed. The line went quiet.

"I'll make a deal," Hunter said. "Names for a conversation."

"With who?"

"You, maybe. How long have you been with the Queensland police?"

"Eighteen years."

"How much do you know about the border patrol?"

"Enough, I guess."

"Are you prepared to give me a straight yes-or-no answer? No comebacks?"

"What's the question?"

"Do you remember the border patrol investigation from twelve years ago?"

"Maybe."

"Was it a whitewash?"

Patterson paused for a long moment before answering with a single word. "Yes."

"I'll call you back," Hunter said and hung up.

Turning over his shoulder to Sally, he asked, "Did you reach Peacock?"

"He's caught up," she replied. "He wants us to wait here until he's done with the AFP."

Hunter shook his head. "We can't stay here. It's too obvious. We need to keep moving. Let's go to him, and then get back on the road."

Sally hesitated for a second. "Are we in serious danger?"

"Nothing we can't handle," he assured her.

She didn't seem convinced.

"You worried?" he asked.

"A little," she admitted. "Actually, a lot."

"You can't afford to be," he said. "I'm going to need your help."

"Why was the lie about the ring different?" she asked suddenly.

"Because everything else was secondhand information. But I found out about the ring for myself—it wasn't a fake. That kind of personal discovery feels very different."

"I still don't see why it's so important."

"It matters because I've built a whole theory, and the lie about the ring messes everything up."

"Why do you want to believe her so much?"

"Because she had no money with her."

"What's this big theory of yours?"

"Remember that quotes from that one from your farming family and Smith?" Sally nodded.

"Well, I've got another one," Hunter said. "Something Sun Tzu wrote."

"Appear weak when you are strong, and strong when you are weak."

"What are you, a walking encyclopedia?"

"I just remember things I read, that's all. And I remember something Ryan McMahon said too, about dingos."

Sally gave him a puzzled look. "You're crazy," she said.

He nodded. "It's just a theory. But we can test it."

"How?"

"We wait and see who comes for us."

She was silent.

"Let's check in with Peacock," Hunter said.

They walked through the humid night air toward the courthouse building. A breeze was blowing in from the north again, damp and heavy with urgency. When they reached Peacock's office, he was sitting alone at his desk, looking exhausted. The desk was cluttered with phone books and scattered papers.

"Well, it's begun," Peacock said. "Biggest manhunt you've ever seen. AFP and state police have set up roadblocks everywhere. Helicopters in the air. Over a hundred and fifty people on the ground. But there's a storm coming, which won't help."

"Hunter thinks they're holed up in a motel," Sally said.

Peacock gave a grim nod. "If that's the case, they'll be found. A manhunt of this scale is relentless."

"Do you still need us?" Hunter asked.

Peacock shook his head. "We should let the professionals handle it now. I'm heading home to get a few hours of sleep."

Hunter scanned the office—the door, the floor, the windows, the desk, and the filing cabinets.

"Guess we'll do the same," he said. "We'll go to Sally's place. Call us if you need us, or if you hear anything, okay?"

Peacock nodded. "I will. I promise."

****

"We'll go as AFP again," the woman said. "It's a no-brainer."

"All of us?" the driver asked. "What about the kid?"

The woman paused. She needed to go because she was the shooter, and if the team had to split up, she wanted the tall guy with her, not the driver.

"You stay with the kid," she decided.

There was a moment of silence.

"Abort horizon?" the driver asked.

It was standard procedure for them. Whenever the team split, the woman set an abort horizon—a specific amount of time they would wait before getting out, every person for themselves, if the team hadn't reunited.

"Four hours, okay?" the woman said. "Done and dusted."

She stared at the driver a second longer, eyebrows raised to make sure he understood what she was implying. Then she knelt down and unzipped a heavy suitcase.

"Let's do it," she said.

They repeated the steps they had taken for Troy Bradley, only much faster this time since the Ford Falcon was parked in the motel's lot, not hidden miles away in a dusty turnout. The parking lot was dimly lit and mostly empty, but even so, it didn't feel entirely safe. They quickly pulled the wheel covers off and threw them in the trunk. They attached the communications antennas to the rear window and the trunk lid. They zipped up blue jackets over their shirts, loaded spare ammunition clips, and adjusted their souvenir caps. They checked the loads in their nine-millimeter pistols, racked the slides, and clicked on the safeties before jamming the guns into their pockets. The tall man slipped into the driver's seat while the woman stood outside the motel room door.

"Four hours," she reminded him. "Done and dusted."

The driver nodded and closed the door behind her, casting a glance at the kid lying in the bed. "Done and dusted" meant no loose ends—especially not living witnesses.

Hunter took the SIG Sauer, the maps of Queensland, and the Auspost Express packet out of the Hyundai and carried them into Sally's house, moving straight through the living room and into the kitchen. It was cool and still inside, with the central air conditioner running at full blast. For a moment, he wondered what her electric bill must be like.

"Where's the scale?" he asked.

Sally pushed past him, squatted down, and opened a cupboard. She pulled out a large kitchen scale and set it on the countertop. The scale was new but had a retro look, with a big white upright face the size of a dinner plate, like the speedometer on an old car. A bulbous plastic window with a chromium bezel covered the face, and behind the window was a red pointer with large numbers around the edge. The scale was marked with a manufacturer's name and a printed warning: *For Personal Use Only*.

"Is it accurate?" Hunter asked.

Sally shrugged. "I think so. My nut roast always turns out fine."

The scale had a chrome bowl sitting in a cradle above the dial. Hunter tapped it lightly, and the pointer bounced up to half a kilo before settling back at zero. He removed the magazine from the SIG Sauer and placed the empty gun in the bowl, which made a metallic clink. The pointer jumped to one kilo two hundred grams—not especially light, but about what he expected. His memory told him the catalog weight was just under a kilo with an empty magazine.

He reassembled the gun and began rifling through the cupboards until he found some food supplies. He pulled out an unopened bag of granulated sugar, wrapped in a bright blue-and-white paper bag labeled "2kg."

"What are you doing?" Sally asked.

"Weighing things," he replied.

He placed the sugar bag upright in the bowl, and the pointer swung to two kilos exactly. He returned the sugar to the cupboard and tried a packet of chopped nuts wrapped in cellophane. The pointer stopped at one kilogram, matching the label on the package.

"Good enough," Hunter said.

He folded the maps and laid them across the top of the bowl. They weighed half a kilo. He removed them and replaced the nuts in the bowl. The pointer moved back up to a kilo. He then placed the Auspost Express packet on the scale, which weighed half a kilo and a few grams. He added the maps again, and the weight rose to one kilo and one hundred grams. Finally, he placed the loaded gun on top, and the pointer jumped to nearly two and half kilos. He could have calculated the weight of the bullets if he'd wanted to.

Saly stared at him the whole time like he was mad.

"Okay, let's go," he said. "But we'll need to get fuel—long ride ahead. You should probably change out of that dress, too. Got something more practical?"

"I guess," Sally said, heading for the stairs.

"You got a screwdriver?" Hunter called after her.

"Under the sink," she replied.

He found a brightly colored plastic toolbox under the sink and clicked it open, selecting a medium-sized screwdriver with a clear yellow handle. A minute later, Sally returned, now dressed in loose green cargo pants and a black T-shirt with the sleeves torn off at the shoulders.

"How's this?" she asked.

"Looks like you and Rhiannon have a lot in common," he said with a smile.

She grinned but didn't reply.

"I'm assuming your car's insured?" Hunter asked. "Could get banged up tonight."

She said nothing, just locked the door behind them and followed him out to the Hyundai. She drove out of her complex with Hunter on high alert, scanning the shadows. They stopped to refuel at a neon-lit all-night station on Yabbie Creek Road, and Hunter paid for the fuel.

"Alright, back to the courthouse," he said. "There's something I need to grab."

Sally didn't ask any questions, just turned the car and headed east, parking in the lot behind the courthouse. They walked around to the street entrance, but the door was locked tight.

"So, what now?" she asked.

The night was still hot, the temperature hovering around ninety degrees, and the breeze had died. Clouds filled the sky overhead.

"I'm going to kick it in," Hunter said.

"There's probably an alarm."

"There definitely is. I checked."

"And?"

"And I'm going to set it off."

"Then the cops will come."

"That's the plan."

"You want us to get arrested?"

"They won't come right away. We've got three or four minutes, tops."

He took a couple of steps back and launched himself forward, smashing the flat of his boot against the door just above the handle. The wood splintered but held. He kicked again, and the door flew open, crashing into the wall inside. A blue strobe started flashing high above them, and an electric bell began ringing loudly—just as Hunter had expected.

"Go get the car," he said. "Start it up and wait for me in the alley."

He ran up the stairs two at a time and kicked open the outer office door without breaking stride. He weaved through the secretarial desks like a running back, steadied himself, and kicked in Peacock's office door. It slammed open, the venetian blinds snapping sideways, shattering the glass pane behind them. Shards of glass fell like ice in winter.

He went straight to the filing cabinets. The lights were off, and the office was stifling and dark, so he had to peer closely at the labels. The filing system was odd, arranged partly by date and partly by alphabet, which would slow him down. He found a cabinet marked "B" and jammed the screwdriver into the lock, hammering it with the heel of his hand. He twisted it sharply, breaking the lock, and pulled the drawer open, raking through the files with his fingers.

The files were neatly arranged, tiny labels encased in plastic tabs forming a diagonal from left to right. All the labels started with "B," but the contents were too recent—nothing older than four years. Hunter moved two paces sideways, skipping the next "B" drawer, and went for the following one. The air was hot and still, the bell was deafening, and the flashing blue strobe's light pulsed rhythmically, almost in sync with his heartbeat.

He broke the lock and slid open the drawer, checking the labels. No luck—everything in this one was from six or seven years ago. He'd been inside the building for two and a half minutes, and now, beneath the constant ringing of the bell, he could hear a distant siren. He stepped sideways again and attacked the third "B" drawer. As the siren drew closer, the noise from the bell seemed louder, and the strobe light even brighter. He found what he was looking for three-quarters of the way through the drawer: a two-inch-thick file of paperwork in a heavy paper sling. He grabbed it, tucked it under his arm, and left the drawer open while kicking the others shut. Then he sprinted through the secretarial office and down the stairs. After confirming the street was clear, he ducked into the alley and hopped into the waiting Hyundai.

"Go," he said, slightly out of breath, which surprised him.

"Where?" Sally asked.

"North, to the cream house," Hunter answered.

"Why? What's there?"

"Everything."

Sally hit the accelerator, and a few seconds later, Hunter noticed red lights flashing in the distance behind them. The Mount Kalka Police Department had arrived at the courthouse, but they were just a minute too late. He smiled in the dark, then caught a glimpse of a large sedan turning left onto the road leading to Sally's house, about two hundred meters ahead.

The car had plain steel wheels and four VHF antennas on the back, likely a police-spec Falcon. He watched it disappear into the darkness.

“Faster,” he urged Sally.

Hunter placed the stack of paperwork on his lap and clicked on the dome light to read it. The “B” stood for *border patrol*. The file detailed crimes committed by the border patrol twelve years ago, along with the actions taken afterward. It was disturbing reading.

The border between Papua New Guinea and Queensland was long, and for about half its length, the distance over the ocean was less than half a day sailing. The theory was that if illegals breached the border there, they could easily disappear into the interior of Queensland because of the tropics. Other stretches of the border had nothing to offer but empty desert, so those areas were rarely patrolled. Standard practice involved conducting random vehicle sweeps behind the border to catch migrants during their week long trek across the wasteland. The strategy worked—by the time migrants had walked fifty kilometers through the scorching heat, they were often too exhausted to resist and would surrender willingly. In some cases, patrols even became mercy missions, with officers offering first aid to dehydrated and weakened migrants.

The migrants were usually desperate, having paid their life savings to unscrupulous operators on the PNG side who promised them safe passage. These operators would sail them to the border, point to a distant outcrop of trees, and claim more transport was waiting just over the other side. The migrants would cross the forest, only to find nothing on the other side. Too scared to turn back, they’d continue walking south, hoping for the best.

Sometimes there would be a vehicle waiting, but the driver would demand more money, which the migrants no longer had. The driver would laugh, take whatever small valuables they had, and drive off, never to be seen again. The migrants would continue their grueling journey on foot. In hot summers, many didn't survive, which made the border patrol's sweeps feel like humanitarian efforts.

But that all changed one year.

For twelve months, the patrols became deadly. Randomly and always at night, utes would arrive, rifles blazing, targeting lone runners. These individuals would be hunted down, shot, and left for dead. The utes would vanish into the night, leaving only stunned silence behind.

Sometimes it wasn't that simple. Some migrants were tortured —one teenage boy was found tied to a mangrove, partially amputated. Others were buried alive or mutilated. Six teenage girls were found dead over a span of five months, their autopsies detailing unspeakable horrors.

None of the survivors' families made formal complaints— they feared interacting with authorities. However, rumors spread among legal relatives and support groups. Lawyers and human rights advocates began to gather evidence. Eventually, the issue was raised at an official level, and a low-level inquiry was launched. Anonymous testimonies established that at least nineteen homicides had occurred, with nine more deaths extrapolated based on missing bodies or those buried by survivors. Young Ratu Longman's name was among the extrapolated cases.

The file included a map showing where most of the ambushes occurred. The area, shaped like a pear and covering about a hundred and fifty square kilometers, was marked on the map. It was located mostly within the giant Four Ways Shire, indicating the victims had traveled at least fifty kilometers before being ambushed, too weak to resist by then.

The border patrol launched a full-scale investigation in

August, almost a year after the first rumors. One more attack occurred that month, but after that, the killings stopped. With no further incidents, the investigation stalled. Preventive measures were enforced, including stricter tracking of ammunition and more frequent radio checks, but no solid conclusions were drawn. The investigation eventually faded into obscurity as time passed, survivors moved on, and immigration amnesties helped dampen the outrage. Five years later, the files were sealed.

"So?" Sally asked, breaking the silence.

Hunter butted the papers together with his palm, closed the file, and tossed it into the backseat.

"Now I know why she lied about the ring," he said.

"Why?"

"She didn't lie. She thought she was telling the truth."

"She said it was a fake worth thirty bucks."

"She believed that because a jeweler in Mount Kalka laughed at her and told her it was a fake worth thirty bucks. She didn't know any better. But he was trying to con her. He probably wanted to buy it for thirty and sell it for sixty thousand. Oldest trick in the book. Same thing that happened to some of those migrants in the file. Their first experience in Australia."

"The jeweler lied?" Sally asked.

Hunter nodded. "I should have figured it out earlier. It's obvious. Probably the same guy we saw. He didn't exactly scream 'honest businessman.'"

"He didn't try to rip us off."

"No, Sally. He didn't. Because you're a sharp-looking white lawyer, and I'm a big, intimidating white guy. But Lahni? She was a small Pacific Islander woman, scared and desperate. He saw an opportunity to exploit her."

Sally was quiet for a moment.

"So what does it mean?" she finally asked.

Hunter clicked off the dome light, stretched, and smiled in the dark. He placed his hands on the dashboard and flexed his shoulders.

"It means we're good to go," he said. "Everything's lined up perfectly. Now, step on it, because we're about twenty minutes ahead of the bad guys, and I want to keep it that way."

Sally sped through the silent crossroads again, covering the remaining sixty kilometers in thirty minutes, which Hunter thought was impressive for a small two-liter import with a bobble head beside the steering wheel. She turned in under the gate and braked hard at the foot of the porch steps. The porch lights were on, and the dust from the Hyundai's tires swirled around them in a cloud of brown. It was close to 2:00 a.m.

"Leave it running," Hunter instructed.

He led her up to the door and knocked hard. No answer. He tried the handle—it was unlocked. Why would it be locked? They were sixty kilometers from the nearest crossroads. He pushed the door open, and they stepped into the cream-painted foyer.

"Hold out your arms," he said.

Hunter pulled all six .22 hunting rifles from the wall rack and placed them in her arms, alternating muzzle to stock so they'd balance. She staggered slightly under the weight.

"Take them to the car," he told her.

There were footsteps overhead, followed by the creaking of stairs. Ryan McMahon emerged from the parlor door, rubbing the sleep from his eyes. He was barefoot, wearing boxers and a

T-shirt, and staring at the now-empty gun rack.

"What the hell do you think you're doing?" he demanded.

"I want the rest," Hunter said. "I'm confiscating your weapons on behalf of the Four Ways Shire sergeant. Remember, I'm an officer now."

"There aren't any others," Ryan said, trying to sound firm.

"Yes, there are, Ryan. No good country boy like you would settle for just a bunch of .22 popguns. Where's the real firepower?"

Ryan remained silent, sizing up the situation.

"Don't mess with me, Ryan," Hunter warned. "It's way too late for that."

Ryan paused, then shrugged in defeat.

"Okay," he said, turning toward a door off the foyer. He padded across the room barefoot and pushed it open, revealing a small, dark space that looked like a study. He flicked on a light, and Hunter saw black-and-white photos of oil wells on the walls. There was a desk, a chair, and another gun rack, this one holding four 30-30 Winchesters. Seven-shot lever-action repeaters with oiled wood and twenty-inch barrels—beautifully kept weapons. Hunter smiled. *Ned Kelly, eat your heart out*, he thought.

"Ammunition?" Hunter asked.

Ryan opened a drawer built into the gun rack's pedestal and pulled out a cardboard box of Winchester cartridges.

"I've got some special loads, too," he added, taking out another box.

"What are they?"

"I made them myself. Extra power."

Hunter nodded. "Take it all out to the car."

He grabbed the four rifles from the rack and followed Ryan outside. Sally was already sitting in the car, the six .22 rifles piled on the backseat. Ryan leaned in and placed the ammunition boxes next to them, while Hunter stacked the Winchesters upright behind the passenger seat.

Turning to Ryan, Hunter said, "I'm borrowing your Nissan."

Ryan shrugged again, still barefoot on the hot dirt. "Keys are in it."

"You and your mother stay inside the house now," Hunter ordered. "Anyone seen outside will be considered hostile, okay?"

Ryan nodded, casting a glance over his shoulder before walking back toward the porch. He looked back once before disappearing inside. Hunter leaned into the Hyundai to talk to Sally.

"What are we doing?" she asked.

"Getting ready."

"For what?"

"For whatever comes our way."

"Why do we need ten rifles?"

"We don't. We need one. I just don't want the bad guys to get their hands on the other nine."

"They're coming here?"

"They're about ten minutes behind us."

"So what's the plan?"

"We're heading out into the desert."

"Is there going to be shooting?"

"Probably."

"Is that a smart idea? You said it yourself—they're good shots."

"With handguns, yes. The best way to defend against handguns is to stay far away and shoot back with the biggest rifle you can find."

Sally shook her head, clearly conflicted. "I can't be part of this, Hunter. It's not right. And I've never even held a rifle."

"You don't have to shoot," Hunter reassured her. "But you do need to be a witness. You have to identify exactly who comes for us. I'm relying on you—it's crucial."

"How am I supposed to see anything? It's pitch black out there."

"We'll handle that."

"It's going to rain."

"That'll help us."

"This isn't right," she said again, her voice strained. "The police should be dealing with this. Or the AFP. You can't just start shooting at people."

The air was thick with the coming storm. The wind had picked up, carrying the scent of low pressure and voltage building in the sky.

"Rules of engagement, Sally," Hunter said calmly. "I'll wait until they make a hostile move before I do anything. Just like the SAS. Okay?"

"We're going to get killed."

"You'll be hiding far away."

"Then you'll be killed! You said it yourself—they're good at this."

"They're good at walking up to someone and shooting them in the head. What they're like out in the open, in the dark, with incoming rifle fire? That's anyone's guess."

"You're crazy," she muttered.

"Seven minutes," Hunter said, checking the time.

Sally glanced nervously at the road to the south, then shook her head and shifted the car into first gear, keeping her foot on the brake. Hunter leaned in and gave her shoulder a reassuring squeeze.

"Stick close behind me, okay?"

He ran down to the motor barn, hopped into the McMahon family's Cherokee, and racked the seat back. He started the engine and flicked on the headlights before reversing into the yard, straightening up, and looping around the barn. He headed down the dirt track that led into open country, checking the rearview mirror to see the Hyundai following close behind. He looked ahead just as the first raindrop splashed onto his windshield, large as a plum.

CHAPTER 16

They drove in convoy for five fast kilometers through the dark. There was no moonlight, no starlight. Low, thick cloud cover blocked everything, though it kept the rain to no more than sporadic splashes—ten seconds apart, six drops every minute, each one hitting the windshield like an explosion, spreading wet patches the size of dessert plates. Hunter hit the wipers to swipe each one clear. He held the Nissan steady at around forty kilometers per hour, following the winding track north toward the approaching storm. The ground was rough, causing the Nissan to bounce and jolt. Behind him, the Hyundai struggled to keep pace, its headlights swinging and jumping in his mirrors.

Five kilometers from the house, the rain had yet to truly start, but the landscape began to change. The once wide desert plain, which might have been cultivated farmland a century ago, started to rise, slowly turning into a plateau. Rocky outcrops appeared in the headlight beams, closing in on either side. Acacia trees grew thicker, funneling them into a tighter path. Before long, the track had become nothing more than a pair of deep ruts worn through the hard ground. Ledges, sinkholes, and dense thorny brush lined the way, forcing them to stick to the narrow route, which twisted and turned like an old riverbed.

Then, the track suddenly leveled out onto a miniature plateau, a stone surface about the size of a football field—roughly 120 meters long and 80 meters wide, oval-shaped. No vegetation grew on it. Hunter swung the Nissan in a wide circle, using the high beams to check the perimeter. Along the edges, the ground dropped a couple of feet into rocky soil, where stunted bushes clung wherever they could. He made another wider loop and liked what he saw. The plateau was as bare as a dinner plate set on a dead lawn. He smiled to himself, timing out in his head what needed to happen. The plan seemed good.

He drove to the far end of the rock table, stopping where the track dropped off and disappeared into the brush. Sally pulled the Hyundai alongside. Hunter jumped out of the Nissan and crouched by her window. The night air was hot and damp, the breeze urgent again, and the big, lazy raindrops fell vertically, as if he could dodge them individually. Sally rolled down the window.

“You okay?” he asked.

“So far,” she replied.

“Turn the car around and back it up to the edge. Block the track’s mouth.”

She maneuvered the Hyundai like she was parking in a tight city spot, reversing until the rear wheels were right against the drop-off. The front of the car pointed directly south, back the way they had come. Hunter parked the Nissan next to her and opened the tailgate.

“Kill the engine and lights,” he called. “Grab the rifles.”

Sally passed him the large Winchesters one by one. He laid them carefully in the Nissan’s load space. Then she handed him the .22 rifles, which he threw into the brush as far as he could. She passed him the two boxes of 30-30 ammunition—Winchester’s own rounds and Ryan McMahon’s hand-loaded shells. Hunter laid them next to the rifles, then walked around to the driver’s side of the Nissan, turned off the engine, and listened. Silence fell. He scanned the northern horizon, hearing only the faint sigh of the wattle brush in the wind, buzzing insects, and the sporadic raindrops hitting his shoulders. Otherwise, nothing. Just blackness and quiet everywhere.

Returning to the tailgate, he opened the ammunition boxes. Both were packed tightly with cartridges standing on their firing pins, tips up. The factory shells were new and shiny, while Ryan's hand-loaded rounds were a bit scuffed, made from recycled brass. Hunter picked one up and examined it under the Nissan's interior light. Ryan had mentioned extra power, which made sense—why else would a guy like Ryan hand-load his own rounds? Not for less power, that was certain. He had likely packed the shells with extra powder, maybe thirty or forty additional grains, possibly even hotter powder. The result would be higher muzzle energy and greater velocity, but at the cost of a huge muzzle flash and potential damage to the gun's breech and barrel. Still, Hunter smiled, deciding that a massive muzzle flash was exactly what he wanted.

He loaded the first Winchester with a single one of Ryan's hand-loads, filled the second with seven more, and alternated stock rounds with hand-loads in the third. The fourth rifle he filled entirely with factory ammo. Laying the rifles in order from left to right across the Nissan's load space, he closed the tailgate.

"I thought we only needed one rifle," Sally said.

"I changed the plan," Hunter replied.

He moved to the driver's seat, and Sally climbed in next to him.

"Where are we going now?" she asked.

"Picture the plateau like a clock face," Hunter explained. "We came in at six o'clock. Your car is now parked at twelve, facing backward. You'll be hiding on the rim at eight. On foot. Your job is to fire a rifle, one shot, then move to seven."

"You said I wouldn't have to shoot."

"I changed the plan."

"I told you—I've never fired a rifle."

"You'll be fine. Just pull the trigger. You don't need to aim, just make noise and create a flash."

"And then what?"

"Then you move to the seven o'clock spot and watch. I'll be busy shooting, and I need you to identify who I'm shooting at."

"This doesn't feel right."

"It's not wrong, either."

"You sure about that?"

"You ever seen Benjamin Blackman's grave?" Hunter asked.

Sally rolled her eyes. "Hunter, Benjamin Blackman was a psychopath. He killed a guy during a robbery just for being slow at counting the gold. There was nothing noble about him."

Hunter shrugged. "Well, we're past the point of backing out."

"Two wrongs don't make a right, you know."

"It's a choice: either we ambush them, or we get ambushed."

Sally shook her head. "Great."

He didn't reply.

"It's dark. How am I supposed to see anything?"

"I'll take care of that."

"How will I know when to fire?"

"You'll know."

Hunter pulled the Nissan to the edge of the sandstone table

and stopped. He retrieved the first rifle, checked his bearings, and ran to the rim of the plateau. Laying the rifle on the ground with the butt hanging over the edge and the barrel aimed into the empty space ahead of the distant Hyundai, he racked the lever. The mechanism moved smoothly with a satisfying metallic slick-slick.

"It's ready," he said. "This is the eight o'clock spot. Stay low below the edge, fire, and then move to seven. Crouch all the way. And watch carefully. They might fire in your direction, but I promise they'll miss."

Sally said nothing.

"Don't worry," he added. "I guarantee it."

"Are you sure?"

"James Bond couldn't hit anything with a handgun from this distance in the dark."

"They might get lucky."

"No, Sally, not tonight. Trust me."

"But when do I fire?"

"Fire when ready," he said.

Hunter watched her crouch below the rim of the rock, positioning herself an arm's length from the rifle.

"Good luck," he said. "I'll see you later."

"Great," she muttered again.

Hunter climbed back into the Nissan and sped across the plateau to the four o'clock position. He spun the wheel and backed the car off the rock ledge, bringing it to a stop in the underbrush. After killing the engine and lights, he grabbed the fourth rifle and propped it against the passenger door. Then, carrying the second and third rifles, he ran back onto the plateau, heading to the two o'clock spot. He carefully placed the third rifle on the rock's edge and ran the rest of the way to the parked Hyundai. Ducking inside, he unscrewed the dome light, left the driver's door slightly ajar, and moved twenty feet clockwise to place the second rifle at what he estimated was twelve-thirty on the clock face.

Hunter crawled back and lay flat on the ground, pressing himself tight against the Hyundai. His right shoulder was wedged under the small running board, his face pressed against the sidewall of the front tire. His left shoulder was exposed to the weather, and every so often, a large raindrop would smack down on it. He shifted closer to the vehicle, settling in for the wait. He figured it would be about eight minutes, maybe nine.

It turned out to be eleven minutes. They were slower than he had expected. At first, he mistook the flash he saw in the distance for lightning, but then it happened again, and he realized it was the headlights of a vehicle bouncing through the rough terrain, catching the low clouds. The ute was pitching and rolling as it made its way toward him, just as he knew it would—it had no choice but to follow the track. The lights flared as the ute's nose rose and fell, the engine working hard. It sounded like a petrol-powered V8, with the sound rising and falling as the wheels lost and regained traction. It had to be Ryan's ute, the one he used to hunt dingoes.

Hunter wedged himself even tighter beneath the Hyundai as the engine noise grew louder. The vehicle's headlights bounced across the landscape, spearing through the mesquite, casting flickering shadows left and right as it approached. Then, the ute roared up onto the plateau, hitting the flat surface at speed. Its engine screamed as all four wheels left the ground. The lights flared and dipped as the ute crashed back to earth, slightly off-course, the beams sweeping the perimeter before the driver corrected. The ute accelerated, coming straight at the Hyundai—forty kilometers per hour, fifty. Seventy meters away. Fifty. Forty.

Suddenly, the headlights illuminated the Hyundai, glowing impossibly bright. The driver slammed on the brakes, all four wheels locking up on the sandstone. The ute skidded to a stop, slewing slightly to the left, coming to rest about thirty meters in front of Hunter. The beams barely missed him, but he remained hidden in the shadows, pressed tight against the ground.

Nothing happened for a second. Then, the ute's driver cut the lights. The bright beams dimmed to weak orange filaments before fading into total darkness. Only the sound of the idling engine remained.

Did they see me? Hunter wondered.

Another moment passed. Still nothing.

Now, Sally, he thought. But nothing happened.

Shoot, Sally. Shoot now, for God's sake! Still nothing.

Pull the damn trigger, Sally!

Hunter closed his eyes, braced himself, and prepared to act. But just as he moved to launch himself out from under the Hyundai, Sally finally fired.

The muzzle flash was huge, easily ten feet long, lighting up the night. A supersonic bullet sliced through the air with a sharp buzzing whine, followed a split second later by an enormous, echoing crash. Hunter rolled out from under the Hyundai, reached in through the driver's door, and flicked on the headlights. Then he dove backward into the brush, rolling six feet away into a low crouch.

The ute was caught perfectly in the Hyundai's headlights, frozen in the glare. There were three people in it—a driver in the cab and two figures crouched in the bed, gripping the roll bar with one hand each. All three had their heads turned sharply, staring back at where Sally had fired from.

For a split second, they were completely still. Then they reacted. The driver flicked the ute's headlights back on, and the vehicles faced off, their beams locked in a duel. Hunter was partially blinded by the intense light, but he could make out that the two figures in the back were wearing caps and blue jackets. One was smaller than the other—a woman, most likely. She was crouched low beside her partner, on his left.

Both of them had handguns, and after a moment, they snapped forward and started shooting into the Hyundai's headlights. Their caps bore the letters "AFP" on the front. Hunter froze for a second—*What the hell?*—but then relaxed. It was all fake. The apparel, the IDs, the tricked-out Ford Falcon they'd used at Sally's place. That was how they had stopped Troy Bradley.

The two gunmen fired rapidly, their powerful nine-millimeter pistols barking loudly. Spent shells clattered onto the ute's roof. The Hyundai's windshield exploded, and bullets ripped through the sheet metal, glass tinkling as it shattered. Then, the Hyundai's lights went out, and darkness enveloped everything behind the ute's glare.

Hunter sensed the shooters were now aiming at where they remembered Sally's shot had come from. Tiny muzzle flashes illuminated the night as bullets whined through the air. The gun in the woman's hand suddenly went silent—she was reloading. *Only thirteen shots,* his mind calculated automatically. *Has to be a SIG Sauer P228 or a Browning Hi-Power.*

He crawled forward to the edge of the plateau and slid left, finding the rifle he had left at the twelve-thirty position. The Winchester was loaded with Ryan McMahon's hand-loads. Without bothering to aim, Hunter fired, and the rifle's recoil nearly knocked him off his knees. A tremendous flame shot out of the barrel like a camera flash. He had no idea where the bullet went, but he racked the lever and hustled right, toward the ruined Hyundai. He fired again, sending two massive flashes moving counterclockwise across the plateau.

From the ute's point of view, it would appear that a shooter was moving right-to-left. Any smart marksman would try to anticipate the next flash and fire ahead of it. They did exactly that. Bullets whined off the rocks near the Hyundai, and one hit the car. By then, Hunter was already on the move again, this time clockwise. He abandoned the first rifle and sprinted to the next one, which was positioned at the two o'clock spot.

The third Winchester had a mixed load, alternating factory rounds with hand-loads. He took careful aim this time, firing a stock round into the darkness about eight feet behind the ute's headlights and four feet above them. He heard nothing but figured the enemies would now believe there were three riflemen: one behind them on the left, and two ahead on the right. His ears were ringing from the noise, but he could make out the woman's voice giving a faint command. The ute's headlights promptly died, plunging the plateau into darkness once again.

Hunter fired a second shot, a hand-loaded round this time. The flame from the muzzle lit up the entire scene as he jinked five feet to the right. He fired again, aiming carefully. This time, he heard a sharp scream. Moving one pace to the right, he fired another hand-load, and the muzzle flash revealed a body falling headfirst out of the ute's bed, frozen in midair. *One down,* he thought. *But it's the wrong one—it's the man.*

He aimed slightly left of where the man had been, racking the lever, but the mechanism jammed on the spent shell from the last hand-load.

Then, two things happened at once. First, the ute lurched

forward, peeling away in a tight circle and heading back north, the way it had come. Second, a handgun started firing close to the Hyundai. The woman was on foot now, moving through the dark, firing rapidly. Her bullets missed by several feet, but they were getting closer.

The ute's lights flicked back on as it bounced away, and Hunter tracked it from the corner of his eye. It jerked and swerved, then disappeared off the edge of the plateau, thumping down and speeding toward the cream house. The noise faded, and its lights dimmed, becoming no more than a distant glow on the far horizon. The woman stopped firing—she was reloading again. The plateau fell into silence, the only sound the growing hum of insects. The rain had shifted from heavy drops to a persistent drizzle, like a shower slowly opening up.

Hunter wiped the water from his forehead and quietly laid the jammed rifle in the dust, which was rapidly turning to mud. Moving left, he tracked his way back toward the hidden Nissan, now about forty meters away. The rain grew stronger by the second, drowning out all other sounds.

The rain intensified, hissing as it hit the wattle bushes all around. The downpour had its advantages—it masked any noise he made while moving. At six-foot-five and weighing two hundred fifty pounds, Hunter wasn't exactly built for silent movement through desert vegetation. The storm was more of a help to him than to her. But there was a downside: visibility was rapidly dropping to zero. If they weren't careful, they could end up bumping into each other before either realized the other was there.

A lever-action repeater was no longer the weapon of choice in such conditions. It was too slow for a quick, reactive shot and too bulky to handle easily. Plus, Winchesters eject their spent shells from the top, not the side, which meant the ejection port could let rainwater in, a problem in the heavy downpour. And Hunter could tell—this storm was going to be bad, like it was trying to make up for ten years of drought in a single night.

He made it back to the Nissan at the four o'clock position and found the fourth rifle still propped against the door, now soaked. Shaking off the water, he aimed across the plateau toward where he figured the eleven o'clock position would be and fired. The rifle still worked fine, so he fired four more spaced-out shots, covering the twelve, one, two, and three o'clock positions—fan fire, a deliberate gamble.

The upside? He might get lucky and hit the woman. The downside? It would tell her he was alone, one guy using multiple rifles. It would also give away his location. If she was paying attention, she might figure out he still had two shells left in the magazine.

Satisfied with the distraction, Hunter slid the rifle under the Nissan and moved west through the brush, stopping about forty feet from the edge of the plateau. He pulled Sally's SIG Sauer out of his pocket, flipped the safety off, then knelt down and smeared mud over his hands, arms, and face, waiting for the storm to give him the break he needed. In hot parts of the world, summer storms like this often brought lightning, and Hunter was sure it was coming soon. The storm clouds were building tension, rubbing together, generating static. He figured five more minutes, and the sky would light up with bolts or sheets of lightning, illuminating the entire landscape.

He was wearing khaki clothing and had smeared khaki mud on his skin. He doubted the woman had done the same.

The rain was pouring down now, and Hunter crouched, waiting for the lightning to come. Every muscle was tense, his senses hyper-aware, the darkness and the storm heightening the danger. He couldn't see her, but she was out there—armed, highly skilled, and more than willing to kill. The two of them were locked in a deadly game of cat and mouse, with the rain and darkness closing in tighter around them.

Finally, a flash of lightning ripped across the sky, briefly lighting up the plateau. The rain fell even harder, pounding the rocky surface and filling the air with a constant roar. He could barely hear his own breathing over the noise, but the storm worked to his advantage—it would help him move without being detected.

As he scanned the landscape for any sign of movement, he stayed low, his muddy hands gripping the SIG Sauer tightly. He didn't know where she was, but the lightning would eventually give him an opportunity. He just had to wait for the right moment.

The storm was about to unleash its full fury, and Hunter knew that when it did, the battle would be decided in seconds.

Hunter worked his way south, moving away from the Nissan and back toward the wrecked Hyundai, keeping about forty feet into the undergrowth. The darkness was absolute, and the rain kept building relentlessly, harder than before. The sandstone sinkholes were already filled with water, their surfaces lashing with raindrops. Small streams were forming, gurgling into deep crevasses all around him. The sound of the rain was deafening, impossible to imagine anything louder. Then it somehow got even louder, the roar of it against the ground filling the air completely.

He realized the mud he had smeared on his skin for camouflage had washed away—there was no way it could have stayed on in rain like this. It was like being in a waterfall. He even started to worry about breathing. How was there air left to breathe with so much water everywhere? Rain poured down his face in solid streams, some running directly into his mouth. He put a hand over his jaw, sucking air through his fingers, spluttering and spitting out the rainwater.

He was opposite the two o'clock position, about thirty feet from the edge of the plateau, when the lightning started. A ragged bolt exploded from the sky far to the south, about five kilometers away, illuminating everything for a split second with intense, pure white light. The bolt looked like an upside-down tree, hurled into the ground by a hurricane. Hunter dropped into a crouch, eyes scanning ahead for any sign of movement. Nothing. Five seconds later, thunder followed the lightning with a ragged, tearing rumble.

Where is she? he thought. *Does she think she's smarter than I am?* In her world, maybe she was slick. Put her face-to-face with someone like Troy Bradley, and she'd probably outsmart anyone. But here, out in the open, in a storm, at night? She was out of her element. *I'm good at this. She's not. She's in front of me somewhere, clinging to the edge of the plateau, scared like she's never been before. She's mine.*

The storm drifted slowly south and east, and three minutes later, another lightning strike lit up the sky, this one a jagged sheet of light a kilometer closer. The flickering lasted for eight or ten seconds before fading into darkness again. Hunter craned his neck, scanning ahead and to the right. Nothing. Then he turned left and spotted her—about seventy feet away, crouched near the ledge. The white "AFP" letters on her cap were visible in the lightning's glow. She was looking straight at him, her gun rigid in her hand, her arm fully extended from the shoulder.

He saw her fire—a tiny muzzle flash, barely visible amid the storm. She missed.

The lightning faded, plunging them back into absolute darkness. Hunter fired a single shot at the place where she had been, but he doubted it hit. Seventy feet away, in heavy rain, was a tough shot. Then the thunderclap came, a booming crash that rocked the ground and rolled away slowly. He crouched down again. Nine bullets left.

He decided to play the bluff. *She'll think I'll move, so I won't.*

He stayed exactly where he was, waiting for the next lightning bolt. It would tell him just how skilled she really was. An amateur would move away. A professional might move closer. A really good pro would double-bluff and stay put.

By now, the rain was as heavy as it could get, he guessed. He'd been caught in jungle storms in Southeast Asia that soaked him faster than falling into the ocean fully clothed. This was just as bad. He was beyond drenched—water poured off him in continuous streams, sluicing out of his shirt's buttonholes like jets. The temperature had dropped by twenty or thirty degrees in less than twenty minutes, and the ground had turned to six inches of slushy mud. His feet were sinking in it. His gun was soaked, but that didn't bother him. A SIG Sauer would fire wet. So would a Browning or a Glock.

The next lightning flash was brighter, closer. A gigantic lateral bolt crackled across the sky. He scanned to the left. The woman had moved closer—now sixty feet away, still pressed against the plateau. Good, but not great. She fired again, missing him by four feet. It was a rushed shot, her arm still swinging inward from the south. *She figured I'd moved away,* Hunter thought, feeling slightly insulted. He leveled his gun and fired back, but the incoming thunderclap drowned out the sound of his shot. It was probably another miss. Eight bullets left.

Hunter recalculated. What would she do next? She'd gotten it wrong before, so now she'd gamble. She would figure he'd move in closer and respond by doing the same, going for the kill shot. He stayed exactly where he was, in a crouch, holding his gun ready, tracking it from left to right in the direction she'd likely move.

The storm was picking up speed, and the next lightning strike came sooner than expected, exploding just half a kilometer away. Thunder bellowed almost immediately, the flash lighting up the desert brighter than day. But she wasn't where he had expected her. She had moved. He jerked left, spotting a blur of vivid blue moving away in the opposite direction. He fired instinctively just ahead of it as the lightning died and darkness closed in again.

Seven bullets left, he thought, smiling. *But now I only need one more.*

Thunder frightened Lahni, reminding her of when Max and Patty had worked on the roof of the motor barn, banging down large tin sheets that boomed as they flexed. Thunder was like a hundred million of those sheets all booming at once. She ducked her head under the sheets, watching the room light up with flashes of lightning from the window.

"Are you scared?" the man asked.

Lahni nodded, though the sheets scrubbed her hair. She figured the man could see her head moving.

"Don't be scared," he said. "It's only a storm. Big girls aren't scared of storms."

She said nothing, and the man checked his watch again.

Hunter stayed crouched, considering his next move. The woman's tactics were good, but not good enough. She was hugging the edge of the plateau, using it as cover, working a pattern of moving in and out. Smart, but predictable. She had moved closer, then away. Now she would move closer again, but instead of pulling back, she'd come in even tighter. She figured he'd start to read her pattern, expecting her to retreat, but she'd wrong-foot him by pushing forward.

He knew what to do. Hunter leapt out of his crouch, sprinting backward and to the left in a wide curve. He crashed through the brush like a wild animal, hurdling over wattle, splashing through puddles, and sliding through the mud. He didn't care how much noise he was making—the rain was so loud it would drown out everything. What mattered was speed. He needed to outflank her before the next lightning strike.

He ran in a wide arc, then slowed, skidding to a stop near the sandstone ledge, about twenty metres south of where he'd last seen her. She should be thirty feet ahead now, right in front of him. Hunter moved in, walking fast but staying loose, trying to anticipate the next flash of lightning while ready to drop flat at a moment's notice.

****

Back in the motel room, the small dark man checked his watch again. Lahni stayed hidden under the sheets.

"Over three hours," the man said.

Lahni didn't reply.

"Do you know how to tell the time?" he asked.

Lahni slowly pulled the sheet down past her mouth. "I'm six and a half," she said.

The man nodded. "Look," he said, twisting his wrist to show her his watch. "One more hour."

"Then what?" she asked.

The man looked away. Lahni watched him for a moment longer, then pulled the sheet back over her head. The thunder boomed, and the lightning flashed again.

****

Hunter crouched low, waiting for the next flash. The lightning lit up the entire landscape, followed by a deafening crack of thunder. But she wasn't there. Hunter dropped to the ground, wondering if she had outflanked him. Had she circled around like he had? He lay completely still in the mud, letting the rain hammer down on him as he thought. Maybe she had gone to ground in a sinkhole or crevasse. Or had she gone for the Nissan? If she'd seen it during a lightning flash, she might have figured he'd eventually have to go back to it. After all, how else was he going to get out of the desert?

Maybe she was waiting there, perhaps even inside it, crouching low. Worse yet, she could be under it, in which case he'd just left her a Winchester rifle loaded with two factory rounds.

Hunter pressed himself deeper into the mud, ignoring the next lightning flash entirely as he weighed his options. His military training told him to eliminate the flanking maneuver. She wouldn't try something that complicated. A soldier might, but she was more likely to aim for a clean, direct hit. Maybe she was lying in wait at the Nissan. He circled around in the mud, keeping his body low.

The next flash of lightning lit the sky, rippling madly like a battlefield flare. The Nissan was far away—too far, he figured, for her to be an immediate threat from there. Even if she had made it to the vehicle, she wasn't close enough to worry about right now. He turned his attention back to the south, crawling forward on his knees and elbows, scanning the area zone by zone, just like basic training. Ten feet. Twenty feet. Twenty-five. Then something caught his attention—a smell.

At first, he thought it was just the scent of the desert after the rain, but as he moved, he realized it wasn't natural. It was perfume—faint, but definitely there, lingering in the air, intensified by the rain. He stopped moving, laying completely still. The perfume was unmistakable, drifting on the wet breeze. He raised his gun, though he could barely see it in his hand—it was pitch black.

Which way is she facing? he wondered. If she was looking east, she'd only see the two-foot wall of the plateau's edge. If she was facing south or west, he'd be fine. But if she was looking north, she'd be staring straight at him. Then again, it was too dark for her to see anything. And she wouldn't be able to smell him either—he was upwind.

He slowly raised himself onto his left forearm, pointing his gun out in front of him. If she was facing south or west, he'd have an easy shot into her back. But if she was facing north, they could be five feet apart, staring directly at each other, waiting for the next flash of lightning.

It was a gamble now. When the lightning struck, who would react first?

Hunter held his breath, waiting for the storm to give him another chance. It felt like the longest wait of his life. The thunder had become more of a constant rumble, rolling endlessly through the clouds, while the rain pounded harder than ever. Water was kicking up mud and grit, thudding against the brush. Hunter's body was half-submerged in water, cold from head to toe.

Suddenly, a massive crack ripped through the sky, accompanied by an immediate, blinding flash of lightning. The desert lit up in stark white. Hunter's eyes darted ahead, and there she was, three feet in front of him, slumped facedown in the mud.

She was already dead.

Her body lay small and collapsed, legs bent at the knees, arms folded under her. The Browning Hi-Power pistol was by her shoulder, half-submerged in the mud, with twigs already gathering around it like a tiny dam. Hunter scrambled for the gun in the final moments of the lightning flash, tossing it far away into the brush. Then darkness swallowed the scene again, and he used the afterimage burned into his eyes to find her neck.

No pulse.

Her skin was cold. She had been dead for a while now.

Hunter had killed her earlier, with his third shot, a deflection round he had fired instinctively as she scrambled away from him. She had run straight into its path. His fingers stayed on her neck, afraid to lose contact in the blackness. He waited for the next flash of lightning, his left arm shaking. *It's just from holding it at an awkward angle,* he told himself.

But then, laughter bubbled up inside him. It built fast, just like the rain, and he couldn't stop it. He had spent the last twenty minutes stalking a woman he'd already shot. Accidentally, at that. He laughed uncontrollably, the sound catching in his throat as rainwater filled his mouth, making him cough and sputter wildly.

****

Meanwhile, back at the motel, the small dark man stood up and walked over to a credenza. He picked up his gun from where it lay on the polished wood. Then, crouching down to a black nylon suitcase, he pulled out a long silencer, carefully fitting it to the muzzle of the gun before returning to his chair.

"It's time," he said.

He placed a hand on Lahni's shoulder, and she wriggled away from him, swimming deeper into the bed and curling up tightly under the sheet. She needed to pee badly.

"It's time," the man repeated.

He folded back the sheet, but she scrambled away, holding the opposite edge tightly between her knees.

"You said one more hour," she argued. "It hasn't been an hour yet. I'll tell that lady. She's your boss."

The man's eyes went blank for a moment. He turned and glanced at the door, then turned back to her.

"Okay," he said. "You tell me when you think it's been one more hour."

He released the sheet, and Lahni quickly wrapped herself back up in it, ducking her head under to block out the thunder.

She closed her eyes, though she could still see the flashes of lightning through the fabric and her eyelids. They looked red.

****

Back on the plateau, the next flash of lightning flickered across the sky, faint and diffuse. Hunter rolled the woman's body over, just to be sure. He tore open her jacket and shirt, examining the wound. She had been hit in the left armpit, the bullet going clean through her body and exiting on the opposite side of her chest. The shot had likely taken out her heart, lungs, and spine. A .40 bullet was a brutal thing. The entry wound was small and neat, but the exit wound was a mess, now being flushed clean by the rain. Her chest cavity was filling with water, looking like a grotesque medical diagram. Hunter could have fit his whole hand inside the gaping wound.

She was medium-sized, with red hair, now soaked and muddied, spilling out from beneath her AFP cap. He pushed the brim up to get a better look at her face. Her eyes were open, staring at the sky, filling with raindrops like tears.

She looked familiar.

Where had he seen her before?

The lightning flickered again, and her face flashed in his mind, like a reversed photograph negative. Then he remembered—the takeaway shop. The Coke floats. Friday, around school quitting time. The Falcon, with three passengers. He'd pegged them as a sales team.

Wrong again.

Hunter stood up, wiping rain from his face. "Okay," he muttered. "Game over."

He slid Sally's gun back into his pocket and walked north, back to the Nissan. The rain was so heavy that he didn't even see the vehicle until he thudded into its side. Feeling around for the hood, he found the door, opened it, then closed it again—just to feel the satisfaction of making the dome light come on, a small patch of light he could control.

Driving back up onto the plateau wasn't easy. The grit that normally provided traction had turned into slick mud. He switched the Nissan into four-wheel drive, letting the wipers beat furiously and the headlights blaze on high. The tires spun for a moment before finally catching, dragging the vehicle up the slope. He steered in a wide curve, heading for the seven o'clock position. There, he hit the horn twice.

Sally emerged from the wattle, stepping into the beams of the headlights. She was drenched, water pouring off her, her hair plastered flat to her head, ears sticking out a little. She ran around to the passenger door and climbed in.

"This must be the storm everyone's been expecting," Hunter said.

A jagged bolt of lightning split the sky far to their left, followed by an explosion of thunder. The storm was moving north, fast.

Sally shook her head. "This little shower? Just wait until tomorrow."

"I won't be here tomorrow," Hunter replied.

"You won't?"

He nodded.

"You okay?" he asked.

"I didn't know when to fire," she said, her voice shaky.

"You did fine."

"What happened?"

Hunter put the Nissan in gear and drove off, zigzagging to fan the headlights across the plateau. About thirty feet from the wrecked Hyundai, he found the first body. The man lay slumped and motionless. Hunter dipped the lights to shine directly on him and jumped out into the rain.

The man had been hit in the stomach with a Winchester round. He hadn't died instantly—his jacket was torn open, his hands clutching the wound. He had crawled a distance before finally succumbing. Tall, heavily built. Hunter closed his eyes, recalling the scene in the takeaway shop by the register: the woman, the two men—one big and fair, the other small and dark.

He returned to the Nissan, soaked to the skin. "Two dead,"

he said. "That's what happened. But the driver got away. Did you get a look at him?"

"They came to kill us, didn't they?" Sally asked, her voice tense.

"That was the plan. But did you see who was driving?"

She stayed silent.

"It's important, Sally," Hunter pressed. "For Lahni's sake. We can't question the dead."

She hesitated before speaking. "No, not really. I'm sorry. I was running, and the lights were only on for a second or two."

Hunter had felt like the lights had been on much longer, but in reality, Sally was probably right. Maybe even overestimating. It could've been less than a second. They had been quick with their triggers.

"I've seen these people before," Hunter said. "Friday, at the crossroads. After they got Bradley, they were scouting the area. Three of them—woman, big guy, small dark guy. I can account for the woman and the big guy. So, was the small dark guy driving?"

"I didn't really see," Sally replied.

"Gut feeling? First impression? You must have caught a glimpse or seen a silhouette."

"Didn't you?"

Hunter nodded. "He was facing away from me, looking toward where you fired. There was a lot of glare, some rain on the windshield. Then I was shooting, and he took off. But I don't think he was small."

Sally nodded too. "Gut feeling, he wasn't small. Or dark. It was just a blur, but I'd say he was big enough. Maybe fair-haired."

"Makes sense," Hunter said. "They left one behind to guard Lahni."

"So, who was driving?"

"Their client," Hunter guessed. "The guy who hired them. They needed someone with local knowledge."

"He got away," Sally said.

Hunter smiled. "He can run, but he can't hide."

They went to check on the wrecked Hyundai. It was beyond saving, but Sally didn't seem too bothered. She just shrugged and turned away. Hunter grabbed the maps from the glove compartment, then turned the Nissan around and headed north. The drive back to the cream house was a nightmare. Crossing the plateau was manageable, but once they were past it, the desert track had become a river. The hard-baked ground wasn't absorbing any of the water, and it all flooded over the surface. What had felt like a dry riverbed earlier had become a real river, with fast-moving torrents surging over the tires. Wattle bushes had been uprooted and were swept along in the current, some even piling up against the front of the Nissan before being torn away by cross-currents. Sinkholes were hidden beneath the floodwaters, making the drive even more treacherous.

Thankfully, the storm was starting to ease up, the rain dying down to a drizzle as the eye of the storm moved northward.

They were almost on top of the motor barn before they even saw it. The place was in total darkness. Hunter braked hard and swerved around it, noticing pale lights flickering behind the house windows.

"Candles," he said.

"The power must be out," Sally replied. "Lightning must've hit the lines."

Hunter braked again, sliding in the mud as he turned the car so its headlights shone into the barn.

"Recognize anything?" he asked.

Ryan's ute was back in its usual spot, but it was streaked with mud and dripping water from the bed, pooling on the ground.

"Okay," Sally said. "So what now?"

Hunter stared into the rearview mirror, then turned his head to look down the road to the north.

"Someone's coming," he said.

In the distance, faint headlights could be seen, bouncing up and down as they drew closer, breaking into thousands of glimmering pieces through the raindrops on the Nissan's windows.

"Let's go say hello to the McMahons," he said.

He pulled Sally's gun from his pocket and checked it. *Never assume*, he thought. But it was fine—cocked and locked with seven bullets left. He slipped it back into his pocket and drove across the soaking yard to the foot of the porch steps. The rain was almost gone by now, and the ground had started to steam. Vapor rose gently, swirling in the beams of the headlights.

They got out of the Nissan and into the humid night. The temperature was rising again, and so was the noise of insects. A faint, wary whirring sound surrounded them, distant but ever-present.

Hunter led Sally up the porch steps and pushed open the door. The hallway was lit by candles placed on every available surface, their soft orange glow giving the foyer a warm, almost inviting feel. He ushered Sally through to the parlor, where more candles burned—dozens of them—glued to saucers with melted wax. A Coleman lantern hissed softly on a credenza against the wall, its bright light illuminating the room.

Ryan and Judy McMahon were sitting at the old stained table. Shadows flickered and danced around them, the candlelight softening Judy's features, taking years off her face. She was fully dressed in jeans and a shirt, while Ryan sat beside her, staring at nothing in particular. The candlelight played across his face, making it seem almost animated.

"Well, isn't this romantic," Hunter said.

Judy shifted uncomfortably. "I'm scared of the dark," she admitted. "I always have been. Can't help it."

"You should be," Hunter replied. "Bad things happen in the dark."

Judy didn't respond.

"Towel?" Hunter asked, dripping water all over the floor. Sally was soaked too.

"In the kitchen," Judy said.

There was a striped towel on a wooden roller. Sally wiped her face and hair, patting down her shirt. Hunter did the same before stepping back into the parlor.

"Why are you both up at this hour?" he asked. "It's three in the morning."

Neither of them answered.

"Your ute was out tonight," Hunter said.

"But we weren't," Ryan replied. "We stayed inside, like you told us to."

Judy nodded. "Both of us, together."

Hunter smiled. "Each other's alibi," he remarked. "That would get some laughs down in the jury room."

"We didn't do anything," Ryan insisted.

Just then, Hunter heard a car approaching. The faint sound of tires slowing on wet pavement reached his ears, along with the faint whine of drive belts turning under a hood. Then came the crunch of gravel as the car turned in under the gate. The sound of pebbles popping under the wheels filled the air, followed by the soft squeal of a brake rotor and the silence of an engine shutting off. A door clunked shut, and footsteps creaked up the porch steps. The house door opened, footsteps crossed the foyer, and the parlor door swung open.

The candle flames swayed and flickered as Tom Peacock stepped into the room.

"Good," Hunter said. "We don't have much time."

"Did you break into my office?" Peacock asked.

Hunter nodded. "I was curious."

"About what?"

"Details," Hunter replied. "I'm a details guy."

"You didn't need to break in. I'd have shown you the files."

"You weren't there."

"Still, you shouldn't have broken in. You're in trouble for that, you know. Serious trouble."

Hunter smiled. "Bad luck and trouble—been my only friends."

"Sit down, Tom," he said.

Peacock hesitated but eventually threaded his way around the chairs and sat down next to Judy. The candlelight illuminated his face, the lantern glowing softly to his left.

"Got something for me?" Peacock asked.

Hunter sat across from him, laying his palms flat on the table.

"I was a problem solver, of sorts, for thirteen years," he began.

"So?"

"I learned a lot."

"Like?"

"Like lies are messy. They get out of control. But the truth is messy too. So, when I see something that's all buttoned up, I get suspicious. Rosie's situation was messy enough to be real."

"But?"

"But there were a couple of things that didn't add up."

"Like what?"

"Like the fact that she had no money with her. Two million in the bank, and she travels three hundred kilometers with only a single dollar in her purse? She sleeps in her car, doesn't eat, and jumps from one service station to another just to keep going? That didn't make sense."

"She was playacting. That's just who she is."

"Do you know who Nicolaus Copernicus was?" Hunter asked.

"An old astronomer, I think. Proved the Earth orbits the sun," Peacock replied.

Hunter nodded. "And more than that. He asked us to consider

the likelihood that we're at the center of things. What are the odds that what we're seeing is exceptional? It's an important philosophical point."

"So?"

"So if Rosie had two million bucks in the bank and traveled with only one dollar just in case she ran into someone as suspicious as me, then she'd be the best-prepared con artist in history. And old Copernicus would ask, how likely is that? His answer is, not very likely. If I meet a con artist at all, it'll probably be an average one."

"So, what are you saying?"

"I'm saying it didn't add up for me, so I started thinking about the money. Then something else didn't fit."

"What?"

"Troy Bradley's people supposedly messengered Warner's financial records, right?"

"Yeah, this morning. Seems like forever ago now."

"Well, I saw Troy's office. It's right across the street from the courthouse. It's literally a one-minute walk. Why would they use a courier? Why not just walk it over for a friend like Warner? Especially if it was urgent. It would take longer to call for a courier than to deliver it themselves."

The candlelight flickered as Peacock responded. "People messenger things all the time. It's routine. And it was too hot to walk."

Hunter nodded. "Maybe. But then there was the collarbone."

"What about it?"

Hunter turned to Sally. "When you fell while skating, did you break your collarbone?"

"No," Sally replied.

"Any other injuries?"

"I scraped my hand pretty bad. Road rash."

"You put your hand out to break your fall, didn't you?"

"Reflex," she said. "It's impossible not to."

Hunter turned back to Peacock. "I rode with Rosie last Saturday. My first time on a horse. My legs got sore, but what I really remember is how high up I was. It's scary up there. So if Rosie fell from that height onto rocky dirt hard enough to break her collarbone, why didn't she have any road rash on her hand?"

"Maybe she did," Peacock suggested.

"The hospital didn't mention it."

"Maybe they forgot."

"It was a thorough report. Art Macalister even commented on how detailed it was. They wouldn't have missed lacerations to her palm."

"Maybe she wore gloves."

Hunter shook his head. "She told me nobody wears gloves here—it's too hot. And she definitely wouldn't have said that if gloves had saved her from serious road rash. She would've been a big fan of gloves after that. She would've insisted I wear them too."

"So?"

"So I started to wonder if Warner broke her collarbone. Maybe she was on her knees, and he hit her with a big, clubbing fist from above. But she claimed he'd broken her arm and her jaw too, and knocked her teeth loose, and none of that was in the report. So I stopped wondering. Especially when I found out the ring was real."

A candle on the end of the table burned out, sending a thin plume of smoke straight up before spiraling off into the air.

"She's a liar," Peacock said.

"She sure is," Ryan added.

Judy shifted uncomfortably. "Warner never hit her," she insisted. "A son of mine would never hit a woman, no matter who she was."

"One at a time, okay?" Hunter said quietly.

He could feel the tension in the room—the shifting of elbows on the table, feet scuffing the floor. He turned to Ryan first.

"You claim she's a liar because you don't like her. You're a racist, and you didn't like that she had an affair with the schoolteacher. So you took it upon yourself to try and turn me against her, out of some twisted loyalty to your brother."

Then he turned to Judy. "We'll get to what Warner did or didn't do real soon. But for now, stay quiet. Tom and I have business to discuss."

"What business?" Peacock asked.

"This business," Hunter replied, setting Sally's gun down on the table, the butt resting on the wood and the muzzle pointing straight at Peacock's chest.

"What the hell are you doing?" Peacock asked, his voice sharp.

Hunter clicked the safety off with his thumb. The sound was loud in the candle-lit room. The flames flickered, and the lantern hissed softly in the background.

"I figured out the thing with the diamond," Hunter said. "After that, everything else started to make sense. Especially the part about you giving us those badges and sending us down here to talk to Judy."

"What are you talking about?"

"You pulled a magician's trick. The whole thing. You knew Rosie pretty well, so you knew what she must have told me. The absolute truth about herself and what Warner was doing to her. But you reversed it all—flipped it on its head. It was simple, really. Neat and convincing, like a conjuring trick."

Hunter leaned in, his eyes locked on Peacock's. "For instance, Rosie told me she was from the Hunter Valley, and you said, 'I bet she told you she's from thei Hunter Valley, but she isn't.' She told me she'd called the ATO, and you said, 'I bet she told you that, but she didn't.' It was like you knew the truth and were exposing lies she'd supposedly told. But it was you who was lying, Tom. You dressed it all up behind your pretense of wanting to save her. You had me fooled for a long time."

"I did want to save her. I am saving her."

"Bullshit. Your only goal was to force a confession out of her for something she didn't do. It was a straightforward plan. Your hired guns kidnapped Lahni today so you could coerce Rosie into confessing. I was your only problem. I stuck around, and I brought Sally into it. We were in your way from Monday morning onward. So you misled us for nearly thirty hours, feeding us lies bit by bit, pretending you were regretfully exposing Rosie's deceit. It was beautifully done. Almost perfect. But not quite. To pull it off completely, you'd have to be the best con artist in the world. And, as Copernicus would remind us, what are the odds of that?"

Silence filled the room, broken only by the sputtering of candles and the soft hiss of the lantern. Five people sat breathing in the warm glow. The old air conditioner wasn't running—there was no power.

"You're crazy," Peacock said.

"No, I'm not. You played me, Tom, with that regretful tone about what a liar Rosie was, about how desperate you were to save her. You were even smart enough to reveal a selfish reason for wanting to save her—wanting to become a judge. That was a nice touch. But all along, you were the one lying. While you were talking to her on the phone, you were the one telling her to confess, threatening her with Lahni's safety if she didn't comply. You were the one who drafted those fake financial statements and the phony trust deeds. You knew what real ones looked like."

"This is nonsense," Peacock insisted.

Hunter shrugged. "Let's test it. We'll call the AFP and see how the search for Lahni is going."

"The phones are out," Ryan said. "Electrical storm."

Hunter nodded. "Okay, no problem."

Keeping the gun pointed at Peacock's chest, he turned to Judy.

"Tell me what the AFP agents asked you tonight," he said.

Judy looked puzzled. "What AFP agents?"

"No AFP agents came here tonight?" he asked.

She shook her head, her expression blank.

Hunter nodded. "You were putting on a show, Tom. You told us you'd called the AFP and Queensland Police, that there were roadblocks and helicopters and more than a hundred and fifty people on the ground. But you didn't call anyone. Because if you had, they would have come straight here. They'd have questioned Judy for hours, brought in sketch artists, crime scene techs—this is the scene of the crime, after all. And Judy is the only witness."

"You're wrong, Hunter," Peacock said.

"There were AFP people here," Ryan protested. "I saw them in the yard."

Hunter shook his head. "There were people wearing AFP hats, sure. Two of them. But they're not wearing those hats anymore."

Peacock remained silent.

"Big mistake, Tom," Hunter said. "Giving us those stupid badges and sending us down here. You knew Judy wouldn't cooperate fully with me, so sending us here made no sense—unless you wanted us out of the way and knew where we'd be at all times. So you could send your people after us."

"What people?" Peacock asked, his voice rising.

"The hired guns, Tom. The people in the AFP hats. The same people you sent to kill Troy Bradley. The same ones who killed Warner. They're professionals, sure, but even pros need a cover. Killing Troy was easy—middle of nowhere, no witnesses. But Warner was tougher. He was fresh out of prison, not going anywhere, so it had to be done at home. Risky. So, you framed Rosie to cover their tracks and coerced them into helping with the kidnapping."

"This is ridiculous," Peacock said, but his voice faltered.

"You knew Rosie had bought a gun. You told me the paperwork came through your office, and you knew why she bought it. You knew all about what Warner had done to her. So, if she wanted to hide a gun in the bedroom, where would she put it? Top shelf of the closet, bedside table, or underwear drawer—common sense. Your people slipped in while she was in the shower, grabbed the gun, shot Warner with it, and were out in less than a minute. Quick and clean. You knew the house well enough to help them pull it off. You probably even drew them a floor plan."

Peacock sat in silence, his face pale in the flickering candlelight.

“But you made mistakes,” Hunter continued. “People like you always do. The financial reports were sloppy—lots of money, hardly any spending. It didn’t make sense. And the messenger thing was another slip. If the financials had really been messengered, you’d have left them in the courier packet to make them look official. You’re smart, Tom, but not that smart.”

Peacock said nothing. The candle flames danced in the dark, and the lantern hissed softly.

“The medical reports,” Hunter said. “You left them in an Auspost Express packet to make them seem urgent. But you should’ve torn the label off. Auspost charges by weight, and I weighed the packet on Sally’s kitchen scale. It weighed half a kilo,but the label said one kilo. So either Auspost ripped off the hospital, or you trashed over half the contents. I’m betting you kept only the reports that helped your case and threw out the ones about the beatings.”

Peacock stayed silent, his expression unreadable.

“But you were mostly good,” Hunter admitted. “When I realized Rosie wasn’t the shooter, you didn’t miss a beat. You spun it into a conspiracy, trying to tie her back to the killings. But your mistake was sending people after me. You underestimated us.”

Peacock stared straight at him, defiance flickering in his eyes.

“Yes, why would I do any of this?” Peacock asked. “What possible motive could I have?”

Hunter smiled. “Something Benjamin Franklin once wrote.”

“What the hell does that mean?” Peacock asked, his voice rising.

"You wanted to be a judge," Hunter said. "Not to do good or make the world a better place. All that was just sanctimonious bullshit. You craved the power, the status. You were born poor, and you were greedy for money and influence. And it was right there in front of you. But first, you had to get elected. And do you know what can stop someone from getting elected?"

Peacock didn't answer, but his body language showed he knew the answer.

"Old scandals," Hunter continued. "Old secrets coming back to haunt you. You, Warner, and Troy—back in the day, you were a trio, inseparable. Did all sorts of things together, you three against the world. You even told me that yourself. But then Warner ends up in prison for tax evasion, and he can't stand it in there. So he starts thinking, 'How do I get out?' He figures, 'My old buddy Tom is running for judge this year. Big prize, big money, big power. What's he willing to do to get it?' So Warner calls you up, threatening to dig up some serious dirt from your past unless you help get him out."

Peacock still said nothing, but the tension in the room was thick.

"You think it over. At first, you figure Warner won't incriminate himself—he wouldn't risk his own neck. So you relax a bit. But then you realize there's a big gap between what could convict you and what could ruin your election. So you cave. You take some of your campaign donations and use them to pay off Warner's debts to the ATO. Warner's happy, for now. But you're not. The cat's out of the bag. Warner's blackmailed you once—what happens next time he wants something? And Troy, Warner's lawyer, is involved now too, so the whole thing is fresh in his mind. Suddenly, your chances of becoming a judge are hanging by a thread."

Peacock stared at the table in silence.

"You know what Ben Franklin said?" Hunter asked. " 'Three can keep a secret, if two of them are dead.' "

A heavy silence fell over the room. No one moved. The candle flames flickered, the lantern hissed, but otherwise, it was deathly quiet.

"What was the secret?" Sally whispered.

Hunter leaned back, still watching Peacock. "Three boys in rural Queensland, growing up together, playing rugby, having fun. But as they got older, they started looking at what their dads did—guns, rifles, hunting. Maybe they started with dingos. Shouldn't have, because they're protected. But hey, if a dingo's on your land, why not? Right, Ryan? 'It's mine to hunt,' you said. Arrogant attitude, like they're worth nothing. But dingos are just dogs—too easy. These boys wanted a real thrill."

Sally's eyes widened as she listened. "What did they hunt?" she asked.

"Pacific Islanders," Hunter replied. "Poor families escaping from PNG and the Torres Strait by boat, landing on empty beaches, heading south through the tropics and into the desert, desperate. What were they worth, really? Were they even human, to these boys? They made great prey—screamed and ran, almost like hunting real people. The thrill was intoxicating."

The room went quiet again, the weight of Hunter's words settling heavily.

"Maybe it started with a girl," Hunter speculated. "Maybe they didn't mean to kill her, but it happened anyway. They panicked. But nothing came of it—no one noticed, no one cared. So they kept going. It became a sport, a twisted game. Better than dingos, at least. They used that old ute, the one still parked in the barn. Warner was good at it—Ryan told me so. And soon, they got plenty of practice. They killed twenty-five people in a year."

"That was the border patrol," Ryan blurted out, his voice shaky.

"No, it wasn't," Hunter said. "That report wasn't a cover-up. It was legit, confirmed by Sergeant Patterson. The investigation got nowhere because it was looking in the wrong place. It wasn't rogue officers. It was three local boys—Warner McMahon, Troy Bradley, and Tom Peacock—out for sport in the desert."

More silence followed as Hunter's words hung in the air, the truth sinking in.

"The attacks happened mostly within Four Ways Shire," Hunter continued. "Which struck me as odd. Why would the border patrol be operating so far south? They weren't. It was three boys from Four Ways heading north."

He leaned forward, his eyes boring into Peacock. "The attacks stopped in late January. Why? Not because they were scared of the investigation. They didn't even know about it. It was because university started in early February. They grew up, moved on. But twelve years later, Warner's sitting in a cell, desperate to get out. He digs up the past."

Everyone stared at Peacock. His eyes were closed tightly, and his face was deathly pale.

"It felt so unfair, didn't it?" Hunter said to him. "All that was behind you. Maybe you didn't even want to be part of it back then. Maybe the others dragged you in. But now it's back, threatening to ruin your life, take away the big prize. So you made a choice. You remembered Franklin's words. Three can keep a secret, if two of them are dead."

Another candle died, its wick hissing as smoke plumed up from the melted wax.

"No," Peacock whispered. "It wasn't like that."

The lantern flickered, casting eerie shadows on the walls.

"Then what was it like, Tom?" Hunter asked.

Peacock swallowed hard, his eyes still closed. "I was only going to take Lahni. Just for a while. I hired some local guys to watch her. I had campaign money. But when I went to tell Warner, he didn't care. Said I could take her. He didn't want her—he was conflicted. He married Rosie to punish himself, I think, for what we did. He thought she could see it in his eyes, like voodoo. Same with Lahni. So, taking her wasn't a threat to him."

"So you hired more people," Hunter pressed.

Peacock nodded. "Yes. They took over, got rid of the first guys for me."

"And then they took care of Troy and Warner?"

"It was a long time ago," Peacock whispered. "We were kids. It wasn't supposed to come back."

More silence followed, the flames flickering around the room.

"You were driving the ute tonight," Hunter said.

Peacock nodded slowly. "Yes. I thought it would all be over once I got rid of you. I knew you'd figured it out. Why else would you take the files and lead us out into the desert? So I drove. I'd done it before, many times."

He went quiet again, swallowing hard.

"But I got scared," he admitted. "I couldn't go through with it. I'm not that person anymore. I've changed."

Hunter watched him, his eyes narrowing.

"Where's Lahni?" he asked.

Peacock shrugged. "I don't know. They're using motels. I don't know which one. They wouldn't tell me—it's safer that way."

"How do you contact them?" Hunter pressed.

"There's a number in Brisbane. It must be rerouted."

The room fell silent again, the tension thick.

"Where is she, Tom?" Hunter asked one last time.

"I don't know," Peacock whispered. "I'd tell you if I did."

Hunter raised Sally's gun, pointing it directly at Peacock's face. His arms were long, and the muzzle came to rest just two feet from Peacock's forehead.

"Do you want to die, Tom?" Hunter asked.

Peacock nodded. "Yes, please," he whispered.

Hunter's finger tightened on the trigger, moving it a fraction of an inch. Peacock's eyes crossed as he stared at the barrel. Then, with a sigh, Hunter slackened his finger and lowered the gun back to the table.

Nobody moved. Then, out of nowhere, Judy McMahon's hand came up, holding a revolver. The small gun wavered in her hand, but the barrel pointed directly at Peacock's head.

"You killed my boy," she whispered.

Peacock didn't flinch. He nodded, ever so slightly.

"I'm sorry," he whispered back.

The hammer clicked, and with a deafening blast, the gun fired. The top of Peacock's head blew backward into the candle-lit room. Smoke and flames flickered from his hair, and his body slumped to the floor. Judy kept firing. Six shots in total. The third hit the wall, the fourth shattered the lantern, and the fifth exploded the kerosene reservoir, setting the wall ablaze. Flames licked upward, hungry and fast.

Hunter sprang into action, shouting, "Out! Get out!"

The fire spread quickly. Blue flames crept up the walls, eating through the old, dry wood with no hesitation. The paint on the walls bubbled and peeled away as the heat intensified. The air inside the house grew hotter by the second. Smoke billowed out, thick and choking, as the fire licked across the ceiling and started to consume everything in its path.

"Get her out of here!" Hunter shouted, his voice cutting through the crackling flames.

Sally was already on her feet, moving fast, but Ryan stood frozen, his eyes wide with fear as he stared at the growing inferno. Judy McMahon remained seated, clicking the trigger of the now-empty revolver, still aimed at the space where Tom Peacock had been.

"We've got no water!" Ryan yelled, his voice panicked. "The pump doesn't work without electricity!"

Hunter didn't hesitate. He kicked chairs out of the way and lifted the heavy table, flipping it over to try and smother the flames. But the fire simply detoured around it, spreading even faster. The ceiling was already ablaze, and the doorframe had caught fire as well. Peacock's body lay near the window, his hair still smoldering from the muzzle flash. The parlor had become an inferno, a roaring wall of flames.

Without another word, Hunter grabbed Judy, yanking her out of the chair and spinning her toward the door. He shoved her through the smoke and out of the room, sending her stumbling into the foyer where Sally was already waiting. The front door was wide open, and Hunter could feel the cool night air rushing in to feed the fire, causing the flames to roar even louder.

He pushed Judy through the front door and down the porch steps, where she staggered onto the wet dirt, still holding the empty revolver in her hand. She stared blankly ahead, clicking the useless trigger over and over again.

Hunter turned back toward the house, the heat from the fire already intense. The foyer was filling with thick, black smoke, and he could hear the loud cracking of wood as the fire consumed the structure. Ryan was still standing near the parlor door, coughing hard as the flames crawled closer to him.

"Get out!" Hunter shouted.

Ryan remained frozen, staring at the fire as it crept across the floor and up the walls, filling the room with yellow light. The windows were alive with flames, and smoke was drifting through the screens. There were loud popping sounds as timbers gave way, and the soaked roof was already beginning to steam in the heat.

Hunter rushed toward Ryan, grabbing him by the wrist and twisting his arm behind his back like he was making an arrest. He grabbed the back of Ryan's belt with his other hand and hauled him out of the burning house, dragging him down the porch steps and into the yard.

"It's burning down!" Ryan screamed, his voice cracking with panic. "The whole house is burning down!"

Hunter released him in the middle of the yard, away from the flames.

"Go live in the barn," Hunter said coldly. "That's where people like you belong."

Ryan collapsed to his knees, still staring at the flames as they consumed the house. The windows were glowing with yellow light, and flames danced behind the glass. Smoke billowed out, filling the night air with a bitter, acrid smell. The fire had taken hold of the entire structure, and there was nothing anyone could do to stop it.

Hunter turned away, his expression hard. He grabbed Sally

by the hand and ran straight for the Nissan, leaving the McMahons behind as their home burned to the ground.

CHAPTER 17

As the storm veered south, the driver knew instinctively that his partners wouldn't be coming back. It wasn't just a feeling—it felt like an undeniable truth. The rain had left behind an emptiness that would never be filled. He turned to face the motel room door and sat there, staring at it for what felt like an eternity. Eventually, he got up, crossed the room, and opened the door. He scanned the parking lot, first to the left, then to the right. The blacktop shimmered with water, and the air carried a sharp, clean scent.

He stepped outside, walking a few steps into the darkness. The only sounds were the distant gurgling of gutters, the trickle of street drains, and the steady drip from the gum trees. But other than that, there was nothing. No one was coming. No one ever would. He knew it. Turning back, he felt the wet grit sliding under his shoes as he re-entered the room, gently closing the door behind him. His eyes settled on the bed, where a child lay sound asleep.

"You're driving," he shouted, "Head south, okay?"

He nudged her toward the driver's seat and sprinted around the hood. She adjusted her seat forward, and he pushed his back, spreading maps across his knees. The house to their left was now fully engulfed in flames, both floors alight. The maid, draped in a bathrobe, emerged from the kitchen door, her face eerily expressionless in the firelight.

"Let's go," he urged.

She shifted into Drive and hit the gas. The four-wheel drive was still engaged, causing the tires to spin and throw wet gravel as they shot forward. She maneuvered around Peacock's Mercedes, sped under the gate without hesitation, and accelerated. He glanced back, watching the flames spread to the roof's edge, where they paused, then flickered horizontally in search of fuel. Steam rose from the soaked shingles, mingling with the smoke, while Judy, Ryan, and the maid stood watching, entranced. He tore his gaze away, rifling through the maps on his lap until he found the one showing Mount Kalka Shire in detail. He reached up to turn on the dome light.

"Faster," he said, his voice tense. "I have a really bad feeling about this."

****

Though the four hours had passed, he hesitated, conflicted. He wasn't a monster, after all. He'd do what needed to be done, but he wasn't going to relish it.

He got up, opened the door, and hung the "Do Not Disturb" sign on the handle outside before locking it. He appreciated the way motel locks worked—a big lever that clicked satisfyingly, smooth and firm. It felt secure. He slid the chain on and moved deeper into the room.

****

Sally drove as quickly as she dared. The Nissan wasn't built for the road—it swayed and rocked violently with each turn, and the steering was sloppy, requiring constant adjustments. But Hunter paid no mind, holding the map high to catch the light from the roof console, studying it closely, measuring distances with his fingers.

"Ever done any tourist stuff around here?" he asked.

She nodded without taking her eyes off the road. "Yeah, I went to the Katter Observatory once. It was cool."

He glanced at the map. The Katter Observatory was far southwest of Mount Kalka, perched in the Selwyn Mountains.

"Too far," he muttered. "Eighty kilometers."

"For what?"

"For today. I think they stayed within a half-hour of Mount Kalka by road—twenty-five, maybe thirty kilometers at most."

“Why so close?”

“To keep an eye on Peacock. He could’ve planned to smuggle Rosie out or bring Lahni in to convince her the threat was real. Either way, they wouldn’t have strayed far.”

“And near a tourist spot?” she asked.

“Definitely,” he nodded. “That’s crucial.”

“Can this really work? Finding the spot in your head?”

“It’s worked before.”

“How often?” she asked, curious.

He ignored her question, turning his attention back to the map. She gripped the wheel, her eyes flicking to the speedometer.

“Oh no,” she whispered.

He didn’t look up. “What is it?”

“We’re out of fuel. The gauge is on empty. The warning light’s been on for a while.”

There was a brief silence.

“Keep going,” he said. “We’ll be fine.”

She pressed her foot down harder on the accelerator.

“You think the gauge is wrong?” she asked, her voice tight.

He finally glanced ahead. “Just keep driving.”

“We’re going to run out,” she said, her tone growing anxious.

“Don’t worry.”

The car rocked over the slick blacktop, the headlights bouncing ahead. She glanced down at the dash again.

“It’s dead empty, Hunter,” she said, her voice urgent.

“Just keep going,” he repeated calmly.

“We’re running on fumes,” she insisted.

"Don't worry."

“How can you be so sure?” she asked.

“That’s why,” he said, pointing as the headlights washed over a parked steel-blue Ford Falcon on the side of the road. It had four VHF antennas and no hubcaps, sitting abandoned, facing north.

“We’ll take that,” he said. “It should have plenty of fuel. They were organized.”

She braked hard and pulled in behind the car. “Is this theirs? Why leave it here?”

“Peacock ditched it,” he explained.

“How did you know?”

“Simple. They came from Mount Kalka in two cars—this one and the Mercedes. They dumped the Mercedes here and took the Falcon the rest of the way. Later, Peacock put the ute back in the barn, drove the Falcon back here, picked up his Mercedes, and drove down again to make us think it was his first visit if we survived.”

“What about the keys?”

“They’ll be inside. Peacock wouldn’t have been worried about losing a rental.”

Sally checked, giving him a thumbs-up when she found the keys. He followed her with the maps, leaving the Nissan idling as it ran out of fuel. They climbed into the Falcon, adjusted their seats, and within seconds, were back on the road.

“It’s three-quarters full,” she said, her relief palpable. “And it drives a lot smoother.”

Hunter nodded. The car felt fast and stable, as a big sedan should.

“I’m sitting where Troy Bradley sat,” he said with a wry smile.

She glanced at him but didn’t respond, focusing instead on the road ahead as they sped toward their next destination.

"Go faster," Hunter said. "No one’s going to stop you. We look like a police car."

She pressed the accelerator, bringing their speed up to seventy-five, then eighty. Hunter switched the dome light back on and resumed studying the maps.

“Where were we?” he asked.

“The Katter Observatory,” she said. “You didn’t like it.”

He nodded. “It was too far out.”

He tilted the map, catching the light as he scrutinized it again.

“What about Duchess State Recreation Area?” he asked. It was still southwest of Mount Kalka, but only thirty kilometers away. A more reasonable distance.

“It’s a big, clear lake,” Sally explained. “You can swim or scuba dive there.”

But it didn’t feel right.

"No, not there."

He shifted his focus northeast, searching for something else within the right range.

"How about the Ironbark Sandhills?"

"Four thousand acres of sand dunes. It looks like the Simpson Desert."

"That's it? And people actually visit?"

"It's popular," she replied.

He fell silent, his eyes sweeping over the map once more.

"What about Three Rivers?" he asked.

"It's just a town," she said. "Not much different from Mount Kalka."

Then, as if remembering something, she added, "But Old Three Rivers is kind of interesting."

Hunter looked at the map. Old Three Rivers was marked as a historic ruin, a little to the north of the town itself, and closer to Mount Kalka. He measured the distance—around forty-five kilometers.

It seemed like a possibility.

"What is it exactly?" he asked.

"A heritage site," she said. "It was a military outpost. The first soldiers stationed here. The place was destroyed by the local indigenous mob, but the soldiers rebuilt it a few years later, I think."

Hunter checked the map again. The ruins were southeast of Mount Kalka, with access via the Burke Highway—a decent, fast road by the looks of it. Likely a typical route.

He closed his eyes, thinking. Sally kept driving, the Falcon gliding smoothly over the wet road. Hunter was exhausted. The car was warm and quiet, and the soft hiss of water spraying from the tires lulled him.

"I like Old Three Rivers," he said.

"You think that's where they went?"

He didn't answer right away. Another kilometer passed.

"Not exactly there," he said. "But nearby. Think about it from their perspective."

"I can't," she replied. "I'm not like them."

"Pretend," he urged. "Try to put yourself in their shoes."

"I don't know who they are."

"They were professionals—quiet, unobtrusive, blending in like chameleons. They were good at not being noticed. Now try to imagine what they were thinking. I saw them and thought they were a sales team. Judy McMahon thought they were social workers. Even Troy Bradley believed they were AFP agents. They appeared normal, respectable, and professional. So put yourself in their place. What would make sense to them?"

Sally sighed. "Okay, but now they have a child with them. So what are they now?"

"They're a normal, middle-class family," Hunter said without hesitation. "At least, that's the impression they'd want to give."

"But there were three of them," she pointed out.

Hunter paused, thinking. "One of the men was probably the uncle. So now you've got a family on vacation, a perfectly ordinary, respectable family, traveling in their Ford sedan. Nothing flashy. They're not the kind of family that goes to theme parks or loud tourist attractions. They're a little more earnest, a little more serious. Maybe they seem a bit nerdy or studious. They look like they might be the family of a school principal or an accountant. They're clearly from out of town, traveling through the area. Now, where would they go that fits that image? Somewhere safe and respectable."

"Old Three Rivers," Sally said, picking up on his train of thought.

"Exactly. They'd go somewhere with historical value, somewhere educational, even if the kid is too young to care. And they wouldn't stay in the expensive hotels—they'd choose something reasonable, where they'd blend in. Somewhere on the outskirts, where the value for money is good."

Hunter opened his eyes.

"That's where you'd stay, Sally."

She looked at him, slightly confused. "It is?"

He nodded. "A place filled with families just like yours—earnest, middle-class people on vacation. It's the kind of place where you'd never stand out, and no one would remember you. And it's only about thirty, thirty-five minutes from Mount Kalka on a fast road."

Sally shrugged. "It's a good theory. But what if they weren't following that logic?"

"I hope they were," Hunter said grimly. "Because we don't have time for a wide search. I've got a bad feeling about this. I think she's in real danger now."

Sally said nothing.

"Maybe the others were supposed to check in," Hunter continued. "If they haven't, the third guy might panic."

"So this is a huge gamble?"

Hunter didn't respond.

"Do the math," Sally said. "A forty-five-kilometer radius covers over six thousand square kilometers. You really think you can pick one spot?"

Another long silence.

"I think they were smart and careful," Hunter finally said. "And their priorities were obvious. They were looking at the same maps we are. That's how I'd do it."

"But are you sure?"

Hunter shrugged. "I can't ever be sure. But that's what I'd have done. You have to think like them. That's the key."

"And does it always work?"

"Not always," he admitted. "But it's worked enough."

The quiet crossroads of a sleepy hamlet appeared ahead—there was a school, a service station, a takeaway shop. Mount Kalka straight ahead, Old Three Rivers to the left

"Well?" Sally asked.

He remained silent.

"Well?" she repeated.

He stared through the windshield, thinking.

"Decision?" she pressed.

He remained quiet. Sally braked hard, skidding a little on the soaked road, stopping at the intersection.

"Well?"

Roll the dice, Hunter.

"Make the turn," he finally said.

The driver decided to take a shower first, feeling it was an acceptable delay. He had time. The room was locked, and the child was fast asleep. He undressed, folding his clothes neatly on the chair, and headed for the bathroom. He pulled the shower curtain across and turned on the water, adjusting the temperature.

As he unwrapped the small bar of motel soap, he took a moment to savor the crisp scent that filled the air when the packet crinkled open. The soap's clean, sharp aroma was somehow comforting. He sniffed the tiny plastic bottle of shampoo—it smelled faintly of strawberries. He placed the soap on the tub's porcelain shelf and balanced the shampoo on the rim, then stepped into the steaming shower, pushing the curtain aside with his forearm.

Meanwhile, the road west out of Four Ways wound along a narrow ridge, tracing the banks of a tributary of the Leichhardt River. The Falcon, no longer ideal for the conditions, felt too big and sluggish, its soft suspension struggling against the rough terrain. Water ran across the road, carving ruts and leaving patches of mud and gravel. Sally gripped the steering wheel tightly, her knuckles pale as she fought to maintain a steady forty kilometers per hour. Her tan skin looked almost ashen in the dim light, as if she were chilled to the bone.

"Are you okay?" Hunter asked, breaking the silence.

“Are you?” she shot back.

“Why wouldn’t I be?”

“You just killed two people, saw a third die, and watched a house burn down.”

Hunter turned his head, looking away. Civilians, he thought.

“It’s done,” he said quietly. “No use dwelling on it now.”

“That’s your answer?” she asked, incredulous.

“Why not?”

"Doesn't any of that bother you?"

"I'm just upset I didn't get a chance to ask them any questions."

"That's all you regret?" she asked, eyes narrowing.

He paused before replying. "Tell me about the house you're renting."

"What's that got to do with anything?"

"I'm guessing it's a short-term place. Probably not well-maintained. Was it dirty when you moved in?"

She hesitated, then nodded. "I spent the first week cleaning."

"Grease on the stove, sticky floors?"

"Yeah."

"Bugs in the closets?"

"Cockroaches," she admitted, grimacing. "Big ones that fly."

"And you got rid of them?"

"Of course."

"How?"

"Poison," she said simply.

"Tell me, how did you feel about that?" he asked.

She glanced sideways at him. "Are you comparing those people to cockroaches?"

He shook his head slowly. "Not really. I like cockroaches better. They're just simple creatures, doing what they have to do. Peacock and his men—they didn't have to be the way they were. They had choices. They could've been decent people, but they chose otherwise. And then they chose to mess with me. That sealed their fate. So no, I won't lose sleep over them. I won't even give it another thought. And if you do, well, that's up to you, but I think it's a mistake."

Sally was quiet for a while, navigating another twist in the road.

"You're a hard man, Hunter," she said softly.

He stayed silent for a moment, then replied, "I think I'm just a practical man. Decent enough, all things considered."

She gave a small, bitter laugh. "I'm not sure most people would agree with you."

He nodded, unfazed. "A lot of people don't."

****

He stood under the warm spray long enough for the water to soak through his skin before he started working the shampoo into his hair, massaging his scalp with his fingertips. Rinsing his hands, he soaped his face, neck, and the space behind his ears. With his eyes closed, he let the water wash over him. He applied more shampoo to his chest, where his hair was thick, and carefully scrubbed his underarms, back, and legs.

Finally, he meticulously washed his hands and forearms, like a surgeon prepping for a procedure.

****

"How much farther now?" Sally asked.

Hunter glanced at the map. "About twenty-five kilometers. We'll cross the road heading north to the Gulf of Carpentaria and then keep going past the bridge over the confluence where the rivers meet."

"But the ruins are on the road leading to the Ironbark Dunes," she said.

"Trust me, Sally. They stayed on the Burke Highway. They wanted easy access."

She didn't argue.

"We need a plan," Hunter said.

"For taking this guy down?" she asked. "I wouldn't even know where to start."

"No, I mean for later—when we get Rosie back."

"You seem pretty sure of yourself."

"There's no use planning for failure."

Sally braked sharply for a curve, the front end sliding slightly before she straightened out and hit the accelerator again, clearly relieved by the straight road ahead. "Habeas corpus," she said. "We'll go to a federal supreme court judge, file an emergency motion, and lay out the whole story."

"You think that'll work?"

"That's exactly what habeas corpus is for. It's been working for eight centuries. No reason it won't work now."

"Okay," he said, "but one thing."

"What's that?"

"We'll need him alive to testify. You'll have to make sure of that."

The driver finished his shower, letting the warm water run over him a bit longer. A new thought had taken root in his mind. He needed money. His crew wasn't coming back, and the job was done. He knew that for sure. Now, he was unemployed, which left him unsettled. He wasn't someone who thrived on his own. He had cash stashed at home, but it wasn't enough. He'd need more, and soon.

As the water flattened his hair against his scalp, he considered his options. Maybe he could take the kid back to Sydney and sell her. He knew people—people who handled adoptions or other, less savory things. The girl was six and a half, brown hair, and caramel skin. That alone would make her worth a good deal of money to the right buyers. Blue eyes might have fetched a little more, but she was still a cute package.

He'd need a way to get her there. The Ford Falcon was gone, but he could rent another car. He'd done it plenty of times before. He could call Mount Kalka or Cairns and have one delivered first thing in the morning. He had enough fake paperwork. But that would mean being seen by a delivery driver—too risky.

Stealing a car might be a better option. He'd done that in his younger days. There were plenty of cars in the motel lot. He leaned out of the shower to check his watch—four-thirty in the morning. If they were on the road by five, they'd be a hundred kilometers away before anyone noticed. He even had spare plates from the Falcon and the rental at Sydney Airport.

He stepped back under the water, his decision made. If there was a white sedan out there, he'd take it. Asian made cars were common in Queensland, and white was the most inconspicuous color. He could hide the kid under a tarp in the backseat. No problem. A Toyota would be ideal, something generic and easy to confuse with other brands. Traffic cops wouldn't give it a second glance. He could drive it back to Sydney and sell both the car and the girl, making a decent profit. Smiling to himself, he rinsed off one final time.

Ten kilometers east of Three Rivers, the road curved sharply before straightening out along a ridge, running parallel to the Leichhardt River once again. The map showed the interchange ahead, where two roads converged, one of which was the Burke Highway leading north towards the Gulf. The highway bridge crossed the river just beyond the town's limits.

"That's the area we're looking for," Hunter said. "Somewhere in that twenty-kilometer stretch. We'll drive north to the bridge, then turn around and come back. See it the way they saw it."

Sally nodded, accelerating down the hill. The tires rattled over the rough road as the big car swayed and rocked.

The sound of the shower woke her. It wasn't thunder, and it wasn't the sound of rain, but the steady beat of water against the tiles. She pulled the sheet over her head, then down again, staring at the window. There was no lightning outside, no thunder—just the man in the shower.

She sat up slowly, pushing the sheet down to her waist. The room was dimly lit, with a faint yellow glow filtering in through the wet window. The bed was empty, as expected.

Of course it's empty, she thought. The man's in the shower.

She climbed out of bed and tiptoed over to the table, where her clothes were neatly folded. She slipped into her underwear and pulled her T-shirt over her head, followed by her shorts. Sitting on the floor, she buckled her shoes, all while listening to the running water.

Once dressed, she crept past the bathroom door, avoiding the linoleum in case her shoes made noise. She kept to the rug, moving silently toward the door. There was a handle, a lever, and a chain. She stared at the chain, puzzled by how it worked. Standing on her toes, she stretched as far as she could and slid the chain along the track until it dropped into the hole. But it wouldn't come out. Frustrated, she tried again, her fingertips barely reaching. With a little more effort, she managed to unhook it, though the chain rattled loudly against the doorframe. She froze, listening.

The shower was still running.

She moved on to the lock, twisting it with both hands until it finally clicked open with a loud metallic sound. Holding her breath, she tried the door handle—it moved easily. But she stopped, realizing the door would make noise when it closed behind her.

Then, the shower stopped.

She froze, her heart racing. He'll hear the door. He'll come after me.

The overpass was a massive concrete structure, a scar in the landscape. Sally flew through it, taking the northwest exit towards the Gulf, the orange glow of Three Rivers fading behind them. Hunter leaned forward, scanning both sides of the road for signs. A few low buildings passed by—motels.

"This could be the wrong place," Sally muttered.

"We'll know soon enough," he replied.

He turned off the shower, pulling the curtain aside, and stepped out. Wrapping a towel around his waist, he dried his face, glanced at himself in the foggy mirror, and combed his hair with his fingers. After securing his watch, he grabbed fresh towels and walked out of the bathroom, the light spilling into the room.

He froze when he saw the empty bed.

Sally passed three motels, none of which seemed right to Hunter. It wasn't about logic anymore—it was instinct. He ignored the over-analysis and let his subconscious guide him. No, not that one. Not yet. Keep going.

The driver took a step toward the bed, hoping for a different perspective, but nothing changed. The sheet was pushed halfway down, the pillow still holding the shape of her head. He checked the window—it was locked. Then he ran to the door. The chain was unhooked, and the lock was open.

How?

He swung the door open, finding the "Do Not Disturb" sign on the ground. She had gotten out.

The third motel had a simple painted sign, its letters carefully shadowed in gold. "I like this place," Hunter said.

"You want to stop?" Sally asked.

"Yeah, pull in."

After circling the parking lot, Hunter new immediately he had chosen the wrong motel.

He hurried back into the room, locking the door behind him. "Come out," he called gently.

No response.

He started his search behind the chair by the window, then under the bed, and finally in the closet. But she wasn't there. He checked the shelves, the high ledge, even a plastic bag from some grocery store. Nothing.

The final motel seemed promising—two rows of cabins, twenty in total, with twelve cars parked neatly beside the doors. Hunter nodded. "Two-thirds minus two. This is the place."

Sally parked, and Hunter stepped out into the warm air, the smell of damp earth all around. He pressed the night bell at the office, holding it down until a man emerged. Flashing his badge, Hunter requested the guest register.

"This is the place," he said to Sally. "I'm sure of it."

"Are you with the police?" the man behind the counter asked, glancing toward the car parked outside.

"I need to take a look at your guest register," Hunter replied. "For tonight's check-ins."

****

It didn't make sense. Completely impossible. She wasn't outside, and she wasn't anywhere inside the room. The man's eyes scanned the space again—nothing. The beds, the furniture, the closet, all empty. She wasn't in the bathroom either, or at least, she hadn't been when he was there.

Unless...

Unless she had been hiding under the bed or in the closet and then slipped into the bathroom while he had been outside. He strode over and flung the bathroom door open, catching a glimpse of himself in the mirror. The steam had cleared. With one swift motion, he yanked back the shower curtain.

"There you are," he said.

Lahni was standing in the corner of the tub, pressed up as far as she could go. She wore a T-shirt, shorts, and shoes. Her right hand was jammed into her mouth, her wide eyes filled with fear, looking impossibly large.

"I've changed my mind," he told her. "I was going to take you with me."

She didn't respond, just stared. He reached toward her, and she shrank back, removing her hand from her mouth.

"It hasn't been four hours yet," she whispered.

"Yes, it has," he said. "It's been way more than that."

Her knuckles went back into her mouth. When he reached out again, she flinched further away. Scream, she thought. Scream like mummy said. She tried, but her throat was too dry, and no sound came out.

"The register," Hunter repeated.

The clerk hesitated, as though there were procedures to follow. Hunter glanced at his watch, then, in a single fluid movement, pulled the SIG Sauer from his pocket.

"Now," he commanded. "We don't have time for delays."

The man's eyes widened as he ducked behind the counter, pulling out a large, old-fashioned leather register and sliding it toward the edge. Hunter and Sally leaned in together to examine it.

"What names are we looking for?" she asked.

"No idea," Hunter replied. "Just look at the cars."

The register had five columns: date, name, home address, vehicle make, and date of departure. The place had twenty rooms, and sixteen were occupied. Seven entries had arrows indicating guests who were staying over from the previous night. Nine cabins were marked with new arrivals, and eleven had vehicle makes listed next to them. Four of the cabins were listed as sharing two cars.

"Families or larger groups," the clerk explained.

"Did you check them in?" Hunter asked.

"No, I'm the night guy. I don't start until midnight."

Hunter stared at the page, then went still.

"What is it?" Sally asked.

"This isn't the right place," he said, voice flat. "I was wrong."

"Why?"

"Look at the cars," he pointed to the vehicle column, running the muzzle of the gun along it. "Three Toyotas, three Mitsubishi's, two Holdens, one MG, one Audi, and one Ford."

"There should be two Fords," he said, "the Falcon and the Explorer already parked outside."

"Damn," she muttered.

He nodded, feeling the weight of his mistake. He had nothing else, no backup plan. The Ford in the register was the Explorer outside, not the Falcon. He had gambled everything on this.

Then he looked at the handwriting.

"Who fills this out?" he asked.

"The owner," the clerk said. "She does everything by hand."

Hunter closed his eyes, recalling their slow circle around the motel earlier, mentally walking through every old-fashioned motel he had ever stayed in.

"Okay," he said, thinking aloud. "She probably glances at the cars herself when they're checking in, writes down the makes. Maybe the guests are distracted, getting out their wallets or talking."

"Possibly. I wouldn't know," the clerk said.

"She's not big on cars, is she?"

"I wouldn't know that either. Why?"

"There are three Toyotas written down, but only two outside. She probably listed the Explorer as a Holden by mistake. They look kind of similar, especially if she's not paying attention."

He pointed to the word "Ford."

"That's the Falcon," he said. "They're here."

"You sure?" Sally asked.

"I can feel it," he replied.

They had booked two rooms, not next to each other, but in the same wing: rooms five and eight.

"All right," Hunter said. "I'm going to check them out."

He turned to the clerk. "Stay here. Keep quiet."

He looked at Sally. "Call the state police and start working on that federal judge, okay?"

"You need a key?" the clerk asked.

"No," Hunter replied. "I don't need a key."

He stepped into the damp night air.

The row of cabins started with number one. He moved quickly along the walkway, his shoes leaving wet tracks behind him. The setup was standard—door, short hallway, closet, bathroom, and a room spanning the width of the cabin. Typical motel layout.

When he reached room five, he noticed a Do Not Disturb sign lying a foot from the doorway. He stepped over it and continued down the row, stopping outside number eight. Pressing his ear to the door, he heard nothing. He moved on, circling the garden at the center of the two wings.

The crushed stone crunched loudly underfoot, forcing him to walk slower. He passed cabin ten, then nine, and crouched beneath the window of number eight. The air conditioner was humming loudly, drowning out any other sounds. He carefully peeked through the window.

Nothing. The room was completely empty. It hadn't been touched, as if no one had ever occupied it. Panic briefly flared in his chest. Maybe they booked multiple motels, giving themselves options. He stood up and ran to room five's window, throwing caution aside. He pressed himself against the glass and peered in.

There he saw the small dark man, wrapped in two towels, dragging Lahni out of the bathroom. Bright light streamed behind him. He held both her wrists in one hand above her head as she kicked and thrashed wildly. Hunter saw it all in a split second—the layout of the room, the gun with a silencer on the credenza—before he acted.

He snatched up a large rock from the garden and hurled it through the window. The screen disintegrated, and glass exploded inward. He was through the window a second later, the frame catching around his shoulders.

The man froze, stunned, and let Lahni go. He scrambled for the gun, but Hunter was faster. He grabbed him by the throat, slamming him against the wall, then delivered a powerful punch to his crotch. The man crumpled, and Hunter kicked him hard in the head, sending his eyes rolling back.

Breathing heavily, Hunter fought the urge to kick him again.

He turned to Lahni. “Are you okay?” he asked.

She nodded, still catching her breath. “He’s a bad man,” she whispered. “I think he was going to shoot me.”

Hunter nodded. “He won’t do that now.”

“There was thunder and lightning,” Lahni said quietly.

“I know. I was outside. Got soaked,” Hunter replied.

She nodded. “It rained a lot.”

“You sure you’re okay?” he asked again, studying her carefully.

Lahni nodded again, this time more confidently. She was calm —too calm, considering what had just happened. No tears, no screaming. The room was eerily quiet, as if nothing had occurred. The large rock from the garden lay in the center of the floor, surrounded by shards of broken glass. Hunter bent down, picked it up, and tossed it back out the shattered window, where it rolled away with a crunch.

“You’re sure you’re okay?” he asked for the third time.

She nodded, and he moved to the phone, dialing the front desk. The night clerk answered, and Hunter told him to send Sally down to room five. Then he walked over to the door, unhooked the chain, and unlocked it, leaving it propped open. A warm, damp breeze flowed through the room, carrying the smell of wet earth.

"You okay?" Hunter asked one last time.

"Yes," Lahni answered firmly. "I'm okay."

Sally stepped inside a minute later. Lahni looked at her curiously.

"This is Sally," Hunter explained. "She's helping your mum."

"Where is my mum?" Lahni asked.

"She'll be with you soon," Sally reassured her.

Sally turned to look down at the small man slumped on the floor, his limbs tangled awkwardly.

"Is he alive?" she whispered.

Hunter nodded. "He's just knocked out. Concussed, maybe."

"QLD police are on their way," Sally whispered back. "I called my boss too—got him out of bed. He's setting up a meeting with a judge for first thing in the morning, but he said we'll need a straightforward confession from this guy if we want to avoid delays."

Hunter nodded. "We'll get one."

He bent down, grabbed one of the towels around the man's neck, and twisted it into a makeshift noose. He dragged him across the floor and into the bathroom.

Twenty minutes later, Hunter emerged from the bathroom to find two QLD officers standing in the room—a sergeant and a constable, both Aboriginal, both looking composed and sharp in their tan uniforms. He could hear their police car idling outside. Hunter nodded at them, then retrieved the man's clothes from the chair and tossed them back into the bathroom.

"So?" the sergeant asked.

"He's ready to talk," Hunter replied. "He's offering a full confession—voluntarily. But he wants you to know he was just the driver."

"He wasn't one of the shooters?"

"No," Hunter said, shaking his head. "But he saw everything."

"What about the kidnapping?"

"He wasn't there for that. He was just guarding her afterward. But he's got a lot to confess to. Stuff from years back."

"In a case like this, he talks, and he'll be locked up for a long time," the sergeant said.

"He knows. He's accepted it. He's looking for redemption."

The officers exchanged glances and headed into the bathroom. Hunter heard the sounds of movement, the clicking of handcuffs.

"I need to get back," Sally said. "There's a lot of work to prepare the writ for habeas corpus."

"Take the Ford Falcon," Hunter said. "I'll stay here with Lahni."

The officers brought the man out of the bathroom. He was dressed now, his hands cuffed behind his back, and both officers held him by the elbows as they escorted him out. He was bent over, pale with pain, already talking quickly. They hustled him to their car, and the door swung shut behind them. Hunter heard the muffled slam of car doors and the engine roaring to life.

"What did you do to him?" Sally asked, her voice low.

Hunter shrugged. "I'm a hard man. Like you said."

He asked Sally to send the night clerk over with a master key, and she headed toward the office. Hunter turned to Lahni.

"You sure you're okay?" he asked again.

"You don't need to keep asking me," she replied, a hint of exasperation in her voice.

"You tired?" he asked.

She nodded. "Yes."

"Your mum will be here soon," Hunter said. "We'll wait for her right here. But let's move to another room. This one's got a broken window."

Lahni giggled. "You broke it—with that rock!"

Hunter smiled. He heard the distant sound of the Ford Falcon starting up and its tires on the road.

"Let's try room eight," he said. "It's clean, and nobody's been in it. We can make it ours."

Lahni took his hand, and together they walked out, along the concrete path to room eight. It was a dozen steps for Hunter, but many more for Lahni, her small feet leaving damp tracks behind them. The clerk met them with a passkey, and Lahni immediately climbed into the bed by the window. Hunter lay down on the other bed and watched her until she was sound asleep. Then he slid his arm under his head and closed his eyes, trying to doze.

A couple of hours later, the new day dawned, bright and hot. The metal roof creaked and cracked as it expanded, and the wooden beams beneath it groaned as the temperature rose. Hunter woke after a brief, uneasy rest, swinging his legs over the side of the bed. He crept quietly to the door and stepped outside.

The eastern horizon, far off beyond the motel office, was glowing with a brilliant white light. A few rags of cloud lingered in the sky, burning away in the early morning heat. There would be no storm today. Despite all the predictions, last night's brief shower had been the only rain they'd get. It was over.

Hunter returned to the room and lay back down. Lahni was still asleep. She had kicked off the sheet, her shirt riding up to reveal a pink band of skin at her waist. Her legs were bent as if she'd been running in her dreams, but her arms were thrown above her head—a sign of security, he remembered an army psychiatrist once telling him. A child who sleeps like that feels safe.

She was a remarkable kid, that much was clear. Most adults he knew would be wrecks after going through what she had. But not Lahni. Maybe she was too young to fully understand, or maybe she was just that tough. Either way, he wasn't sure. He closed his eyes again.

He woke again about half an hour later to find Lahni standing next to him, shaking his shoulder.

"I'm hungry," she said.

"Me too," Hunter replied. "What would you like?"

"Ice cream," she said with a grin.

"For breakfast?"

She nodded.

"Okay," he said, chuckling. "But you've got to have some eggs first. Maybe bacon. You need something nutritious."

Hunter found a truck stop cafe listed in the guide book, about a kilometer closer to Three Rivers. He promised the driver a fifty-dollar tip to bring breakfast out to the motel. While they waited, he sent Lahni to wash up in the bathroom. By the time she came out, the food had arrived—scrambled eggs, bacon, toast, juice for Lahni, and coffee for Hunter. There was even a large dish of ice cream with chocolate chips.

Breakfast changed everything. As Hunter ate, he felt some of his energy return, and the same was true for Lahni. They propped the door open to let in the fresh morning air, dragging two chairs outside to sit in the warm sun.

They spent the next four hours waiting. Hunter lounged in his chair, passing the time with the ease of someone used to waiting. Lahni, on the other hand, treated it like a serious task, her usual earnest concentration evident. They talked occasionally, ate a second breakfast that Hunter ordered from the same cafe, and took turns going in and out of the bathroom. Most of the time, though, their eyes were fixed on the road, looking to the east where it disappeared into the horizon. The dust from the storm had settled, but the dry heat brought it back quickly, hanging in the air like a haze. Traffic was light, with only the occasional vehicle breaking the stillness.

Around eleven, Hunter stood a few paces into the parking lot when he spotted a car emerging from the heat shimmer in the distance. The Ford Falcon crept slowly toward them, dust trailing behind. The fake antennas on the back wobbled as it approached.

"Hey, kid," he called to Lahni. "Look at this."

She shaded her eyes with her hand and watched as the car slowed and turned into the lot. Sally was in the driver's seat, with Rosie beside her. Rosie looked pale and worn out, but her face was lit up with joy. Before the car had fully stopped, she was out, skipping around the hood as Lahni ran toward her, leaping into her arms. They spun around in the sunlight, laughing, crying, and shrieking all at once. Hunter watched for a moment, then stepped back, giving them their space. He knew reunions like this were best left private.

Sally, seeing his retreat, lowered her window and placed a hand on his shoulder.

“Everything squared away?” he asked.

“For us,” she said. “The police have a mountain of paperwork ahead of them. They're looking at over forty-five homicides across six different states and territories—everything from what happened twelve years ago to Bradley, Warner, and even Peacock. They’re going to arrest Judy for shooting Peacock, but I think she'll get off lightly, given the circumstances.”

“Anything about me?” Hunter asked.

“They had questions about last night,” she replied. “I told them I did everything.”

“Why?”

She smiled. “Because I’m a lawyer. I called it self-defense, and they didn’t argue. It was my car, my gun—it was easier that way. They would’ve given you a much harder time.”

“So we’re all in the clear?”

“Especially Rosie,” Sally said, nodding.

Hunter glanced over at Rosie, who was holding Lahni tightly, her face buried in the girl’s neck as if she needed that closeness just to breathe. She was walking in slow circles with Lahni in her arms, her smile wide and full of happiness. Hunter couldn’t help but smile along with her.

“What’s next for her?” Hunter asked.

“She’s planning to move to Mount Kalka,” Sally said. “We’ll help her sort through Warner’s affairs—there’s bound to be some cash somewhere. She's thinking about getting a place like mine, maybe working part-time. She's even considering law school."

"You tell her about the cream house?"

Sally grinned. "I did. Told her it was probably burnt to the ground, and she just laughed. I've never seen anyone so happy about losing their home."

By now, Lahni was leading Rosie around the parking lot, pointing out the trees she had inspected earlier, chattering excitedly. They were a perfect picture—Lahni bursting with energy, Rosie serene and beautiful. Hunter stood up and leaned against the car, watching them.

"You hungry?" he asked Sally.

"Here?"

"I've got a connection with that cafe. They probably have something with vegetables."

"Tuna salad works for me," Sally said.

Hunter went inside, called the diner, and ordered sandwiches, promising yet another fifty-dollar tip. When he came back out, Lahni and Rosie were looking for him.

"I'm going to a new school soon," Lahni told him, bouncing on her toes. "Just like you did."

"You'll do great," Hunter said, smiling. "You're sharp as a tack."

Rosie released Lahni's hand and stepped closer to Hunter, a little shy and awkward. Then she broke into a wide smile and wrapped her arms around him in a tight hug.

"Thank you," was all she said.

Hunter hugged her back. "I'm sorry it took so long."

After a while, Rosie, Lahni, and Sally went inside to freshen up before lunch. As soon as the door clicked shut behind them, Hunter simply walked away. It felt like the right thing to do —no goodbyes, no long explanations. He jogged to the road and started walking south. After about a kilometer, a farm truck pulled over, driven by an old man who didn't have much to say. Hunter climbed in, rode as far as the Bruce Highway interchange, and got out.

He stood on the highway on ramp for ninety minutes in the heat before a road train smelling of animals pulled over. Hunter walked around the front of the massive truck and looked up at the driver's window. The faint sound of AC/DC played over the rumble of the diesel engine. The driver leaned out, a burly man in a Cowboys T-shirt, with about four days of stubble on his chin.

"Gold Coast?" the driver called down.

"Anywhere," Hunter replied.

If you loved this novel, please subscribe to our newsletter for the latest updates:

www.bigstretchpublishing.com

Other novels in the Mick Hunter series:

Dark Alibis (novella)

Subway Winds (short story)

Dire Warning

Made in the USA
Las Vegas, NV
11 June 2025